Declan

THE BRASH BROTHERS BOOK FOUR

JENNA MYLES

Publishers Note:

This is a work of fiction. Names, Characters, places and incidents are a product of the author's imagination. Locales and public names are sometimes used for atmospheric purposes. Any resemblance to actual people living or dead, or to businesses, companies, events, institutions, or locales is completely coincidental.

Published by Myles High Publishing

authorjennamyles.com

THE BRASH BROTHERS READING ORDER

- For me
Here's to twenty years of self-doubt and daydreams.
I got there, but I wish someone would have said,
"For fucks sake woman, just write the book!"

AUTHORS NOTE

Most of the events of this book run concurrently with Colton's book. If you haven't read it yet, then visit this link to find it at your favorite retailer: https://mybook.to/colton brashbrothers.

Content Warning: Cara and her sister experience an attack off the page, and deal with the aftermath throughout the book. I make prolific use of swears and there is some violence on the page.

I love hearing from readers. If you spot a typo, or you just want to complain about how long it's taking me to get to Ransom's book, email me at: jenna@authorjennamyles.com

CHARACTERS IN THE BRASH SERIES

Ransom Kyle: The 'dad' of the group. He brought together a group of misfit boys and turned them into a family. He's the big idea guy.

Kade Dixon: The CEO, in charge of operations. Favorite word is Fuck and he manages to work it into nearly every sentence. Girlfriend is Becca

Becca Tyler: A teacher at a Dojo and runs a lot of self-defense classes. Colton trains with her, and she makes him cry at least once a week. Often referred to as a Ninja.

Micah James: Works on custom projects out of the Knight Street garage. Was beaten by his father as a child, and suffered brain damage. He will often use ASL to supplement his speech. Big reader, has a kitty named Minnie (as in mouse). Girlfriend is Holly.

Holly Clarke: Escaped her abusive husband and hid from him for two years. He's now in prison with Joker. Holly works at Knight Street with Micah.

Colton Miles: He's the overprotective Golden Retriever of the group. Had a history of underground fighting. Girlfriend is Evie.

Evie Collins: ER nurse and mom to Mia. She has a no-bullshit attitude that the guys find equally terrifying and hilarious. She's the one that helped Holly escape her abusive husband, and as a result, had her life torn apart.

Declan Wilder: The hacker/computer geek. He can find anything on anyone. Obsessed with video games. Notorious for losing bets with his brother Jonas, leading to Mohawks and ass tattoos.

Zach Lee: Head of marketing. The playboy of the group. Very image-focused and loves his expensive suits and beautifully decorated home. His younger biological brother is Jonas.

Jonas Lee: The CFO, the numbers guru. On the Autism Spectrum. He tends to be reserved around new people. Huge fan of puzzles.

Nick Diaz: The fixer. He could convince a nun to marry him in ten minutes flat. No official title, he goes where Ransom needs him to.

Maverick Walker: The lawyer. He and Nick are often sent out to handle problems that Cara can't solve.

Johnny (Joker) Miles: Older brother of Colton. He's been in prison for eighteen years.

1

CARA

This idiot actually believes he can charm me into lying to my boss. I would be insulted if he wasn't so predictable. I give him a sultry smile. The one I practiced in my room as a teenager. The one that made the high school boys go crazy and the one that still drives men wild. It makes them stop thinking with their big brain. It also makes them underestimate me. And that suits me just fine.

As expected, the stuffed shirt's eyes go hazy. He gives me a smarmy smile and smooths back his hair. "You are a stunner," he mutters, staring straight into my cleavage. There's only a hint of revulsion left in me as his eyes linger. I learned a long time ago to set aside my feelings in the moment. I trade the disgust, the revulsion, and the disappointment, for the satisfaction of taking them down a peg, or twenty, in the end.

He thinks this is his game. He's wrong.

I've had a lot of practice, first as a teenager with a very healthy curiosity, then as a woman striving to be more in the world. I learned early that most men are simple and I'd have to play the game sometimes to get ahead. But when that gets old? I drop the act and show them the real me.

I'll admit, that spilled into my romantic relationships

sometimes. My itch was getting scratched, and that's all I cared about. Bree would tell me that's fucked up, but I don't really mind. It makes me the odd one out, though. No husband and no babies when most of the women in my high school class have both.

I didn't care. I never wanted anything more. At least until I met *him*.

I let out a tinkling laugh, leaning forward and letting my blood-red blouse gape open a little more. "So...what am I supposed to do about this?" I ask, channeling my inner airhead, tapping the contract on the boardroom table with a black manicured nail.

He tugs down his tie, loosening his top button. I have no doubt I'm driving him wild. But he's a classically handsome man. He's played this game before. He's used to women falling over him.

He's never played with me, and he's about to discover I always win.

"Just don't mention it, honey. There's a big present in it for you as soon as this deal is signed."

I widen my eyes, batting my triple-thick mascara-coated eyelashes. "Really? How big? I love...big presents."

I let my mind drift as we trade sexual innuendos. Keeping up with him requires only a tiny fraction of my brain power, so the rest of me can think about all the things that really matter today, like the liquor shipment that should be arriving at the club right about now. And the ache in my toes from my stilettos. And the raise I'm going to demand from Ransom when I save him from this fucking deal.

And, of course, as my eyes travel idly over the playboy across the table from me, I can't help comparing this man to Declan and him coming up short. Smooth playboy has never been my favorite.

Don't get me wrong, I like all men. But ever since I met

Declan, I'm all about stuttering, nerdy, and playing hard-to-get guys.

Well, guy. It's only him. From the day I started working here, it's just been him.

The energy of the room shifts. Playboy straightens up, unconsciously puffing out his chest in some show of...I don't even know what. Ransom walking into a room has that effect on people. He makes most men feel inferior at six-foot-three, with dark hair and eyes, and cufflinks worth more than most people's cars. The whole package screams successful, cold billionaire. It's accurate marketing, except for the cold part. He may be cold in this room, but for the rest of his life, in this company he built with his brothers, he's anything but.

"Are we ready to wrap this up?" Ransom asks crisply. He has an air of indifference in his voice like he doesn't care if this deal happens or not. Sometimes it's an act. This time, I don't think it is. Sure, he'd like this land, but Ransom always has a backup plan and a backup for the backup. He loves his contingencies. That's one of the best lessons I've learned from him. Never set your heart on one thing. In business, there's always the next opportunity.

Too bad I can't seem to apply that same principle to my love life, or lack thereof.

Playboy shoots a secretive smile at me. I wink back, then turn to Ransom, savoring the twitch at the corner of his mouth as I continue the airhead voice. "On page ninety-six it states Environmental cleanup of the site isn't covered. My guess is he's found out there's some contamination he wants to put the burden on you to handle." I glance over the table at playboy, blinking innocently as his face reddens.

I drop the act, letting my absolute indifference show. "I'm not for fucking sale. Especially not for the kind of present you're offering."

Then I stand, strolling out of the office like I can't hear his

6 | JENNA MYLES

cursing and Ransom's evil chuckle as the door shuts behind me.

I stride through the offices on the executive floor, nodding at coworkers as I pass. We're all friendly here, but I haven't made any real friends with any of them. I don't have a lot of friends, period. When you live with your best friend/sister, it's easy to get lazy about trying to make new ones. But that's not why I have no tight relationships here. It's because of Ransom and the boys. They've pulled me into their group, and they're all-consuming. I'm on call 24/7, and sometimes, it can be exhausting. But the payoff more than makes up for it.

I kick off my shoes in my office, flopping into my eight-hundred-dollar ergo chair. I strolled into Ransom's office the day after he hired me and demanded his credit card. No fucking way was I going to work in the old piece of shit chair they had at my desk. He turned it over without a peep, smart man. When my new chair showed up later that afternoon, he spent an inordinate amount of time playing with it. Then he called all the brothers in, and all nine of them tested it out.

When Jonas and Declan started talking hydraulics and plastic molding, my little heart went pitter-patter. I was hooked on them both. Then Declan made eye contact with me, blushed, and fell out of the chair, and I had my new fixation.

Later that month, the entire twelve-story building was in an uproar as nearly a thousand ergo chairs were delivered, all in one day. That's the day I knew I wasn't going to move on from this job. I'm really fucking good at what I do. I get emails and calls from other companies weekly, desperate to hire me. And for a long time, I needed that rush of being chased. But The Brash Group is the first company I've worked for that puts their employees' needs above their own. I don't know where that came from. How did nine orphan men succeed in business and still stay good guys? It just doesn't compute. But they did. They started with a single garage and now have a fucking empire.

It's something I aspire to someday. Oh, I don't need to be a billionaire. But financial security and being the master of my own destiny are pretty powerful motivators. I don't ever want to struggle again.

It's past five by the time Ransom fills my doorway. I saw him coming, of course, because the whole office is glass, but I relax back in the chair, lifting a brow at him. "So? Are we moving on to plan B?"

He smirks. "Nah. He knocked another million off the price, so I wouldn't walk away."

I narrow my eyes. "You already knew about the contamination."

I see his surprise in the widening of his eyes and the way his body stiffens. "How the fuck do you do that?" He cracks his neck. "Yeah, I already knew. I had a team in there testing a few weeks ago. I already have a quote on the cleanup."

"Let me guess, it's a lot less than a million?"

"Yep," he says with a wink, turning to his office across the hall.

"I still expect a reward for noticing the clause and dealing with his smarmy ass!" I shout. It's not the first time I've told him to reward me. The first time I saved him a hundred grand, I asked for a raise. He fought me on it, but he smiled the whole time.

I wasn't always a go-getter, but I changed pretty damn fast a decade ago. I had to. So the first time I asked a boss for a raise, I worried about it for a month first. I got it. It got easier and easier. Now, I'm indispensable, and I know it.

He spins, crossing his arms over his chest and leaning in his doorway, smirking my way. "Really? You deserve a reward for doing your job?"

"Damn straight, I do. Call it a commission on the money you saved on the deal."

"And what will this reward entail?"

"I get the jet for a weekend. Bree and I want to go somewhere sunny and work on our tans. Maybe Miami." I can picture it now, the heat on my skin, a cold slushy drink in my hand. The only thing that would make it better would be a certain geeky cabana boy at my beck and call.

"You're a pain in my ass, you know that? You are aware there were other applicants for your job. Professional, composed, well-spoken applicants."

I raise my hand, not trying that hard to hide my yawn. I didn't get enough sleep last night, but that's pretty much my norm. "Yeah, you'd scare them off within the first week. No one else could handle your annoying ass."

His warm chuckles roll down the hall across the mostly empty offices. "You're probably right. You don't scare easily. That makes you pretty damn invaluable."

"I know," I say, no trace of conceit in my tone. It's a fact. I am invaluable to him. With me around, shit gets done. I handle the shit, so he has time to focus on the big picture. It works really fucking well.

"Take the jet. Have fun. Use my card to book a suite on the beach." He wanders into his office, his mind already on his next move. The man's brain never seems to shut off.

The dollar value of this trip is less than my last raise, but I'm overly excited about this one. The cold is rolling into Chicago, and I can't wait for some sun and sand.

With a small squeak of excitement, I pull out my phone and text Bree.

> We're going to Miami! Girls only, no Tyler.
> Look at your schedule and let me know when
> you can go.

I don't bother waiting for a reply. She's constantly running late with her physiotherapy clients and doesn't carry her phone on her. I can't wait for some boyfriend-free time with her. Her boyfriend's a douche, and I've had to bite my tongue more than once around them. I do not get what she sees in him, but it's her life, and it's none of my fucking business.

I hang around my office a little while longer, hoping that I'll see *him*, but eventually, I just feel ridiculous. Pushing my feet back into my way too high, way too sexy, way too expensive stilettos, I grab my bag and my jacket and head down the hall, eyes peeled. My usually stellar self-esteem takes a hit as I creep toward his office, but I need my fix.

Declan is like no man I've ever been around before. Men, don't ignore me. Ever. I always attract attention wherever I go. I have the hips and the boobs that bring all the men to the yard, most of them desperate to get their hands on me. But not Declan. No, he seems to be the opposite. Completely uninterested in me. Well, not completely, but completely unwilling to do anything about it.

I know men, and I know for a fact that he is *very* happy to see me most of the time, despite how hard he might try to hide it. But I can't figure out why he won't act on it. I've thrown myself at him at every opportunity over the last few years, and he can't get away from me fast enough.

At first, it was funny. It became a bit of a game, seeing how far I could push him before he bolted. Now, it's not funny anymore. I feel more and more pathetic every time I see him, but I'm powerless to stop.

The routine is predictable. Every day after work, the brothers gather in Ransom's office for drinks and to decompress. If Declan's not here yet, that means he's still in his office playing with his computers. When it comes to tech, I get by, but I really don't understand what it is that Declan does most of his day. All I know is that he's got way too many monitors and seems way too excited anytime a new gadget shows up.

I slowly make my way down the hall, passing the other brothers' executive offices, stopping just before the doorway of Declan's. My heart is racing, anticipating seeing him. My palms are sweaty, which annoys the fuck out of me. I'm supposed to be calm, cool Cara, but around him, I revert to a nervous sixteen-year-old. Which is stupid since, at sixteen, there were no nerves to be found. I had confidence for days.

I take a chance and peek my head around the edge of the doorway, and there he is. It's still weird seeing him now. From the back, he looks mostly the same with his hood pulled up over his head, but the width of his shoulders is new. When I first met him, he definitely wasn't scrawny, but he was never built like this, muscle on muscle. Somehow in the last few months, he seems to have matured, and his whole body has changed. I can't decide if I like it. I mean, yeah, he's gorgeous. But I really liked the old Declan too. The new one is taking some getting used to. Of course, if I got him naked, I wouldn't kick him out of bed.

I stand there, unashamed to be creeping on him, watching him work. His fingers flying over the keyboard. The little triumphant hum he makes when he's hacked some government or whatever the hell he does on that computer all day makes the back of my knees tingle. It makes me wonder what sounds he might make when he's exploring my body.

He's so cute. Why won't he love me?

I mean, I'm completely lovable and banging. He's the only one who doesn't seem to realize that. The way he stutters and panics when I talk to him sometimes makes me wonder if he's a virgin, but that seems a little outlandish. Besides, I've seen him with women in the past. Well, a woman. I'm not proud of how long I followed them, how I ducked into doorways downtown as they walked down the street. But it hurt. It made me feel like I was the problem, which I guess I am.

I know I should move on. But I can't.

He starts packing up, turning off his monitors, shutting down his equipment, and so I step out of the doorway, leaning against the hallway wall, waiting for him like the obsessed woman I am. When he comes around the corner, I put on my very best flirty expression, sticking my chest out, making sure the girls are on full display. I pretend that the way his eyes widen and the way he steps back doesn't hurt me, and I paste a sultry smile on my face. "Well, hello there, handsome. Fancy meeting you here."

2

DECLAN

I can feel her behind me. I swear I could be in the middle of a crowd of a million people and still know exactly where Cara is. I'm that drawn to her. She's been watching me.

Again.

I tell myself that today is the day that I get over it and finally ask her out. I'm going to be smooth, speak clearly, and whatever I do, don't run away.

It seems pathetic to have to give myself a pep talk before I can talk to a woman, but she's not just any woman. She's *the* woman. The object of my obsession for the last three years and the one woman in the world that makes me turn into a teenage boy every time I see her. I swear I've dated women before. I've had full conversations with them. But no one like Cara.

She's been the sole occupant of my mental spank bank since the day I met her. I'm a fucking billionaire. Women come on to me all the time. Somehow I manage to handle them just fine. But the day I caught a glance of Cara across the room, the day she started working here, everything changed. Any skill I might've built up around women, any experience I may have had, just flew out the fucking window.

I spotted her as Ransom was getting her settled in her office, and I broke out in a full-body sweat. I had never seen anything like her. She was tall, so fucking tall in those stilettos. Nearly eye to eye with Ransom. From the top of her blonde hair to the tips of her pointy-toed stilettos, she oozed sex. She had the kind of body that I had drooled over since we managed to steal a bunch of adult magazines from the corner store when we were kids. The lush big breasts, the nipped-in but still thick waist, a luscious ass, and thick, strong legs. It's like everything about her was custom-made to match my dream woman.

I'm not proud of it, but when Ransom and Cara started down the hall toward my office that day, I dove into an empty cubicle and hid under the desk. A man as tall as I am should not be trying to wedge himself into a space that small. It was pathetic and painful.

I quizzed Ransom that night about the new girl and got all the details. And then, I mentally ran through all the things I wanted to say to her the next day. I had such grand plans. But instead, we all ended up in her office admiring her new desk chair. I have no idea what I said when we finally met, only that the way her hand felt in mine was earth-shattering. I do think I hung onto it a little too long. I distracted myself after that by playing with the chair. Jonas and I were fiddling with the hydraulics, geeking out a bit, and she fucking leaned over and smiled at me. My whole body twitched like it had been hit by lightning, and I fell out of the fucking chair.

It only got worse from there.

Closing my files, I grab my shit and head for my empty doorway, hoping like hell that she hasn't left the building already. *Today's the day. I'm going to actually talk to her. I'm getting that date. Guaranteed.*

I should have known better.

When I turn into the hallway, she's right fucking there. My dream, and my nightmare, smirking. I startle, clench my ass cheeks in fear, and step back, heart racing.

"Well, hello there, handsome. Fancy meeting you here." Her voice is low, raspy. I want to hear that voice scream my name. I'd fucking give anything for it.

I search for all my well-rehearsed words. And come up with nothing. "Cara," I force out, my throat tight. My fingers reach for the zip on my hoodie, sliding it up and down, over and over. The zipping sound is the only one between us as we stare at each other.

She smiles, and it lights up her face. Helen of Troy was a fucking gremlin compared to this woman. She takes a step closer, and I'm hyper-aware of her scent. The lemony fragrance is always a shock. I don't know what I expected her to smell like when we met, but it wasn't this fresh, clean scent she wears. The contrast of that smell with the way she radiates sex just throws me off balance.

I freeze as she reaches up, brushing my long hair off my forehead. She snorts delicately. "You're always hiding behind that hair." The touch of her hand makes my cock try and shoot through my jeans. I rear back, banging my head on the wall, desperate to get away from her touch. I'm losing control.

Her hand, still hovering where my forehead was, curls into a loose fist before she drops it to her side. She tosses her hair, laughing lightly, but it sounds off. I scramble to say something. Do something. *Think asshole. Think.*

"Ah...what are you up to tonight?"

I got the words out without stuttering. I. AM. AWESOME.

Her smile is back. "I'm heading to the club. Maybe you want to come along?" She steps closer, running her pointy black fingernail down my zipper. I watch that finger, completely blanking on anything she just said. What the fuck did she just ask me?

"Ah. Yeah, no. Clubs aren't really my thing."

Her eyebrow arches. "Pretty sure I heard Zach talking about taking you to the clubs."

Fuck. I have been going to the club with my brother Zach, but I really didn't want her to know that. It's not like that's my scene. It never has been, but I had some stupid idea that if I could practice talking to women, I wouldn't be so nervous around her. Zach's taken me out a bunch of times, and so far, nada.

I don't think it's ever going to work. Because the problem is not women. It's this woman. The woman occupies all of my thoughts. *Come on Declan, think of something to say, for fuck's sake.*

"Why are you always going to the club?" I don't mean the words to sound the way they come out, but I still want to know. From what I can tell, she spends most of her nights at clubs. It kills me to think about what she might be doing there. She's not mine. Not yet, at least. So I have no say over what she does. But I really wish she was home reading a book instead of out at the fucking nightclubs wearing God knows what. That's completely un-evolved, I know, but I can't help it.

Truthfully, I wish she was doing anything, in my home, with me. She lives a life that makes me sweat just thinking about it. The people, the noise, it's all a lot. Wishing I were different, wishing I could be the kind of guy that would fit right in at those clubs, has gotten me exactly nowhere. So somewhere along the way, I started wishing she were different. Which is fucked up since I really like her just the way she is. It's me, and my reactions I don't like.

She frowns, stepping back. But that hand, that nail, stays on my chest. Our bodies aren't pressed together anymore, and I can think again, at least a tiny bit.

"Is that such a bad thing?"

"Not bad, exactly. I don't know. I just thought maybe there

might be other things you'd like to do. You know something better than going to clubs, I mean."

"Better? I don't really know what that means."

"I don't know. It's just...you're smart, Cara. It seems like you'd have better shit to do. Clubbing is something people do in their twenties." I hate the fucking clubs. It always feels like Zach and I are a decade older than everyone in there. I don't like how packed they are, I don't like the way the women come onto me, and I really don't like the music.

Her hand drops from my chest, and I take a full breath for the first time since she touched me. Her eyes drop to the floor, and she takes it a few steps away, planting her back against the opposite wall.

"I see," she says softly. She exhales and raises her head, a wide smile on her lips. "Well, I guess I'm young at heart. Good night Dec."

She turns, walking away before I can get a word out. I wouldn't be able to speak anyway. All thought has left my brain as I watch that majestic ass sway. I swear every song ever written about amazing asses was written about Cara's.

"You're so stupid." Colt's voice scares the shit out of me, and my butt clenches. Again.

I spin on him, aiming a punch at his stomach. Fucker doesn't even try to block, laughing as I connect. I do get a little grunt out of him, which shocks the hell out of me. He's a fucking wall of muscle, but all the lifting I've been doing lately is clearly having an effect.

"What the fuck, man? Why are you skulking around? And how the fuck do you do that. You're the size of a fucking tank. You should make noise when you walk."

"It's a gift, brother, what can I say?" He shrugs, smirking. "Why the fuck did you just call Cara old?"

"What? I didn't say that." Did I? I mean, I was barely conscious during most of that interaction, but I'm pretty sure I didn't call her old.

"You said going to clubs was for young people. How else was she supposed to take that?"

I turn and bang my head on the wall a few times, finally stopping to rest with my forehead pressed to the rich wood paneling. "Fuck."

"Yeah," he says, laughter lacing his words.

"Why the fuck can't I just talk to her?" I spin, dropping to a crouch, ass against the wall. "I don't know how to talk to her. I don't know how to be what she needs. And I hate that she spends all her time out at those places. They're full of assholes hitting on her, I'm sure of it."

When I glance at Colt, there's something on his face I can't pinpoint. "What?"

He rolls his lips, planting his hands on his hips. "Have you ever bothered to talk to her about it? Or have you just made a bunch of assumptions about her?"

"I've known her for years, Horsey. I'm not making any assumptions." He doesn't even flinch at the nickname. His woman's little girl, Mia, calls him that. We've all been doing it, but he doesn't seem to give a shit, which honestly takes most of the fun out of it.

"You don't think so?" He shakes his head. "You're wrong. And you just hurt that woman. Get your head out of your ass Dec. She's not going to give you many more chances."

He walks away before I can pin him down and ask him what the fuck he's talking about. His implication that I hurt her sits uncomfortably. Cara is fucking teflon. Nothing I could do or say would bother her. Of that, I'm sure. Sometimes, I wish she wasn't. I wish she was as affected by me as I am by her.

But as I climb into my car, I can't shake the feeling that I've fucked up somehow. So I do what I always do when I'm uncomfortable...crank the music and let my mind loose, sorting through every moment of our conversation and everything I should have said and done instead.

I roll my windows down, pull out of the back garage on our compound, and head down the lane past our building. Some days, I can't fucking believe that all of this is ours. The day I left the group home for good, I thought it was the best day of my life. Then we made our first million. Then two. The good days just kept rolling in. I had all the money I could ever want. I bought the shit I'd always dreamed of. I thought I was living the life.

I was satisfied with my gamer friends and the occasional girlfriend I met while gaming. Honestly, I didn't get it. What was the big deal? The women I dated were sweet and nerdy. I thought that was my type. But then Cara showed up, and I realized that I had no fucking clue who I was.

Cara is the complete opposite of every woman I've ever dated. She has more confidence in her pinkie than all of them put together, and I don't know how to handle her. I feel like a fucking loser every time I'm around her.

I thought bulking up and having Zach take me to clubs would help me build my confidence, but it hasn't done a fucking thing. I am who I am, and that man will never be good enough to keep Cara's attention. She loves fucking with me. Has from day one. But to actually date someone like me? Someone who likes computers and hanging out with his family? I'm too boring for her.

I hit the accelerator, trying to shake off my mood. My life is good. Great even. I just need to get my head out of my ass. As I pass the strip mall my barber's in, I pull a U-turn. Dealing with the fucking mop on my head is the perfect distraction.

Two hours later, when Colt knocks on my door and sees my close shaved head, his eyes pop out of his fucking head. I didn't plan on cutting it like this. My hair's always been long. But I'm sick of being me. Sick of feeling like I'm not enough. Sick of hiding behind it.

I should've looked into a personality transplant instead.

3

CARA

Taking the last corner too hard, I screech into the parkade of my building. I'm still stewing over Declan's words. That's not new. I obsess over anything he says to me. He talks to me normally when we're all in a group. He's even nice. But get him alone, and he clams up...usually.

But today? I've never felt small that way. Not physically, but like my life has been judged ... immature. He basically told me to grow up.

It's a tough pill to swallow.

When he spoke to me, I was so thrilled. Until I actually processed what he said. The talking was new, but I wish he'd kept his mouth shut, so I could continue to dream that he was in love with me too.

A horn blares beside me, and I flinch, fumbling my purse, the contents flying into the air. A tampon lands in my hair. Looking over, I'm not at all surprised to see Bree sitting in her old Jeep, laughing her ass off. I shoot her the finger, hiding my smile, and climb out of my car. That's the one downside of being tall with a significant ass. You have to actually climb out of a sports car like mine. It's a trade-off I'm willing to make, though. The car is hot and totally my style.

It could be worse. I could be as tall as Declan. And there I go again, thinking about Declan and the stretch and flex of his muscles as he exits his luxury car.

Bree strolls around the car, meeting me in the middle. We are so different in so many ways, but anyone looking at us would know in a heartbeat we're sisters. Same blonde hair, same blue eyes, same thick bodies. But where I dress to impress in leather and lace and uncomfortable shoes, she lives in sneakers and track pants. She spends maybe ten minutes getting ready in the morning.

I can't decide if I'm jealous of her natural look or just of the extra hour she gets to sleep each day.

It's really the sleep.

I love dressing the way I do. It used to be for other people, but now, it's just for me. Ok, and maybe, in my heart, I really want Declan to like it too. And judging by the tightening of his pants when I'm around, he does.

Difficult, contrary man.

"Stop mooning over that man and get your ass inside. I'm starving."

Bree's voice cuts through the chaos in my head.

"I'm not in charge of meals anymore, smartass. No one's stopping you from cooking your own supper."

I know it's coming. We've had a decade together in close quarters, and I know her better than anyone in the world. But it still hits me in the gut when she rolls her lip out into a pout.

"Please, Care Bear. Please? Can you make your spaghetti?"

I heave a sigh. I am way too easy to manipulate. But secretly, I love that she's here with me instead of asshole Tyler's house. I don't see her nearly enough, and I miss her. A lot.

As I putter around our ancient kitchen, I sip a Corona and

listen to Bree ramble about her day with one ear. When the words 'cock' and 'face' penetrate, I choke on my beer.

Coughing, I pin her with a glare. "What the fuck did you just say?"

She leans back at the tiny two-top table in the corner of the kitchen, giggling. That table has seen so much. We picked it up on the side of the road one night, and it's been with us ever since. We've had blowout fights at that table. There've been tears and so much laughter.

This place was all I could afford when we moved in here a decade ago, and it's tiny and run down, just like that table. There's no good reason we're still here except we're comfy. And busy. And we're saving a ton of money.

Ok, so there are lots of good reasons.

"I said...I was working on his leg mobility, and every time I pressed his leg into his chest, his cock was right in my face. I mean, I didn't get an in-the-flesh look, but what I did see was impressive."

"Who is this guy?"

"Just a guy with an ACL injury. He plays football, I think."

"You think? Did you ask him? He sounds hot." And he's got to be better than her loser boyfriend.

"He is. But no, I didn't ask."

I shoot her a look, but she doesn't rise to the bait. She never does. The raging, hormonal, emotionally damaged teenager that moved into this place with me is gone. In her place is a messy, loving, professional woman.

"I'm really proud of you," I mumble, blinking furiously, taking a sip of beer to wet my dry throat. No need to get emotional here.

She smiles, shaking her head gently, eyes warm. "I know. I'm really proud of you, too, Care Bear. We've come a long way. I mean, look at us, the Davis sisters, kicking ass and taking names."

Grinning, I plate our food and drop into my seat. "Yeah, we're pretty awesome."

IT'S A MADHOUSE TONIGHT, AND I'M ALTERNATING BETWEEN doing a mental happy dance and worrying that the Fire Marshall might show up.

"Promise me, Shorty, one out, one in from now on. I can't risk getting shut down."

Shorty grins down at me from his impressive seven-foot height, bright white teeth gleaming under the flashing sign at my door. *Curves Ahead* is my baby, and my baby is a moneymaker.

"Promise, boss. One out, one in. I got your back. Plus, ain't no way I want us getting shut down. I got mouths to feed."

Winking, he turns back to the line outside the door, and I head back in to survey the space. It's packed, bodies pressing, mouths touching ears to be heard over the sensual music. Dancers, up on their platforms, sway and grind with the beat, toeing that line between dancer and stripper with finesse.

Bree waves me over from the bar, looking frazzled. She's been here since day one, painting and sanding, then waitressing, then bartending. She's always been my biggest supporter, chipping in whenever I need a shift covered, even though she has a degree and a great-paying day job. I don't take it for granted. Ever. And if she's frazzled, it's serious.

I weave through the crowd, ducking under the bar flap rather than lifting it. She's on me immediately.

"Two of the taps won't pour. I'm out of Vodka in my well, and the garnishes are nearly gone."

"On it," I assure her, slapping her on the ass. "Flirt with them, distract them from the fact that there's no booze."

She flashes a sultry grin at me, "Baby, I'm always flirting. You know those boys can't resist me." Ponytail swinging against her neck, she *Jessica Rabbit* walks her way back to her suddenly riveted customers. Chuckling, I head to the back to deal with the supply lines. If the beer's not flowing, neither is the money.

All my staff is in constant motion for the next few hours. I don't take a breath or a moment to rest until the crowd at the bar has dwindled to one deep. As I circle it, I spot Tyler sitting at Bree's end of the bar. She's been dating him for months. He didn't seem that bad at first, but now he's turned into a bit of a possessive ass, and I'm not a fan.

Judging by the tension in Bree's body as she leans over to talk to him, she's not either.

I tap out Robbie, sending him for a break as I take over his well, filling drink orders, flirting with the men and the women, and taking money with one half of my brain. The rest of it is on Bree and Tyler.

Finally, she pushes off the bar and heads my way, lines of frustration etched in her face. "Are you ok if I cut out?"

I scan the crowd, still busy but not packed like it was. "Yeah. I can handle it if you need to go."

She nods, moving to the register to cash out. I slide in next to her, glancing briefly at Tyler. "He seems pissed. Is everything ok?"

She groans. "Yeah. He's just being a bit of an ass. Nothing I can't handle." I clamp my mouth shut, and she laughs. "I know you don't like him. But he has his good moments. Besides, we can't all have billionaire boyfriends."

Scowling, I stick my tongue out at her. "Keep making fun. I'll get him, Bree. The man has to give in, eventually. When he does, I'll make damn sure he never wants to leave."

She laughs and rises to the toe of her sneakers, leaning in to press her forehead against mine. "He would be so lucky to have you. He's a complete fool, Care Bear, and one day, he'll be at your feet begging you to give him a chance." She presses a kiss to my nose and bumps her hip against mine. I get one glimpse of her and Tyler's arguing faces as they leave the club, then she's gone.

CLOSING DOWN THE CLUB IS ACTUALLY ONE OF MY FAVORITE parts. I love the routine of cleaning and restocking, tallying the receipts, and laughing with my staff. Every time I do it, I'm grateful again for what I've built. And yes, really fucking proud.

By the time I pull into my spot at home, my eyes are nearly crossed in exhaustion. I drop my head back on the headrest and close my eyes. It's times like this, when I'm so tired I seriously consider sleeping in my car, that I wonder if I'm making the right choices.

Running the club...well, owning my own business, has been my dream for a long time. It replaced any other dreams I might have had in the years after my parents died. Being a parent is hard. It's painfully hard to be a single parent. And it's devastating trying to parent a grief-stricken sibling while you yourself are grieving.

With a groan, I climb out of the car, slamming the door and leaning against it for a minute. Stupid fucking shoes. I truly do have a love-hate relationship with them. I love the way they make me feel, and my legs are killer in them, but holy fuck do I pay for it at the end of the day.

Lifting one foot, then the other, I pull my shoes off and plant my bare feet on the cold concrete. They'll be filthy by the time I get upstairs, and I don't care. My ears are ringing as I step into the elevator. They always are after a night at the club. The cacophony of voices, glasses, and music, all blend into this low-level hum that echos in my head for hours.

Maybe that's why it takes me so long to realize I hear screams.

And that they're coming from my apartment.

4

CARA

The bright lights of the Emergency Room make my eyes water. I grip the gurney the paramedics are rolling even tighter, using it to propel me forward. I can't let go. I can't let them take her away from me. My whole body hurts, I'm limping, and I'm pretty sure my feet are bleeding, but none of it matters. Only she does.

I vaguely notice the big body coming towards me, but it's not until he's right in front of me that I register Colt's presence. For the first time since I heard Bree scream, I feel like everything might be ok. It won't be. I know that. But I'm going to ignore the consequences of tonight for as long as possible.

"Tell me where you're hurt, honey." His voice is a soft rumble, and I let myself fall apart, crumpling into his arms. I let every fear, every panicky thought, every painful moment of the last half hour out. With Colt here, I know I'll be ok.

I've been the grown-up, the responsible one for most of my life. It's just been Briana and me for so long that I don't allow myself to depend on anyone. I wasn't her big sister for a lot of her life. I was her mom. But Colton feels like a brother to me. Like the brother I always wish I had.

Colton's a wall of muscle, but he's also gentle and kind and so sweet. He lifts the hem of his t-shirt and wipes my face. I glare at him a bit because, ew, but it's also very caring, so I drop the attitude fast, blowing out a breath full of pain, regret, and fear.

Letting Colt hold my weight, I scan the room to find Bree, landing on *him* instead. Declan. I do a double take, registering his cropped hair. It makes him look so different. So much older and harder. The intensity on his face right now, the murderous rage, is new too. But I can't focus on him right now. Bree is my priority.

She's there, being tucked into a cubicle. I pull away, needing to go to her. Colton gently stops me. "Ok honey, you're limping, though. Let me carry you over."

I don't object because I hurt. My ankle is sending bolts of fire all the way up to my knee. Colton is Paul Bunyan huge and will have no trouble carrying me, so I let him.

I vaguely register Declan's growl as we pass, which is also new. Since when does sweet nerdy Declan scowl and act all growly?

Colton lowers me carefully. I'm thankful he keeps his arms around me as I watch them slide Briana from the gurney onto a hospital bed. There are so many people around her, and she's not waking up. She has to wake up. I won't survive without her.

I grip Colton's arms tightly, letting my tears fall. I have a reputation as a tough bitch, so if anyone saw me right now, they'd be shocked. I don't give a fuck.

"What happened, Cara? Who do I have to kill?" Colton whispers against my temple.

A slightly hysterical laugh escapes me. "I don't think that's going to be necessary." I don't think Tyler's going to be a problem again. It's my sister they rushed to the ambulance. Tyler, they covered with a sheet, right there in the middle of our apartment floor, surrounded by pieces of our shattered lamp.

"Who did this to you? What the fuck happened?" I vaguely register Declan's words, but they sound like they're coming from a long dark tunnel. I can't focus on them more than to wonder why he sounds so upset. I mean, I don't look that bad, do I? All my attention is on Briana and the way the doctors are hovering over her bed. *Please be ok. Please be ok.*

"I was out tonight at the club," I mutter, answering his question. "I could hear the screaming from the elevator." My throat is so dry. It hurts so much.

"He had her pushed up against the wall...his hands were on her throat, and he was banging her head on the wall." She looked half dead, and he didn't care. He just kept hurting her. Hurting the person I love most in this world. I can't hold back the sobs. They force themselves out of my body, despite my efforts to hold myself together.

Colton pulls me closer. I feel his cheek on my head. "Finish it," he whispers.

I'm so tired. "Briana's softball bag and bat were by the door. I'm always tripping over the fucking things. I picked up the bat and swung at him. I got him in the ribs, then the head when he dropped her and turned on me." The fear and the panic of those moments shudder through me. "She slid down the wall when he let go...just flopped like she had no bones. I thought she was dead. I should have swung at him harder." The fear of those moments is making my hands shake. "He came at me and tried to take the bat. He was punching me, and we ended up on the ground."

The heat from Colton's body is soothing, warming my back, keeping the shivers at bay. Declan's tucked in close, too, listening to every word I say. Any other time, I'd be so into having his attention. But right now, I don't care.

I'm on the verge of a meltdown. I can feel it. I let myself slump in Colton's arms, trusting him to hold me as I tell him the worst of it. "Bree crawled to the table, grabbed a lamp, and hit him with it. I was able to get up and…hit him with the bat again. He fell, and he didn't get up."

The words sound mechanical. Matter of fact. I leave out the part where I crawled past him to get to Briana. The part where we hugged each other crying. The part where she slumped in my arms, and I couldn't get her to wake up.

The way Colt's arms tense tells me that even though I may not have said it, he understands what I just told him.

I killed a man tonight.

And I can't seem to muster up any regret about it. Maybe it will hit me later? I mean, it's supposed to, right? You can't just take a life and then be totally ok, can you?

"Cara honey, go to Declan. I'm going to make a call."

I tense up but don't object as Colton passes me into Declan's arms. He feels weird. He's so much bigger and harder than he's always been in my fantasies. He's holding me so carefully, though, his arms banded around my back, pulling me into his chest.

I register Colton telling us he's calling their other brother Maverick. Good. I'm pretty sure I'm going to need a lawyer. It won't matter that Tyler tried to kill my sister. The cops are still going to investigate. I don't care. Let them come after me. As long as Bree is ok, I can handle anything else. Live through anything else.

"Breathe, Cara. Just breathe," Declan whispers.

I thought I was breathing. But as I try to match his steady in and out, I realize I'm on the verge of blacking out. Eyes locked on my sister, my head resting on his shoulder, I follow his lead, breathing in and out with him.

"Good," he murmurs, stroking my hair. The longer he holds me, the more of my weight I let him take. He doesn't stumble. He doesn't tire. Just holds me up as easily as Colton does.

Maybe I could get used to this new body of his.

"Why are you guys here?" I ask. Huh, my brain's online again. Enough to wonder, at least.

"Colt's freaking out about Evie's safety. He's been prowling the ER all night. He dragged me along to check out their systems."

Sounds about right. He'd want Declan's computer expertise here, though how the hell he got access to the hospital systems, I don't know. Colt's protective as hell, even of me, and I'm just his friend. I can't imagine how bad he'd be with his girlfriend. I'm sure he's considered wrapping her in bubble wrap each time she leaves the house.

I straighten as I spot the doctor coming toward us. I'm holding my breath as he speaks.

"How do you know this woman?" he asks.

"She's my little sister. Is she going to be ok?"

His eyes tighten, a mask slipping over his face. A kind mask, but still a mask. "We don't know yet. We're going to send her upstairs for some scans. We're worried about bleeding and swelling in her brain. We'll know more in the morning."

He says more, but as he walks away all I can focus on is *bleeding and swelling*. That sounds really bad. A moan forces its way out of me. "Oh, no." My legs feel wobbly. Declan's arms tighten around me until I get my feet under me again.

"Goddammit. What the fuck happened, Cara. Who was this guy? Who did this?" Declan doesn't talk like this. Not to me. He stutters and mumbles and blushes.

"Tyler. He's Bree's boyfriend. I didn't like him. They were at the club tonight, but they left early." I'm a broken record, repeating the same shit over and over.

"Seriously, Cara? So you stayed behind and partied while your sister went home with her abusive boyfriend?"

He's saying exactly what I've been thinking, but somehow it doesn't feel right when it's coming out of his mouth. I'm at the club because that's my business. My future. That's where Bree and I are all the time.

"I've never seen him hurt her. She never told me he was. I thought he was just an asshole. She's twenty-six. She has her own life. And she can usually handle her own shit." I sound defensive because I am.

"How the hell did you miss it? Maybe you should spend less time in the fucking club and more time with your sister. Your priorities are fucked up, Cara."

Years ago, I read a book that talked about love like a garden. The first seed is planted, and that seed needs to be nurtured and watered. And it will grow. I loved that metaphor, and each time I saw Declan, every time he came to my desk to fix my computer, every time I showed him how attracted to him I was, I pictured that love growing.

I was a fool.

This isn't love. Declan doesn't love me. He doesn't even like me. He thinks I'm the kind of person that chooses to party at a club while her sister is beaten. How could he ever love that kind of person?

I wouldn't.

That little seedling of love, the one I was carefully tending, watering, watching grow, shrivels up and dies in the center of my chest. I was so wrong. In that seedling's place, a tower of rage forms.

Raising my hands, I plant them on his chest, shoving him away. He's big, but so am I, and I manage to take him by surprise and knock him back a couple of steps. My disappointment and anger make my legs steady under me. "Let go of me, right fucking now." I use my work voice. The one that lets everyone know not to fuck with me. "You don't know a fucking thing about me. Turn around and walk the fuck away. Now."

He moves back towards me, eyes wide, and I show him how much I don't want him here. I show him my disgust with myself for being so stupid. He staggers back, shaking his head. "Fine. You want me gone? I'm gone."

He turns and walks away, not stopping. Not looking back. I'm not surprised, but it hurts. Colton's tugging a nurse towards me. I've never met her, but I've seen her picture a few times. Evie. The woman Colt's obsessed with. He's been hounding me to meet her, but I barely have a spare second between work and the club.

I watched Evie with my sister. The gentle way she touched her, how she spoke to her, even if Bree couldn't hear her.

I love her. I love her because she's taking such good care of Bree. And I love her because she looks at Colt like he's the most incredible man in the world. He deserves that.

Colt's face radiates concern. "What just happened? What did he do?"

He's such an amazing friend. He loves so big, so deeply, you never have to guess where he stands. I smile, thankful he's here on this completely shitty night. "He fixed me."

"I don't understand, honey."

I shrug. "I thought I was in love with him. And he just made it very clear how he feels about me. So he fixed it. I'm done with him. He set me free."

I turn away, moving to my sister's bedside, blocking out Colt's confused gaze and Evie's sympathetic one.

My stupid heart is broken, but it doesn't get any more attention from me right now. Because the rest of my heart is lying in this bed. She's all that matters now.

5

DECLAN

The ER doors shut behind me, separating me from her.

"Fuck!"

Most of the people in the waiting room startle, but a few are slumped over, not moving. Somebody better fucking check on them. The security guard in the corner is eyeing me like he's sizing me up, trying to figure out if he can take me or not.

It's not.

He's big, but I've been trained to fight by tougher men than him.

I'm not looking to start a fucking brawl in the ER, though, so I head out the second set of doors into the crisp night air. Pacing, I peer into the waiting room, wishing I had Superman's X-Ray vision so I could see into the ER itself. So I could see Cara.

Everything fucking stopped when I saw her come through those doors, but not in a good way. Not the way it stopped when I saw her the first time. But like I might be about to lose everything.

I've lived through some scary shit, but I've never been this scared, and that says a fuck of a lot about how big my feelings are for her. So, of course, I fuck it up.

I used to do that. Lash out and let shit spew when I was overwhelmed. But I haven't done it in a long time, and I've never done it like that. Yeah, I have an issue with some of her choices, but to spew that shit all over her when she's hurt? When she's in pain and has been through something horrible?

That's low.

I want to go straight back in there, drop to my knees, and tell her how sorry I am. It is not her fault that her sister was attacked. It's not her job to predict that someone might go off the fucking rails. And for me to say so was inexcusable.

But if I go back in there right now, it's all about me. Her attention needs to be on her sister right now. Not on the asshole who spouted shit at her. But my words hurt her. Badly. And I'm desperate to fix it, and I don't fucking know how.

I can still feel her in my arms, on my skin. That was the first time I actually held her, and for a minute, I felt like a superhero. Like I could and would protect her from the world. It felt so right.

She felt so right.

I don't know how long I stand here, staring in the window. Long enough to be chilled. Long enough to see those slumped-over people get woken up and taken through the double doors. Long enough to see the security guard go on break, a shorter woman taking his place. I vaguely consider pushing past her to get back to Cara, but a closer look at her lined face convinces me to stay where I am. She has seen some shit, and she'd be a fuck of a lot harder to take down. Plus, I'd be no better than the fucker that hurt Cara's sister.

How did I not know she had a sister? The woman's not shy, so I thought I knew everything there was to know about her. But clearly, I don't.

I see his reflection beside mine the second before his hand drops on my shoulder. "Hey, Mav."

Maverick tightens his grip, standing next to me silently. Minutes later, Colt exits the ER. We watch him stride through the waiting room and out the automatic doors. He stomps to us, face a mask of rage that grows the closer he comes.

I deserve it. I know it's coming. I'm ready for it. I don't fight it. But the sheer force of his fist connecting with my stomach doubles me over.

"You are a fucking asshole."

I can't stand up straight, my stomach still clenching. I have to swallow the bile down to speak. "I know."

Colt turns to Maverick, already done with me. I don't blame him. I am a fucking asshole.

"It's bad, brother," he says. "From what I can tell, Cara killed her sister's boyfriend tonight."

Maverick has his game face on, not a flicker of reaction showing. "I've made a call to one of the top criminal defense attorneys in the city. For now, I'll stay with her. Make sure she doesn't say anything to the cops until Marty gets here."

"I can see if Evie can run interference. Cara's fucking wrecked, man. She's in no condition to answer questions right now. And her sister..." His voice trails off as he stares into the parking lot.

"Is she in rough shape?" Maverick asks.

"She's got bruises around her neck from his fucking hands. She's not waking up. It's not good."

Shoving my hands against my knees, I manage to stand upright. I always feel a bit like a kid next to Colt, but right now, standing between my brothers, I feel like an immature asshole. But I have to know. "Did you guys know she has a sister?"

They both turn to stare at me like I'm dumb. It's Mav who answers. "Yeah, of course, I fucking knew. I work with her every day. I know a fuck of a lot about her life."

"I didn't know," I say quietly. I work with her every day too. But still, I didn't know.

Colt curses under his breath. "You don't fucking talk to her. You don't know her."

I open my mouth to...I don't know, defend myself? Agree? Either way, it doesn't matter.

"Fuck," Colt says, grabbing Maverick's arm. "Cops are here. Let's go." He pulls him through the doors into the waiting room and, with a smile and a few words, gets past the security guard and back into the ER.

I stand, one hand on my aching stomach, watching as the two detectives walk past me. Their badges aren't out. They're dressed in jeans, but everything about the way they walk, the way they scan their surroundings, spells cop. We've all got a lot of fucking experience spotting them. The way we grew up, it's a skill necessary for survival.

Waves of regret and shame wash through me. My brothers are in there supporting Cara while I stand out here, useless. They're capable, powerful men. They'll take care of her, I have no doubt. But it should be me. I should be the one comforting her. Protecting her. But I fucked that up.

My phone chimes with a text, and I dig it out of my pocket.

Colt: Find everything you can on this fucker. Make this right.

He's right. I have nothing to offer here. Not right now. My brothers are far more capable. So I'll go home and do the only thing I can do. The only thing I'm good at.

Reluctantly, I turn and hail one of the cabs idling nearby. Resting my head on the window, I watch as the hospital gets smaller and smaller. When it's gone from my sight, I turn my attention to the problem at hand. I may not be able to be there for Cara, but I can tear this fucker's life apart and find every bit of dirt on him I can.

I will not allow her to be punished for protecting herself and her sister.

6

DECLAN

I slide another document into the folder labeled with her name, Cara. I'm fixating, I have been for weeks, but I don't know what else to do. Gathering up any dirt I can on anyone remotely connected to that Tyler guy and the cops investigating his death is all I can do.

I flick my monitor off at the soft knock on my door. I know that knock. None of my brothers would ever ask permission to enter, so that's a dead giveaway. And they've never done anything softly.

Well, that's not totally true.

They're total marshmallows with their women, but here, when it's just us? It's slaps and swears and shouting down the hallway.

"Come in, Janey."

She cracks open the door, peeking in first, then coming in the rest of the way. I hide my involuntary grin. I don't know what she thinks I'm doing in here, but she comes in the same way every time, like I might be naked or some shit. But not in a judgmental way. More like she doesn't want to interrupt my happy time. It's one of my favorite things about her.

"Hi, Declan. I just wanted to say goodnight. How was

your day?" She's wearing one of her favorite outfits. At least, I think it's her favorite since I see her in it all the time. A simple gray silky shirt and those tight black pants women wear. She fills them both out really nicely. And I feel like a dick now for thinking it.

"My day was ok, Janey. How about I walk you out?" I mean, what else am I going to say? *I'm drowning in guilt and feel totally powerless to help the woman I spend every night obsessing over?*

Her nose crinkles when she smiles, and I can't hold back an answering grin. She's so fucking adorable. How did she fly under our radar for so long? She's worked for us for years, answering the phones at the front desk. Greeting people. But recently, we promoted her to head of HR. I don't think there's an official name for what she does, but People Fixer comes close. There's something about her that just sucks you in and makes you want to spill your guts. And she's about the most people-smart person I've ever met. She sees connections and patterns in people that the rest of us miss. We're not stupid, so we created a position for her to take advantage of her skill set.

I put my hand on the small of her back, escorting her down the long hallway. All my brothers' offices are on this side of the building, one next to the other. My feet slow automatically as we approach Ransom's office. His door is open, and I can hear my brother's voice. But that's not why I slow. It's because she's there, Cara, in the office right across from his. We haven't spoken, not a single word since the hospital. Not since I opened my fucking mouth and let stupidity pour out.

"Things are still hard between you two," Janey says softly. Her eyes are on Cara, too, as she moves around her office.

"Yeah. I thought I might be able to fix it, but I haven't been able to get her alone. Between her sister and her work here, it seems like she never has a spare minute."

Janey hums, tilting her head. "Sometimes broken things

can't be fixed. If you don't figure out a way to fix your friend-ship soon, it might stay broken."

My mouth dries up. "It's only been a few weeks, though. So not really that long."

Janey's blue eyes narrow on mine. "Do you understand where you went wrong with her?"

"Yeah, I said some shit I shouldn't have."

"Why shouldn't you have said it?"

I go to run my fingers through my hair, the movement a reflex. Only there's nothing there.

"Because it's none of my business that she spends all her fucking time at clubs. She's allowed to, and I shouldn't have judged her for it."

"But you did judge her. You don't like the way she spends her time, do you?"

Christ, Janey's eyes feel like laser beams. "No, I guess I don't." Or, more accurately, I wish she was someone who would be happy hanging out with a guy like me. A guy who breaks out in hives in big crowds. But that's not fair, even I can admit that.

Janey smiles sadly. "Maybe that's the bigger problem then. You've looked at her life and decided she's not living it right. So why does it matter if you barely speak anymore? You don't seem to respect her or like the way she spends her time. And that's ok. You don't have to have anything to do with each other. There's no rule that says you have to be close with your employees."

Employee. Yeah, technically, Cara is an employee, but she was never in that box. From the day she started here, she was always crossing the professional line with me. The guys made fun of me for it, and I didn't always handle it well, but she was bright and sexy and in your face all the time. I fucking hate seeing her so withdrawn.

"She's not just an employee," I admit.

Janey nods, unsurprised. "Then, if she's more, you need to

stop avoiding the problem. I've learned that the longer you leave a wedge between two people, the harder it is to fix. Unless …" She bites her lip, studying me. "Do you think she did something she needs to apologize to you for?"

"Fuck no. I was an ass. She had just been through something awful, and I said some shitty things to her. It doesn't matter whether I believed them or not. I should never have said it."

She smiles slightly and pats me on the arm. "Then fix it. Don't wait any longer. I'll ask one of the security guards to walk me out." She turns and leaves me standing there, staring at Cara like a creeper.

Fix it. It's not that hard. Just go up to her and tell her I was a colossal ass, and say sorry. Then we can go back to the way we used to be. I can do that. But my feet don't move. I stand there, like a fucking idiot, taking her in.

She's always been stunning. A wild mane of blonde hair and sharp blue eyes. From day one, she dressed like a sex goddess with deep v-necks and tight skirts that emphasized her curves and her soft belly. She favors leather, lace, and silk. She always looks touchable, fuckable.

She's changed since that night. She's been doing more buttons up in the last few weeks, wearing pants, pulling her hair back. She's dimmed her light. I didn't realize I'd miss it so much.

As she pulls her coat on, I move towards her, stopping in the doorway of her office. "Cara."

Her expressive eyes shutter, mouth firming. "Declan."

We stare at each other, and my fucking throat closes up the way it always does. But this is too important. I clear my throat and shove my hands in my jeans pocket. "Cara. I'm so fucking sorry. I should never have said...what I said at the hospital. I was completely out of line."

Her eyes drop to the floor. "Yeah, you were."

"I'm really sorry."

"Ok," she whispers, briefly meeting my eyes before turning to grab her purse. "I need to go. Goodbye." She turns, raising an eyebrow to get me to move. She steps into Ransom's office to say goodbye, and I follow her. She accepted my apology. So why doesn't it feel all better?

All my brothers are here except Micah. He's across town at the garage, working on one of his customs. But the rest of us are crammed in this room like we usually are at the end of the day. Looking at us, you'd be forgiven for thinking we're blood. All big, dark-eyed with dark hair.

We're not.

We're a bunch of lost boy misfits that Ransom brought together to make a family. Now, we're brothers in every sense of the word.

"Cara," Ransom says softly, "can you come sit for a minute?" She nods, falling into one of the chairs across from him. Maverick occupies the other one. "Mav was just filling us in on the investigation. They're still dragging it out. I'm so fucking sorry."

The lines around her eyes soften. "You don't have to be sorry."

"Yeah, I do. They're making this painful because you're connected to us. It's pretty fucking obvious that if you hadn't...done what you did, your sister would be dead. It's clear-cut. If you didn't work here, the case would already be closed. But Jackson's been holding a grudge for eighteen years."

Cara grins, but it's a shadow of her old one. "I've used your name to get my way, your way, a lot over the years. It's been a mostly good thing. It's ok if it comes with a little bad now." Ransom looks grim but doesn't object. He should. This is way too much bad. It would be different if it were one of us under the gun. We've all earned it. But her? An innocent? It's not right. "Why...why does he have a grudge against you guys? What am I caught in the middle of?"

Ransom rubs the back of his neck, and glances at Colt, who gives him a small nod. "Years ago Colton's brother killed Jackson's cousin. The family was full of losers, so it honestly didn't occur to us that he would make something of himself. Now that he's worked his way into a position of power as the District Attorney, he's trying to find anything he can on us."

"I'm confident things will go your way, Cara. It's just going to take a little while longer. How are you holding up?" Maverick asks. He's not a criminal lawyer, but he's been working with the top one in the city to take care of her.

"Fine," she murmurs, and it's total bullshit.

Colt leans forward on the couch, eyes begging. "You're not fine, Cara. We can all see it. And it's ok if you're not. You've been through something shitty, you and Bree both. But you don't have to do this alone. Let us help you?" He's a big fucking teddy bear, and he wants to take care of everyone all the time. Cara looks like she's about to object, but his "please" brings her to a stop.

She runs her fingers down the crease of her pants. "Maybe I could take the day off tomorrow? I'd like to go look at some new apartments."

"Of course, you can have the day off," Ransom says. "What's bringing this on now?"

It's a testament to their relationship that she answers honestly. If anyone else had asked, I'm not sure she would have been as truthful.

"Ah, Bree and I are having some trouble sleeping. Every time we go into the living room, all we can see is his body on the floor. We just...I just need to not be there anymore."

Jesus. Of course, they're having trouble sleeping. I'm shocked she's managed to stay for the last three weeks. But the stress of finding a new place and moving? That's a lot too. "We've got a two-bedroom on the same side as Evie's. Why don't you move there?"

Shit. I shouldn't have been the one to say it. I know we're

all thinking about it. We still have three empty apartments on the thirty-fourth floor of our high-rise. Why shouldn't she use one? But coming from me? I doubt it will go over well. Her eyes flash up to mine, a wrinkle in her brow. She's already shaking her head. I glare over at Colt.

He clears his throat. "That's a great idea, actually. They're just sitting empty. They cost us money every month. We can have you guys settled in there in a couple of hours."

Cara's frowning. "I don't know if that's such a great —"

"Sounds good," Ransom says, slapping the top of his desk. "We've got Kade and Colt's trucks and Jonas's minivan. We can have you packed up and moved over in no time."

A smile blooms over her face as she shakes her head. "Pushy bastards. You guys realize you're billionaires, right? You're supposed to pay people to do shit like this. Do you even know where to find moving boxes?"

Colt hoots, throwing his arms up in the air. "Me! I know."

She shoots him a dirty look, but her eyes are laughing. It makes my stomach ache to see it. "Only because I arranged it when you went to get Evie, and I told you where to pick them up."

He sits back smugly. "Doesn't matter. I recognized the place. We have a bunch of them here...one not too far away if I'm not mistaken. What the fuck would you guys do without me?"

And that's how I end up standing in the middle of Cara's bedroom, holding her panties.

7

CARA

"Bree," I yell, throwing myself through the door. It's an echo of that night three weeks ago, and it sends a shiver down my spine, even though I know she's ok. "Bree, we've got company coming. All my bosses are on their way." That last bit may have come out slightly panicked.

I don't care who you are. No woman wants a bunch of men invading her space without having time to clean up first. Brianna and I don't live like pigs, but even so, a bunch of fucking billionaires are coming through that door any minute and I'm freaking the fuck out.

I have to admit I'm grateful, though. Ever since that night, everything has felt harder, more unbalanced. I told the guys that I was uncomfortable going into the living room, but uncomfortable is too mild a word for the way I feel. I can't even go near the spot where Tyler's body was covered with that sheet. Every time I do, all I hear is Bree's screams and the dull thump her head made every time he banged it on the wall. I remember the fear, the panic, the terror.

Bree comes out of her room, hair standing up on end. She's been sleeping a lot, but the doctor says it's normal. She's not back to the old her, but I'm so fucking grateful that she's here, standing, able to talk. It doesn't matter what other deficits she might end up with. She's alive.

"What? All your bosses? What is happening?" She looks completely confused, and I don't blame her.

"I kind of mentioned to Ransom that we weren't sleeping very well. I just wanted a day off so I could go and look at some new apartments for us, but the guys decided we should move into their building in one of the empty apartments they own. They're on their way to help us pack up everything and move us." I'm running around frantically picking up the shit we've left lying around. My bedroom is a mess since Bree, and I are basically living in our rooms. More nights than not, we're both sleeping in the same bed.

That could have something to do with why we're so tired. We're both bed hogs, we both talk in our sleep, and ever since she was a kid, Bree's thrown punches when she's dreaming. Dad always teased she must be fighting off all the boys who love her.

"Wait, they have empty apartments? Just sitting empty, waiting for what?"

"They built the whole fucking building, and they own all the apartments under the gym. I don't know why exactly. All I know is they're empty except for the one Colton's girlfriend lives in."

"So what, we're just gonna go live in one, just like that?"

I drop my pile of laundry on my bed and move back to the doorway of her bedroom. There's something in her voice that makes me slow down and really look at her. She looks terrified, and she's trying to hide it. Before this month, I hadn't seen that look on her face in years.

"Oh, Bree, I'm sorry this is happening so fast. I didn't plan on any of this happening tonight, but they asked how we were doing, and before I knew it, I had just told them the truth. We're not sleeping, Bree. We can't use our own living room, and I know you're having nightmares. I am too. I can't help thinking that the quicker we get out of here, the better it's going to be for both of us."

She wraps her arms tight around her body, hugging herself. She used to walk with her shoulders back, confident in the world. And I fucking missed it when she started to change. It changed when Tyler came along. It's his fucking fault.

"No, I guess we aren't sleeping. But this is all happening so fast."

"I know. How can I help you? How can I make this easier for you? Because eight very large men are about to descend on us. And all of them are determined to help." My voice shifts to a whisper. "And honestly, Bree, I think we need it."
Bree shuffles forward, tucking herself into my body. I wrap my arms tightly around her, worrying all over again about how thin she's getting. We've always been thick, right from when we were kids. But since that night, it feels like Briana is wasting away. We need to leave here for so many reasons.

The knock on the door lights a fire under my ass. "Go brush your hair, throw it up in a pony. Then come meet the guys. I promise they'll be good to you."

I take a few deep breaths, looking back to make sure Bree's in her bedroom, then I swing open the door revealing a sea of men. A chuckle escapes me as I take in the wide shoulders, tall frames, and smiling faces. "Why on earth do you look so happy to be here? I have a lot of shit, guys. This is gonna suck." But I know why they're smiling. They've been worried about me. It's been obvious. There hasn't been a single snarky comment or bit of teasing in weeks. And I'm woman enough to admit that I'm soaking up their concern. I need to be taken care of right now, just a little bit.

I wave them in, and they file into the living room, filling it.

Not eight bodies. Nine. They all came, and I have to choke back the tears. I can't worry about what used to be on that floor they're standing on because they're all looking at me with raised eyebrows. I shake off the memories and clap my hands together.

"So, first of all, thank you. I appreciate this. Ransom, we'll work out the rent details later. For now, I need you guys to hear me." I move closer to them, lowering my voice. "Bree's struggling a little bit with how fast this is happening. Since the...that night, she's been dealing with a bunch of concussion symptoms, as well as some memory issues. She's having a hard time with sounds and lights. So I'm going to bring her out to meet you, then she'll go into her room and pack as much as she can. When it's time for her stuff, I'll take her to the car or something."

The guys are nodding, smiles gone. Their eyes shift over my shoulder. I turn, waving Bree forward. She approaches slowly, shoulders back. I can see the effort it takes to put on a brave face. "Bree, I want you to meet the guys." Her eyes lock on the towering men in front of us. I introduce them one by one.

"This is Ransom, the best boss in the world. He's like the daddy of the group." The guys muffle laughs behind their hands, and Ransom rolls his eyes.

Bree gives him a soft, "Hello."

"Next are Jonas and his brother Zach. Jonas is the financial wiz and has a whole sexy accountant vibe going a lot of the time." Jonas's eyes widen, a blush staining his cheeks. "Zach is head of marketing and a total man-whore. Stay away from him." Zach smirks, radiating pure sex for a second. I glare at him, and he turns it off, putting his everyday smile on. Bree's cheeks are red, but she's smiling. Thank god. The guys are coming across as total pussycats, which isn't an act when it comes to the women in their circle.

"Micah here is a car wiz. He does beautiful restorations and custom work. And I didn't know he was going to come. Thank you so much."

He gives me a gentle smile and Bree a soft, "Hi, Bree."

"Bree, you've met Maverick. Lawyer extraordinaire. Saver of my butt. And next to him is Nick. Nick's kind of a problem solver, I guess? I don't actually know what your job title is, but he could convince a nun to marry him in ten minutes, flat."

Bree's voice is deadpan. "So you have excellent oral skills?"

The guys all freeze, eyeballing her, until her lip twitches, and she gives herself away. The guys howl with laughter, slapping Nick and reaching out for high-fives from Bree. She's smiling as she returns them, blushing when a laughing Nick kisses her hand.

This crazy whirlwind of a plan now seems like a stroke of brilliance, despite who suggested it. He's there, his presence, like a buzzing along my skin. Why does he still affect me like this? And why the fuck is he staring at me like that? Like I kicked his puppy. He's the one who was a dick. I've wasted way too many days obsessing over him.

As the laughter dies, I clear my throat and finish the introductions. "Kade's the operating officer, he keeps things running smoothly, and his girlfriend is a ninja. She's awesome. Colton, you know of course. He's the biggest, sweetest teddy bear in the world. And Declan fixes computers."

Take that. Thank god Bree's my ride or die. Other than a slight widening of her eyes, she doesn't let on that she knows exactly who Declan is. That she's listened to me on more than one very drunk occasion wax poetic about his beautiful eyes and long fingers. She doesn't let on that I've confessed some very secret...wishes to her.

The guys are so gentle with her, speaking softly but

teasing her in a way that lets me know that they've taken her under their wings. In a way that tells me, I can start breathing again. That other people will worry about her too and care if she gets better.

When I can tell Bree's getting overwhelmed, I send her back to her room. And in quick order, the guys have moving boxes assembled, and they've split up to carefully pack my apartment. Well, carefully is a relative term. I snatch a few of my glass figurines out of Colton's hand, wrapping them myself. Shooing him away from all my breakables so I can make sure they get to our new place in one piece.

The chaos takes my mind off what happened here completely. I have no time to think about the blood or the screams. I'm too busy running around trying to direct the guys. They disappear with box after box, and soon I'm left in the nearly empty apartment.

I knock on Bree's door, sticking my head in. "Ready?"

She nods, dropping a handful of clothes in the box at her feet. "I got most of it packed. Just a bit of bathroom stuff left." I let Colton and Micah in to cart things off. Colton doing what he does best, putting Bree at ease. She follows them out the door, chatting, not a glance backward. Clearly, my worry over her was a little misplaced.

Knowing Colton will take care of her, I scan the empty living room Before everything happened, this place was our refuge. We moved in here in pain and loss. Clinging to each other as we mourned our parents. It was a place of healing for us. A place where we figured out how to be a family without mom and dad. A place where we grew and developed into the women we are now. It was our safe little nest, but it's not anymore. But I do feel a pang as I realize we're gonna walk out those doors and never come back.

I mentally say goodbye, thanking this place for sheltering us. I know it's an apartment, but it still feels appropriate somehow to show some gratitude. Then I turned to do one last check of my bedroom. My feet glue themselves to the floor I take in the large man standing in the middle of the room, the man I thought I loved, clutching...yep, a pair of my panties in his hand.

Fuck my life.

8

DECLAN

"I swear I wasn't being creepy," I shout to Cara. She stands, mouth open in the doorway. My fist tightens around the red satin. I should probably hand them to her or drop them, but I can't get my fingers to unclench.

"Why the fuck are you holding a pair of my panties?" Cara's voice is tight, an angry red flush on her gorgeous cheekbones. And, of course, I lose my fucking words, stuttering, mumbling, and getting nowhere. I close my eyes, counting to ten as I breathe. I can't afford to fuck this up anymore. I give myself a mental pep talk. *Man the fuck up. Just speak to the woman.*

"The guys took your bed and all the boxes. I was just checking, and I noticed something on the floor. I didn't know what it was, and I picked it up. I'm sorry." I stretch out my arm, the red satin panties twisted through my fingers. "Here." She blows out a breath, making her bangs flutter, then stomps towards me, grabbing the fabric from my hand. But I don't let go. I can't.

"Cara. Wait. Can we please talk? Please. We can't go on like this." Her fingers tighten, and her lips firm, and I think she's going to deny me. But she doesn't. She nods. I release the fabric immediately. I can't look at it in her hands, instead focusing on those heartbreaking eyes of hers. They stole the thoughts right out of my head the first time I saw them.

"I fucked up really badly that night. I know you accepted my apology earlier, but it didn't feel like enough. I should never have said what I said. I was completely out of line."

Cara's lips twist into a grimace. "Declan, you said that already. But not once have you said you were wrong." She wets her lips. "Why would you say that to me? Do you really believe that?"

Christ, I can't look at her. "Not really. I know nothing that happened that night was your fault. I do. And it was stupid of me to ever say that it was. My only defense is that I was freaked out to see you there. You were hurt and bruised, and I didn't handle it well."

"You didn't handle it well," she echoes, rubbing the corner of her eye. "That's an understatement."

"I know. I'm sorry. Again."

"What do you want from me, Declan?"

"I want things to go back to the way they were. At work, I mean. I want us to go back to being friends."

"You think we were friends?"

"Well. Yeah. We saw each other every day. We talked."

She's shaking her head, a sad laugh on her lips. "Declan, we weren't friends. Did you even know I had a sister before that night?"

I shift uncomfortably. She reads the answer on my face, unsurprised. "Yeah. You don't know me. You don't know anything about my life."

"That's bullshit. You didn't tell me about your sister. How was I supposed to know?"

"You could have asked Declan. You could have tried to get to know me. You never did."

I rake my hands through my nonexistent hair. Maybe this is why Colton's always running his fingers through his beard.

I move my hand to my beard and try it, and while not quite as satisfying, it'll do.

"Cara, you were kinda...always right there," I say, putting my hand in front of my face.

Her cheeks redden further, and she turns away. "Yeah. I guess I owe you an apology for that, too. I behaved inappropriately with you at work. I should never have...done that."

"That? Do you mean the cornering me at work, the rubbing up on me? The touching me." There was so much touching. I loved it, but it killed me. The way she'd run those pointy nails of hers over the collar of my shirt or down the zipper on my hoodie. It was sexy as fuck, and I would blank every single time she did it, unable to think of anything but backing her into the wall, lifting her skirt, and pushing into her.

"I am well aware that my behavior was out of line," she says stiffly. "You would have been within your right to report me for harassment." I nearly laugh at that. Why the fuck would I report her for something I looked forward to every day?

"Why did you do it?"

"It was a mistake. I was teasing, but I realize now I crossed a line."

Shit. My chest deflates. I always hoped she liked me. I was just too fucking insecure to do anything about it. But I was wrong, and it's way too late. "So...you don't like me anymore? That's what you're saying?"

"You asked me if we could go back to the way things were. I'm answering you. No. No, they can't go back. I won't act like that anymore. You're my colleague, and I should have always been treating you more professionally. I will from now on."

I don't want professional. I don't want distance. I don't want her doing what she has been doing for the last three weeks, ignoring me. I want her fucking hands back on me.

"Can we...can we just slow down for a minute?"

She crosses her arms under her breasts, eyes heavy. "Declan, I don't think there's anything more to say. You don't owe me anything. I don't owe you anything. We work together, and that's it. Right?"

"But why can't we be friends?"

"You think I'm the kind of person who would choose to party, over my sister. Why would you want to be friends with someone you think so little of?"

"Fuck! I told you I was sorry."

Cara ignites, dropping her arms and pushing into my space. "Do you respect the way I live my life, Declan? Yes or no?"

"I respect you, Cara, but don't you talk about going to clubs every night?" I need to stop. I should stop. But of course, I fucking don't. She asked me a question, and now, of course, I have to answer it. "Maybe there's something else you could do. Maybe take up a hobby or join a club or something." Holy fuck, I'm so stupid. Why the fuck do I do this?

"You condescending fuck. Want me to get a hobby? Sit at home and knit booties for my imaginary children? Maybe find a boring stuffed shirt and marry him? Pop-out some real babies to make booties for? How should I be spending my time exactly? Oh wait, maybe I should sit at home and play video games like you? Live in an imaginary world and make friends I can only talk to online." She sneers. "Yeah, your way is so much better."

My ears are on fucking fire. And my defensiveness rears its ugly head. I feel it coming, and I'm powerless to stop it. Three weeks of worry and stress, and frustration pour out. "At least I have real friends, Cara. Instead of spending my time with a bunch of random men at clubs all over town."

She presses a hand to her stomach and steps back. "So wrong. How could I have been so wrong?" she mumbles, almost to herself. Her hard eyes lock on mine. "I think we're done here. You've made it very clear what you think about me. And I have no interest in standing here while you slut shame me." I flinch at the word 'slut' coming from her lips. I never once thought that, but it obviously came out that way. I want to crawl into a hole and let her shovel dirt on top of me. That would feel better than standing here, knowing I just destroyed the last bit of hope I had for us.

Her eyes sweep the room one last time, then she tosses the panties at me. "Here. A little something to remember me by." Then she sweeps out of the room like the world didn't just explode, leaving me in the wreckage.

"Brother." Colton's voice brings my head up. He's standing in the doorway, rubbing his fingers through his beard. "What was that?"

How the fuck is he always right there every time I fuck up? Asshole must be psychic.

"Nothing." I don't want him digging into my head and pulling all my secrets out. He's too fucking good at it.

"Didn't look like nothing. I haven't seen Cara look like that...ever. What the fuck did you say?"

"It's automatically my fault?"

He puts his hands up defensively, but he's not backing down. "Cara's one of the most level people I've ever met. She handles shit that would send me through the roof. She handles it with an attitude, yes, but underneath it all, nothing gets to her. Nothing bothers her. She looked really fucking bothered just now."

"She didn't like me calling her out on her social life."

"Social life?"

"Yeah, all the fucking clubs. The guys she's always mentioning. I swear there's a rotation of them."

Colt winces, closing his. "Fuck. Tell me you didn't."

"Didn't what?"

"Say something stupid."

"I just told her she should find something better to do with her time than go to fucking clubs."

"Oh, you did it. Oh, god. You're never getting in there now. Never."

"What the fuck is the big deal? I called her out on her shit. Why is that so horrible?"

"Because you don't know what the fuck you're talking about." He leans against the doorframe, nearly filling it with his big, fat body. Ok, not fat. But he's still a stupid head. "You've made a fuck of a lot of judgments about Cara. I can almost see why, with the way she would corner you at work. But seriously, man, I don't think you could have said anything worse to her."

My righteous indignation is failing me. Something in Colt's eyes says I've fucked up so badly that I'll regret it for the rest of my life. "What do you mean?"

"I mean, brother, that she may be hell on wheels, but she's never paid anyone the kind of attention she did to you."

"She likes to fuck with me. That's all. She knew she made me nervous."

"She knew, I think, but she wasn't fucking with you. She was teasing, maybe. Being a little forward, but," he winces, "I'm pretty sure she had a thing for you. I never saw her get that close to anyone else."

I wish he was right. But she just told me she didn't. It's all just wishful thinking on my part and delusion on his. "She's a walking wet dream, Colt. She gets attention wherever she goes."

"Yeah, she does. She uses it to her advantage when it suits her, but she never crosses that line. Never." Rubbing the back of his neck, he wanders closer. "I don't know how or why you made up your mind about her. You didn't used to be so judgmental. I thought you liked her, man. Didn't you?"

"I do like her. A lot."

"Then why the fuck did you blow it up?"

Great question. I have no fucking clue. Or maybe I do, and I don't want to admit it to myself. Or to Colton. Maybe I wish she would have done more than tease me. Maybe I wish I would have been enough for her. Been better. Been someone who could handle her. I was fucking trying, but apparently not fast enough.

I end up shrugging because how the fuck do you say that you're jealous, and you handled it like a little shit? Because I did. The knowing look Colt gives me makes me think he's got me figured out.

"You handled things like a pussy. Face it. And move the fuck on. But honestly, brother, you'll have to move on with someone else. I don't think Cara will ever give you another chance." He heads out of the bedroom, stopping to drop one more bomb on me. "She's my friend. And I'll keep her confidence. But I will say this...she hasn't been on a single fucking date since I met her. And not once...not at the club or anywhere else, did I ever see her rub up on another man, especially not the way she did to you."

9

CARA

I t's a relief to close our new front door behind the last of the guys. Ever since that conversation with Declan, my nerves have been strung tight. I can't take one more sideways look from him. I turn, leaning my back on the door to take in our new place.

It's a serious upgrade from the old one. The floor-to-ceiling windows, the view of the lake, and the granite countertops are all stunning. And nothing I would ever pay for. For so long, Bree and I struggled. Now that I'm making good money at my day job and the business is running smoothly, I could maybe afford a place like this, but I'd rather spend the money building up our nest egg. Every time I see the balance in my investment account tick up, I feel a little more secure. A little more settled.

Heading to the main bedroom, I take in Bree, curled tightly on the bed. "Come lay down," she mumbles, eyes closed. She doesn't have to ask me twice. I lay with a groan, so thankful to be off my feet.

"We didn't carry a single box, and I still feel like I got hit by a truck. Moving is exhausting."

She hums out a laugh. "We haven't done it in a decade. But you're right. Last time was hard too."

Hard is an understatement. Last time we were grieving, in pain, and missing the people who had anchored us in this world.

"Yeah," I murmur.

"Do you need to go in tonight?"

"No. Avery has it covered. She'll call me if they need anything." I'm too tired to go in and deal with being the boss. The club is my baby, but I'm not a masochist. I hire great help, and I pay them well. I learned that from Ransom. Tonight, I just want to lie in this bed with my sister. "Bree, do you think you'll be happy here? I mean, do you think you'll be ok?"

Her eyes slit open, studying me. She reaches out and takes my hand. "It wasn't your fault. I didn't tell you what was going on. You gotta stop running over it in your head."

"I'm not," I say defensively. She gives me a look, and I cave. "Ok, I am." I slide closer until we're sharing the same pillow. "I just don't understand. Why didn't you tell me? How did it get so bad, and I never noticed? How did you let..."

Her mouth tightens, and I regret my words immediately. "How did I let him hurt me? That's what you really want to know, isn't it? How would I let my boyfriend treat me that way?" There's a bite in her words, but we've been dancing around this for weeks, and I think it's time. Time to say all the painful things. Time to purge them.

"Yeah, little Bee. How?" A small smile curves her lips when I use my nickname for her. She loved bumblebees when she was a baby. She used to insist I walk her around our backyard, clinging tightly to my finger, so she could find them.

"It was mostly good, Care Bear. It just snuck up on me. I thought it was cute that he always wanted to know where I was. He would get me to text him when I got home safe.

There weren't any red flags for a long time. Then he started to get jealous, and I realized he's not who I thought he was."

Her words echo my earlier thoughts about Declan. He's not who I thought he was, either. But I can't imagine he would ever be someone like Tyler.

"When did the...when did he start hurting you?" The words are ashy in my mouth.

Her hand tightens on mine. "That was the first time. I swear. I never expected it, Cara. Maybe I should have, looking back, but it never once occurred to me he would get physical with me." A single tear trickles over the bridge of her nose, falling to the pillow. "I was getting ready to leave him. He was extra possessive that night. I didn't like the way he was looming over me at the club. He was acting like a jealous ass. So we left, and we fought the whole way home." Her eyes drift closed, her lids almost translucent. "I told him I was done. That's when he grabbed me."

I snuggle even closer until we're nose to nose, breathing the same air. "I was so fucking scared that night, Bee. I thought you were dead."

A shudder runs through her body. "I thought I was dead, too. Then he turned on you, and I thought we were both done."

Her eyes open, locking on me with an intensity that I haven't seen from her in forever. "He doesn't get to break us, Cara. I won't let him. We've been hurting, but we're done now. I won't give him any more of my life. Not even a minute." Her hands tighten on mine. "You saved us. Don't you ever regret it. You don't have to be happy he's dead, but you should be damn happy that we're alive."

"When did you get so smart?" I ask, brushing her blonde hair off her forehead.

She snorts. "I'm trying something new."

We dissolve into giggles, something we haven't done in a

long time either. This move is feeling more and more like the right decision.

We relax, dozing for a while. Her curious voice breaks the silence. "So...Declan's hot. Somehow I pictured a long-haired geek. He is so...not that."

"He used to have long hair. He even had a bright red mohawk too. He lost a bet." Not the first time, from what I've heard. I've heard a whisper or two on the cost of losing other bets to his brother Jonas. One involving a tattoo on his ass cheek. I really hoped I would get the chance to verify that one for myself. Not happening now. Not with a man who thinks so little of me.

"Things seemed weird between you two."

"Weird is an understatement. We're...nothing."

"What happened?"

The ache is back in my stomach. "He said some things that showed me what he really thought of me."

She pushes up on her elbow, looking down at me. "Like?"

"Like I'm too old to spend all my time in clubs. Like I should have followed you home sooner that night instead of staying at the club." I can't look at her. "Like you got hurt because I wasn't there for you."

Bree drops back to the bed, tucking back in right next to me. "That's total bullshit, you know that, right?"

"It doesn't feel like bullshit. I should have seen that something wasn't right with you. I should have known." Bree reaches out, stroking down the bridge of my nose, then pinches the tip. "Ow. Fuck."

"Listen up," she says, letting go. "I'm an adult. I know our dynamic got twisted when mom and dad died, but you haven't been responsible for me for a long time. I made a choice, and I am the one that was living it. You're not a fucking psychic, Cara." I let her words penetrate that wall of guilt I've been carrying around for weeks. The one that formed at the hospital and wouldn't fall, no matter how much

I tried to convince myself I wasn't at fault. I put so much stock in Declan and what he thinks of me that I let his words carry more weight than they should have.

"I don't get how someone can know you for years and think that about you. He's so wrong." She's shaking her head, and something about the way she says *know you* stops me in my tracks.

"I'm not sure he actually knows me," I say slowly, rolling the words around. Testing their truth. "I mean, I saw him every day, but he never really talked to me. It was always me approaching him." My stomach is churning. "I made a fool of myself, Bree. I threw myself at him every time I saw him. Maybe he was just too polite to ask me to stop. If a man had been doing that to me, I probably would have reported him to HR."

"But he didn't report you, though."

"No, but he ran away from me. More than once."

She pops up, eyes wide. "He ran away from you?" Her lips are twitching. "That six-foot-three hunk of a man ran away from you? Fuck Cara, I thought you had game."

"Shut up," I grumble. "It's embarrassing. I've never been that girl. The one who chases the guy. I think I just lost my head for a while."

"You've never had to chase anyone. You're delicious, and all the men know it. So maybe he's just not for you? Maybe it's time to move on."

"I see him every day, though. Moving on is not really an option." I don't tell her I still look for him around every corner. That I can't go through the day without seeing him, even from a distance. I don't tell her because I don't want her to know how pathetic I truly am.

"You and I both know you could get another job in a heartbeat."

"Did you forget I killed someone? I can't see a future employer being stoked about hiring me." Do you have to put something like that on your resume? Where would it go? Maybe under miscellaneous?

"You're delusional. Even the news was saying it appeared to be self-defense. You're going to be cleared any day now. But even if it was a barrier, the club is doing well enough to support you. You know that. The job is just gravy." She crosses her legs, placing her palms on her knees. "Is that the only reason you were staying there?"

"No." At her raised eyebrow, I repeat it. "No. He's part of the reason. At least he was. But I really like it there. I love the rest of the guys. I feel like I earned a place there. If I left..."

"You'd lose them all."

"Yeah," I murmur. "It feels like I got to be a part of their family. I really liked it."

"So then, it sounds like you only have one option."

"Yeah, what's that?"

"Go back to work, and make him wish he'd realized how great you were before. You can rub his face in it a little. And outside of work? Get back on the fucking horse. Ride a cowboy or some shit. I don't know. Just find a new man and ride him."

I'm laughing, and it feels so fucking good. "I can do that."

I can. It would be easy. There's not a night at the club that I don't get an offer. Problem is, I don't want to. But I also don't want to spend the rest of my life wishing Declan would give me the time of day. So something's gotta give.

It might as well be my panties.

I can find someone else. Someone who thinks I'm amazing and wants to be my everything. It doesn't have to be him. It won't be him.

"Why don't we order a pizza? Watch *Magic Mike*. Maybe eat some ice cream while we're at it."

"That sounds like heaven. Why don't you—" The club's ring peals on my phone. I send an apologetic smile to Bree.

We both know if they're calling me, I'm going to end up going in.

She waves me off, snuggling back down into the bed. "I'll save some for you."

"You're getting pizza without me?"

She snickers, "Fuck yea. Bye-bye. Catch ya later."

I take her laughter with me into the night. Taking a minute when I hit the silence of my car to appreciate the spark lit in her. The one I thought would be permanently snuffed out by that night. I push the flutter of panic, of fear, that rises like a tide when I think of it. Of him. Tyler. Of what could have happened and of what I did. I let my tears fall there in my dark car, just like I did yesterday. And the day before. Someday, it'll feel better, right? Someday, I won't have to carry this guilt.

Someday. I hope.

10

DECLAN

She barely looked at me as we unloaded her stuff into the apartment. Not once did she make actual eye contact. I fucking tried to get her alone again, but my brothers were in the way. Colt's words are still ringing in my ear as I pound on Zach's door. Is it actually true? Cara's fucking dynamite, and I guarantee she gets offers. Why would she not be dating anyone? Colt has to be wrong.

Zach swings open the door, still in his tailored suit. Fucker carried boxes in a five thousand dollar suit. He's always dressed like he's going to be on the cover of some fancy magazine. His hair is always fucking perfect. His suit is never wrinkled. He's a full-on grown-up.

I, meanwhile, only bought new jeans because my new workout routine had my thighs busting out of my old ones.

"You heading out tonight?"

He studies me, seeing way too fucking much. "Come in." He turns, heading into his place. I follow behind him, careful to keep my hands in my pockets. More than any of us, Zach appreciates nice things. He fills his walls with expensive art featuring...I don't know what. It's all squiggles and slashes and looks kind of like someone just yeeted the paint at the canvas. But I keep my hands in my pockets because I broke a $30,000 vase in this apartment once, and I don't plan to repeat it. His whole apartment looks like it would fit neatly inside a museum for art or other expensive shit.

"I take it you want to go out tonight?" He mirrors my pose, hands tucked in the pockets of his suit.

"Yeah. I think I just need to get the fuck out of here for a little while."

"Colton told me about a club he invested in. We can go there. I just need a few minutes to freshen up."

Freshen up? He already looks fucking perfect. What is there left to freshen? And since when do guys say *freshen up*? The man has always been obsessed with the mirror. He used to pose and make model faces when we were kids.

I follow him to his bedroom. He heads into his closet, flipping through the packed contents. I've never been in here before, but holy fuck. "Dude, seriously? Do you really need this many suits?"

He smirks, sliding me his signature panty-dropping smile over his shoulder. The same one he used to practice in the mirror. Well he practiced that and what Colt calls his *sexy man lips*.

"I can afford them, and I look fucking amazing in them. Besides," he mutters, pulling off his shirt, "the ladies love them."

Do the ladies love them? I suppose they're an upgrade from my everyday wardrobe of jeans and hoodies. "Is that my problem, then? The way I dress?"

His face turns serious. He stops, shirtless, holding a thin sweater. "There's nothing wrong with you, Dec. When the world looks at you, they see a rich, successful guy who's not too hard to look at. The world isn't the problem."

It's an echo of what I've been thinking lately. I've been in my own fucking head for too long. I let my obsession with Cara, my fixation on her, take control of me.

"So, what is my problem?" I make sure my voice conveys curiosity and not a big old fuck you because I honestly feel like I need another perspective at this point. Maybe Zach sees something that I don't.

He pulls his black sweater over his head. "Why are you so scared of Cara? I mean, she's hot as fuck, and if she was rubbing up on me the way she does to you, you can be damn sure I'd have her in my bed. But you've spent more time running away from her than actually talking to her. Your problem is in your fucking head."

"How the fuck did you know this is about Cara?"

He laughs, shaking his head as he exchanges the expensive watch on his wrist for another equally expensive one.

"We all know you've been fucking with her computer so you can see her every single day. And I've been with you at these fucking clubs for months. Not once have you taken anyone home, even though you've had plenty of offers. Why?"

I can feel my cheeks heating as he looks at me. I shrug, hands still in my pockets. "It just wasn't right, man. I don't know how else to explain it." Plus I wasn't going to pick anyone up. I just wanted to try and be the kind of guy Cara would like.

He nods, looking unsurprised. "I can't pretend to know what it's like to be obsessed with one woman, but I would imagine that's pretty normal. You want her, and nobody else is going to do. So where does that leave you?"

"That's the fucking question, isn't it? I said some shit to her I shouldn't have, and now she seems to want nothing to do with me." He winces in sympathy, then glances in the mirror to double-check his perfect hair is still perfect.

"And I take it you've tried to fix it, and nada?"

"Yes, I fucking tried to fix it. I apologized over and over. But she doesn't look at me the same anymore."

"What do you really want from her? Because the days of her rubbing up on you at work are over, aren't they?"

"That's the fucking problem. I didn't want it to be over. I just wanted to be something different, someone, who could be with a woman like her. And for her to stop spending every free minute in clubs. I'm never going to be the kind of guy that can live that life. I don't really like going out that much."

Zach puts his hand on my shoulder, squeezing it. "Then maybe she's not the right choice for you. Have you thought of that? That you should be with someone that you don't need to change for?"

"I want her."

"You might want her, but after three fucking years, I think that ship has sailed, brother. Maybe you need to realize that she's not the woman for you and actually show some fucking interest at these clubs. There are dozens of women who would happily go home with you. Why the fuck aren't you spending time with one of them? Because Cara? That's not gonna happen."

IT'S NOT GONNA HAPPEN. THOSE WORDS RING THROUGH MY HEAD over and over as I drive us to this new club, Zach riding shotgun. The man has a car as expensive as mine, and he'd still rather ride shotgun in Jonas's minivan than drive himself.

The sexy red sign above the clubs door flashes *Curves Ahead*. It's clear by the line stretching down the block it's gonna be fucking hot in there. "Where did you hear about this place again?"

"Colton mentioned it to me earlier today. He said we might enjoy it. Apparently, he's an investor. I have no fucking idea when that happened." It's news to me too, but not surprising. Colt has a fuck of a lot going on.

I pull up to the valet, my Mercedes drawing everyone's attention as we pass the line. At first, I bought it for the attention it brought me. It's flashy as fuck and turns heads everywhere I go. It felt good to be seen. But that wore off fairly quickly. I'm not sure who I was trying to impress with the car, but it's got one feature that keeps me driving it. It goes fast. Really fucking fast. I love taking it to the track and opening it up. Seeing how far I can push it. I think I've always been a bit of a thrill seeker, but with money came the opportunity to feed the need. And feed it I do, with many, many cars.

I follow Zach up the steps to the velvet rope. The man standing there clocks us from our heads to our toes. I can see him mentally calculating the value of my watch and Zach's and coming up with dollar signs. Though my $300,000 car was probably hint enough that we're high rollers. He opens the rope and ushers us in with a smile.

Now, this is my kind of club. The music is loud and throbbing, which is typical. But the women on raised platforms around the room aren't. They're lush, curves overflowing, bellies and thighs on display. They're all sexy, all moving to the bass line. The sign out front makes a lot more sense now. Zach looks like it's Christmas morning. Laughing, I'm about to guide him to a booth when one of the waitresses approaches us.

"Gentlemen. Why don't you join me in our VIP area?"

Yep. They clocked us. We follow her to a raised area at the back of the club, passing two very large security guys who give us a nod. We relax back on the black velvet couch as she hurries away to grab us a bottle of Macallan 30.

"It always feels like these VIP areas are missing the point of coming to a club, aren't they? I mean, the women are down there. We're up here. It just doesn't compute."

Zach grins, resting his arm on the back of the couch as he surveys the tops of the heads in the full crowd. There are plenty of eyes on us, and more than one woman is smiling. "It's not about the women being up here. It's about having them see us up here. And if I want one, all I have to do is call her over."

"You sound like a douchebag." He laughs but doesn't disagree. We are on display up here. I wonder why they do that? "Do most VIPs want to be seen? I don't really get it."

Zach drops the arm, turning from playboy to brother. "I think it's a little like fishing, for the club and for us."

"How so? And what the fuck do you know about fishing?" The man lived his whole life in this city.

"I saw it on TV once. Did you know people fucking compete for fishing titles?"

"That's the weirdest fucking thing I've ever heard." What exactly is the competition? Like, is the heaviest fish the winner? Or is it like dogs, and there are certain breed details they're looking for? Are there breeds of fish? Is the plural of fish fishes? Zach's voice stops me from getting lost thinking about fishing. Thank fuck.

"Right? Anyway. For the club, the VIP section is a money-maker. There's an expectation we'll order premium and tip well. But for the VIPs, it's an opportunity to flaunt their wealth. To reel in the people they want."

"Reel in?" More fishing. "You mean women?"

"Can be. Or men. If you're after a fuck or some arm candy for the night. But those guys," he says, nodding towards a table full of suits, "aren't here for women. They're here to close a deal. They're giving their clients what they think they want. It's calculated. Most clubs are."

"That's cold."

He shrugs, winking at the waitress as she sets down our bottle and glasses, pouring us a finger each. "Maybe. But it's all marketing. People coming in here want something. They're looking for a hookup, or maybe they want to dance, or maybe they just want to be seen. They market themselves appropriately. Take her, for example." He points to a woman around our age in a strappy gold dress. "She's on the prowl tonight."

"How the fuck do you know that?" I don't see anything different about her. She looks the same as all the other women in here.

"She's dancing, just like the others, but watch her face. She's calculating, looking for the audience, showing off for the men she's targeting. Right now, that's us."

Oh fuck. Yep. She's looking right at us. Somehow staring at both of us as she dances. It's seductive, I suppose, but I'm just not feeling it. Zach though? The smirk on his lips seems to be leading her on.

"We just sat down, man. Already?"

He groans, grabbing his drink and leaning back on the couch. "Have you learned nothing in the last few months? I don't come to clubs for the booze. I've got the same bottle at home. I come for the women. I come to flirt and touch and, eventually, let one take me home. That was the whole point of this, but you don't seem to be getting with the fucking program. Get your ass down there, flirt, make out with a couple of women. There's nothing holding you back anymore. Cara is not yours. She's never going to be."

Every fucking time one of my brothers tells me to move the fuck on, I want to punch them in the face. I don't think there's ever going to be moving on from Cara. I swear, she's fucking haunting me. I see her everywhere.

It takes me too fucking long to realize the tall blonde moving through the crowd isn't a figment of my imagination.

Cara's here.

She's fucking here.

11

DECLAN

I can't take my fucking eyes off her as she moves across the room. She's inches taller than most of the other women in here. She stops to chat with the staff at the bar, smiling and laughing. They're all looking at her like she's wearing a fucking halo.

"Zach, Cara's here. At the bar." He sits up, eyes scanning the room, finally landing on her. He whistles.

"Shit, man. Looks like the Universe is out to fuck with you tonight."

Sounds about right.

We both watch her circulate through the room, smiling, laughing, and winking. She looks completely at home here and a version of herself we haven't seen at the office in a while. And I was right. The men fucking gravitate towards her, drawn in by her. I don't fucking blame them. She's a bright light, even in this sea of glitter and gold. She teases and casually flirts as she moves through the waves of admirers, never stopping for long, eyes always scanning.

It's on one of those scans that her eyes lock on the VIP area. On us. I watch as her smile dims and her shoulders fall. It's only for a second. She straightens and plasters a smile back on, but I can see the difference. Seeing us...seeing me, hurt her.

The bouncers nod at her respectfully as she climbs the stairs. She visits the table full of suits first, and they fall under her spell immediately. How the fuck does she know everybody? She must spend a fuck of a lot of time here. She turns, strolling over to us. I hate the way she focuses on Zach. She won't even meet my eyes, and I regret every stupid thing I ever said all over again. She leans her back against the rail, propping her elbows on it. To the outside observer, she looks relaxed, completely at home. But I can see the tightness in her eyes, in her smile.

"Well, what brings you gentlemen here tonight?" Her tone is light and flirty.

"Colton said we should check it out. I can see why. This place is killer."

A warm smile creases her face. "Thank you." The words are shy, making me sit forward. I nearly fall off the fucking couch at her next words. "I'm really proud of it."

"This place is yours?" How the fuck did I not know this about her?

Her eyes dart to mine. "Yeah. I leased the space a few years ago. A little after I started working for you guys, actually. Colton's an investor."

Zach slides toward me, leaving room at the end of the couch. "Sit your ass down, Cara. I have so many questions."

She grins at him, turning to survey the floor. She motions to someone, then curls into the spot next to Zach, facing us.

"Cara, Cara," he says with a teasing smile. "You've been keeping secrets. I want to know all about this place. Was there a club here before you took over the space?"

"There was. It was a shithole. I'd been keeping an eye on it. I knew it wasn't going to be open much longer, so I did some research and reached out to the landlord."

"So it closed, you scooped it up, and then?"

"It wasn't quite that easy. But yeah. I knew I had to find some investors. I approached a venture capital firm. Colton happened to be working with them at the time. He approached me privately, and we worked out a deal." She snorts. "He tried to help with some of the Renos, but he's fucking useless with tools." We both nod at that because, yep, he is. He hauls his purple toolbox around, but there are more toys than actual tools in there. He is enthusiastic, though, you gotta give the guy that.

Zach studies the space with his marketing guy eyes. "The concept and the layout are killer. I would know. I go out...a lot. Was it already like this, or did you design it this way?"

I'm pretty sure she's blushing. I've never seen her look like this. Almost...vulnerable. "I designed it. I studied a lot. I read everything I could get my hands on, and I spent a lot of time at the popular places, learning what was working for them."

Zach's voice is filled with admiration. "Jesus. Good for you, Cara. I had no idea." They dive into the science of clubs, and I zone out as I watch them. Watch her. She's so engaged, so excited about what she's built here. And she fucking should be.

The more she talks, the clearer my mistake becomes. Finally, I have to ask. "Every time you said you were going to the club...I thought you meant you were going out to party every night. But you were coming here?"

She finally looks at me. "Usually. I still check out other clubs at least once a week. I need to pay attention to what the competition is doing."

"You knew what I thought?" She could have told me she was going to her own club. Everything could have been different if she'd said something. But that's the fucking problem, isn't it? I keep expecting her to just volunteer everything about her life without putting a speck of effort in.

"I didn't tell anyone about this place, so I suppose, yes, I knew what you thought. I didn't realize you were judging me so harshly for it, though." She looks as though she wants to say more but changes her mind. Then, changes it back again. "I have a lot of customers that are here multiple nights a week. They come because they like being in a place that's fun, with bartenders who remember their names and their favorite drinks. For a lot of them, they dance, they socialize, and they go home alone. They're good people."

I open my mouth to explain myself. To apologize again, but I don't. Now is not the time, and this is definitely not the place. But I hate that she feels she has to defend herself to me.

"This place is different from most of the places we've been to," I say instead. It is. It's sexier and seemingly more people-focused. Not as much of a meat market as the other clubs Zach took me to.

Zach pulls her attention with another question, leaving me with my spinning thoughts. I fucked up. Big time. There is no doubt about it. The question is, can I recover from it? Cara doesn't seem like she's interested in giving me any more chances, but fuck if I'm willing to just roll over and give up. She showed us a part of herself tonight that I've never seen before. I didn't know she owned a business. I didn't know she'd built something like this for herself.

As shitty as it might have been of me, I honestly looked down on her a bit when I thought she was a partier. Maybe I was comparing her a little to the women Zach attracts at the fucking clubs. The vapid ones. The ones that are all about the good time. Maybe I'm too fucking old, but none of that inter- ested me. Sure, I could talk to them, but there are only so many superficial conversations I can have without losing my mind. And it never seemed to line up with who I knew her to be at work. I couldn't reconcile the driven, take-charge woman I know with the after-hours party girl.

"How are things going with Maya? You convinced her to come work for you yet?" she asks Zach. I lean back, eager to hear his answer. Happy to think about something other than my dumbass self.

Irritation makes his words crisp. "No. She still won't take my fucking calls."

"Have you considered she just doesn't want to leave her job?" Cara asks.

"Why the fuck would she want to stay? I'm offering her more money and more creative control. What else could there be?"

Cara leans back, absentmindedly rubbing her bottom lip. I can't take my eyes off her. "Have you considered what else, other than work, might be keeping her in New York? Maybe there's another reason she doesn't want to move."

Zach looks thoughtful. "No, I hadn't thought of that." He turns to me. "Dec, can you do a little more digging? See if you can find out more about her?"

"Yeah, man. I'll look into her some more tomorrow." I already have a file started on her. I only looked her up at first because Zach was so frustrated by the mysterious M. Miller. Fucker didn't realize he was headhunting a woman.

"Look into her habits. Maybe she has a tie to the city that you just won't be able to sever. At least if you know, you can move on and stop obsessing over her."

"I'm not obsessing. I just wish she'd reply to a fucking email or answer the fucking phone. Why does she have to be so difficult?"

"You don't really do 'difficult' when it comes to women, do you?"

Zach scowls at Cara, making her laugh. She pats him on the leg.

"I've got to get back on the floor. My manager called in sick tonight, so I need to keep an eye on things." She hesitates, looking between us. "I'll see you at work tomorrow." She uncurls herself from the couch, and I pop up when she stands. I almost bow but stop myself. Why am I such an awkward fucker?

She gives me a funny look, then strides off, confidence back in full force.

"How late do you think she'll have to work?" I ask Zach.

He shrugs. "Club probably closes after three. I wouldn't be surprised if she's here right up till then."

"How the fuck does she do that? Work till three, then show up at the office by nine? When does she sleep?"

"Makes you wonder, doesn't it, how much she's sacrificed to build this place? Seems like her whole life is work right now."

"Sacrifice," I mutter, eyes still on her blonde head. "We understand sacrifice. Nine of us slept in a studio apartment for years. We hustled for every dollar. Everything we have is because of those sacrifices early on."

Zach eyes me. "Sit down, you awkward fuck."

"Fuck you." There's no heat in the words. I'm barely aware of Zach. My mind is fucking spinning. When Cara heads down a hallway, out of sight, I drop to the couch.

"What's going on, brother? What's happening in your head?"

"I fucked up. But I'm going to fix it. I'm going to woo her. I'm going to make her mine."

Zach groans and leans his elbows on his knees, studying me. "Did you just use the word 'woo'?"

Fucker's laughing at me. I don't care. "Yeah. Our dynamic was fucked up. She came onto me, and I froze and ran. It's my turn to chase her."

"So you just decide to go after her? What about the freezing?"

"I'll figure it out. I spoke complete sentences tonight, didn't I? This is too big for me to keep acting like a pussy."

"I don't disagree, but it sounded like Cara was pretty done with you. Do you really think you can change her mind?"

"You tell me? You're the one who's been taking me to the fucking clubs, trying to help me build my confidence. Am I going to be able to change her mind?"

He winces. "It's completely different. You have no trouble getting those women wrapped around your finger. You have no history, and most of them came around because they smelled money when we walked in."

He's not wrong. Cara is in a completely different league, and I clearly have a lot to fucking learn.

"Dec...maybe trying to build your confidence the way we did was a mistake. Maybe you should treat this like one of your projects. You're a single-minded bastard when you're digging for dirt on those computers of yours. What if you turn that focus to learning, Cara?"

"Like, dig into her life. Wouldn't that be—"

"Not on your computer, dipshit. In real life. Get to know her, pay attention, be present." He rises, moving to the railing, mimicking Cara's earlier pose. "I've never wanted anyone the way you seem to want Cara, so I shouldn't be giving you advice. But I will. Anything you picked up from me at the clubs...ignore it. What I do at those clubs has nothing to do with love...at least, not the kind you're talking about. Now," he says, rubbing his hands together, "I've got a gold goddess to meet. I'll find my own way home."

And he's gone, weaving through the crowd, eyes locked with the woman in gold from earlier. To each his own, I suppose. Not nearly enough curves there for me, though. Shaking my head, I scan for our waitress, signaling her over to switch out my drink order. I'm in it for the long haul tonight.

I SPEND THE NEXT FEW HOURS SIPPING SODA AND RESEARCHING club design on my phone. The more I learn, the more I understand why Zach was so impressed. She's designed this whole place to make people collide, but in a good way. Forcing them to rub up on each other and interact with each other. It's brilliant, and I had no idea it was a fucking thing.

I somehow know it every time Cara's near. We make eye contact several times throughout the night, her gaze getting more and more puzzled. As the lights go up and people pour out, I make my way to the bar and sit at the end.

The very large bartender stops wiping down bottles, moving to me. "Sorry, buddy. Time to go home."

I nod. But don't take my eyes off Cara. "I'm waiting for Cara. I'll walk her out when she's ready."

He frowns, moving back to the other end of the bar to talk to her. There's a lot of head shaking, and she scowls my way a few times, but I hold fast. I'm not going anywhere. I need to talk to her one more time.

She doesn't rush. She doesn't look my way again. She just goes about her business, doing what she has to do. I expected nothing else from her. Finally, she comes toward me with her jacket and purse. I half expected her to disappear on me when she headed down the hallway. I'm glad now I didn't act like a suspicious fuck and follow her. I really fucking wanted to.

I rise, putting my hand on her back as we walk out. I'm not imagining the subtle jolt that goes through her when I do. She's not as unaffected by me as she seems, and I almost fold in relief. There's a chance. She's not completely done with me. I hope.

The valet has our cars waiting, my black car behind her sexy white GR86. I thought I'd get a little more fucking time. But I'm not letting her leave without saying my piece. I've been fucking practicing. Time to man up.

"Cara." I wait for her to look at me. "I wanted to say I'm sorry one last time. I shouldn't have said what I said. My head was up my ass, but I think you deserve an explanation, as dumb as it might be." Her eyebrows rise, and she folds her arms across her chest, hopefully because she's cold and not because she's done with me. I shift so my body's blocking the wind, sheltering her. And I tell her every fucking thing in my head. I own every pathetic embarrassing bit of it.

"I'm not proud of this. But every time you said you were going to the club, I was jealous as fuck. I hated the idea that you were out dancing and flirting with other men." I lock my eyes on the top of her head, ears hot. "I am not a smooth man. I don't have game. And I will never be someone comfortable in this world. Knowing you were, just made me feel like I wasn't good enough." I peek at her wide blue eyes and finish. "I was really fucking pissed at myself for not asking you out. And that night, at the hospital, all of that jealousy and frustration poured out in an epic bout of jackassery." Her lips quirk at jackassery. "I am really fucking sorry I was a dick. I wish I could tell you I didn't mean it...but at the moment I did. I think we both know that. But I truly am sorry."

I step back, taking my keys from the valet. "I fucked up, but I won't again. I'll spend however long it takes to make it up to you. I don't want to lose you, and even though we'll never be more, I can be a good friend if you just give me a chance." I give myself a second to savor her wide, tired eyes and rosy cheeks before I turn and make my escape.

Maybe it's cowardly, but I don't want to give her a chance to tell me no. I don't want to pressure her to give me another chance. Not yet. Not until I flesh out the rest of my wooing plans. But starting tomorrow —well, today— I'm going for shock and awe. And if I can't change her mind, well, at least I'll know I really fucking tried this time.

12

CARA

I squeeze in a couple of hours of sleep and am plagued by dreams of Declan. Sexy, annoying dreams. Trying to put him out of my mind and ignore the fact that I'll see him any minute now, I stop abruptly in the doorway of my office. There are flowers on my desk. A wild explosion of color, only partially contained by the vase holding them. Tucked into the sweet-smelling array is a card. I stand there, staring a little too long. Finally, when Colton's walked past my office three times, nosey bastard, I grab the card.

Cara,

I thought about getting you roses, but this
arrangement seemed more like you.
Bold. Untameable. Beautiful.

- Declan

GOD.

I sink down in my chair, mind spinning. Isn't this what I always wanted? For him to notice me? It is, but not like this. Not in apology. I don't want flowers because he's sorry. I want flowers because he's thinking about me and wants to brighten my day.

As much as I wish I could put my feelings for him away, I haven't been able to. I'm realistic enough to realize my emotions can't just disappear overnight. I'm not built that way. I fall deep and hard. But in the past, when I was done, it was easy to move on. This time, it hasn't been. As much as I tried to convince myself that night in the hospital cured me of my obsession, it didn't.

But I'm not going to let myself get sucked into his orbit again. I'm done throwing myself at Declan Wilder. Despite tossing and turning in bed this morning, replaying his words in my head, 'I was jealous.' Not once in the weeks since that night did I expect him to tell me that. In some way, having him be a dick because he's jealous is comforting. It soothes a part of me that was really hurt by him. The part of me that believed he said that stuff only because he didn't respect me.

I move the flowers to the edge of my desk and focus on work. But I look at them way too many times and spend most of the day anticipating the moment my computer breaks and Declan comes to fix it. Other than the last few weeks, that's been our pattern. Every day, without fail.

I always knew he did it on purpose. There's an entire tech team here, and they keep everyone's computers running smoothly. But somehow, mine got fucked every single day. And Declan was always the one to show up. Every single time. He still barely spoke to me, but the daily ritual kept me on his fucking hook. I thought it was him showing me he liked me back. I'd corner him in the hallway or his office, and he'd freeze. I'd back off, and the next day, he'd show up like clockwork.

What a fucked up dance we've been doing.

But today, my computer works perfectly, and I don't see Declan. By five, I'm grumpy and actively talking myself out of walking past his office. I'm proud of myself for leaving the long way, and I'm on guard the whole way down the elevators and out the front door. I hurry to the car, bundled against the frigid October air. It's not until I'm sitting in my car that I notice the flower under my wiper blade. I grab it, my heart fluttering pathetically in my chest. It hasn't been here long. The petals are still soft, and undamaged. I don't have to guess who left it, and I'm more confused than ever.

The takeout at my front door from my favorite Chinese place is the icing on the cake. I forgot that this elevator is secured for our floor and the ones above it. Only the brothers, Becca, Holly, and Evie, have access to this floor. It's comforting and also infuriating. There's no escaping him.

I push into the apartment, slamming the takeout on the counter. Bree rises from the couch, setting her book aside.

"Are you ok?" she asks, eyeing me as I slam doors and drawers, hunting for cutlery and plates. Bree's done some unpacking, and I find them easily.

"Fucker bought us Chinese," I mutter as I slam the containers onto the counter.

"That complete asshole. How dare he!" Bree gasps, pressing her hand to her chest. Her dramatics make me laugh, breaking the tension I've been carrying all day. "Who's the asshole?"

"Declan. He showed up at the club last night. Then he left me flowers today, in my office and on my car, and now he bought food." I'm whining. I can hear it. And I don't care. Bree won't judge me...much.

"Oh my god. Why? What did he say?" I can't tell if her excitement is for the food or if she just wants more gossip.

"He told me that part of the reason he said all that shit was because he was jealous."

She cackles. "Doesn't excuse it, but it's interesting."

"Interesting," I echo. And infuriating and maddening. I think I should be creeped out by the fact that my bosses, one of which happens to be a man I'm trying not to be in love with, have access to my front door. But I'm not. I've faced danger, horrifying, scary, real danger, and there is none of it here. They're loud, they're annoying, but I know for a fact that I'm safe with all of them. Physically, at least. I pick up his note for one last look before tucking it into the kitchen drawer.

Cara,

I got all your favorites.
Hope you and Bree have a relaxing weekend.

—Declan

BREE AND I SPEND THE WEEKEND UNPACKING THE REST OF OUR shit and doing what we do a lot of the time, sleep. But our sleep over the weekend is different. It's healing. No nightmares plaguing us. It's like now that we're in a new space, our bodies can finally relax. Our minds can finally relax.

I stay home and let my staff handle everything at the club. With the exception of the last few weeks, I've always gone in anyway. Even when we're fully staffed, and now I'm wondering why. Shit is handled. But it's almost like I don't know what to do with my life if I'm not running full tilt at the office and at the club. But if that terrifying night has shown me anything, it's that Bree is not replaceable. I wanna make sure that we are solid. Because if anything happened to her, I would not be ok.

By Sunday night, the dark bags under Bree's eyes are

nearly gone, and we've plowed through the Chinese food, all ten containers of it. She hasn't eaten that much in weeks, and my irritation over Declan's little gift is completely gone. We have enough energy to finish unpacking our place and then head out to have a stroll by the lake.

The brothers built this place before I came around. I'm sure they paid a pretty penny for the land, with its proximity to the lake. The views are killer. Bree and I walk around the waterfront, checking out all the little shops and restaurants. This neighborhood is a serious upgrade from where we've spent the last decade of our lives. The rent conversation should be interesting because I know for a fact the rent on this place would be at least half of my salary, and I get paid really fucking well.

I already know, walking into that discussion, there's no fucking way they'll accept full market rent from me. And I don't have a problem with that. If someone wants to help me, I'm not gonna fight. I've spent too long doing shit on my own, taking care of people. I'm not going to argue with anyone wanting to give me a break.

By the time I walk into the office on Monday morning, I feel lighter and brighter. I've barely got my coat off when Colton barrels into my office. He's bouncing, eyes wide, nearly vibrating with excitement.

"I'm fucking getting married," he sings, throwing his arms out wide. "And you're coming."

Laughing at his enthusiasm and really happy for him, I go in for a hug. "Congratulations, big man. Of course, I'll come. I wouldn't miss it for the world."

He hugs me tightly, bouncing us both up and down. My giggles are rolling. I'm thoroughly enjoying Colton's excitement when I spot Declan over his shoulder. He's leaning against the wall across from my office, wearing his standard jeans and a t-shirt. His favorite hoodie, because of course I've watched him so much I know which one is his favorite, is unzipped, showing his chest, outlined by this tight t-shirt. He's so much bigger than he used to be.

But that's not what makes my traitorous heart pitter-patter. It's the wide, happy smile on his face that does it. Not once, in more than three years of working here, has he looked at me like that. With pure joy.

I pull away from Colt, smoothing my hair. Colt's eyebrows furrow when he looks at me, but he smirks when he sees Declan in the hallway.

"Dec, fancy meeting you here. Outside Cara's office. So weird. Can I help you with something?" His tone is sugar-sweet and super annoying, but Declan doesn't bite.

"Nah, man. Just came to say good morning to Cara."

"Well, don't let me stop you." He crosses his arms and rests his butt on my desk, nearly knocking over the flowers from Friday.

I slap him on the back of the head. "Get your gargantuan ass off my desk. Who told you it was ok to do that shit?" Declan's choked laugh makes my toes tingle.

Colt stands up, pouting. "When did you get so mean? I was going to ask you to walk me down the aisle, but now? No way. You're off the roster."

"I'm heartbroken. Really. Can you see the little tear in my eye? It's right there." I lean forward, tapping the bridge of my nose. The dumbass leans forward, still pouting, putting his nipple right within my reach. I grab it, giving it a healthy twist before he yells and yanks away. He slaps both hands on his nipples, eyes wide and betrayed.

"I can't believe you, Cara. You dare to manhandle me? I am an engaged man. Wait till Evie hears about this. You're gonna be in so much trouble." He would fit right in with a bunch of third graders.

"I'm so terrified," I say flatly, trying my damndest to keep my lips from twitching. Declan's not trying to hide his amusement, belly laughter rolling from him.

Colton pivots, still clutching his pecs, and makes his way down the hallway muttering about ungrateful employees. Laughing, I sit, eyeing Declan. His laughter has tapered off, but he's watching me with hooded eyes, a small grin still gracing his lips.

Maybe thanks to his apology, the awkwardness of the last few weeks is gone. I'm not ready to jump up and run into his arms, but then I don't think that's where this is going, anyway. But I am happy that we've managed to clear the air a little bit. I didn't like him judging me. I get it, but I didn't like it.

Declan's smile grows as we just stare at each other. Finally, tucking his hands into his back pockets, he murmurs. "Morning, Cara," then he turns and walks away. I suddenly wish my office had windows that opened, so I could stick my head out and scream. Why the hell does a simple hello from him still make me so damn happy?

And why am I so disappointed that he didn't bring me something?

An hour later, when I'm searching for my stapler, I realize he did. There, tucked into my second drawer, is a present. Unwrapping it, I laugh when I find a twenty-pack of hair bands wrapped in tissue paper with another note.

Cara,

You have the most stunning hair,
But it's not the most beautiful thing about you.

—Declan

Jesus, I'm in trouble. Roses and chocolates wouldn't get to me. But wildflowers, Chinese food, and hair bands have me hooked. I'm constantly using pencils and chopsticks to get my hair out of my face when I'm working. And he noticed.

I'll never admit it out loud, but I spend the walk to my car trying not to get my hopes up. I shouldn't have bothered because there, under the windshield wiper, is a single tulip. Who the fuck does that? And how long will these apologies last? And why do I wish he were giving me things because he liked me, not because he's sorry?

13

DECLAN

I t's too quiet. The executive floor is not exactly a hive of activity, but when my brothers are here, there are always voices booming or music filling the hallways. I drop my headphones on my desk, standing with a stretch. I have the best setup money can buy, but sitting at a computer for as many hours a day as I do is crap for my body. Wind-milling my arms to loosen my shoulders, I open the door and wander into the hallway.

The entire executive floor, except for our offices, is made of glass. From my office door, I can see around the corner and down the hallway to Ransom's office. The light is off, which is weird. We usually gather in there every night to decompress, check in, and generally bullshit. Even if it's only for a few minutes, we always pop in. And even if Ransom isn't in, we still all meet there.

Tonight, especially, I expected we'd meet up. We're all supposed to head straight to the airstrip for our flight to Vegas. Colton and Evie are determined to get hitched as soon as possible, so Colt's been a manic mess all week.

But all the executive offices are empty. Every one. I don't think I've ever seen it like this on a workday. The elevator dings, drawing my attention. There she is. Cara. She stalks off in those pencil heels, a sway in her hips that is fucking mesmerizing.

I visited a museum in London years ago and saw some paintings by a guy named Rubens. He painted women with thicker thighs and rounded stomachs. One painting was of a beauty contest. The winner got a golden apple.

Cara? She'd win all the apples. Every one of them. She's fucking stunning.

She slows, then comes to a stop. I'm blocking the hallway, arms still windmilling. I didn't even notice. Letting them flop to my sides, I take a deep breath, letting it out slowly.

"Hi, Cara."

The wariness that she'd been watching me with for weeks has been weakening this week. I think my wooing plan is working.

Her lips curve in a tiny smile. "Hi, Declan. What's up?"

"Nothing." I stand there, staring for too long before my brain comes online. "Fuck, sorry. Let me take that." I reach for the duffel bag on her shoulder. She gives it over with a murmured 'Thanks.' I just stand there, holding her bag, looking at her.

"Think we can go to my office with that, big guy?" Yeah, she's smirking. Why do I do this? Just freak the fuck out around her? I mean, aside from the fact that my dick is trying to hammer its way out through my jeans, and it's distracting as hell, I should be able to have a fucking conversation with her. But every time I see her, the stakes just feel huge. I've never felt this way for anyone, and it's terrifying and exciting all at the same time.

I follow her down the hall. She peers into Ransom's dark office. "Where is everyone? I thought we were leaving from here for Vegas?"

"I have no fucking idea. I thought the cars were picking us up from here, too."

Grabbing my phone, I hit the speakerphone button and dial Colt. Cara nudges in closer.

"My brother," he crows when he picks up. I can hear muffled voices in the background.

"Where the fuck is everyone?"

"On our way to Vegas, baby! Where the hell did you think we'd be?"

"What the fuck, man? You left us behind?"

"Dude, no. I would never." He snorts a laugh. "Well, I did. But there's a car coming to pick you and Cara up soon. We had to charter another jet, and you guys drew the short straws."

Cara and I exchange a *what the fuck* look. "We didn't draw any straws, Horsey."

"Right," he mutters, sounding completely distracted. "I drew them for you. Anyway, you'll only be about an hour behind us. See you at the hotel. Byeeee." I stare blankly at my phone before meeting Cara's narrowed eyes.

"Do we really want to go to this wedding?" Cara asks, rolling her eyes. "He's obnoxious as hell, and I doubt that's going to get any better this weekend."

Tempting. Really tempting. "We'd never hear the end of it. He'd whine about it for years if we missed it."

Cara groans, running her fingers through her hair, scratching at her scalp in frustration. "You're right. He would totally do that."

Resigned, we grab our stuff and head down to the lobby. Cara drops into a chair at reception, propping her elbow on the arm and resting her head on her fist. She looks exhausted.

"Are you and Bree doing ok? Sleeping, I mean? You seem a little tired." I hoped that being in the new apartment would make her feel safer, so it kills me to see her so tired.

"We're doing way better, actually. It's not that. Ransom had me running all over town today, picking up the most random shit ever. I don't know why the fuck he needed me to do it instead of a courier, but there you go."

That doesn't make much sense. Cara's way too valuable to waste on errands, but what the fuck do I know?

A blacked-out Escalade pulls up, the driver hopping out. And just like that, we're on our way to the private airstrip outside the city. I rack my brain, trying to find something to talk about, but Cara seems lost in thought, gazing out the window, eyes hazy. Instead of talking to her, I spend the trip staring at her legs and trying to figure out the next step in my apology tour.

The jet waiting for us is smaller than ours but plenty big for the two of us. The pilots and steward introduce themselves, then disappear in the front once we're settled.

I'm pissed that we're on this little plane. There are no side-by-side seats, only ones across the aisle from each other. On our jet, we could have sat together. Course, it would also be filled with the rowdiest, most annoying group of men I know. So maybe this is ok.

Cara asks for a blanket, and as soon as we're airborne, she's out like a fucking light. Guess I don't have to worry about trying to have a conversation. Her head's leaning against the window, the flashing lights from the wing creating a halo around her face. I don't like her resting on the cold glass. Grabbing another blanket from the overhead storage, I lean over her, carefully pulling her head into my chest as I put the folded-up blanket against the window.

"Declan," she murmurs, freezing my body in place. She nuzzles against my chest, and I hold my breath, worried she's going to wake up and think I'm fucking creeping on her. She's so fucking soft, so warm, so...everything. This is the very first time I've ever held her like this. Sucks that she's asleep, but it's also amazing. I'm not worried about acting cool or saying the right shit or what she's thinking of me. I'm just...holding her. She's always so dynamic, and in my face, I always feel like I'm three steps behind. I felt like a fucking loser each time she touched me. What thirty-three-year-old man can't hold a conversation with a beautiful woman?

It's me. I'm the loser.

I don't know how long I stand there, drifting in the scent of her shampoo and the warmth of her breath on my skin. But eventually, I slowly, carefully lean her back towards the window. She settles her head on the blanket with a sigh, and I back away, falling into my seat.

She looks different like this. Softer, more vulnerable. Smaller somehow. When she's awake, she keeps everyone around her on their toes. But this version of Cara brings out a protectiveness in me that I've only felt one other time, that night at the hospital. Colt's woman Evie has a little girl, Mia. She has all of us acting like protective uncles, but it's different. With Mia, I want to coddle her and protect her from everything.

With Cara, I want to be her muscle. The enforcer that helps her get whatever she wants. And ok, maybe protect her a little too. She's so fucking capable that I know she doesn't need me at all. But I can't help imagining what it would be like to be the man Cara turns to. To be the first one she calls on when she needs backup. I may be a computer geek, but my brothers have made sure I can more than take care of myself.

I can take care of her.

Maybe, if I keep my head on straight, I can convince her to give me a chance.

Dropping my head against the headrest, I let my mind ponder how I'm going to get her alone when we're in Vegas. I need to keep wooing, and I'm out of fucking ideas.

A few hours into the flight, the steward enters. "Mr. Wilder. I'm sorry to inform you we need to make an unscheduled landing. There's a warning light on that requires immediate attention. There's nothing to worry about, but I'll ask you to fasten your seatbelt." He moves to touch Cara's shoulder, but my snarl sends him scurrying back to the front.

Crouching next to her, I take her fingers in mine, stroking the back of her hand with my thumb. "Cara. Wake up, honey." She frowns, the V between her eyebrows pronounced. Not a happy camper.

After a little more nudging, those electric blue eyes open lazily. I keep rubbing the softness of her skin, marveling at how right it feels to hold her hand in mine.

Her fingers flex in mine, then carefully tighten. We're holding hands.

My ears are hot.

"What's happening?" she asks, voice husky.

"We need to land. There's something mechanical going on. The pilots have to check it out. Everything's ok, but we're going to be a little off schedule."

"Fucking Colt," she says with a roll of her eyes.

"Yeah," I murmur with a smile. "Fucking Colt."

THE PILOTS PROMISE TO CHECK IN WITH US AND SEND US INTO THE small terminal. Cara and I find a small diner and grab a table at the back.

"I'm so hungry," Cara says, grabbing the plastic menu and studying like she just might unlock the secrets of the universe inside it.

Chuckling, I grab a menu too, and before we know it, we're wolfing down our burgers and fries. Judging by the moans coming from Cara, she's found greasy heaven. Me too.

When the worst of our hunger is dealt with, we sit, carefully avoiding each other's eyes. Sick of myself, I finally just blurt. "I was hoping we could get to know each other." I'm so stupid. "I mean, we know each other, but obviously, there's a lot about you I don't know. I haven't been a good friend. I'd like to do better."

Something chases across her face, but it's gone too fast to pinpoint. "Friends. Right." She leans back in her seat, crossing her arms over her chest. "What do you want to know?"

My mind flips through a million different questions, finally landing on probably the most cliche one of them all. "What do you do for fun?"

Her eyebrow quirks, and I resist the urge to run my fingers through my nonexistent hair. I really wish I'd kept it long. I didn't realize how much of a crutch it was. It wasn't just a nervous habit. I would also hide behind it, letting it fall in my face and shield me from the world. Now, there's nowhere for me to hide.

"I don't have much free time. I work a lot, so my downtime is mainly hanging with Bree or sleeping."

"It's great you have her with you. Nearby, I mean. Have you guys lived together for a long time?

"A decade. She came to live with me when I was in university."

I frown. "She must have been young. Why did she move in with you?"

She drops her crossed arms and tilts her head questioningly. "You didn't look this up in your files? I know for sure you ran me before you hired me."

I sit up straighter. "I ran you, but it was pretty standard, and I haven't looked at those files in three years."

"Why? Why wouldn't you look again?"

"Because it was none of my fucking business. I wouldn't invade your privacy like that."

"I see," she says, gaze searching. She stands, moving for her wallet. My scowl stops her. I drop a hundred-dollar bill on the table.

She didn't answer my question.

We walk silently back to the tarmac doors, just in time to see our plane taxi down the runway and take off without us. We both stare at the plane as it disappears from sight.

What. The. Fuck.

"Sir. Mr. Wilder." The hesitant voice breaks through my confusion. Swinging around, I take in the small woman wearing a safety vest, holding a cart with our luggage.

"What the hell is going on? Our pilots just left without us."

"Yes sir. I've been instructed to give you this." She reaches out, dropping a set of car keys and an envelope with my name scrawled on the front into my hand. She turns, moves our luggage off the cart onto the floor, and wanders off.

"Declan," Cara asks, staring down at our luggage. "What the fuck is happening?"

14

CARA

We're in a tiny town somewhere in Colorado, and our plane just left without us. I wish I could say this is the worst thing that could happen to us, but honestly, I've had a few fantasies about being stranded with Declan. Most of them involved a sandy beach and us being the only ones capable of repopulating the earth. Only in those fantasies, he didn't want to just be friends.

Fucking friends.

His way too thoughtful gifts this week have been chipping away at that wall I thought I had built. The wall that was supposed to stop me from obsessing over him. Stop me from wishing he loved me back. Stopped me from loving him. It's crumbling before my eyes, and he wants to be friends.

Rationally, I know being friends is good. It's better than me coming onto him and him running away from me every chance he got.

Friends is better than him breaking my computer and coming to fix it, barely saying two words. Friends is better than icy exchanges in the hallway and avoiding each other.

But it's still so much less than I hoped for, so it's a bitter pill to swallow. If I let myself dwell on it, it'll send me into a spiral of wondering what's so wrong with me and why he can't love me. It's dumb and not productive. I'm not his type. Simple. Except I see him every day, and that's not so simple.

Declan's still staring down at the letter in his hand. Stepping closer, I slide the envelope out of his grasp, tear it open, and pull the card out. He turns his body into mine, and the busyness of this little airport fades away. All I'm aware of is him. With effort, I pull my focus to the card in my hand.

Fucker,

You screwed the pooch with Cara. Now's your chance to make it better.

There's an SUV outside, gassed up and ready to go.

You're about seven hours from Vegas. Drive the car, have the talks, and I'll see you later tonight at the hotel.

You're welcome.

—Colton (Motherfucking) Miles

A STRING OF CURSES FALLS FROM DECLAN'S MOUTH. NONE OF it's earth-shattering, but I've never heard him talk like this before. He always has this mild-mannered, shy, geeky way about him. The muscled, slightly ragey look he's got going right now is really working for me. His head is tilted back as he stares at the fluorescent lights of the terminal. He brings his hands up to his head, clasping at the back of his neck, making the muscles in his arms bunch. I sneak a peek down, and a sliver of abs is revealed.

My sister took me to the male strippers once. I saw way more Dong that night than I ever wanted to, and not one of those men got me as excited as Declan does, showing that one tiny strip of skin.

I'm so fucked.

"So," I say, trying to control the squeak in my voice. "Colton basically set us up. He wants us to spend the next seven hours trapped in a car together because..."

I know exactly why he'd pull something like this. Because I stupidly confessed that I was in love with Declan. I love Colton like a brother, but I'm going to fuck him up so badly when I see him. I'm talking atomic-level wedgie.

Declan groans, scrubbing his hands over his face. "He thinks he's helping. That if we spend some time together, just the two of us, we'll be able to get past...what happened." He winces, glancing at me. "I'm sorry. I don't know what the fuck he's doing. It never occurred to me he would put you in a position like this."

"It's not like him. I mean, he's nosey and opinionated and loud, but he's also really thoughtful most of the time."

"I know," Declan mutters. "It's Evie and Mia. He's turned into a total love addict. He wants everyone shitting out rainbows and unicorns, just like him."

My heart's in my throat. "Love addict. So he wants us to talk because...?" Please say because you're madly in love with me and just need time to prove it.

Who am I kidding? As much as I might have dreamed about that. About Declan falling to his knees and declaring his undying love for me, I'd probably freak out and run as far and as fast as I could. I know how to obsess. I know how to be the aggressor. I have no idea how to be chased by him.

Declan shifts, eyes wandering the terminal. "Probably, so we stop acting awkward around each other."

"You've always acted awkward around me," I say flatly. He flushes, eyes meeting mine before darting away again.

"Yeah. Well, I've been working on that."

I suppose he has been. This *wanting someone who didn't want me, then said shitty things to me, then starting giving me presents thing* sucks.

"We have other options," he says, planting his hands on his hips, keys dangling from his fingers.

"Like?" Go ahead, tell me all the ways you want to get rid of me.

"Like we can call another charter and wait for a new plane to come get us. We don't have to go to the wedding at all. Fucker can't blame us after he pulls this shit." He wanders over to the windows facing the parking area, frowning. He pulls out his cell, studying something on the screen for a while.

I join him at the window, watching a few people darting to their vehicles, dodging a few small raindrops. I haven't spent much time in places like this. The surrounding mountains are so high it feels like they're looming over us, blotting out the sky. I spend all my time in the heart of a city, skyscrapers doing the same thing, but somehow, there, I always feel in control, in my element. Here, in these mountains, I feel smaller.

Declan bites off a curse. "There's a storm system coming this way. In a few hours, this place is going to be shut down."

"So, no plane."

"No plane," he echoes.

"If we go now, can we beat the storm?"

"We're heading west. It's coming from the north. In theory, yeah, we'll beat it." I don't like the sound of *in theory*.

"What happens if it turns?"

"Then we're going to have to find a place to stay until it blows over."

"Hypotheticals aren't my favorite. Can we try some real talk?"

He squints at me. "Real talk? We haven't been really talking so far?"

"You're the one that said 'in theory.' So real talk, right now the storm is headed right here, where we're standing. If we do nothing, we'll be sleeping on the floor in this terminal. I don't sleep on the floor. Ever. Or we hit the road. The storm forecast shows it should miss us. Seems like an obvious choice, doesn't it?"

He tightens his grip on the keys, bringing them up between us, studying them. Finally, blowing out a breath, he nods. He's got our luggage in his hands, and he's leading us out to the parking lot within minutes, hitting the alarm until we see the lights flash on a black SUV.

He throws our bags in the backseat and opens the passenger door, looking at me expectantly.

I raise my eyebrow. "Why don't I drive? You can sleep for a bit, then we can trade off."

"Get in I'll drive."

The way he says 'get in' puts me on edge. "I'm a great driver," I say, proud of how level my voice is.

"I'm sure you are, but I'm still driving. Non-negotiable." Is he fucking kidding me? I open my mouth to argue with him. He steps into me, nose to nose.

"You will not win this. In most things, I'll give you whatever the fuck you want. But not this. I'm driving. End of discussion. Get your pretty ass in the car, Cara. Now."

His intensity, the force in his words, shut me up. I can't remember why I was arguing in the first place. I mean, why wouldn't I get my pretty ass in the car?

TWENTY MINUTES LATER, I FINALLY SNAP OUT OF MY DAZE. Declan's hands are loose on the wheel, handling the curving mountain roads with confidence, but his shoulders are bunched around his ears.

"I really am a good driver," I say into the silence between us.

Declan blows out a breath, his shoulders dropping. "I don't doubt you, Cara. Not for a second."

"Then why don't you want me to drive?" He glances at me briefly, hands flexing on the wheel.

"Did you know I have a garage full of cars?"

"No. I only ever see you drive the one." That actually always struck me as strange. If I had as much money as he does, I'd drive a new car every year. So, a garage full of cars makes a lot of sense.

He nods. "Well, I do. I love driving, always have. Stole my first car when I was eleven. Took it for an epic joyride before the cops caught me. That wasn't the last time I did that. But I got better at not getting caught."

"What happened when the cops brought you home?"

"My foster parents at the time kicked me out. I ended up at a small group home."

I have so many questions for him. Like, why did they kick you out? How many foster homes did you live in? What happened to your parents? But I drop them and focus back on him.

"When we finally had crazy money. Money we could blow. I spent it on cars. And on driving lessons. When I was about fifteen, I developed an obsession with stunt driving. So I lived out that teenage fantasy. I paid the best stunt drivers in the world to teach me. Then we moved on to tactical driving."

"What's that?"

"It's the kind of training security and military personnel get. It's basically how to handle an attack on the road. How to get out of the situation, and how to disable other vehicles. That kind of thing."

"Wow."

Declan flashes me a grin. "I've spent thousands of hours behind the wheel learning everything I could about how to control a vehicle, Cara. I've been trained on icy tracks and through whiteouts." He glances at me, his eyes intense. "If that storm hits us, I will keep you safe."

Jesus. He's protective. I honestly did not see that coming. What happened to shy, unassuming Declan?

"I thought you were being a chauvinistic dick."

He chuckles. "I know. We didn't have time to discuss it. We had to get the fuck out of there."

"You could have said something once we were on the move."

"Could I? You seemed pretty in your head. I thought it would be better to let you bring it up when you were ready."

"Bring it up when I was ready?" I echo. Is it better? I'm not so sure. "I don't think biting your tongue, waiting for the right moment, is a good strategy. I did that with Bree, and look how that turned out."

He frowns, glancing at me. "What do you mean?"

"I saw some things with her in the month leading up to...that night. I was a little worried about how she was being treated, but I didn't say anything. I didn't want to interfere in her life like that. I thought she'd come to me when she was ready." Instead, everything went to shit.

"But she didn't, and you ended up having to fight for your fucking life."

The dash lights play over his face, creating a pattern of shadow and light. His face is tight. He looks how I feel.

"Yeah," I whisper. "I did." I don't want to think about that night. Or about what I had to do. Swallowing down the bile trying to climb up my throat, I play with the seat recline until I'm laying back a bit. "I'm going to sleep for a bit. Wake me if you need me."

15

DECLAN

I'm going to murder that motherfucker. Why the hell did he think trapping Cara and me together was a good idea? She can barely look at me. I'm still so relieved she's talking to me. I thought I fucked everything up when I ordered her into the car. I knew I sounded like an ass, but I was too freaked out by the idea of taking her into a storm to slow down and convince her.

And I was right. This fucking storm has turned. I would give anything to have the rain back, instead of this. My speed ticks lower and lower as the snow blows harder, making visibility nearly nil. I haven't seen another car on the road in twenty minutes. We're the only idiots out here now, and my brain is going over all the *what-if's*. I checked the trunk back at the airport, and the emergency roadside kit is tiny. Cara was already shivering from the terminal to the car. She's not dressed for a fucking snowstorm. Neither am I, but at least my legs are covered by thick denim. She's in those tight thin black pants and a light coat. It's bordering on crazy for the temperatures back home, but a snowstorm...fuck no. And the four-inch stiletto boots are going to give her less than zero protection in the snow.

"Cara, wake up." I reach out and give her shoulder a little shake. She groans, clearly not happy. "Cara. I need you awake."

She turns to me, blinking owlishly. "What? How long have I been...holy fuck." She sits up, fumbling at the side of her seat, raising it. Her eyes are huge, staring out at the wall of snow illuminated by the headlights.

"Holy fuck sounds about right," I mutter.

"Declan...are we okay?" I hate the fear in her voice. I could tell her everything's going to be okay, but if we don't get out of this soon, we're fucked. In so many ways.

"Yeah. We're okay for now. But I need you to pull out your phone and see if there are any towns nearby. I don't know if I should stay on the highway or pull off. We need to find a town, fast. The fucking storm found us, and I don't think it's going to let up. We need shelter now."

"On it," she mutters, fumbling around for her phone. We're damn lucky there's still service. She's in Cara mode pretty quickly, her panic forgotten as her hands fly over her phone. I love it when she's like this. She could be in the middle of a hurricane and be completely unbothered. It's the same kind of focus I have when I'm at my computer, digging up dirt.

She twists in her seat, facing me. "Okay, found one about twenty miles from here. There's an exit coming up, and I can guide you from there. The town looks tiny, but our next option would be another fifty miles past that."

"Tiny it is," I say grimly. "Dial Colton, please."

She nods, putting it on speaker. He picks up, clearly in the middle of a crowd.

"Don't be mad. You guys needed some time, you know that you—"

"You're on speaker," she shouts. Colt stutters to a stop.

"If we make it out of this in one piece, brother, you and I are going to have words." Cara's eyes widen at my tone. To his credit, Colt must hear something in my voice that alerts him not all is well. Soon the noise behind him quiets.

"I knew you'd be mad, but what's happening?"

"We're in the middle of a fucking snowstorm. I can't see more than five feet in front of me."

"Goddamn it. The forecast was clear. I swear. What can I do?"

"There's nothing you can do. Nothing can get to us right now. Cara's found a town twenty miles from here. At the speed we're going, it'll take us at least half an hour to get there. I'm hoping we can find a hotel or somewhere to ride out the storm."

"Send me your location now." The gravity of our situation is in his sober tone. "I want to see where you are and where you're going."

Cara follows his directions, downloading an app and giving him real-time access to our route. He's in full protector mode, refusing to get off the phone with us until we see lights in the distance.

There's a collective sigh of relief as I pull into the tiny town. The main street is mostly a ghost town. It's really fucking late, so that's not a surprise. At the far end of town, I spot a motel and what looks to be the only pub in town attached to it. Judging by the cars around both businesses, I'm guessing a lot of people were caught by the storm.

I swing into an open spot as close to the office as I can and turn the engine off. My entire body is tight, my tension ratcheted up as the snow came harder and harder. As prepared as I might have felt back at that airport, I've never had to drive in shit like this for this long, with someone so important in the car with me. Worry over Cara, making sure she would be okay has been consuming my thoughts. She matters. A fuck-of-a-lot. Fingers aching, I flex them, trying to get the blood flowing.

Cara's soft hands take mine, pulling on my fingers and kneading my palm. I sit, hands completely relaxed, soaking in her touch. This is the first time she's reached for me, touched me since I screwed everything up. I missed it so much. I didn't know how much I craved the way she'd run her fingers over me at work, or lean into me.

I just sit, breathing, gaze on the top of her bowed head, willing my dick to behave. I don't want anything to ruin this, especially not my body.

"Thank you for getting us here in one piece." She glances up, bites her lip, then looks back at our hands. "I've never had to drive through anything like that. Being a passenger was bad enough. I can't imagine having to handle it by myself."

I wrap my hands around hers, for a moment lost in the contrast between us. Her hands are soft, nails painted a glittery gold. My hands are tanned and calloused and so much larger. What was I going to say?

"Thank you for being a great navigator. We made a pretty good team."

Her head comes up, and she smiles at me. I don't think I've ever seen this smile before. It somehow makes her seem softer, younger. Thank god she didn't use this on me before. I would have spent the rest of my life following her around like a dog. Now? She's definitely stuck with me...at least if I have anything to say about it. The problem is, it's not just my choice.

A wheezing...something comes out of me. "Ah. So, maybe we should get some rooms?"

"Rooms are a good idea." She moves for the door handle.

"No," I shout. Her eyebrows shoot up.

"Sorry, it's just, you aren't dressed for this. I have no fucking idea how you walk in those on an average day. In the dark with all this snow, they're not safe."

"I will have you know, I can run for blocks in these shoes."

"Why the fuck would you do that?" I know my eyes are wide, but seriously, why would anyone run in those? "Anyway, I'll go. Be right back."

I make my escape, shutting the door on her laughter, so the blowing snow doesn't pelt her. I thought I knew what cold was, what winter was. Chicago winters are no joke. But the Colorado cold is sinking straight into my bones. The driving need to get Cara safe and warm pushes my discomfort back.

I shove open the door to the tiny office. It's beat-up, and rundown, but clean. As long as we don't have any creepy crawly visitors in our rooms, it'll do just fine. A harried woman in her fifties comes out from the back room.

"Oh dear, you look frozen." She's radiating concerned grandma energy.

"Yes ma'am. We got stuck. Looks like a bunch of us did." I say, waving to the cars filling the parking lot."

"Oh honey, we've been hopping for the last hour. We haven't had this many guests in years."

My stomach drops. The details I'd been cataloging all coming together. Thirty-plus cars, plus maybe twenty rooms, equals we're fucked.

I plant my hands on the desk separating us, dropping my shoulders. "Please tell me you still have rooms."

Her tinkling laugh rings out as she slaps an actual key on the desk. "Last one, honey. Must be your lucky day."

It is. It really is. My head drops in relief. I have no fucking idea what we would have done. No way we could sleep in the car. We're on a quarter tank of gas. That would not keep us warm till morning. My relief is short-lived as the reality of that one key hits me. One key, two of us. I hand over my ID and cash, nodding distractedly as the clerk gives me the rundown.

"The bar will be open 24/7 until the storm passes. We

have a lot of folks in the outlying areas that have lost power. The older ones usually come and hunker down here during storms. It turns into a bit of a party, but usually nothing too rowdy. So you come by and get food anytime. My Cliff is a great cook."

I thank her, then, head spinning, trudge through the calf-high snow to the passenger side of the SUV. Cara's lips look almost blue through the window. I pull it open, hand her the key, then tug her out.

"Did you get roo—" Her words cut off with a yelp as I duck down and throw her over my shoulder.

"Don't you dare drop that key. We'll never find it again." I mutter against her backside. We're in the middle of a snowstorm, I can't feel my feet, it's so fucking cold, but my body still reacts to having her ass right in my face. I don't know if that says more about my attraction to her or how sexy she is.

I trudge the thirty feet to our door, putting her down right in front of it. The sidewalk is mostly bare, thanks to the overhang. "Be right back."

I make quick work of grabbing the rest of our stuff, thankful that Jonas challenged me to that stupid bet all those months ago. I was always in shape, but never like this. I appreciate my body more than ever right now and its ability to take care of business. I hustle back to Cara. She's just standing there, eyes wide, key dangling at her side.

Sliding it out of her hand, I pop the door open and nudge her in, then push in after her, slamming the door shut. I drop my head against it, relieved to be in the warmth of the room. My cheeks tingle from the temperature change.

"Jesus. They only had one room left. We're lucky as fuck." I'm shivering. Cara must be colder.

She's cold, alright. Her lips are definitely blue, and she's shivering. But she doesn't seem to notice. Her eyes are locked on the bed.

The.

Bed.

Singular. A single queen-size bed, right there in the center of the room.

"Fuck."

16

CARA

Declan's ass is spectacular. Grade A.

I'm sure I should be worrying about the fact that we're stranded in some middle-of-nowhere town in a fucking blizzard, but I can't seem to care. Because Declan's ass is staring me right in the face. I panicked for a minute when he threw me over his shoulder, but I should have had more faith. New Declan has got me just fine. So fine.

My hand, holding the key, is dangling, casually brushing his butt. Tap, tap, tap with every step. Would he notice if I added a little rub in there? I'm vaguely aware of the wet snow falling on my ass. Combined with the howling wind, my butt's completely numb. But I've got a key in my hand, and before you know it, I can climb into the shower and have a little me time while fantasizing about this moment. Being manhandled this way is definitely going into the permanent rotation.

I'm spinning, then I'm suddenly on my feet. He takes a second to steady me, then dashes back to the car. The blood is rushing every which way in my body, and my head's not really sure what way's up. Maybe next time, I'll opt for a piggyback. I could get behind that. Climbing up on that muscled back, legs wrapped tight around him.

Before the end of this trip, I'm going to get a piggyback ride. I've decided.

Daydreaming about riding Declan, I barely register it when he takes the key from me and ushers me into the room. It's not until the door closes and we're out of the wind that I register how cold I really am. My face is numb.

"Jesus. They only had one room left. We're lucky as fuck."

I hear him, but I can't respond. I'm struck dumb, staring at the middle of the wall. There, covered in an ancient floral spread, is a single queen bed. One bed.

Oh my god, I'm in a romance novel.

"Fuck," Declan mutters. He's rubbing his beard, staring at the bed. Guess I'm not the only one floored by this little development.

"I guess it could be worse," I murmur. "It could be a twin."

Declan snorts, a surprised chuckle rolling from deep in his chest. The panic and worry of the last half an hour releases, and I'm laughing too. Our laughter gradually dies, and our eyes meet. The moment is charged. I know we're both wondering what the hell we're going to do. What's the etiquette here? Do we roll for it? Rock-paper-scissors for it? Do we make a wall of pillows like in some stupid movie? Do I just crawl onto him an—.

Whoops. Got carried away there.

Declan clears his throat and pulls his eyes away. He picks up my bag and carries it into the bathroom.

"Why don't you jump in the shower and warm up? I'm going to call Colt and tear him a new asshole."

"Are you sure? You're soaked."

Declan's face is grim. "Cara, you're shaking. Get in there." I am shaking. How did I not notice that?

"Okay, I'll be quick."

Closing the door, I drop to the edge of the tub. What a fucking day. We were supposed to be in the guys' hotel in Vegas by now — because, of course, they own a hotel — sipping drinks and gambling. We were going to be in a big group, helping Colton celebrate his wedding. Now, thanks to that lunatic, I'm stuck in a motel room, alone with the man I've been crushing on for years, while a terrifying storm rages outside.

It could be worse. We could be dead. But I'm afraid by the time this storm ends, one of us will be. I don't know how I'm supposed to get through this. With him. The man who wants to be friends.

I don't want to be his friend.

But maybe that's been part of the problem all along. I've been fixating on Declan, but we didn't really know each other. Other than he loves his family and he plays video games, how much do I really know about him? I had no idea he'd stolen cars. And why does the idea of him hot-wiring a car get me so hot?

I rush through my shower, skipping the 'me' time. No way can I do that with him right outside the door. The walls are so thin I can hear the guy next door singing in the shower. For sure, Declan could hear me. I don't care about giving some stranger a show, but not Declan.

I paw through my bag, discarding one item after another. I have Vegas clothes, not snowstorm clothes. And I really don't have *share your hotel room with your boss* pajamas. This would be easier if I was one of those Victorian ladies who wore nightgowns that touch the floor and button to the neck. Instead, I'm stuck with my favorite satin babydolls. They're sexy as fuck, but I love them because they only fall to mid-thigh. Long nightgowns or top sheets end up wrapped around me, and I wake up screaming, convinced I'm being swallowed whole by a boa constrictor.

I throw one of the babydoll sets on, and yep, sexy as fuck.

Vegas was my chance to get wild and crazy. To try and put aside the worry of the last month and just breathe. I was going to try and find myself again. And maybe find someone to get on top of. Hence, the sexy wardrobe.

As I dry my hair, I run through my options, which honestly aren't many. Every item of clothing in my bag is sexy and tight. Why the hell didn't I pack at least one of my lounge sets? Because I was supposed to have my own hotel room, that's why.

My blonde hair, now dry, is a wild mane around my head, my hazel eyes glittering, cheeks rosy, and breasts totally on point. I look like a woman who's been thinking about sex, and I'm supposed to go out there?

A soft knock on the door. "Cara, are you okay?"

"I'm okay," I say, clearing the panic from my throat. "I, uh, just didn't pack for any of this."

"Do you need something? I've got another hoodie in my bag."

Do I need Declan's hoodie? No. Do I want it? "That would be great, thanks."

I crack the door, peeking out to watch him dig through his bag. He finally turns, holding a black hoodie, and freezes when he sees me peeking out. The little devil on my shoulder makes me push the door open and walk to him for the sweater. Did I plan on making his eyes bug out of his head? Did I want his breath to catch in his throat? Did I hope his eyes would roam over me, looking hungry?

Yep.

Even if I didn't fully admit it to myself, I wanted all of those things. And oh my god, did I ever get them. Stopping a couple of feet from him, I let him look his fill. The way he's looking at me right now gives me back the equilibrium I lost when he said all those awful things to me. I know how to handle a man wanting me like this. I know sexy hooded eyes. I know want. Coming from Declan, though, it's a revelation.

Men love me. I don't care what the beauty ideal is. Men look at my curves, and they want. Always. It's predictable. It's reliable. But Declan never seemed to, not really. That hurt more than I would like to admit. What good is being stacked if you can't attract the one man you're starving for? Or were starving for. Okay, that's a lie. I'm still starving.

I watch Declan watch me. Finally, his eyes rise to mine. He flushes, caught, dropping his gaze and flapping the hoodie in the air toward me. I should take it. I should pull it on and break this tension, but instead, I turn slowly, giving him my back. His choked inhale makes me smile, but he gets the idea and comes to me. He slowly pulls the sweater up my arms, his fists pulling the fabric closed at my throat.

We stand frozen, both breathing faster than we should be. I keep waiting for him to pull away, to dash to the bathroom, but he doesn't. Instead, he steps into me, making my breath catch in my throat. I can feel all of him. The cold of his damp clothes through the sweater. The zipper of his jeans is just at the top of my ass. My head is spinning with sensation, and I'm nearly overloaded when his arms come around me, reaching for the zipper. Slowly, so slowly, he pulls it up, using his thumb between the zipper and my satin nighty, making sure it doesn't catch.

Is he teasing me on purpose? I've been touched more intimately by other men, and not one of those moments generated this kind of heat. The tip of his thumb is grazing slowly up my belly, the tiniest back-and-forth motion barely noticeable. To my eye, at least. To my body, it feels like his whole hand is stroking me. I can feel his beard brushing my cheek as he looks over my shoulder. We're both breathing, watching, feeling as he grazes the valley between my breasts. I'm either about to hyperventilate or attack the man. This tension has to break somehow.

"Colton is very sorry." His breath rasps against my cheek. "Evie's pissed at him. And Ransom wants you to call him."

He pulls away, grabs his bag, and enters the bathroom without a backward glance. He places my bag outside the door and closes it firmly, not looking at me once. Meanwhile, I'm reeling, wondering if my legs are going to support me long enough to get to my phone. How can he be so unaffected?

All those insecurities are roaring back. I don't like this version of me. The one so desperate for a scrap of his attention. It was almost easier when he was avoiding me. This though? The teasing, then walking away, hurts worse. I couldn't have been more obvious about what I wanted, what I was offering, and he just...passed me up. Again. I am so done.

Angrily blinking away my tears, I grab my purse, pull back the covers on the bed, and drop down into the crisp white sheets, tucking my cold feet under the covers gratefully. It's past midnight, but I dial Ransom, knowing he'll be waiting for my call. He picks up on the second ring.

"Cara. Are you okay?"

His concern makes the tears well again. I didn't know I'd be getting this, any of this when I took this job. I've never worked for anyone like these men. As soon as I became Ransom's assistant, I got a bunch of truck-sized big brothers. The men checking on me, teasing me. Making me feel like I was part of their family, even though I'm not.

"I'm okay," I hear the break in my voice. I know he does, too, from his quick inhale. "It's just been a long day, and the roads were so scary."

"Fucking Colton. I can't believe he did this. It's not like him to put anyone in danger like this."

"He would never put us in danger on purpose." It's true. He's overprotective to the max. He'd never put me in a dangerous situation. "But I don't understand what he was thinking." Ransom's silence is telling.

"What do you know, Ran?" A shiver runs up my back. All those dumb errands he had me running today flash through my mind. Things are starting to make more sense. He was fucking in on it.

"I didn't know he had all of this planned, I swear. We were just going to get the two of you on the plane together. That's all. I thought it would give you a few hours to straighten things out. I didn't know about the stop, or the car, and the rest of his stupid plan."

He's sorry. I can hear it. But knowing he had a part in this, in angling to get us together, hurts.

"I trusted you," I say calmly. Evenly. It's that, or scream at him. "You went behind my back and fucked with my life."

"I was trying to help. I swear that's all it was."

"Because I'm so incapable of running my own life?"

"I know you're not incapable." His words are low and measured. Cautious.

"Then it must be Declan. You knew he wanted to make amends, so you wanted to give him time to do that. You betrayed me." I think my heart is breaking a little. I thought I mattered more than this. "I guess when it comes down to it, I'm not family, and he is. I shouldn't be surprised that you'd do what you think is best for him."

"Fuck, Cara. That's not it. I just want—".

I press the end button, unable to keep it together anymore. He calls back immediately, and I switch my phone to silent as my tears fall steadily.

I didn't realize how much I depended on Ransom and the rest of the guys caring about me. They always make me feel like I matter. But for the first time, I feel like an outsider. This hair-brained plan wasn't about what I confessed to Colton all those weeks ago. It's about Declan and his guilty conscience. So they moved and manipulated me because that's what they thought was best for him.

It was stupid of me to believe I was just like family. I was wrong, and I try to convince myself it's better I know it now, so I can adjust my expectations.

I don't believe it.

17
_____

DECLAN

I almost blew everything up with that sweater. I'm supposed to be earning her trust. And as fucked up as this plan of Colton's is, I need to make the most of it. I've never had this much one-on-one time with Cara, and now that I'm not worried we're about to freeze to death or drive off the fucking road, I can appreciate it.

But when she walked out of the bathroom in...that. God. I nearly swallowed my tongue. Cara, in her lace and leather, in her death-defying shoes, is hell on wheels and sexy as fuck.

But Cara, in a tiny scrap of satin, feet bare, is a fucking dream. My dream. She's been starring in them for years, and holy shit, she's better than I ever hoped.

I should have just handed the fucking sweater to her, but nope, I had to push it. When she turned, and I was faced with that creamy back and glorious ass, nothing could have kept me from going to her. There's something so seductive about a woman giving you her back. It shows a level of trust, of vulnerability that I don't think I've ever been given.

I shouldn't have pushed it, though. She's alone in a hotel room with me. Is she even okay with that? I didn't ask her because I was too fucking relieved to have a room, I didn't

question it. But there's one fucking bed, and suddenly an intimacy she wasn't prepared for is being pushed on her.

I'm going to be a fucking gentleman if it kills me, though.
Starting with offering to sleep on the fucking floor.

I rush through my shower, eager to get back to her. I'm
still buzzing from the drive, but I bet she's exhausted. I don't
want to put off this conversation.

I'm mentally patting myself on the back for my amazing
plan as I pull on a pair of sleep shorts. I second guess myself,
but decide throwing a t-shirt on is my best play. Going out
there bare-chested, even though I'm finally proud of my body,
seems a bit creepy.

A billow of steam escapes when I open the door. I lock on
her immediately.

She's curled in the bed, back against the headboard,
covers pulled up to her shoulders. Her eyes are swollen and
red. "You were crying?"

"Brilliant deduction, Dec," she mumbles, eyes on the awful
blue floral bedspread. I'm off balance. I don't know how to
handle sad Cara. Or any sad woman. If it were my brother
looking like that, I'd go over and slap him on the back. Ask
him what the fuck was wrong. That doesn't seem like the
right approach here. But fuck if I know what I should do.

"Did something happen? You talked to Ransom?"

"Yeah," she says, her voice a dull monotone.

"Can I...help?"

She laughs bitterly. "I don't think you can, Declan. We're
in this fucked up situation thanks to your brothers. They
manipulated everything to get the two of us alone." She
clamps her mouth shut, glaring at me. "Do you know how
scary this could be? Aside from the fact that we could have
been in big fucking trouble in that snowstorm, I'm a woman
alone in a hotel room with a man I really don't know
anything about. But they didn't consider that. They didn't

think about how I might feel. They just manipulated and maneuvered."

I flinch at the ice in her words and the idea of her being unsafe with me. I would never fucking hurt her. How the hell did we go from touching ten minutes ago, to this?

"What am I missing?"

"Ransom was in on it. He kept me busy all day, so I'd miss them leaving early."

"Oh." Shit. The whole world is upside down. No way would Ransom normally do something like this. What the fuck was he thinking?

"What does that say about me? Am I really that disposable?" Her eyes are welling with tears again. I want to go over there, take her in my arms, and explain to her how vital she truly is. Not just to Ransom, but to me. But I can almost see the giant fuck off bubble she's sitting in.

"No fucking way would anyone say that about you. You are not disposable, Cara. Get that thought out of your head. They love you, you know that."

She laughs a far-from-happy sound. "Sure they do. So much, they didn't think twice about fucking with my life and putting me in danger."

"They fucked with both our lives, Cara. It's shitty of them, for sure. But their hearts were in the right place."

Her gaze sharpens on mine, hints of the terrifying Cara from work appearing in her eyes. "The right place. Gotcha. They were doing what they thought was best...for you."

I open my mouth to defend myself, but I'm not sure I can. My brothers know what a fucking loser I am when it comes to Cara. It's not at all outside the realm of possibility they pulled this crap to give me a chance to fix the shit sandwich I made for myself. Colton may have planned this because he wants everybody to be in love, but Ransom didn't help for the same reason. As much as he might love all my brother's women, he's a lot more cynical —about love and everything else—when it comes right down to it.

"They think I have no game. That I can't talk around you and that without their help, I won't be able to repair this." Might as well just spill my guts. I doubt any of this is a surprise to her. "They have no faith in my ability to fix this between us. It's all about me."

She smiles sadly. "That's the problem, though, isn't it? It's all about you. They didn't once consider how I might feel as a woman, stranded alone with a man, a near stranger."

"Wait, a fucking minute. I'm not a stranger. You know me, Cara. You've known me for years. There's no fucking way I'd do anything to hurt you. You have to know that." Too late, I realize how stupid my words are. Because I did hurt her. Maybe not physically, but I did hurt her with my stupid jealousy and shitty actions. Her shake of the head shows me she's aware of that, just as much as I am.

"I don't know you, Declan," she whispers. "Not at all."

She could kick me in the balls, and it would hurt less than this. "Do you honestly believe you're not safe with me? Because if you do, then I've fucked this up worse than I ever imagined."

Her hesitation kills me. "I don't think you'd physically hurt me or force me to do anything."

"Well, that's something, I guess. You know I wouldn't hit you or rape you. Pretty low fucking bar." Backing away, I slide down the wall next to the bathroom until my ass is on the floor. I cover my face with my hands, so fucking done with all of this. Why did I believe Colt when he implied Cara had feelings for me? She very obviously doesn't. Or if she does, it's a wisp of a feeling, easily set aside.

"Are you okay," she asks quietly.

A humorless laugh escapes. "Sure. Just peachy." I shove the heels of my hands into my eye sockets, willing my eyes to stop watering. "I'll end this. I promise. When we finally get to

Vegas or home or wherever the fuck you want to go, I'll make sure they stop interfering."

I drop my hands, resting my head on the wall. "I am very aware of the power dynamic here. I might not be your direct boss, but I am aware that you're my employee. I always have been. And you shouldn't have been put in this position. I'll handle it. I promise."

Her flinch when I say *employee*, clearly hits a nerve. We've never treated her like an employee. We've always, all nine of us, blurred that line with her. Have since the beginning. But for me, the idea of being her boss was laughable. She's far more suited to being a boss than I am. I figured out how to handle my group of IT geeks, and only there do I feel in charge. I understand my place, and I have no fucking problem running it. But with her, honestly, she felt like the boss. But I can't ignore the unequal power dynamic anymore.

"Right. You're right. You're my boss." We sit, staring, the weight of this conversation hanging between us. Both exhausted, physically, but more so emotionally. Pushing up, I grab my bag, pulling some sweats on over my shorts. Then my last hoodie. I check my coat, hanging on the back of the chair. Still soaking wet.

Cara's eyes widen as I cross to the bed. I give her a tight smile as I pull a pillow off the bed, and drop it on the floor near the door, then drop and stretch out. I feel better having my body between the door and the bed. It's unlikely we'll have trouble, but who the fuck knows who else is out there. I won't let anyone, or anything, get to her.

"Declan...are you going to be okay on the floor?"

"Yeah. I spent more than a year sleeping on the floor, remember? We all had sleeping bags when we started Knight Street. I'll be fine." There were a half-dozen of us crashing in the studio apartment above our first garage. It was a fucking puppy pile. For years.

"You're in your thirties now, Declan. I don't think it's going to be the same."

I search for a thread of humor. A tiny bit of levity, though a boulder is sitting on my chest. "You calling me old, woman?"

Finally, I get a hint of a smile. "Fine. Be a martyr. Sleep on the floor...there are no extra blankets."

"Go to sleep, Cara. I'll be fine."

She hums, reaching out to flick off the hideous bedside lamp, plunging the room into near darkness. I lay, staring at the light playing on the ceiling, the blowing snow turning the sky a dusky purple, listening to her sigh as she snuggles in. She may have worried about me sleeping on the floor, but unspoken between us is the knowledge that she didn't invite me to share the bed. She doesn't trust me. There's a canyon between feeling safe enough to sleep in the same room and knowing I'd never hurt her. A canyon I don't know how to cross.

"Declan."

The voice registers at the same time as I feel her hand on my shoulder. I'm moving before I realize it, reaching for her.

"What's the matter? Are you okay?" The room is so much darker than it was when I fell asleep. I can only see a faint outline of her crouched next to me. The frigid temperature of the room registers next. Her skin is like ice. "Jesus, you're freezing." I'm up and guiding her back to the bed.

"I'm fine. I can't get the heat up any higher, though, and I can hear your teeth chattering from over here. You can't stay on the floor, Declan. It's too cold."

Pausing, I realize she's right. I'm shaking. She guides me to the edge of the bed, then moves away, coming back with the pillow.

"Get in. Under the covers. Come on."

I follow her instructions because I am really fucking cold. The bed doesn't feel that much warmer, but when she crawls in on the other side, my body starts generating heat all by itself. I'm afraid to move. To spook her. To make her change her mind. Checking my watch, I see it's only been an hour since we fell asleep.

"Is this okay?" I whisper. "I don't want you to be uncomfortable."

"This whole trip has been uncomfortable, Declan. But I don't want you miserable on the floor all night." I would argue, but she's right. No way would I have stayed asleep much longer. My entire body is quaking.

"I don't think I've been this cold since I was a kid." I can't stop fussing with the blankets, trying to make sure she stays covered while I wiggle around until I feel them drop over my back. "And you're right...I am not built for the floor. I've gone soft. Money's made me soft."

She laughs, "So soft. I mean, you sleep in beds now and everything." I laugh with her, thankful the tension between us is broken.

"You're safe with me. I promise. I would never physically hurt you. I know you know that. But I'll be careful with all of you. I swear it."

She's quiet. I can feel the heat radiating from her, even over the foot that separates us. I'm on the bed, but as far as I can get to the edge without falling off.

I startle when I feel her hand on my arm. The touch is hot, even through my sweater. She slides it down until her palm is pressed to mine, our fingers interlacing on the mattress between us. Her simple touch grounds me like nothing else has in weeks.

"Okay," she whispers into the darkness.

18

CARA

The man is a furnace. I may not have been as cold as he was, lying on the floor, but the room was chilly. As upset as I was last night, I couldn't handle listening to him shiver. Moving him to the bed was for my comfort. So I could sleep. But laying with him in this bed, holding his hand, is the most settled I've felt since the night I killed Tyler.

While everything I said last night is true, on the surface at least, now in the light of day, I can admit that underneath, there's a hell of a lot more going on. Ransom may not have been trying to hurt me, but he still did. I don't think I fully realized how much I depended on him to have my back until yesterday. He's my boss, but I always felt like he needed me. Like I wasn't replaceable. Maybe I turned that into something more than it actually was. I'm not his sister, we're not family, so of course, he'd put Declan's needs above mine.

And yes, of course, I'm safe with Dec. I know that. The man spent three years running from me. Pretty sure my non-existent virtue is safe with him. It's still embarrassing, wishing someone loved you the way you love them. Because I do. This isn't a crush, as much as I've been trying to convince myself it is.

Laying here, as the rising sun turns the room shades of orange, I'm woman enough to admit that the man laying beside me, the one that held my hand all night and —twice that I was awake for— pulled the covers tighter over me, has my whole heart.

And that's a problem.

A problem I'm going to have to do something about. I can't be this girl anymore. The pining one. The one throwing herself at a man. Yes, he hurt me, saying that shit to me at the hospital, but then he reeled me back in with his apology, telling me he was jealous. Sure, it's a caveman move. But I must be part cavewoman because that sign of jealousy filled my pathetic heart with so much hope. Just like that, I was hooked again. My mind went immediately to *maybe he does love me*.

Until he said he wanted us to be friends.

So what's a girl to do when she's in love with a man that doesn't seem to love her back, but she still has to see him every day at work?

I can find another man to ride like Bree suggested, but my heart's never been involved in a one-night stand before. No reason to think it would be now. So I fuck around at night and come to work and obsess over Declan each day? That's a stupid plan. Besides, I haven't met a man in years who makes me pant the way Declan does just standing across a room.

So do I leave my job? I love my job. I love working with Ransom. Or I did. But maybe that's broken too. Maybe I don't respect him as much as I used to after the shit he pulled.

I don't technically need the job anymore, but I don't know if I want to lose the safety net it gives me. If I want the club to be successful, I'm going to need to keep pouring my profits back into it.

There are way too many *I don't know's* for me to process

right now. These are all decisions for another day. I've always operated from my gut, but being responsible for feeding Bree taught me quickly to be deliberate when I make decisions. Can't fly off the handle and quit when you've got a teenager to feed and put through school.

I also really like Declan's face. Do I really not want to see it every day? Staring at him like this, vulnerable and unaware, is something I do a lot. I stare. But never this close and never when he's asleep. I thought I knew his face. I thought it was familiar, but in the last few months, it's gotten harder, the lines of his face maturing somehow. With the short hair, the beard, and all those muscles, he's like a different person. That sweetness, that geekiness that sucked me in at the beginning is muted.

He tenses, shifting on his pillow, and I resist the urge to slam my eyes closed and pretend I'm sleeping. That's not me. Instead, I watch as he comes awake. I memorize the way his nose scrunches up, how he scratches at his beard as he yawns. It's endlessly fascinating.

Even more fascinating? The tightening of his fingers around mine and the slow strokes his thumb makes against my skin.

I expected a slow blink awake. Instead, his rich brown eyes lock on mine, completely aware. Unprepared for the force of his stare, I feel a flush rising. I don't look away, though. The silence between us stretches, and I'm about to snatch my hand back and roll off the bed when he speaks.

"You're so fucking beautiful." His words are low, reverent. There's no stopping my flush. It flows across my skin like a wave, heating everything in its path.

"You have to stop saying stuff like that." My heart can't take it anymore.

He frowns. "Why?"

"Because you're fucking with my head."

"I don't mean to."

"Maybe not. But the result is the same." I tug my hand from his, rolling to my back, staring at the popcorn ceiling and questioning all my life choices.

"I never know what to say to you," he mutters.

Turning my head, I arch an eyebrow. "I'm really not that complicated."

His face scrunches up. "That's the biggest fucking lie to ever come out of your mouth."

Shoving up onto my ass, I pin him with a glare. "Seriously? What the fuck, Declan? There's no mystery here." I wave my hand up and down my body. "What you see is what you get. Always."

He sits up. He doesn't use his hands, just a quick ab crunch, and he's in my face. "Bullshit. You're always hiding behind the clothes and the attitude. I never felt like I could get to know you. Whenever we ran into each other at work, you took my fucking breath away."

He's lying. He has to be. "You couldn't get away from me fast enough. We both know that. You're rewriting history." I hop off the bed, probably flashing him my panties, and dig in my bag for my phone. Maybe we can get the hell out of here this morning. I could really use a drink or twelve.

"Fuck Cara, that's not..." He groans, dropping his head in his hand.

I stand, phone clutched in my hand, but forgotten for the moment. "Why do you do this?" I ask him quietly. "You never say what you mean. What you want. The closest you came was the night at my club. You told me you were jealous. You told me you want to be friends. What else do you want to say? Why can't you just talk to me?"

He drops his hand, pinning me with the biggest glare to ever grace his face. It's the fiercest I've ever seen him. "You're intimidating as fuck. You're a walking wet dream, and I spend the entire time you're near me trying to not come in my pants. I feel like a fucking idiot around you."

He's off the bed and slamming into the bathroom before I can take my next breath. Of all the things I imagined coming out of Declan's mouth, that wasn't even in the top hundred.

Staring blankly at the phone in my hand, toes freezing, mind spinning, I just breathe. When my mind settles, my feet take me straight to the bathroom door. I'm about to knock to say...I don't know what, when the shower comes on. Slumping back onto the bed, I slap at my phone, willing its display to change. But it stubbornly refuses to. That fucking *No-Service* message is where my bars should be.

Not only am I stuck in the middle of nowhere with him, but I've also lost contact with everyone I know and love. I've lost contact with Bree. That thought is the one that breaks me. I haven't gone a day without talking to her in a decade. I'm not fucking starting now.

Diving for the ancient phone on the table, I scream in frustration at the lack of a dial tone. I am not letting this storm fuck with my life like this. I rifle through my bag, and after a quick check that the shower is still running, strip and throw on the warmest clothes I have, leggings and a t-shirt. Then I throw Declan's hoodie back over it. All that's running through my mind is getting to Bree, or at least getting to a working phone to talk to Bree. It's not just for her. I have to know she's okay. I have to.

I'm panting, slapping at the stupid locks on the door, trying to get out when powerful arms wrap around my waist.

"Cara, what the fuck? Stop. Stop. You can't go out there like this." I'm fighting, trying to peel those hands away from me so I can get out. Get away. Then I'm spinning and being dropped onto the bed. Declan backs away, planting his back against the door. Logic would have me sit here, calm down, and come up with a plan to reach Bree. But the panic, the overwhelm, the same ones that I've been struggling with since that night, are in full control.

I'm jumping off the bed and running at Declan before I

even realize it. Pushing, pulling, trying anything I can to get him out of my way. Other than rocking him slightly, I can't get him to fucking move. He doesn't fight back, doesn't react, just stands there like a fucking wall as I burn myself out. When I have nothing left, I fall to the floor.

My knees never hit the rust-colored carpet. Instead, I'm pulled into Declan's bare chest, and he drops to the floor with me curled in his lap.

I'm not sure when my panting breaths turn to sobs, but they tear through my body with the force of a hurricane. I'm so fucking scared. I have been for weeks, but I've been keeping it together in front of Bree. Not letting myself fall apart until I'm in the silence of my car. It's always been my job to make sure she's okay. To be the strong one. I am not okay, but knowing she was, that she was alive and breathing, helped me keep my shit together. But I think I'm cracking, crumbling.

And the man who ran every time I cornered him at work is humming to me, petting my hair, and rocking us. The beat of his heart is steady, where mine is racing. Everything about him seems solid and in control. When I so am not.

Whatever fucking planet I'm on right now, I think I want to move here.

19

DECLAN

I ran to the fucking bathroom. What am I? A teenage girl?

I flip the shower on, letting it warm while I mentally beat my head against a wall. Why the fuck do I just blurt shit out like that? Christ, watching Zach pick up women is like watching an elite gamer. Me, on the other hand? A mom playing Pac-Man at an arcade. There is absolutely no comparison.

I strip off my hoodie and t-shirt, bracing my hands on the sink. I look like a grown-ass man. Why the fuck don't I act like it? Time to stop hiding from this shit and just tell Cara what's going on in my head.

Decision made, I slap off the shower and wrench open the bathroom door, ready to man the fuck up, when I spot Cara at the door, feet still bare. It's not until I get closer that I realize she's gasping, freaking the fuck out. I don't know what the fuck happened, but she can't go out there like that.

I wrap my arm around her waist, trying to get her to calm down, but it's like she doesn't even hear me, pulling and tugging at my arms. I'm freaked she's going to hurt herself. I lock my fingers, making it impossible for her to get loose. Old me might have had a hard time holding onto her. New me doesn't.

Picking her up, I drop her onto the bed, then back up and block the door. She's not getting out of this fucking room in the state she's in. My stomach clenches when I get a good look at her face. Her eyes are red, mouth twisted. Her blonde hair, already mussed from sleep, is tangled and staticky. Whatever the fuck happened must have been bad. I've never seen her like this. Not even the night at the hospital. She was wrecked then, but still present. But not now. Now? Cara's left the building. It's just pure desperation left in her.

I've seen this before, in one of the other kids at my sixth foster home. He'd been hurt pretty badly...he never told us how, but I imagined the worst and probably wasn't far off. He used to get triggered by the littlest things, and he'd fucking bolt. Didn't matter where we were or if where he was running to was safe. He just...ran. Into the street. Into traffic. Into a field. His body was pure flight, trying to escape the perceived threat.

She flies back at me, trying to move me, but she's got no fucking chance. Not in this state. I have no doubt, if she was thinking clearly, she'd be able to make me hurt. But not right now. Not like this.

Finally, she runs out of steam, her hands dropping, head falling forward. She drops. I can't let her hit the floor, pulling her into my arms instead. Then together, we curl onto the ancient carpet. Her heaving breaths change to sobs, and I pull her closer, humming some stupid video game theme stuck in my head. Then we rock.

Jonas always liked the rocking. We didn't always get to help him when he was struggling, sometimes being touched was too much. The best thing was to leave him alone. But other times, he'd let us sit with him, holding the back of his neck, and we'd rock. It helped him process whatever he was struggling with in the moment. Maybe it will help Cara.

Whatever is happening, I need it to stop. I can't fucking bear seeing her this hurt without knowing what I can do to help. To make it better.

I don't know how much time passes, but the room lightens, and my ass is completely frozen from the cold air coming under the door. Thank fuck she didn't make it out there in this weather.

Finally, her sobs slow. She's boneless against my chest, trusting that I've got her. Something about her vulnerability settles me. Balls to the wall Cara turned me into a teenage boy. Vulnerable, crying Cara has stripped that kid away, leaving only the man.

Stroking her hair, I press my cheek to the top of her head. "What's happening? Talk to me."

"Nothing," she mumbles, halfheartedly pulling away. I tighten my arms, and she gives in right away, dropping her head back to my chest.

"It's not nothing. We both know that. I promise you can talk to me."

She heaves out a shuddering breath. "There's no service."

"Room service? That's ok, we'll go over to the pub." Maybe she's Hangry? That's a thing, isn't it?

Slightly hysterical giggles leave her. I laugh too, but I have no idea why. I'm just so relieved she's not in the dark place she was before.

"Not room service. Cell service...I can't call Bree."

Finally, something I understand. "Do you need to talk to her? Are you worried about something specific?" I can't magically make a cell tower appear or chase this storm away, but I can talk.

"No...I just," she shrugs, staring down at her lap.

"Is she still struggling after Tyler?" She jumps when I say his name. I can see the pulse in her neck flutter faster.

"Um...yes. I suppose she is. I just like to check on her."

"You guys have been on your own for a long time, huh?"

"Yeah," she murmurs. I want her eyes on me. I'm tempted to say or do something shitty just to bring that fire of hers back.

"How are you doing after that night?" I mean, she's not ok. But she's so good at masking how she's feeling.

Another giggle. This one sounds wrong, though. An edge of hysteria coloring it.

"That night. That's what I call it too. It sounds better than..." she trails off, a lone tear rolling down her cheek. She drags in another shuddering breath. "It sounds better than the night I killed him."

That word makes me flinch, and I know she fucking feels it. I tighten my embrace and pull back to look at her. "Killed him sounds wrong, Cara. The night you defended yourself, is more accurate."

"Maybe," she says hollowly, "but I don't think it matters what you call it. In the end, he's dead, and it's my fault."

Cupping her cheek, I tilt her face until she's forced to meet my eyes. "You didn't start anything that night. But, yeah. He's dead. And I'm really fucking grateful for that."

The crease between her eyes deepens. "Why?"

"Isn't it obvious?" I ask. But I can tell by the lingering confusion in her gaze that it isn't. "You're still here. Still breathing. Still in one piece. He's dead, and you're here, and I'm glad."

"You're glad he's dead."

"I'm sure it's not PC for me to say that. But he attacked your sister. He attacked you. He was not a good guy. I can't imagine anyone would blame you for what happened that night."

Another tear falls. "The District Attorney wants to blame me."

"Yeah, he does. And that has nothing to do with you. Nothing. But you don't need to worry about that anymore. I'll take care of it."

I mentally will her not to ask how. I've been sitting on a pile of shit, hoping the D.A. would do the right thing. But I'm done waiting for him. Cara's hurting, and I won't allow that to continue. But I should have known better because Cara is not the type of woman to let a comment like that go.

"Explain," she orders me, making me smile despite the seriousness of this moment.

"You don't need to know the details. Just know that all of this will be over, and you won't ever have to think of it again."

Her mouth scrunches up. "I wish that were true."

"It's true, Cara. I will handle it. I'm done sitting by."

"It doesn't matter if I end up in prison or not. I'll still have to live with what I did. He's someone's kid, you know. There's some mother out there crying because he's never coming back. That won't just go away because I'm not charged with a crime."

"No," I say stiffly. "I guess it won't." That doesn't mean I don't wish it would. "Are you still struggling with sleep? Moving didn't help?"

She wipes the sleeve of my hoodie over her eyes, then drops her hand back to her lap. "It helped. Sort of, anyway."

"You were awake when I woke up. Did you sleep any last night?" I crashed immediately. It didn't matter I was in a bed with Cara. The stress of the drive and the warmth of the bed combined to knock me the fuck out.

She shrugs again, and I want to push her some more, but I bite my fucking tongue. The glimpse I had outside guarantees she and I are going to have some time together. It's a fucking whiteout, with at least two feet of snow on top of our car, added to everything that fell while we were driving. No fucking way is all of that getting cleared quickly. We've got another night, at least, to figure our shit out.

She sits, seemingly content to stay in my lap. And I'm not going to do a thing to make her move. Not when I finally have her in my arms. I finally feel like I can be the man she needs. One who can be here for her when she's struggling. Now I just have to figure out how to keep being this man. Not the regular computer nerd version of me.

I'm composing sonnets in my fucking mind, odes to her beauty and wit, when my stomach takes the opportunity to howl like a starving wolf. "Sorry," I mumble.

She smiles weakly. "It's ok. I'm hungry too. I usually put snacks in my bag, but I packed light this time."

I shoot her a look, and she slaps at me halfheartedly. "One suitcase is packing light."

"It weighs fifty pounds, at least. We were going for a fucking weekend, Cara."

She scowls at me. "I packed the necessities." She rolls off me, plants her hand on the carpet and pushes up to stand. I sit, staring up at her, admiring the view of her face past the mountains of her breasts. I should write some sonnets about those...or maybe some limericks.

She catches me staring, a smirk covering her face. And for the first time in three years, I don't blush and shy away from that look. Instead, I give her a slow smile, making sure I let her see every dirty thought I've ever had about her in it. Her eyes widen, and she takes a small step away before rolling her shoulders back. It was a tiny retreat, but still a retreat. I'll take it. Declan: 1. Cara: 5,673. I'm on the fucking board.

20

CARA

He's zipping up my coat. Who is this man?

My eyes, still gritty from my earlier tears, are watering as he swings the door open, revealing the peaceful white landscape in front of us. I know there's a parking lot right in front of us, but the cars are just large white blobs, completely hidden below the deep snow.

"Oh my god," I whisper into the hush of the morning. "I've never seen anything like this." Chicago gets a fuck of a lot of snow, but I live in the middle of the city. It's mud brown before you know it. And it's never this peaceful. Maybe I'm starting to understand why people live in places like this.

And also, holy fuck, is it cold. My stiletto boots are not built for this temperature. Or this kind of snow. Jesus, I almost ran out into this in my bare feet. I'm really fucking lucky Declan stopped me. I could have been in a world of trouble.

Declan shakes his head. "We're so fucking lucky we found this place. I don't even want to think about what might have happened if we'd gotten stuck out there." The way he echos my thoughts about luck is a bit jarring. But he's right. We're safe, and we're lucky. No thanks to a bunch of interfering idiots.

Declan claps his hands. "Ok. The walkway to the pub is covered, but there are still drifts. Those shoes of yours aren't going to cut it." He dips down as if to throw me over his shoulder, but I hop back.

"Nope. Not doing that." He scowls, about to scold me, I'm sure, when I raise my hand and twirl my finger. "Turn around. I'm going to ride you...I mean piggyback." Shit. I wish I could call the words back, but they've already hit Declan. Hard, judging by the wide eyes and choked sound he makes.

Rolling my eyes, I spin him, pulling the door shut behind me, then grab onto his shoulders.

"Ready? Here we go." I jump, trusting him to catch me. He shakes out of his stupor, thank fuck, and catches behind my knees, pulling me tight to him. I freeze as my pussy is pressed against his back. I did not think this through. At all.

"Okay...let's go," he says hoarsely, heading towards the pub.

Trying to distract myself from the strength of his hands and the warmth of him through his coat, I peek into the hotel rooms we pass. Most of the curtains are closed, but the odd one isn't, revealing little slices of life. A man in his boxers sitting at the end of the bed, remote in hand, as a woman sleeps on the bed behind him...only the top of her brunette hair showing. A mother curled up in bed with her kids, watching cartoons. It all looks normal. Like they planned to be here. But I doubt any of them had this place as their destination. It's off the beaten path between two bigger towns. Not exactly a tourist mecca. But just like us, their luck held out, and they ended up somewhere warm and safe for the night.

Declan stomps up the step to the wooden porch of the pub. Bar? Restaurant? I'm not really sure what this place is, and I don't care. Because the smells coming from the building would convince an angel to fall, just for a taste.

Releasing my legs, he lets me slide down his back. Though thanks to the stilettos, there's not far to go. We push through the doors and stop to take in everything in front of us.

It looks like there was one hell of a party here last night. People are sleeping in booths and on the floor. A couple of people even have sleeping bags covering them. There's a smiling older lady weaving around the bodies with plates of food. She catches our eyes and hollers out, "Sit wherever kids," then continues on her way. Dec and I share a look at 'kids.'

He pulls me towards a small unoccupied booth in the back. We both dive at the menu, starving. The waitress comes by, shaking her head.

"Sorry kids. With this storm, and all the extra people, we're not really working off the menu anymore. My Cliff has pancakes and sausages on, and he'll fill you up a plate. Coffee?"

"Please! And anything you bring out, I promise I'll eat. It smells amazing," I say.

She laughs, takes Declan's drink order, and she's off.

"You don't want coffee? I honestly don't understand how people function without it."

His mouth twists. "We survived on shitty coffee for a long time. I can't fucking stand the stuff now."

"Aren't gamers all caffeine addicts? How are you getting your fix?"

"Way too many energy drinks. I'm trying to cut back. Colt thinks the way they make my heart race isn't healthy." He scrunches up his nose. "He's probably right." I smile at that, then turn my attention to the room. This restaurant would probably best be described as a dive. But it's clean and warm, and right now, that's pretty damn close to heaven. I grab my phone, hoping for a signal, but get nothing.

"The storm might have knocked out a tower," Declan says, studying me. "But Bree can call the guys, and they'll let her know we're safe. If she needs anything, they'll take care of her."

"How is she supposed to call anyone? No one's at the office until Monday."

"I gave her all our cell numbers earlier this week."

"Wait. You did? Ransom made it pretty fucking clear those numbers were never to be given out, on pain of losing my job." I get exactly why. Some of the staff have a habit of running to the guys to solve problems they should be handling themselves. It's better they come through me, and I can tell them to figure their shit out themselves.

He shrugs. "That's only for staff. You and Bree are different."

"How is she different?"

"You know," he says, eyes somber. "She's one of ours now. She's living in our building."

"And me?"

"You were always ours. I think you wormed your way in there from the first day." The memory of Ransom's part in getting us here rises, and he must see it. "It's me. Ransom moved you around like a chess piece. But it's because of me." He takes a deep breath and grips the edge of the table. "You're pretty much all I think about, Cara. Have been for years. Ransom knows that. And maybe...they thought you might like me too."

I'm frozen in the booth. My worry over Bree, already calmed by Declan's assurance that his brothers will look after her, fades away as his words reverberate in my chest. It doesn't make any sense. But also, maybe it does?

"I'm all you think about? I...that doesn't make sense. You run. Like, bolt from me."

He winces and nods but doesn't drop his eyes. Or run

from the table. No, he just sits there, looking at me. It shocks the shit out of me.

"Yeah. Not my finest moments, for sure. Pretty embarrassing, honestly."

"Why? Why do you run?"

He rubs his hand down his beard nervously. "I...have no frame of reference for you, Cara. Women coming onto me isn't new. It's been happening since we made money. But those girls...women. Shit. They're not like you."

"Not like me." I'm not sure I like where this is going.

"No. I haven't dated much. Not really."

My eyes widen. "Are you a virgin?" Because that would explain a lot. I could totally teach him. I black out a little bit, thinking about practicing all the positions with him.

He groans, slumping in the seat. "No. For fuck's sake. Why does everyone think that?"

My face flushes. "I'm sorry, it's just you said you hadn't dated much..."

He raises an eyebrow, the corner of his mouth curled into a grin. "Now Cara, dating, and fucking aren't exactly the same thing. You know that. If I just wanted to fuck you, this would have been so much simpler."

My thighs clench at the way he says 'fuck you'. I'm thinking all kinds of naughty things now. Crap. "Simpler?"

"Yeah. It might have been a little awkward, but if all I wanted from you was sex, we'd have already done that...unless you're telling me you aren't into me? That you coming onto me every day at work was just a game for you?" His face shutters as he says the words.

"I wasn't playing a fucking game."

"Ok. Right. Good." He swallows. "Good." Is it, though?

"Dating?" I prompt, wanting this conversation back on track. Shit is getting interesting.

"Yeah. Um, I've dated, but most of the women I've dated are...similar. Kinda geeky. Sweet. Into video games. When we'd go out, we'd go to the movies." He snorts. "Most of them I met gaming. We'd talk online more than in person. We were usually friends first."

"But I'm different."

"Yeah, you are. You are way more confident than they are."

"This isn't computing, Declan. You told me you get hit on all the time."

"Well, yeah, I do. But usually, it's when my brothers take me out, and it's pretty fucking obvious we're rich. They see dollar signs when they look at me, and it's easy to play that game. They're all the same, and they all want the same thing from me."

"Money."

"Money," he echoes. "But when I —."

We're interrupted by the waitress as she puts down our drinks. "Be right back with your food."

I doctor my coffee, adding a bunch of creamers and sugar, taking a sip, and letting the creamy goodness flow through me as I ponder his words. What must it be like to know that people are only after you for your money?

"Did the women you dated before, the gamer girls, know you were rich?"

"Not at first. When they found out, it got...weird, usually." Color rises on his face. "Honestly, that was usually when we'd break up. I'm not sure why, but when they found out about my brothers and me, they either stopped returning my texts and calls, or they changed."

"Changed how?"

"Like they'd dress differently. Start asking me to take them to those trendy restaurants...changed."

"You didn't enjoy going to those places?"

"Not really, but I would be happy to take them. But they'd spend the whole time looking around at the rich people and talking about how much everyone's worth." He frowns.

"There weren't many like that, honestly. Only two. Those were easier to handle than the women who just blew me off. I'm still not sure why that happened."

"Because they thought they were getting a simple gamer boyfriend. Not a billionaire with eight brothers and a pretty serious day job. Maybe it was a bit of false advertising."

He leans back in the booth, crossing his arms over his chest. "I wasn't pretending to be anyone else."

"Maybe not, but you only showed them one part of you. The geeky, video game-playing guy. When it was time to show them more, maybe they felt a little deceived. Maybe the world they want to live in isn't the same as yours."

"We live in the same world, Cara."

A laugh bursts out of me at that statement. "Do you honestly believe that? Seriously? Because no, you definitely don't live in the same world as the rest of us." Has he truly forgotten how the rest of us live? With our car payments and jobs and scraping by on minimum wage.

Ok, I don't scrape by anymore. But I did for a lot of years.

The arrival of breakfast interrupts our conversation, and we both dig in. And the food is fucking spectacular. Fluffy pancakes, greasy breakfast sausage, and a mound of fluffy scrambled eggs. We stuff our faces, but I throw in the towel before Declan. Smiling, I push my plate closer to him.

He swallows his bite and frowns. "That's yours."

"I'm full. It's ok. Finish it." He reaches for it, then pulls back, looking torn. "Oh, my god. Declan, just eat it! What is the problem?"

"I don't want you to be hungry."

"I'm full. I promise." When he doesn't look convinced, I remind him. "Besides, I'm sure we'll be back in here for lunch in no time."

Finally, he seems satisfied and digs into the not-small portion left on my plate. There's something in that interaction that I can't put my finger on. Something that feels bigger under the surface. Besides caring that I had enough, which is sweet, it seems deeper somehow.

Though maybe it's not that deep. A man who grew up in foster care might know a thing or two about being hungry.

I watch him plow through the plate, looking like he hasn't eaten in weeks.

"I don't remember you eating quite this much...before."

He swallows and wipes his mouth with his napkin. "It's Jonas's fault. He made a stupid bet with me, and I started working out. Then I kinda got into it and started lifting with Colton. Now I'm always hungry."

"The Mohawk bet?"

"Yeah, that's the one."

"It suited you. It was edgy and cool."

His mouth drops open. "Seriously? Those words have never been used to describe me. Not in my entire life."

"What words normally describe you?"

"Pasty, geek, nerd, boring. All of those."

Does nobody know this man? How the hell can people really think that of him?

"I think you're the most interesting person I've ever met."

21

DECLAN

I'm gaping, I know. But how the fuck can she say that with a straight face?

"There's nothing interesting about me, Cara. I wish there was."

She chokes on her sip of coffee, slapping her chest. I rear up, panicking. Reaching for her.

"I'm ok," she says, waving me off. She gulps in a few breaths, finally calming. Only then can I sit down. She sits back in the booth, looking at me questioningly. "Do you really think that? That you're boring?"

"I know I am."

"Huh," she mutters, her head tilted. Studying me.

As always, when the full force of her is focused on me, I want to squirm. But she shouldn't have any illusions about me. I want her. I want to be someone special to her. But the truth is, I'm boring as fuck, and she'll get sick of me quick.

"Why did you run away from me all the time?"

Shit. We'd kinda dropped this earlier, and I was hoping she'd forget to pick it up. Busying myself stacking our plates and lining up the cutlery, I give her the truth.

"The other women I dated...my feelings for them

were...simple. We liked each other, it was easy. My feelings for you aren't simple. At all. On top of that, I always feel a little out of my league with you." I stop fiddling with the cutlery and move on to the salt and pepper shakers. "You're so confident, Cara. You know exactly who you are. And I didn't really know how to...fuck. I don't know the right words here. Not compete, not handle...I didn't know how to be the kind of man who could be with someone like you."

"Someone like me?"

"Yeah. You seem to know exactly who you are, and until...that night, you seemed like you could take on the whole world and win."

Her fingers are tight around her cup as she clutches it to her chest. When I finally get the guts to look at her face, my shoulders relax at her wide eyes. She's not completely disgusted by me. First hurdle cleared. Now for the next. Being this honest should get easier, shouldn't it? So far, I still feel like I've stripped naked and I'm doing squats in the middle of a church service. Exposed.

"I've been...working on myself over the last few months."

"What do you mean, 'working' on yourself? Do you mean physically?" she asks, waving her hand in front of her.

"Sort of. That's part of it. But it's mainly about being more...confident. I thought if I felt more comfortable in my skin and out there in the world, that maybe we..."

I don't even know how to finish that sentence. Maybe we'd date. Maybe you'd love me. Maybe you'd want me.

"Holy fuck," she whispers, eyes wide. "You're shy."

My face heats, but I nod. She's not wrong. "Yeah. And I have a highly developed flight response when it comes to you."

"The running."

"Yep."

She carefully places her coffee cup on the table, leaning in.

"So you're telling me that you've...liked me all this time? But you were too shy to do anything about it?"

"It sounds even lamer when you say it like that," I mutter, dropping my hands to my lap.

"And that night at the hospital, you were..."

"Jealous. Years of thinking you were out at clubs with other men. I let it spill over. Not my finest moment."

"Jesus," she says, her voice a hush.

Jesus is right. I just laid my cards on the table...well, some of them, anyway. The question is, what does this mean? If anything?

We're silent, Cara looking lost in thought. I'm freaking out a bit, alternating between wishing I hadn't been so honest and being glad I was. I've never let myself be this vulnerable with anyone except maybe my brothers. It could all blow up in my face now. But I think I would rather that than spend the next decade of my life wondering what could have been.

"I wasn't teasing you. Or toying with you," she says suddenly, crossing her arms over her chest.

"Good. That's good. Do you...did you have feelings for me?" There. That wasn't so awful. I didn't beg her to love me back. I'm cool.

She bites her lip, a slight frown on her face. Then, slowly, she nods.

I want to jump up and celebrate. I want to dive across the booth.

"Do you...do you think you might still have feelings for me? Even though I was a dick. Would you maybe consider...me?"

"Consider what...exactly?"

"Giving me a chance to," *don't say it, don't you dare say it*, "Woo you." *Ah, fuck. You said it.* It's one of the hardest things I've ever done in my life, but I don't slide off the bench and curl up into a ball of shame under the table. But it's really fucking close.

"Woo," she whispers under her breath. My leg starts bouncing under the table. I'm too fucking embarrassed to look at her, so I study the people around us instead. Some of the sleeping bag people are sitting up, yawning, sipping coffee right on the floor. Our waitress —the lady from the front desk last night— is handling it all with ease. It looks like she's done this before. Most of the people in the room are dressed comfortably, little piles of things around them. One older lady already has her knitting out.

My gaze lands on a couple of men who don't seem to fit. They're dressed in expensive suits, wrinkled, but clearly worth some change. And they're staring at Cara. I stare at them, waiting until they notice, which takes them way too fucking long. As soon as I've got their attention, I make it clear how much I don't appreciate them looking at my woman. And, as expected, smirks cover their faces. I don't break. I don't blink. This isn't my first fucking stare-down. Also, as expected, their smirks fall, and they busy themselves with their food. I keep my eyes on them a minute more, then slowly lean back in the booth.

"What was that?" Cara asks, eyes darting from the assholes to me. I freeze, completely unaware that she caught our little stare-down.

"I didn't like how they were looking at you. It wasn't respectful."

"You just cowed two men from across the room. I don't get it. I thought you were shy?"

"That," I say, nodding towards the suits, "has nothing to do with being shy. That's about respect."

"I really don't understand the difference."

"Being shy? That's a Cara thing. Not my whole life thing. Fuckers like that are a blip in my world. I grew up in foster care, Cara. I've been bullied and picked on since I can remember. When Ransom built our family, I had brothers to look after me. Brothers who made sure I could take care of myself.

I can handle shit like that without breaking a sweat. I can demand respect when I need to."

"You're confident."

"In my ability to handle them? Absolutely."

"They've been staring for a while. Casually flashing their expensive watches. Being lame. It didn't bother me. I'm used to it."

"You may be used to it, but nobody gets to disrespect you like that while I'm around."

She's silent, considering me. I let her look while I look right back. She's so beautiful. Hair a mess, and no makeup. Still perfect. I think I like her like this the best. No armor, none of her usual I don't care attitude. Just...her.

"I handle guys like that all the time. It's a part of owning a club that I had to figure out really fast." She looks uncomfortable, whereas before, she was relaxed.

"I know you're capable. You don't need to be defensive about it. Your ability to handle your shit is one of the things I admire most about you. But when you're with me, you don't need to worry about crap like that. I'll take care of it."

"Isn't that a little caveman?" Her voice sounds...funny.

"Probably," I admit. "I'm not looking to change you, Cara, or make you smaller. But I also won't tolerate anyone disrespecting you."

"Ransom doesn't ever say anything about it."

"True," I say, smiling. "But that's different. He likes to brag about what a Rottweiler you are in business. It's one of his favorite things about you. But I know for a fact he'll shut down anyone who tries to talk shit about you when you're not around to handle it yourself." Leaning forward, I clue her in. "He's your boss. He won't tolerate anyone disrespecting you."

"You're not my boss. I mean, you are, but you aren't."

"I know. But right now, I'm not acting as your boss."

"Then what?"

"Like a man, protective of a woman. It's not that complicated."

She presses her palms to the table. "Let me get this straight. You're shy, but only with me. You like how confident I am, but you still stare down anyone who's looking at me funny. You go all protective alpha when it comes to driving. You're a reformed car thief, and you're going to make the D.A. back down by being a computer god." A bright giggle comes out of her. "And you think you're boring?"

Her laughter breaks free, rolling from her like waves. She's clutching her stomach, and her head is thrown back. Every eye in the room is on her, and I don't blame them. She's stunning.

She finally winds down, shaking her head and wiping her eyes with the back of her hand. "Do you hear how stupid that sounds?"

I tug at my earlobe. "Ah, well, I didn't really think of it like that."

"Then what made you think you were boring?"

"I think, maybe, it had more to do with what I think your life is like. You seem to thrive at your club. Up till three, always socializing. And I'm just...not like that."

"What do you like doing, then? You've been going out more. I heard Zach talking about it. You're not enjoying it."

"No. I don't like the clubs."

"Then why are you going?" Her eyes turn, knowing because I can't fucking hide my expressions around her. "Me? It had to do with me?"

"This is going to sound stupid," I warn her. She leans forward, eyes wide. "Colt figured I needed to build my confidence somehow. So he thought if I went to the clubs and practiced talking to women, it would help."

"Did it?" she asks, a sharp edge in her words. "Did picking up other women make you feel more manly?"

Even an idiot could hear the danger in those words.

"That's what the plan was. Turns out, I have no problem talking to other women." Her mouth tightens, and I like the hint of jealousy. At least, I hope it's jealousy. It feels good to not be in it alone. "Also, turns out I'm not interested in other women. Figured that out pretty quickly."

"Oh," she says softly, propping her chin in her hand. "Then why did you keep going?"

"Partly because it was a distraction. Partly because I kept hoping I'd see you."

I thought she was beautiful before, but when she blushes, I feel like I've been punched in the stomach. I've never once, in nearly three years, seen her blush. I don't know this woman as well as I thought I did. I want to know so much more. I want to know all of her.

It's time. I'm going to do it. No more waiting. No more running.

"Cara, would you go on a date with me?"

22

CARA

You know how you feel when you've been singing along to a song for years, then someone points out you've got the lyrics wrong? And everything you thought you knew in the world gets shifted? That's how I feel right now.

I've been asked out more times than I can count. They're simple words, *will you go on a date with me*? But suddenly, everything is different.

He's staring at me, mouth pulled tight, and I realize I haven't given him an answer. But the answer, which would have been a screaming yes only a month ago, isn't as obvious now.

"I do like you a lot. I have for a long time. I started looking for you at work every day because I liked you. I didn't realize you were shy." Shit. I wince. "Okay, that's a lie. I thought maybe you were once or twice, but then I'd see you talking with other women in the office, and you didn't react the same way with them. I thought it was just me. That you didn't like me."

He's already shaking his head, which is soothing. "It's easy to talk to other women, Cara, because they're not you."

The words are harsh, but the emotion behind them is stunning. "Why...why didn't you ever give up on me? If you thought I didn't like you the same way?"

Twisting in the booth, I rest my back on the wall and pull my feet up onto the bench.

"That's not an easy answer."

He rests his crossed arms on the table, settling in. "We've got nowhere else to be. And I think we've put this shit off long enough, haven't we? We've spent so long dancing around each other instead of just owning up to the shit in our heads."

"It makes sense. It does." But having his attention like this? The way he looks at me like I'm the only person he sees is unnerving and really hot at the same time.

"Then talk to me. Why didn't you give up on me? I know you had other offers...and Colton said something last week that made me wonder..." He trails off, and I hold my breath, wondering if he'll drop it or if he'll actually ask the question. Something tells this new-to-me Declan's going to go there.

"He said he hasn't seen you with anyone else. That he didn't think you were dating. Is that true?" Yep, he went there.

"Sort of. I...dated some." Banged and ran, really. "At the beginning, anyway. But I haven't in a really long time."

"Was that because of me?"

"You mean, did I sit at home pining for you, blind to all other men?" I ask with a wink. His face reddens but he grins. It's so freaking adorable, even with the beard and his more mature face.

"Something like that."

Rolling my eyes, I lay a little truth on him. "I started the club two and a half years ago. It's been my love, my obsession, my ball and chain for a long time. I didn't have time for a relationship."

"Oh," he says, nodding, looking almost disappointed.

"But I had plenty of offers, anyway. None of them caught my attention."

There's that grin again. Jesus, the way that hits me? It should be illegal.

"Good. That's good. Great." He clamps his mouth shut, making me laugh.

"That. Right there, that's why I kept coming to you. Because you were kind and funny when everyone was together. Then I'd try all my best moves on you, and nothing. I felt pretty pathetic, honestly. Only you're telling me my moves worked?"

He groans, dropping his head onto his folded arms. "They really did. You nearly killed me."

"Good," I mutter. I'm glad we both suffered then. And that I wasn't the pathetic, mooning woman I thought I was. I'm tempted to toy with him. I could slide into the booth on his side and press up against him. Maybe I'd get a different reaction this time. Maybe he'd crush me into his arms and kiss me like he means it. But maybe he won't. "What do you want, exactly?"

Raising his head, he studies me, his arms and shoulders tense. "What do I want? Other than a date, you mean?"

"We work together. Dating, doing anything really, could be a problem if it doesn't work out. It could get messy."

"What if we don't let it get messy?"

"How would we do that, though?"

He shakes his head, sitting back. "I've wanted you for years. You've been interested back for years. And now that we're talking about exploring that, you're backpedaling."

"Jesus. Maybe I liked you better when you were shy."

He cracks a smile. "You just don't like being called on your shit."

Raising my hand, I rub my eyebrow with my middle finger. He laughs but sobers quickly.

"I am very aware of the power dynamic here. I don't ever

want to make you uncomfortable or pressure you, but I want the chance to spend time with you. Get to know you outside of the office. And see if we could be more."

"I think I'd like that too, but your family is full of interfering assholes. What chance do we have of figuring this thing out with them in the mix? Do you think you can ask them to back off, and they'll actually do it?"

He frowns, lip curling into a snarl. "Fucking Colt."

"Fucking Colt," I agree. I can see it on his face. He knows as well as I do that they are incapable of minding their own business. The brothers that are coupled up are even worse, wanting everyone to be all loved up, too.

"Cara," he says, reaching across the table. I could no more stop myself from reaching for him as I could stop my heart from beating. My hand is in his before I even realize it. Heart racing, I watch as he trails the pads of his fingers across my palm.

"What if we stop worrying about everything else? We're stuck here. What if we date now? Today? It's just us right now."

"Date today?"

"Yeah. Date one is lunch. Date two dinner. Date three...well, maybe we just start with dates one and two and go from there, yeah?"

"That's actually a really great plan." I'm sweating. Pulling my hand back, I unzip the hoodie, revealing the lacy tank underneath. We could totally date. Easy. I can do this. Only now that it's real, I'm scared shitless. What if this goes horribly wrong? What if I fuck it up? What if I embarrass myself so badly that Bree and I have to go live in a cardboard box because I can never look at him again and I stop going to work?

"Cara," he calls softly, laughter in his voice. "Where did you go?"

Wetting my lips, I tell him. "I really don't want to fuck this up."

"Neither do I."

"What if..." I can't even finish the question. There are so many what if's running through my head right now.

"I know. But Cara, I promise you that if you change your mind, if for some reason you decide I'm not the guy for you, I will make sure it doesn't interfere at work. I care about you too much to ever want to make you uncomfortable or pressure you into anything."

"I know it might not seem like it, but I really don't have thick skin. Not when it comes to you. My self-esteem has taken a few punches lately, so just be careful with me, please."

His eyes soften. "I will. Promise." He watches me seriously, running his hand over his beard. "Speaking of thin skin. Can...can you tell me what happened this morning? It felt bigger than just missing your sister. This last month you've been different, and I've been really worried about you."

I run my fingers over the frayed cuff of the hoodie. Declan's always cycled through hoodies, wearing one out before a new favorite takes its place. This one must be his current favorite. It still smells like him, surrounding me in a blend of soap and the minty beard oil he uses.

"I'm having a hard time with everything right now."

"Everything," he repeats, eyes kind and patient.

"Yeah. Tyler. And Bree. She's still having a hard time."

"She seems a little better, though."

"She is better. She's sleeping a little less. She's even taken a few shifts at the bar."

"Are you feeling better?"

I pick at a loose thread. "Sort of. I'm not thinking about it all the time, anyway."

"Have you talked to anyone?"

"They gave me some names at the hospital. Bree's gone a few times."

"You should go, Cara. It will help to talk to someone."

Maybe, but opening up to a stranger is not something I'm comfortable doing. But most of the last month has been uncomfortable, so what's one more thing? A tear falls, and I wipe it away quickly, but another follows, then another.

Declan groans, popping up and dropping some cash on the table, then holding out my coat.

"Let's get out of here."

I scooch out of the booth into his arms, letting him wrap me up, turning obediently so he can zip me up. Then, with a hand on my back, he guides me outside. Someone's shoveled, so we're able to walk back to the room easily. I'm a little sad that I didn't get to ride him again. That was honestly the highlight of the last year, maybe the last three years, and I'd really like a repeat.

My cheeks tingle as we enter the warmth of the room. It's still colder than I would like in here, but nothing like outside. The ancient heating system has probably been a little stressed with a full house and freezing temperatures.

Declan guides me to the bed, kneeling to pull off my shoes, then unzips and takes my coat. He pulls back the covers, nudging me in, then tugging them up until I'm snuggled in on my side, facing him. Still kneeling, he crosses his arms on the bed and rests his chin on them, his warm brown eyes a foot from me.

"Talk to me, Cara."

My tears well again, and I let them roll over the bridge of my nose and onto the pillow. Declan makes a soft, sympathetic sound.

"I just can't get his face out of my head. He was lying there. His eyes were open." He reaches out, brushing my tears away with one gentle finger. "I was so scared that he was going to take her from me. But I never wanted him to die. I just wanted him to stop."

"I know. Everyone knows that Cara. The cops, the media, all of us. We know."

"It doesn't make it better, though. I still feel so awful."

"I would do anything to make it better. I wish I could take it away. Just build a time travel device, zip back in time, and make sure none of it ever happens."

It's an intriguing idea, and I welcome the distraction. "What would you use? Like a phone booth?"

He grins, looking all kinds of geeky. "Nah. I'd go with a Delorian. I've actually got one in my warehouse."

"Of course you do," I say with a laugh. "I'd really like to see it."

"I'll take you some time. We can take it out to the track." He rests his hand on my head, his thumb making slow sweeps across my forehead. My eyelids get heavy immediately. So much better than a sleeping pill.

"I get to drive," I mumble. "I'm a good driver. I drive a fast car." Pretty sure I also say 'zoom, zoom,' making him laugh, but I'm already too far gone to know for sure.

"We'll see," he murmurs. I'd like to argue with him, challenge him. But I'm out.

S he talks in her sleep. So far, she's mumbled about lettuce, pinchy shoes, and snakes. I don't know what the hell she's dreaming about, but it's fucking hilarious.

I've been sitting here next to her, watching her sleep for hours. Her confession running through my head the whole time. I know she's been talking to Janey, but she clearly needs more help. And I'm going to make sure she gets it. In the meantime, she's got me. I'm not a fucking professional, but I can take anything she needs to tell me. Anything she's feeling.

She's given me an in. A small one, but I'm going to run with it. Starting with our first date. Throwing on my coat, I slip out of the room, making sure I don't let the cold air hit her and wake her up. I need a little more time to get things organized.

I check my phone —no bars— and I can't help feeling relieved. My brothers are overbearing, full of opinions, way too nosey, and guaranteed to interfere. They've been on my case for months, giving me helpful —ok, not so helpful— unsolicited advice. I'm over it.

I push into the pub, giving my eyes a second to adjust to the dim lighting. Beelining for the owner, I grab a bunch of dirty dishes off the table she's clearing, stacking them in my arms. She smiles, and I follow her to the kitchen. She's rosy-cheeked, her gray hair falling out of her bun.

"Thank you, young man."

"I haven't been called that in a while," I say with a laugh.

She chuckles, patting me on the arm as she efficiently loads a tray and slides it into the huge dishwasher. "When you get to be my age, everyone under fifty is young. Now, what can I do for you? Is the room ok?"

"The room is great. I'm grateful to have it. But I was hoping for your help."

"Of course," she says without a hint of hesitation. Shaking my head, I wonder when I got so cynical. I came in here prepared to bribe this woman to help me. But she's clearly in her element, running around taking care of people. I don't meet many people like her anymore. Everyone in the city knows who I am and expects me to pay, which is fine. I don't mind paying my way. It's the assholes who think because I have a metric fuckton of money, that they can take advantage of me, that I have a problem with. People like this, though? People like her and the grizzled old man at the grill? I'm going to leave them better than I found them.

"My...Cara." *Girlfriend* nearly slips off my tongue. "I'd like to do something nice for her. I was hoping you could help me?"

A blinding smile covers her face. "Anything."

I'M FIDDLING WITH THE BLANKET ON THE FLOOR WHEN CARA groans and pushes up in bed. Her hair is falling in her face, and she sweeps it over her shoulder with a brush of her hand. Her eyes blink slowly, taking in the room before sharpening on me. She shoves the covers off and crawls towards the end of the bed, silky top dipping dangerously low, and I choke on my own spit.

Eyes wide, she doesn't notice my sputtering as she gazes at everything I've put together.

I don't know what to do with my hands. Finally, I shove them into my hoodie pockets and sit back on my heels. "I wanted to do something...special for our first date. I know it's a little cheesy, but would you have a picnic with me?"

"I am in so much trouble," she mutters under her breath as she leans forward and slides off the bed headfirst, landing curled in a ball in front of me. It should have been funny. It's not the typical smooth Cara I'm used to. But I'm not laughing because her mouth is right at my knee, and I want to drag her up into my lap and have her straddle me. I'm not going to do that, obviously. But I need my hands on her, so I cup her under the arms and straighten her up. She's still staring at the spread in front of us. At the picnic basket, the champagne glasses and the bottle of sparkling juice in a big pot filled with ice.

"I might have gone a little overboard. I just wanted it to be nice, but I didn't have a lot to choose from. It is cheesy. I'm sorry—"

Her hand curling into the front of my hoodie shuts me up. The way she pulls me to her and lines up our mouths makes my thighs tense. And when she presses her lips to mine, my brain shuts down.

Cara, her mouth on mine, has featured pretty heavily in my dreams over the last few years. I expected to be wrecked. I expected to want.

I didn't expect my ears to tingle. Or to feel like a thousand fingers are running up and down my back. Nothing in my entire life has prepared me for her.

Pulling her closer, right into my lap where I wanted her, I let her play, loving her soft nips and teasing licks. But all too quickly, teasing isn't enough. I thread my fingers through her hair and angle her head, so I can take over.

Groaning, we fall into the kiss, tongues teasing, diving. I've never felt anything this good in my entire life. I never knew people could feel like this. I know, for sure, that I'm an idiot, thinking I knew what attraction was. The subtle shift of her hips against me has my brain melting. This is so fucking big I can't get a full breath.

I'm mentally calculating the quickest way to get her undressed when she pulls back with a gasp, hands pressed to my shoulders.

"Oh my god. Oh my god." She scrambles backward, off my lap. I lunge, trying to catch her, but she's crazy fast, crab-walking until her back hits the bed. "Sorry. First date. Woah. Too fast."

Her 'too fast' turns my brain back on. She's right. It's been three years, but it's also been only a couple of hours. It is too fast, but holy fuck. Nodding, trying to control my erratic breathing, I sit back on my ass.

"Right. You're right. But," I say with a snort, "I guess you like the picnic?" I'm teasing her, maybe expecting her to laugh or tease me back. I should have known better. This woman is far from predictable.

"I've never had someone do something so sweet for me." Her hands press to her chest. "I love it."

"G—good," I stutter, distracted by that chest and by the sincerity of her words. I was hoping she didn't hate it, but I didn't realize she would react this way. "So you don't think it's cheesy?"

"Oh, it's completely cheesy. But it's also really thoughtful, Dec."

I can't wrap my head around her surprise. She has men falling at her feet. Why wouldn't they do something like this for her? Their fucking loss. I'm relieved I don't have to worry about competing with some other guy. Some other memory. For sure, I'd come up wanting.

I busy myself unpacking the picnic basket onto the colorful blanket. Grace, the owner, let me borrow one of her handmade quilts. The bright squares create a zig-zag across the entire surface. I'm slightly terrified we might spill something on it. I can tell she loves it by how carefully she had it packed away. I get it.

I mean, I don't.

I don't have anything like this. Handmade with care and could be passed on to generations. I don't have a history. My life before I was two years old is a blank slate.

Cara, oohs and aahs over everything I unpack. The jam, the fresh biscuits, the sliced ham, and salad. It all looks amazing. There are even homemade chocolate chip cookies at the bottom. Grace and her husband deserve a great tip. Maybe I can pay off the mortgage on their hotel or something.

Cara crawls back over, settling onto the blanket with me. Fingers tracing over the blanket, a small smile on her lips. She still hasn't brushed her hair, she's got a crease from the pillowcase across her cheek, and I've never seen anything more beautiful.

I serve her a little of everything, then myself, and we tuck in. "This is the best thing I've ever tasted in my life." I feel like I can't get it in my mouth fast enough. Who knew food could taste this good?

Cara giggles, nodding, trying her jam-covered biscuit. Judging by the way her eyes roll back in her head, she agrees. "Maybe she'll give us the recipe."

"Do you know how to cook? Could you make these?" I ask hopefully.

Cara snorts. "They're biscuits. They're pretty hard to fuck up."

"Oh. So you could make them, right?"

She laughs, licking jam from the corner of her mouth.

"Why can't you guys cook? I mean, I know how you grew up, but don't you get tired of eating out all the time?"

"I don't eat out all the time," I say defensively.

Cara's eyebrows raise. "Really? What do you eat at home?" My cheeks heat, and she cackles. "Let me guess...cereal, fruit. Anything ready-made."

I scoff, but she's bang-on. Except, "I eat frozen pizzas too. I know how to turn on the oven and everything." I don't mention that the first time I turned it on, I forgot I had stored some computer parts in there, and my whole place smelled like burned plastic for a month. Why the fuck I thought that was a good storage place, I do not know.

"Well, that's so much better." She leans forward. "But seriously, I don't get it. You took driving lessons. You learn stuff all the time. Why not cooking?"

"I went...once. I didn't go back." I shudder, remembering that night.

"Why not? What happened?" She leans forward. My thoughts drift away as I take her in. The light streaming through the window behind her, combined with her wild mane, creates a halo effect. She looks like an angel. My angel. Every moment with her feels like a miracle. For a man who never believed in God, that's pretty fucking earth-shattering. *What are we talking about? Right...cooking.*

"It wasn't what I thought it was going to be. It was a basic cooking class. I thought there would be people like me there. But there wasn't."

She frowns. "Who was there?"

"Ah, a bunch of older women. They were drinking pretty heavily, and it got...uncomfortable."

Cara chokes, and I rush to fill a glass of sparkling juice. She's laughing, coughing, and I want to pat her back, but I'm afraid whatever she's choking on might get lodged further in her throat. She's got to be more careful with this choking shit. My heart can't take it.

She lets out a wheezing breath. "You're telling me you got chased out of a cooking class by a bunch of cougars?"

For some reason, my brain gets stuck on 'bunch of cougars.' "What do you call a big group of cougars? It's a murder of crows, a pride of lions." *I'm such an idiot.* Why do I have to spew stupid shit like this? I'm always doing this, going off on a tangent about random shit. Not exactly a great first-date conversation. But Cara's not looking at me like she thinks I'm dumb. She's tapping her bottom lip, deep in thought.

"I honestly have no idea. And this is when I'd normally pull out my phone and Google it." Her smile is bright and wide. "Why don't we name it ourselves? How about a harem? A harem of cougars?" She giggles at her own suggestion. "A swarm of cougars."

Her joy in this moment is completely disarming. I put aside my attempt to be cool and play too.

"A gaggle of cougars? A school of cougars. A flock of cougars?"

"Oh my god, I'm imagining you being chased out of a cooking class by a gaggle of cougars."

"Chased is about right. I didn't even take my apron off. I just bolted."

I love watching her fall apart. Her laughter is so big, so disarming. I spend a lot of time in my head. And around her, I'm usually worrying about what she's thinking of me. But those worries have mostly dissolved, evaporated into the ether. Watching her fall apart this morning helped. I hated that she was hurting. Still do. But I got to see a part of her that's less than perfect. I had her on a pedestal as this perfect, confident woman. But she's not that. She's human. Flawed. And I love her all the more for it.

"This is a pretty great first date, Dec," she says through her laughter. "What's up for date number two?"

24

CARA

Nothing about Declan is boring. The man wore a red mohawk for months. His mind is going a mile a minute all the time. And his brown eyes are gorgeous, with deeper flecks of black mixed with a dash of gold.

He's never been boring to me. But until this fucked up trip, I didn't know he was a caretaker. It's so much a part of him, and I had no idea. As an unattainable guy I work with, Declan was hot. But as the man who refuses to let me drive into a snowstorm, throws me over his shoulder so I don't slip, and puts his hand on my back when we're walking through a room? He is scorching.

The Declan that wraps me up and holds me, stroking my hair and humming to me when I'm falling apart, is impossible to resist.

I've never had that with a man. Not once.

Ever since my parents died, I've been the strong one. The rock. I had to be, for Bree. Everything changed for her when they died. New home, new school, new friends. So no way could I fall apart. She needed me strong.

And this Tyler thing? I'm trying to keep cool. Reassure her

and me that it'll be ok. That I won't be going to prison. But I'm having a hard time believing it.

As we settle back into our booth —we've sat here twice, so it's ours— I marvel at the changes in here. This morning there was some daylight coming in through the small windows. Now, hours later, the windows are dark and the bar is hopping. The same cast of characters from this morning are here. The knitting lady has a whole blanket in her lap, leaning forward to catch her straw in her mouth, hands busy the entire time.

The suit guys are back, a little further from us this time. They're looking more rumpled, less stiff. And judging by the number of glasses on the table in front of them? Drunk as hell. But I don't really care. I don't care about any of them. Because Declan is smiling at me in a way that makes me light up. He's the only one I care about in here.

"I don't know why I'm so hungry. We've done nothing but sit all afternoon, and I'm starving." He rubs his hands together, warming them.

He's right. We've done nothing but sit on that blanket all afternoon and talk. He went off on tangents more than once, on video games and the technology in winter clothing. It was completely nerdy, so why was I so happy to sit there and listen to him? Because I was. I would happily sit and listen to him wax poetic about anything as long as he stayed that animated.

"Me too. Maybe it's the panic from yesterday? Or the colder temperatures?"

He looks intrigued. "Maybe it's evolutionary. A part of our lizard brain, forcing us to pack on weight to survive the winter."

"I'm already well equipped for the winter," I tell him with a wink. He blushes, and I sit back, letting him look his fill. I like the way he looks at me. A lot.

"I suppose you're well equipped for famine, but your skin

is still so delicate and soft. Frostbite could be a real concern."

All he needs is a pair of glasses, and he can star in every geeky fantasy I have.

"Good thing you're here to help me stay warm," I purr, enjoying the flush of color over his skin. His throat bobs with his swallow.

"Yes. Well...yes. I am. I can. I'll do that."

Laughing, I reach for his hand, half worried he'll freeze up on me and run. But I only have to go halfway, and his much larger hand is there, wrapping around mine.

"It seems like such a simple thing," I murmur, "holding hands. But it feels really big."

"I know," he says, flipping my hand over and running his fingers along the lines of my palm. "I've wanted to touch you forever. But it felt like a line I shouldn't cross."

"Because you're my boss?"

"Mostly."

"Because you are, but you also aren't. I answer to Ransom and nobody else."

His lips quirk. "We answer to you is more like it. You know you're in charge."

"Maybe," I tease. But there's a lot of truth to what he's saying. Ransom rarely asks me to do anything. I'm usually operating like the other half of his brain, doing things before he even needs to ask.

"I wouldn't have minded, you know. I was looking for any scrap of attention from you. Pathetically, I hoped you would touch me."

He scowls, leaning in, tightening his grip on my hand. "Not pathetic. There are so many things about you I admire, Cara. How strong you are. How smart. How open you are about how you feel. I've never been that open with anyone."

"It's not always an easy thing. Doesn't feel good some-times," I admit softly.

His mouth twists. "Yeah." I can almost see him running

through the last few years, thinking of all the times he turned me away. Ran from me. Made me feel like he wasn't interested, only to reel me back in with a hint of attention the next time I came around.

"I've only had three girlfriends," he blurts, sneaking looks at me.

"You're expecting what from me? For me to look shocked? You ran away from me more than once. I kinda figured you weren't a ladies' man. Besides, you told me about the kinds of women you date."

He shifts uncomfortably. "Right. Yeah. It's just...now that we're officially on our second date, I thought maybe we could do the relationship chat."

"The relationship chat. Is there something specific you want to know?"

"I get the feeling that you're a little more experienced than I am."

"Probably," I say cautiously. I'm not sure where he's going with this.

"And my girlfriends were my friends first. We hung out for a while before we eventually decided we were a couple. We didn't date or anything...not officially."

"Ok."

"So, I guess I was wondering," he wiggles in his seat, "when can I start rounding the bases? I'm not entirely sure what's first and what's second. I missed most of that crap in high school."

Giggling, I drop my head onto the table. "Oh, my god. You want a feel. You're such an idiot."

"No, but seriously. Is there like, a rule? Like, three dates, and I get under the shirt?" He's trying to hide his smile, but he's doing a crap job of it.

"No," I say through my giggles, loving his teasing. "You get under the shirt when I'm ready. Not before."

He smiles. "Ok."

The waitress swings by with glasses of water, ready to take our drink order. "Supper's a stew tonight. It'll stick to your ribs." My mouth is already watering. She rushes off, swinging back with our beers before disappearing into the kitchen. Declan's eyes are glazed over, and I think I see a little line of drool right there in the corner of his mouth.

"Why don't you hire a chef, for fuck's sake? You obviously love to eat."

He wipes his mouth with his hand, shaking his head. "I don't know. It just seemed ridiculous, you know? I'm a single guy. Why should I have someone come in and cook my meals?"

"You guys could have gotten someone for the building. They could have come in and cooked for all of you."

His eyes widen, and I laugh. Clearly, that didn't occur to him or anyone else.

"You guys are so weird. It took me a while to figure you all out. Well," I say, "I thought I had you all figured out."

"What did you think about me?"

"I thought you were an aloof, quiet guy. Clumsy. Shy. Not great with women, and really super smart."

"That's all mostly right."

"I know, but I was missing some things."

"Like?"

"I think I had you built up into a bit of a perfect guy. So when you said that crap at the hospital, it hit way harder than it normally would have." He winces. "But you're not perfect. You're bossy. You're protective. And you're funny. I didn't know you were funny."

"Colt's funnier. He uses humor to disarm people. All my brothers are really fucking quick, so I had to learn to keep up. You know what they say about those who laugh last?" I nod, and he continues. "I laughed last, but not because I was slow. It's just my brothers were really fucking dirty, and I was way behind the curve when it came to women."

"You were innocent," I say.

"The way you say it, it doesn't sound like a bad thing."

"I don't think it is a bad thing. Being a kid as long as you can is where it's at."

"I grew up too fast in a lot of other ways. But not…that way."

"I get it. I wasn't stealing cars when I was a teenager, so you're way ahead of me there."

His lips quirk. "Maybe. It did give me some street cred."

"It would. Your brothers, they didn't tease you about your lack of experience, did they?"

"Not once. We picked at each other constantly, but never about things that might hurt. For each of us, that was a little different."

"What do you mean?"

He spins his glass on the table. "Like Micah. We never teased him about his speech. Not once. We all have something like that."

"Or like Kade's woman troubles?"

"Right. We'll rib someone forever when it's small. Like this Horsey thing with Colt, but never the big things. Aren't you and Bree like that?"

"Not really."

"Is that a girl thing?"

"No. I mean, women can be vicious with each other, but the dynamic between Bree and I is different."

"How so?"

"She was only sixteen when our parents died. I was already at school. So when they passed, everything changed for her. I left the dorms, and I got our place in the city."

"That must have been hard, going to school and supporting both of you?"

"I didn't finish school then. I dropped out and started working full-time as a bartender. I couldn't afford the apartment and everything else otherwise."

His eyes soften. "Shit Cara. What were you at school for?"

"I was two years into a business degree."

"Did you ever get to go back?"

"After Bree finished high school, I started back. It took me a couple of years, but I got my degree." Exhausting, grueling years.

"How did you end up with us? To go from bartending to a company as massive as ours is not a small thing." He's right. It's not. Being assistant to the CEO of a multi-billion dollar company is a big deal.

"There was a visiting professor in my fourth year. He took a liking to me. He said he liked my drive and my out-of-the-box thinking. So when I graduated, he had a job waiting for me in his executive office. I worked my way up there, but I hit a bit of a ceiling."

"Ceiling how?"

"I wasn't going to be promoted any higher. I had the credentials to be an assistant, but at that level, I needed more schooling."

"So what did you do?"

"I quit and found a job with a smaller company. One that needed me to jump in all over the place. It was the smartest thing I could have done." His eyes widen when I name the company.

"They designed some of my favorite video games." I hear the fanboy in his voice.

"Yeah. It was awesome working there. I realized I liked running around and doing a bit of everything. So once they went public, I moved on to another company. Then I did it again. Before I knew it, I had developed a bit of a reputation as an asset to up-and-coming companies."

"So what made you sign on with us? We're not small. We're not bootstrapping anything."

"Honestly? Your story. I was getting antsy at my last job. I felt like I'd done all I could. This job popped up the day I was looking. I don't know what made me apply. Even though I have a ton of experience, I've never worked in a setting like this, and I didn't have all the qualifications I'm sure the other applicants had. But the way he framed the ad, it somehow seemed like a fit. I didn't expect much, honestly. So getting an interview was great."

He laughs. "I remember those days. Ransom was a pissed-off bear for a week. He kept complaining about ass-kissers and stuffed shirts. Then one day, he came in smiling. Told us he'd hired a tiger. Seemed quite pleased. I always wondered what you said in that interview."

I smile, remembering the attitude I walked into Ransom's office with that day. I had nothing to lose, so I didn't try to pretty up my words or mask my true personality like I have in other interviews. I went in there balls-to-the-wall. "I didn't think I'd get the job, so I did my research, and I told him some things he wasn't doing very well."

"Told him?" he asks, lips twitching.

"Well, I told him he was a dumbass for going with some of the suppliers he was working with. We ended up talking for a couple of hours. He gave me the job on the spot."

"No wonder he hired you. We all knew it was a good fit the next day. That whole chair thing convinced us."

"Seriously? How?"

"All of his previous assistants were afraid of him. No way would they demand anything from him. Which is stupid. We've never been a company to pinch pennies...at least not once we had some money."

"I didn't really think of it that way. I just knew I'd be working a lot, and the chairs you guys had were shit."

"They were," he says with feeling.

"That's the day, you know," I say, studying him over the lip of my beer bottle.

"The day what?"

"The day I fell for you. You and Jonas were playing with the chair."

His ears redden adorably. I wish his hair had been shorter all this time. I might have caught onto that tell before. The only time I would have had the chance was when he had the mohawk, but every time I got near, all I could think about was what it would feel like against my inner thighs.

"Yeah, I remember. I remember how sexy you were. You leaned down while I was sitting in it, and I got a view down your shirt."

I stare at him, dumbfounded, before the laughter bursts out of me. "That's why you fell out of the chair?"

"Well, yeah. They were right there," he says, putting a hand in front of his face. "It's like they jumped out and hit me in the face.

I dissolve into giggles. He rolls his eyes, watching me with a grin on his face, then stands.

"Be right back. Just heading to the washroom. Maybe when I get back, you'll have gotten yourself together?"

"Not likely," I say through my laughter. He groans but presses a quick kiss to my palm before sliding out of the booth. I curl my fingers over the spot he kissed and watch him walk across the room and disappear down the hallway. Everything is tingly.

Gray fabric blocks my view. Annoyed, I look up into the bloodshot eyes of one of the suits. He's leering at me, licking his lips. I peek around him, spotting his buddy still at their table, eyes on me.

"Hey, thought you might want to trade up, honey. Why don't you come sit with me?"

Jesus. I'm so tired of dealing with assholes like this. Every night at my club, I deal with a variation of this. At least there, in my leather, with my bouncers seconds away, I can usually flirt my way out of it. But I'm not on duty tonight. I don't have a spec of makeup on. My usual armor is put away, not needed with Declan. But it's backfiring on me. Now, when I shoot this guy my fuck off look, he doesn't look intimidated. Instead, he slides forward, pushing his body into the space between the wall and the table, looming over me.

I clench my teeth and pray I can send him back to his table with his tail tucked between his legs before Declan gets back.

25

DECLAN

I s this what dating is supposed to feel like? This weird mix of gut-clenching attraction and nerves? It's foreign, but I like it. I like the anticipation. I like staring into her eyes across the table. I like the way her smile hits me right in the chest.

Turning the taps on and soaping my hands, I study my reflection in the mirror. I'm still getting used to the new me. The beard, the short hair. I look more like Colt than ever. I don't ever think I'll be his size, though. Fucker's muscles have muscles. But I like what I see. I feel like a grown-up for the first time in my life.

Which is weird.

I've had adult responsibilities and an adult role in my family for years. But outside of that, I was the video game-playing, junk-food-eating geek. It's mind-blowing how hitting the gym has changed everything. Though maybe it's not the gym. Instead, I've just realized what actually matters to me. It's amazing how much clarity almost losing every-thing brings.

Swinging open the door, I admit to myself that Cara has a big part to play in the changes, too. I wanted to be the kind of man she wanted. Turns out, I didn't need to change anything. Life is fucking weird.

As soon as I hit the hall, my eyes dart around, searching for her. Needing my fix. Just looking at her makes me so fucking happy. But she's blocked by a guy in a suit. My hands clench and my heart rate speeds up. I don't like the way he's looming over her. I recognize this guy, even from the back. He didn't fucking get the message this morning, apparently.

My eyes scan the room, getting a lock on his buddy. The first thing I learned from my brothers was to always know where your enemies are. Buddy's still at the table, and when he locks eyes on me, he shrinks back a bit, but only for a second. Things get tense, he thinks he's going to run in and be the hero.

He's wrong. He'll just end up on the floor with his fuck-tard of a friend.

I weave through the crowd, shifting until I can get a look at Cara. She looks slightly pissed but not panicky yet. That's good. That means we might avoid bloodshed. But the suit guy is leaning further into her space, despite her clear fuck-off vibes.

She sees me coming. There's a hit of relief in her eyes, but also some wariness I don't really understand. I press close, inches from the asshole, putting my back to the booth.

"Looks like you're lost," I say calmly, crossing my arms over my chest. The suit turns, startled. His eyes widen before he puts on a cocky smile.

"I'm just having a conversation. You can't blame the lady for wanting to talk to someone that can speak in full sentences."

Baffled, I swing my gaze to Cara. "Did he just call me stupid?"

The corner of her mouth twitches. "I think so. Must be the muscles."

My mouth drops open. I can feel it rising like a wave. I can't do anything about it. It just bursts out of me.

Full-on belly laughs.

I can't stop them. It's too fucking funny. I have an IQ in the stratosphere, but now that I'm ripped, I'm assumed to be stupid? How awesome is this? It's like I'm wearing a disguise.

The suit guy shifts uncomfortably. This little scenario is not playing out the way he imagined.

"Jesus," I sputter, wiping my eyes. "That's the stupidest thing I've ever heard."

Sighing, I look at Cara. "Anything else you wanted to chat with him about?"

Shaking her head, she leans back into the booth. "Nope. Been asking him to leave, quite politely, I might add, for a while. I'm done."

"Got it." Turning to the suit, I drop the humor and let him see how fucking seriously I take his disrespecting Cara. "A man who ignores a woman when she asks him to walk away? You got *entitled asshole* written all over you. Turn around and go back to your friend. You are not going to get anything good standing here."

He sneers, puffing himself up. He's a big guy, I suppose. But when my regular sparring partner is a giant, well, I'm not impressed. I'm no slouch, either. Fact, I've got a couple of inches on him. And I sure as fuck am in better shape.

"Or what? You going to make me?"

"Is that really your play here?" I ask with a grin. It confuses the fuck out of him. He has no idea how much fun I'm having with all of this. He's a fucking ant. I handled dicks bigger than him when I was a pimply-faced teenager. "You want to start shit here, in the middle of this bar? For what? What the fuck do you think you're going to accomplish? It sure as fuck isn't going to impress my lady. Sure as fuck isn't going to impress me. The way I look at it, in the end, if you push this, you're going to end up bleeding. Sounds like a fucking waste of an evening, if you ask me."

His eyes are darting around the room. At the mostly silent tables. At the eyes on us. The motel owner and her husband are watching carefully. He's got a butcher knife in his hand. I shoot them a wink, watching as she relaxes, patting her husband on the arm.

"You really think you could take me in a fair fight?" he mutters, taking a step back.

"Fair fight? Why the fuck would I be interested in a fight with you? You're in my way. You're disrespecting my woman. So you push this, I'm putting you the fuck down." I lean in, my smile dropping. "Your only option here is to walk the fuck away. Any other choice, you're going to be bleeding on the floor. Trust me, you don't want to tangle with me. You're going to end up in a world of hurt."

It must finally get through to him. He mutters a "whatever" and strides back to his table with a scowl. I wait until he's seated before sliding in next to Cara. I press close, lining up our thighs. Part of it is instinct to stay between her and any threat. But mostly, I just want to be near her.

"You okay?" I ask. She's tough, but she's been through a lot in the last month. I don't want some asshole giving her a flashback or something.

She's studying me, a small frown on her face. "I'm okay. I just..."

"You just what?"

"I was worried he was going to start something with you."

"Nah," I say, sliding my beer toward me and taking a sip. "Guys like him aren't dangerous alone. He wasn't going to do much more than talk."

"How can you know that, though?"

"Have you forgotten how I grew up?"

"But, I mean, your brothers were always around, right? You didn't get into that many fights, did you?"

I shift around on the worn vinyl seat. "No," I answer her truthfully. "I didn't get into many fights. But my brothers made sure I could handle myself. No way would Colt let any of us walk around unprotected. He and Micah are the shit, so they worked with all of us."

"So, you're telling me that if that had escalated, you would have been able to handle it?" Something about the disbelief on her face gets to me. Puts me on edge. The kid in me wants to stride across the room and punch that fucker out so she finally understands I can protect her. But the man knows better.

Still stings, though.

"Yes, Cara. I can handle myself. And I can sure as fuck protect you."

Her cheeks redden. "I wasn't...I mean—"

"Yeah, you were," I say, cutting her off. "It's fine." Drumming my hands on the table, I look to the kitchen, hoping for a distraction. Thank fuck, Grace is heading over with two steaming plates.

"Here you go, kids. Beef Stew and garlic bread. Enjoy."

I catch her arm, gently tugging her back. Leaning down, she lets me whisper to her. "The guys in the suits ... they're not going to drop this. Where's their room, so I can keep an eye out?"

Her mouth tightens, but she nods, the movement so tiny I almost missed it. "You're right. They're four doors from you, closer to the bar."

I tug her a little closer, giving her a peck on the cheek. "Thanks, Grace."

She pats me on the cheek, "Welcome, honey." Then spins and disappears back into the kitchen.

Cara's eyeing me, spoon hovering over her bowl. "What was that?"

This stew smells fucking amazing. "What was what?" I ask as I spoon up a big bite. I'm burning my fucking tongue, but it's so worth it.

"What were you whispering to her?"

I shove a couple more bites into my mouth, chewing and hissing. Then put the spoon down. "I just needed a little more information from her. That's all." Her gaze turns mulish, and I'm fucked. No point in dragging this out. She will not let this go. I recognize that look. "I just needed to know where the asshole's room was. That's all."

"Why do you need to know that?"

"Because there's a chance he's not going to let this drop, and I want to be prepared for that."

"Wait, what? You think he's going to come after you? Why would he do that?"

"Because he gets his self-worth from being richer and tougher than anyone else. His ego isn't going to let him walk away and forget it."

She frowns. "I deal with assholes like that at my club all the time. They usually brush it off."

I tap the side of my bowl, trying to put into words how dicks like him think. "It's different, Cara. When a guy like that gets shot down by a woman? He might not like it, but it's easier for him to brush it off, call you a cunt and move on to his next target. It doesn't hit him at the core. Backing down from another man? That's not going to sit right. The only variable is if he works up the nerve to do something about it or not. But this," I say, waving my hand at the people laughing and eating around us, "Is going to make it harder for him to walk away."

"Because of the audience?"

"Yeah. It's not like he can leave this place and never have to look at these people again. We're stuck here. And that's going to grate on him."

"So what do you think he'll do?" Her fingers are nearly white around the spoon clutched in her hand.

"I don't know, Cara. Honestly. But I'd rather be prepared and anticipate his attack than be caught unaware. I can handle him, I swear. I'm just being careful."

She glances over at them, then blows out a breath. "Okay. So we just watch him. Pay attention, and see?"

"Yep. Now can I please eat my food? I'm dying."

She laughs and lets it drop, thankfully. We dig in, chatting and laughing, for way too long. The people camping out here are mostly asleep, tucked into their sleeping bags or booths. Grace, still looking thrilled with all the company, is moving tirelessly around the bodies.

"I wonder what her life is like? Not during storms, but just everyday life?" Cara's leaning against my arm, eyes at half-mast.

"I don't know. She looks so happy, doesn't she? Like running around taking care of this many people just lights her up."

"Yeah, she does. This town is so tiny and off the main road, I can't see it ever being this busy normally. It's like she's exactly where she wants to be and wouldn't change a thing."

"Do you think you could say the same?" Would I? Knowing I'd end up here, in this bar with Cara, would I change anything about my past? Nah.

Cara hums, frowning. "Sometimes. I wish my mom and dad hadn't died. Bree could have finished high school, and I would've stayed at university. Maybe gone to grad school."

"How did your parents die?"

"Just back luck. They got in an accident on a busy highway."

"Shit, I'm sorry, Cara. That's how Jonas and Zach lost their parents, too."

"I know. It happens too often." She looks up at me, her hair a golden halo, lit by the light over our table. She's so beautiful. And technically this is our second date, so holding my breath, I make my move. I gently shift her, pulling my arm out to wrap around her shoulders. Maybe that was too forward? I could have faked a yawn and a stretch, but even for me, that feels too corny. She just smiles and tucks herself closer to me, resting a hand on my chest. Her warmth carries through my sweater, but I wish I wasn't wearing it and that only the thin layer of my t-shirt separated us.

"What happened to your family?" she asks softly.

"I have no idea. I was left at a fire station when I was two. I don't know who left me there or why."

"Declan," she murmurs, eyes sympathetic. She presses her cheek against my shoulder. She's beautiful, but the sympathy is unnecessary.

"It's okay, Cara. I didn't know any different growing up."

"Did they try to find them? Did you? You must have the skills to figure it out?"

"No, there was no clue. There are a lot more cameras around now. It's harder for parents to just disappear. But the fire stations have always been a safe, no questions asked place to take kids. It's better than dumping them on the side of the road." Kids aren't things to be disposed of, but unfortunately, it happens a lot.

She frowns. "Doesn't it bother you? Not knowing?"

"It used to. I used to wonder who they were and make up these elaborate stories about why they left me. I used to wonder what I'd done to make them leave. But not anymore."

"Why not anymore?"

I shrug, running my fingers up and down her arm, remembering the years of wondering and wishing. "Reality is, my parents were probably pretty messed up to leave me. I didn't have things easy, but I was fed every day, and I had my own bed to sleep in at my foster homes. I didn't get beaten or starved regularly like some of my brothers. The alternative could have been so much worse. The *what if's* would make you crazy if you let 'em."

"I guess," she says faintly, frowning into the distance.

"Hey," I say, bringing my free hand to her chin. "Where's your head at?"

"It's hard to let go of the *what-if's*. I knew exactly what I was missing."

"Colt's always playing the *what-if* game with us, and he can take it to some really dark places, but in the end, it comes down to this. We're where we are, with the people we're with because that's where we're supposed to be." I mentally repeat it to check, but yep, makes sense.

"Convenient. I'm sure he uses that to justify all the shit he pulls on other people. Like he's just helping the universe along or something."

Snorting, I shake my head. "You're probably right."

Grace and her husband move around the kitchen, turning off the lights. "What do you say we get out of here? Head back to the room."

Her eyes are suddenly apprehensive. "What then?"

Her anxiousness makes me feel so fucking protective. I don't ever want her to feel like this around me. "Geez, woman. I'm exhausted. You're going to have to keep your hands off me so I can get some sleep."

She rolls her eyes and rewards me with a small laugh. Her fingers wrap around mine, squeezing gently. "Idiot." She reaches up, tracing the shell of my ear with one finger. The room full of snoring people disappears as I tune into the storm of sensation she's creating in me with her simple touch. Her eyes are knowing as she traces a path from my earlobe, down the cords of my neck. She stops, and I gulp in a breath. I'm battling with myself. *Don't drag her out of the booth. Don't be pushy.* I'm getting a hold of myself when her fingers tug on my beard, bringing my chin down. Her ocean-blue eyes are laughing. I should be cool. I should say something witty.

I wheeze and give in. Slowly, carefully, taking that plump lower lip of hers between my teeth. Her gasp flutters against my mouth as I bring my tongue out to lick against the flesh I have trapped. I give her top lip the same attention. The hours stretch out before me. We have nowhere to be. Nothing to do. But sink into each other. But the hesitancy in her eyes a minute ago flashes through my mind. She's not ready for more.

Reluctantly, I pull my lips from hers. She follows me, the tiniest bit, and I almost shout at the sign of acceptance. She's coming to me. Slowly, but I will wait as long as she needs me to. I can live on that little movement for a year if I need to. I press one last kiss to the corner of her mouth. "Let's go."

I slide out of the booth, then take her hand to help her up. When she's standing, I help her into her coat. Something about her allowing me to do that hits all my buttons. She turns, resting her hands on my biceps, grinning, waiting for me to zip her up. It's our new routine, and I don't want to miss a second of it. I keep my eyes locked on hers as I slide the zip up slowly, carefully easing the material of my hoodie out of the way. I love that she's still wearing it. I don't think I'll ever fucking wash it after this. I'll just keep it next to me, so I can get a hit of her whenever I want. That's not creepy at all.

Waving our goodbyes, I tuck Cara into my side, glancing one last time at the booth the suits were occupying. They cleared out a couple of hours ago, and while it's unlikely they've been laying in wait this whole time, we still have to get past their door. I mean, they'd have to be fucking idiots to camp out at their door for hours, just waiting for a shot at me.

Turns out, they're fucking idiots.

26

CARA

He's doing it again. His hand is on my back, and he's guiding me out the door. He stops suddenly, and carefully moves me to his other side, the side opposite the hotel room doors. He leans over to whisper in my ear.

"You sure you can run in those things?"

"Yes. I'm sure. I've done it more than once."

He nods, eyes sweeping in front of us. He presses the key into my hand. "If there's trouble, run to our room, or go straight back to the bar. Whichever route is closest. Do not hesitate. Don't wait for me. Just go."

My fingers tighten on the key reflexively. He's serious. I have about twenty questions and as many objections to this plan, but we're moving, his body positioned slightly in front of me. No way these guys are going to jump out at us. No way.

His tension ratchets up as we pass door after door. He shifts his hand from my back to grip my elbow and propels me in front of him as we pass what I assume is their room. I'm starting to relax, only a few more steps to the safety of our door, when the squeak of a hinge behind us makes me turn.

There they are. Suit jackets off, looking mean. They were waiting for us, just like Declan said. Dec throws his arm across my body and pushes me toward our room. "Cara. Go. Now."

I open my mouth to argue, but the determination in his eyes and the tension in his face convince me to back up. He moves with me, never taking his eyes off of those guys until I have the key in the door and swing it open. I back in and try to pull him in with me.

He gently shakes me off, nudging me in. "You don't open this door for anyone but me or the owners of the motel." He pulls the door shut. "Lock it, Cara," he orders, his voice carrying clearly through the wood.

I obey numbly, which is totally not me. But flashes of that night are playing behind my eyes. Echoes of Bree's screams run through my ears. I don't think I can be tough. The men out there want to hurt him. Maybe hurt me. Tyler wasn't as big as them, and still, when he came after me, I barely managed to get away. Against both of them, I wouldn't stand a chance.

I'm a woman. Walking through the world, there's always a niggling feeling at the back of my mind that I'm vulnerable. That some men still see me as prey. Daddy drilled it into us to be smart, to protect ourselves, but he didn't really understand what it's like to live with that low level of fear all the time.

There are so many things I should have done differently in the last couple of months. The second I met Kade's woman and heard about her self-defense class, my ass should have been there. How was I so stupid, living in this little bubble of protection? I work with large, protective, alpha men. At Brash and at my club, I depended on them and trusted them. And when it came right down to it, at the moment I needed protecting the most, it left me vulnerable.

I have no skills here. Compared to a lot of women, I'm a handful. But against those two guys out there, I'd have no chance. I should stay right where I am and pray somebody notices what's happening. Someone who can actually help. But as I watch Declan turn towards the danger approaching, I know I'll never leave him to face this alone. But my feet feel frozen to the floor. I can't go out there. Yet. For now, I peek at the edge of the curtain and pray this doesn't escalate and that he can talk them out of this testosterone-fueled stupidity.

"Gentlemen. Predictable as always." Declan greets them cheerily. Why the fuck is he provoking them? And why does he sound so happy?

"You think you're so fucking smart. We're about to wipe that smug smile off your face."

Declan groans. "Seriously. Did you get that out of the tough guy handbook? Why the fuck can't you be just a little bit original?"

Apparently, being called unoriginal is the final straw for this guy. Head asshole lunges at Declan. In the full moonlight, I see the curve of Declan's smile, then he's moving. I don't think I've ever seen anyone move that fast. He's dodging fists, moving around, but never letting them get between him and the door to our room. Both guys are coming at him, and the fucking lunatic is laughing. I see his head snap back. He yells, "good one," then throws an elbow that makes the guy curl up into a ball.

Realization dawns. This is not a fair fight. Not at all.

I was worried he would be outnumbered. And yes, despite what he said, I was worried geeky Declan wouldn't be able to handle himself. But these guys are so out of their league against him, Declan's power making them look like inexperienced children. My fingers, curled tight around the doorknob, gradually relax. I step more fully into the window, so I can see it wrap up.

The guys are both on the ground, groaning. Their breath visible in the cold night air. Their noises and swearing tell me that they're hurt, but not badly. Declan rolls them, patting their pockets until he's pulled their IDs out.

He tosses the wallets back, keeping their driver's licenses in his hand. "Boys, enough of this bullshit now. It's done. Yes?"

Apparently, suit guy never learns. He sputters out a laugh, spitting toward Dec. "It's not done till you're bleeding, and we have a little fun with that cunt in there."

Jesus. Declan was right. Why the fuck are some men like this? I'm ready to go out there and smash some heads now that I'm sure Declan will have my back when he casually walks up to the guy and, in one sudden motion, raises his foot and smashes it into his crotch. The howl of pain that comes from him makes the hair on my body stand up. I hold my breath as Declan crouches down next to the guy, pulling one hand from his crotch, casually pulling the pinkie away from the guy's other fingers, and with a snap, breaks it.

I slam my hand over my mouth to keep my scream in. It's so sudden. So unexpected. He did it without hesitation. Without blinking. Without emotion. But when he speaks... there's the emotion.

"See, I was going to let this go. Chalk it up to too much booze. I was going to let you crawl back into your room and lick your wounds. Let you save face. But you had to go and threaten my lady. Not cool, man." Wrapping his hand in the guy's hair, he pulls him up until Declan's standing. The guy's head is at crotch level. "So please understand, this was just a little behavior correction. To make sure you understand that from this moment forward, you don't look at her. You don't think about her, and you sure as fuck don't speak about her. To anyone. Because I know who you are. By this time tomorrow, I'll know everything there is to know about you, right down to the brand of diapers your mommy bought for you. And if I hear of you so much as catcalling another woman, I'll tear your fucking life apart."

His sinister grin sends a shiver down my spine. I can't decide if I'm afraid or really turned on. "And I'll enjoy it. Do we understand each other?"

The suit guy groans, "Yeah, I get it." Declan turns to buddy, who's gone silent, watching his friend get stomped.

The guy tucks his chin in, trying to get as far away from the dangerous man looming over him. "Yeah, man. You've made your point. We'll stay away."

Declan drops suit guy, smiling again as he backs up. "I almost hope you don't. It's been months since I got to destroy someone's life. I'd love a chance to do it again. Now get the fuck away from my door."

He stands sentinel, arms crossed, expression relaxed as they slowly make their way inside their room. The one guy supporting his injured friend. When they're out of sight. Declan turns his head, meeting my eyes through the window. "Let me in Cara."

I hesitate. Just for a second, but it's there. Declan's mouth tightens at the corner, but he otherwise waits patiently while I unlock the door for him and cross the room to put the bed between us.

His eyes are locked on me as he closes the door behind him. His jacket is steaming as the cold on the surface hits the heat of the room. He shrugs out of it, carefully draping it over a chair. Then he stands still, watching me. Waiting for…something.

I can't take the tension anymore. "You…ah…you still have their IDs."

"Yeah," he says, nodding slowly.

"Why?"

"So I can keep eyes on them." He says it so casually, like monitoring them would be a simple, everyday thing.

"What does 'keep eyes' mean?"

His jaw clenches. "It means that I'll learn everything there is to learn about their lives. I'll monitor their homes, their work, their credit cards, and their bank accounts. I'll know them better than they know themselves."

"Why would you do that?"

He slides his hands into the pockets of his track pants. "So I'll know if they're a danger to me and mine."

My mouth is so dry. "Is that something you do a lot?"

"Yes," he says flatly. Not a hint of emotion in his voice or on his face.

"So, you have...files on people?"

"Yes."

I shouldn't ask. I shouldn't rock the boat. I don't want to burst the bubble we've been in today. But I have to know. "Files on Bree and me?"

His calm breaks. His mouth twists into a grimace. "Yes, but not the way you think." He rushes on before I have time to freak out over his admission. "I have a standard background check on you from when you started. I only ran one on Bree after everything happened. And your files are being updated because I'm monitoring the cops and the D.A.'s office. I am not doing anything to invade your privacy. I swear it."

I believe him, maybe stupidly, but I do. "Do you have a file on Tyler?" Saying his name still makes my stomach twist. Will that ever go away? Will the guilt lessen? Will it be just a faded memory one day?

"Yeah, Cara. I do."

I sink down on the end of the bed.

"What's in the file? I need to know."

"What, specifically, do you need to know?"

"Had he done it before? The stuff he did to Bree?" Had he systematically torn someone apart before? Taking someone bright and full of life and dulling them, making them smaller?

Declan exhales heavily, head bowed. "Yeah, he did, Cara. I found a few police reports and a restraining order. Nothing ever came of them."

"Why? Why was he allowed to keep doing this? Why didn't he get punished?"

"From what I can tell, he came from money. He had great lawyers too. Either he paid the girls off, or the lawyers got the charges tossed."

"So he could come after my sister. And hurt her. How is that justice? If he had paid for what he did, he never would have been in our lives."

I force the panic away, breathing deeply and steadily, willing my heart rate to slow.

"Yeah, baby, he should have been taken care of a long time ago. I'm so fucking sorry you were the one that had to handle him. You never should have been in that position. Bree should have been safe, always."

I'm spinning out, but that word, baby, resonates through me. "She didn't tell me, Declan. And that guts me."

"Cara," he says, pleading. "Can I please hold you?"

Startled, I study him. The tense lines of his shoulders, the tight jaw, those hands, now clenched into fists, arms corded with power. That power caused so much damage to the two men outside.

Those hands also stroked my hair so softly. Those hands feel so right in mine. Maybe I should be worried. Maybe I should be cautious. I did just watch him explode into violence. And yet, explode isn't really the right word to describe what happened.

"You told me you can take care of yourself. I didn't realize you would be so...efficient."

His shoulders slump. "I wasn't playing Cara. No way would I risk them ever getting near you."

"You were so calm, though. How can you stay so calm?"

"Practice," he bites out.

Images of Declan running around town beating up people play through my mind. "You've beaten up a lot of men?"

"I've been in a lot of tense fucking situations. I'm an excellent poker player when I need to be." He winces. "When I have to be."

"Oh," I murmur, head still spinning.

"Cara, please, baby, can I hold you? That's all, I swear. You're over there looking spooked, and I can't fucking stand it."

I want to be held. I want him to go back to the geeky guy I thought he was. But everything feels off. I need a minute to just…reset. "I'm tired," I whisper. "I want a shower, and then maybe…we can go to sleep."

His throat bobs with his swallow. "Together?"

The squeak in his voice breaks me out of my daze. "Together. It'll be warmer if we share."

"Right. Gotta stay warm."

Moving to my bag, conscious of the sway of my hips, and the brush of my hair at my collar, I tease him a bit. I slowly unzip and slide his hoodie off my shoulders, leaving me in my silky t-shirt. Then I bend, ass out, and fish out my nightie. It's mean, but teasing him, taking control this way, makes me feel steadier. It's familiar, and I need that familiarity right now.

Shooting him, an only slightly wobbly smile over my shoulder, I head into the bathroom. Only when I'm inside, do I drop the act. I have to crawl into that bed. With him. And I can't figure out if I'm excited or terrified by that idea.

27

DECLAN

She's curled under the covers, head on the pillow, tracking me as I move around the room. I'm stalling, I know it. But the tension in the room is thick. How the hell did I forget to consider what seeing me stomp that fucker would do? She doesn't know me like that. I've never once shown her that piece of me. There are a lot of pieces of me she hasn't seen.

Fighting has always been a part of who we are. On the streets, we had to be stronger than anyone else. Both individually and as a brotherhood. The cards were fucking stacked against me. Sure, I was tall, but I was always starving. There weren't enough Big Macs in the world to fill me up. And I spent all fucking day screwing around with computers. As our business got bigger, I could've passed a lot of that shit on, but I thrived on being the smart guy. Not Jonas-level smart, but out of all of us, I'm the information god.

So breaking my fingers on some guy's jaw wasn't smart. Didn't mean I stayed out of the fights, though. I just learned to use my elbows and knees more effectively. And hey, a bodyslam goes a long way to disarming your opponent.

"Are you afraid of me now?" I ask her. I wasn't vicious. I didn't toy with them.

She doesn't move other than a slight crease on her fore-head. I'm going to crack under the weight of her gaze. The weight of her judgment. Finally, she lifts the edge of the covers, "Come, lay down, Declan."

I'm sliding into the bed before my brain even registers it. She could tell me she wants me to pat my stomach and hop on one foot, and I'd be doing it before I even realized. I don't know how to do this, be this guy so wrapped up in a woman. I didn't come close to this level of obsession in any of my previous relationships. I thought it would get better now that we've had some dates, but no, it's so much worse. It's like now that I know I have a chance, I'm completely fixated on her. It doesn't help that we're in this fucking bubble right now. No phone, no work. Nothing to do but her...I mean, think about her.

No, I don't.

I'm thinking about getting in Cara. Problem is, it feels more like a possibility now than ever, so I've had to have words with my cock.

A lot of words.

"Declan," she says quietly, bringing my eyes to her. She always has my attention, even when we're not in the same room.

"Are you afraid of me?" I ask again, needing her answer. Needing it to be no. She wiggles closer until inches separate us, and our faces are lined up.

"I'm not afraid of you. You just...surprised me."

"Surprised. Right. Because you didn't think I could protect you?"

She winces but answers honestly. "I didn't know you could handle yourself like that. I have no frame of reference for what you just did. I mean, you crushed that guy's balls like it was no big deal."

"Should I have let them beat the shit out of me? Maybe let them get through our door and hurt you? Is that more like what you were expecting? Did you want—"

"Shut up, Declan," she orders with a frown. I clamp my mouth shut to stop the firehose of words I want to spew. "I can clearly see your body has changed over the last few months. I can see how strong you are. You can stop sounding so defensive." I glare at her forehead, but I'm somewhat mollified. "You've just been this sweet, geeky guy who avoids any kind of attention. My attention, anyway, so seeing you walk toward danger blew my mind a little bit."

"I don't usually run from shit, Cara. That's unique to you." I bunch up the pillow and shove it further under my neck. Okay, maybe I do run from shit a little. But I have so many brothers, I don't often need to get my hands dirty. Plus, they're better at it.

"I can't decide if that's depressing or flattering," she says with a snort.

"I can't decide if it's embarrassing or pathetic."

Everything about her softens. "It was hard on my ego Declan, but I don't think you should be embarrassed for being shy. If anything, I should be embarrassed for coming on so strong."

"You were just being you, though. There's nothing wrong with that. You're a confident woman."

Her face screws up. She starts to speak, stops, then finally says, "I guess." There's more there, I'm sure of it, but am I supposed to dig?

"You have your shit together, Cara. Other than this stuff with Tyler, you've been the master of your destiny."

Her lips curve into a smile. "Master of my destiny. You do play a lot of video games."

There it is again. That feeling. The one that says grow the fuck up and stop playing kid games. Maybe I need to find some new hobbies. What do grown-ass men do for fun? Organize their tie collections? Watch sports? What?

Cara's smile falls. Slowly, deliberately, she brings her hand to my face, running the pads of her fingers over my eyebrows, down the bridge of my nose, and to my beard. "What made you grow this?"

"I just wanted a change. It's way easier than shaving." I don't tell her that I did it to make myself look more mature. That I agonized over it for weeks, hoping it would grow in thick. Not an unfounded worry since I had fucking peach fuzz until I was twenty-five.

She hums, stroking over the hair. This is why I invested way too much money into beard products. If I ever had the chance to get Cara's hands on me, I wanted it to be soft. I wanted her to like touching me. Thank fuck it worked.

She's tracing the line of my jaw, eyes sleepy, and I'm so fucking hard for her it hurts. This level of want is disorienting. The room is spinning, and the only thing keeping me from breaking is her touch. Only when I feel like I'm on fire do I cover her hand with mine. "I can't...you have to stop." I'm about to crash over that edge of self-control, and that would be an epic mistake with her. She's not ready for more with me, and I can't risk pushing her. I'm playing the long game, and my body needs to get on board.

She withdraws, her whole body pulling away from me, giving me some relief. I bury my head in my pillow, every muscle in my body tense as I try to will my dick to behave. It's useless. There's no way it's going to calm down with Cara in this bed. Every shift and wiggle is making me tenser. Finally, she settles, and with a lot of deep breathing, I get myself a little under control. Lifting my head from the pillow, I turn to her.

She's curled away from me on the edge of the bed, covers pulled up to her nose. A tiny sniffle, quiet, but unmistakable, does what minutes of breathing couldn't. My cock deflates like a popped balloon. "Cara. Are you okay?"

She chokes out a hard laugh. "Sure. Totally fine."

She doesn't sound fine. She sounds like she's crying. Have I fucked up again? "You don't sound okay, Cara. If I did or said something, I'm really sorry." She's a flurry of movement, getting tangled in the blankets, grunting and muttering to herself until she finally throws them at me. Sitting up in bed, cheeks flushed, eyes fiery, round, creamy shoulders bare except for the tiny straps of her nightgown, she's everything I've ever wanted in one perfect package.

"Enough with the apologies, Declan. I'm so over it," she snaps. She doesn't look over it. She looks ready to gut me.

"I'm sorry I..."

She growls at me, tipping towards me, planting her hands on the mattress between us. The weight of her breasts pushes into the cups of the nightgown, exposing the shadowed valley between them. "Stop fucking apologizing! It feels like that's all you do."

"I don't know what I'm supposed to say." I also have no idea where to look. I want to dive between her breasts. I want the right to lick and suck. I want to leave my mark on her.

She exhales a sigh, sitting back on her heels. She doesn't look angry anymore, but I think I'd take the anger over the lost look on her face. "I guess that's the problem, Dec. It feels like you're mentally rehearsing every word before you say a damn thing. It's like trying to get to know you through bullet-proof glass. Like you're on the defensive with me." She reaches out, pulling her pillow to her chest, eyes on the bed between us. "Why is there a *supposed to*? Why don't you just speak?"

I straighten the pile of covers on me as I ponder her words. "I guess this feels like a dance I don't know all the steps to."

She frowns. "What do you mean? What feels like a dance?"

"Figuring out what I should and shouldn't say. I don't want to say something that upsets you or makes you change your mind about giving me a chance. And I really don't want to scare you or push you."

She props her chin on the top of her pillow. "There's no script for this, Declan. And if you keep acting like there is, we're going to be doomed."

"What? Why?"

"Because you're hiding."

I shift uncomfortably, her words hitting me hard. "I'm not hiding exactly."

"Then what do you call it?"

"I'm just trying to be...better."

"Better than what?"

"Better than me! I don't want to be that loser anymore. I need to figure out how to be smoother."

"Smoother?" she echoes, frowning. "You want to be smoother?" Her fingers loosen, letting the pillow droop in her lap.

"Yeah. More like the kind of guy you're used to."

Her eyes widen briefly, then flash in a way that makes me drop my hands to protect my junk. Leaving me completely defenseless as she rises up and starts beating me with her pillow. "Stop. Being. So. Stupid," she yells between hits. She's got some fucking stamina, and her hits are no joke. I wonder if she's had a lot of practice. And now I'm thinking about college-age Cara and pillow fights, and I'm hard as a fucking rock again. She doesn't seem like she's in any mood to stop, but she's getting really close to the edge of the bed, and I don't want her falling over.

I dive under her next strike, yanking her to me. Rolling us to tuck her under me. The pillow drops from her hands as she stares up at me in shock. Not questioning my impulse, not second-guessing myself, I wiggle until I've made a spot for myself, right between her legs, keeping my hips away from her core. I pull my arms from under her, taking her hands in mine and pressing them into the bed. She seems to shake herself out of her daze, the attitude screaming back.

"You're dumb."

The fire in her eyes and her heaving chest are seriously distracting. "Clearly. Can you spell it out for me? Use little words."

"I liked the old you. I like the new you. What makes you think I want you to be different? If I wanted to be with someone like the men that hit on me at my club," she lifts her head, getting in my face and grits out, "then I would date someone from the club." She drops back to the bed, frowning at me.

Right. Cause she could have anyone she wants. But as crazy as it is to me, she wants me. "How do I fix this?"

She arches a brow. "You want to fix it? Might be easier to give up."

It's my turn to growl. I know what she's doing, and I fucking deserve it. She's giving me a chance to run, just like I used to, but running is not an option. I drop a little more of my weight on her, thrilling at her gasp. "I'm not going to give up. Tell me what you need from me. Please."

"Stop policing every word and every action. I'm a big girl, Declan. My reactions and my feelings are not your responsibility. I can take you being honest."

"That's where you're wrong," I say softly, dipping my head until my mouth is next to her ear. Her hands flex in mine. "What you feel...making sure you're good is all that matters. I don't ever want to say something to hurt you like I did that night at the hospital."

"That was jackassery." Her words a faint whisper against my cheek. "And assumptions. You gotta stop assuming you know what I'm thinking or feeling and just talk to me."

"I can do that," I mutter distractedly. I am so far gone, lost in her lemony scent and the feel of her body lined up with mine. And I can't resist dropping a little more weight on her. It's a miscalculation because now I'm nestled up against her core. I can feel her heat through my shorts, and all I can do is wonder if she's wearing panties.

"You...you're," she stops, wetting her lips. "You're hard... you want me."

"No shit, Sherlock," I mutter, pressing my lips against her neck.

"No shit, Sherlock," he mutters, his breath sending shivers down my neck. Then he nuzzles in, pressing his lips against my skin. If anyone asked me, I'd swear I was in another dimension right now. No way is he actually here, in this room, nudging at my core.

"Ah, maybe I need to take my own advice," I say, breath catching at the soft brush of his beard on my shoulder.

"What do you mean?" He sounds distracted, using the same tone of voice I've heard him use with his brothers when he's working through a problem. But he's never been like this with me. He's always been too on guard for that with me. Too wary.

"When you asked me to stop earlier...I thought you didn't want me. I assumed."

He rears up, studying me with surprised eyes. "The fuck? Why would you think that?"

"Um, because you used to always pull away from me, and I have a bit of a complex now. I got sucked back in time a bit, I think."

"Right," he says, the dazed look clearing as his eyes sharpen on me. "Dumb, but not I guess?"

Truly mature, I stick out my tongue at him. Thank god my hands are pinned, so I don't do something awful like stick my thumbs in my ears and say nana nana boo boo. It would be impossible to look him in the eye ever again if I did something that childish.

His reaction chases any childish thoughts out of my mind. His focus locks on my mouth and his hips thrust powerfully against my mound. We both moan.

"Cara," he says, wetting his lips. "I don't know what to do here."

"What do you want to do?" I ask breathlessly. I know what I want him to do. I also know I'm probably not ready for what I want.

He winces. "See, this is where I feel like I should be smooth."

"Don't be smooth. Just be honest."

"I want to be buried so deep in you, I can't tell where you end, and I begin."

My core clenches, and I flinch up into him, pressing us together. "Oh."

He groans, but his face turns serious. "You're not ready for that."

Sorting through everything I'm feeling right now, the hope, the excitement, the worry. I finally shake my head. "No, I'm not."

"Okay," he says on an exhale, dipping down to press a kiss on my temple before raising up. The second I feel him pulling away, my legs wrap around his waist and pull him back into me.

"Whoops." Hadn't planned that.

He makes a noise somewhere between a choke and a laugh and drops onto me. "You're not making this easy. You said you're not ready, and I'm trying to fucking listen."

"I know, I know. Just...wait." His hips move again, slowly,

sensuously, and I groan. "I can't think when you do that. Stop."

He freezes, and I'm still overloaded with sensation, but the lightning racing along my skin shifts to tingles.

"Just because I'm not ready for all of it doesn't mean we can't do some of it." He wheezes out a 'like,' making me laugh. "You were supposed to get to first base...pretty sure we blew past it, but we can go back."

"I don't remember what first base is, but it probably has something to do with putting my mouth between your thighs."

My legs tighten on him. "Jesus, tell me that wasn't first base in your school?"

My question seems to break the tension in him. He shakes with laughter. "I graduated from high school when I was thirteen. But I guarantee most of the kids at my school skipped the bases and went straight for the home run."

"You graduated at thirteen? But...how?"

"You really want to have this conversation now? Like this?" He tightens his grip on my hands for emphasis. At my nod, he shakes his head. "What the fuck did you ask me? How does a kid in foster care graduate early?"

"Or graduate at all, in your case. You told me you were stealing cars. I guess I just assumed you ended up dropping out."

"I did," he says with a grin, "but Ransom set me straight pretty quick. He found a way for me to challenge the grade twelve exams, and when I passed, he had me start some classes at Tech. After a while, I was going full-time."

"What was your degree in?"

He wrinkles up his nose. "We got too busy, so I dropped out. Can't say I minded."

"Why didn't you mind?" There was no way I could give up on my degree. I knew that was my only chance to get out of the hole that raising Bree dug for me. Teenagers are fucking expensive.

"I was bored out of my fucking skull. And the social shit was hard. I was younger than everyone else, but I was smarter, too. The administration wouldn't let me challenge a bunch of classes, and I just lost interest. The timing worked out."

"Your IQ must be off the charts." What is it like to have everything come so easily?

His eyes shutter. "I don't know. It doesn't really matter."

It does matter. Why isn't he proud of who he is? If I was as smart as he is, I'd probably get it tattooed on my forehead, so everyone knows. Okay, maybe not on my forehead, but definitely somewhere near my boobs. Then people would know I'm stacked and smart.

I giggle-snort at the stupidity of that thought. Declan tilts his head in confusion. Before I can explain or ask him more questions, I hear it. He registers the noise at the same time. We stare at each other in horror as it escalates.

The moaning and banging of the headboard next door clearly broadcast what's happening. But the "yes, yes, more" coming clear as day through the wall seals it.

The panic in Declan's eyes sets me off. I lose it, my legs dropping from around him, laughter rolling through me as the chick next door gets railed. Wriggling my hands free of his, I reach for my pillow and clamp it over my face.

I feel Declan's laughter before I hear it, his body shuddering over me. He rolls off me, and I sneak a peek at his face. His arm is thrown over his eyes, only his mouth is visible. His chest is bouncing.

I want more of this. More of laughing Declan. This is the first time I've really seen him let go around me, and it's irresistible. "You have a really good laugh."

He drops his forearm over his head and turns to smile at me. "Nick says I sound like a hyena."

"Oh my god, you do!"

He groans and covers his eyes again. "So I guess the mood is officially ruined."

"Little bit. Unless you want to give them a little show of our own."

"Strangers listening to us? I've officially lost my woody." He rolls, propping his head on his arm. "But maybe, one day soon, when we have some privacy..." His eyes trail over my skin, heating me everywhere he looks.

"That sounds really good."

He smiles, seeming content to look at me. Last night we fell asleep so quickly, we didn't do this. Sit in the intimacy of this room and just be together. I'm tempted to reach out and touch him again, but the caution is back in his eyes, as I'm sure it is in mine. It's been twenty-four hours, and everything's changed. But only in this room. What happens when we go back to our real lives? Can this continue?

"Don't look so worried," he says, brushing my hair off my shoulder with one fingertip.

"What happens after this?"

"When the roads open?"

"Yeah."

He hums, dropping to his back on the mattress. "We still want to keep this between us, right?"

The idea is still logical. All the reasons we made the decision still apply, but the reality of pretending is starting to set in. "Yeah, I think that might be smart."

"Maybe. So we just try to find time together, wherever we can then, right? Could be kind of fun sneaking around at the office."

"Fun, sure." Sounds great. Pretending we're just friends while pining after him. Sounds familiar. But I won't be in it alone this time. And if Declan is to be believed, I wasn't last time either. This should be simple. Report to HR, to Janey, and tell her we're dating. That's the end of it. Except his brothers are interfering twats, and I have blurred the boundary between friend and co-worker so often with them that it's basically non-existent.

Proving he's far more intuitive than I ever gave him credit for, he takes my hand, bringing it to his mouth. "It's different now. It's just about us, and we don't owe anyone any piece of this. Not until we're ready."

"You're right. You are. It'll be fine. And if things go well...then we tell them when we're ready."

"Except Colt. No way will he ever let up if he figures out this shit worked."

"It didn't work yet." I remind him with a raised eyebrow.

He grins adorably. "We're in a way better place, though. Trust me, that'll keep him going for years."

"If we really want to fuck with him, we could."

He sits up. "Oh, hell yes. What's the plan?"

"Simple. He wanted this to bring us together. Instead, let's show him how much worse it made things. We could move from a truce back into hate. It would make his in love little heart miserable."

"We never hated each other, did we?" he asks stiffly, the small grin on his face falling away.

"No, not entirely," I say deliberately.

"Shit. You did a bit, then?"

"Well, you said some shitty things. I moved somewhere in the neighborhood of hate. Hate adjacent." He opens his mouth, and I slap my hand over it. "No more apologies."

He clamps his hand over mine and blows the longest, loudest raspberry of my life. I'm sure they heard it in the next room. In fact, I know they heard it when the sex show pauses.

"Eww," I hear through the wall. I roll into Declan, giggling uncontrollably, burying my head in his shoulder. He pulls me into a hug, laughing silently. It's moments like this, moments I didn't even dream of that are everything right now. Making me believe that we can do this. We can figure out our relationship...or build one without the world interfering.

"You going to give me more dates tomorrow?" he murmurs against the top of my head.

"Yeah, but you're going to have to work to top the picnic today."

"I've got all night to think up something awesome."

"Do you think we'll get out of here soon?"

"I can't imagine we'll be here much longer. The roads have to be open soon."

Hopefully, we'll get a few more days in this bubble. A few more days to just be us.

29

CARA

He snores.

Just a little bit. But it's there. I slept better last night than I have in a long time, and I'm not ready to get up, but his mouth is right next to my ear, and I'm afraid my eardrum is going to blow.

I haven't done this, sleep in a man's arms, maybe ever. And I really like it, except for the snores and the fact that my bladder is minutes from embarrassing me. *Must pee!* I wiggle and slide, slowly maneuvering out from under his arm. I'm almost out when his snores stop. I peek up, a smile at the ready, but his eyes are glazed as they stare down at me. I follow his gaze down to my chest and the boob that's jumped right out of my nightgown.

I freeze for a minute, staring at the mound resting against Declan's arm. As I watch, my nipple pebbles. "Ah. It's cold in here," I mumble, not making any move to cover up. I'm a whore. Or maybe my brain is offline due to embarrassment. Either way, my nip is there, standing straight up, apparently liking the attention.

Declan makes a low sound in his throat and brings his hand

to my stomach, slowly sliding it up, cupping the underside of my breast. Millimeter by millimeter, he slides his palm up. There's plenty of time for me to say no. To brush him off and tuck my boob back into my nightgown. To stop him. I clamp my mouth shut instead, wanting to see where this goes. I'm half afraid he's going to back off. If he does, I will lose my shit.

But holy hell, he doesn't back off. Instead, his warm hand is cupping me. His hands are big, but my breast is bigger, so he can't grasp it all, but oh my god, does it feel good. His calloused fingers brush against my skin, his palm circling over my nipple.

A wheeze escapes me, the sensation too much and not nearly enough. He makes a low sound in his throat, then slides his hand back so he can rub his thumb over my skin, teasing me with wide, slow passes. Nothing in his touch is hesitant, and I'm suddenly really glad he's not a virgin. I roll into him, meeting those brown eyes, and open my mouth to...I don't know what. Beg him to fuck me, order him to kiss me. Something like that. Something...more.

His eyes widen a second before I register the sound. I've heard it more than once, the whap of a helicopter. When the brothers don't take a jet, the helicopter is their favorite mode of transportation.

"What are the chances?" I ask, frozen, Declan's thumb still making those maddening circles.

He groans, dropping his forehead to mine. "It's my fucking brothers. Guaranteed. Cockblocking assholes."

Well, shit.

"Cara, I am very sorry you were stuck. Are you alright? Is there anything you need?" Jonas is concerned, and it thaws the chill I've been feeling for the last half hour. I shoot Declan a glance and find him staring at the helicopter, ignoring his

212 | JENNA MYLES

brothers and me. It's what we decided, so I shouldn't be upset. But I am. I don't want to be a secret.

I don't know what the hell to do. Declan's whispered reminder of our plan to pretend like we hate each other came just as Jonas and Zach stepped out of the helicopter.

Zach shoots me his playboy smile, more out of habit than anything, then lets it stretch into a genuine one. "We were worried about you," he says, gaze darting between us. I nod, still reeling over the suddenness of their arrival. Would it be wrong to ask them to leave? But wait, would people who hate each other want to stay trapped? See, stupid plan. On all fronts.

What the hell was I thinking, suggesting it?

"We're ok," I murmur.

Declan hums in agreement. "I'm surprised Ransom and Colton didn't come."

"They wanted to," Jonas says, "but I reminded them that you were unlikely to be happy to see them since their actions directly contributed to this situation."

"And they listened to you?" he asks with a raised brow.

"Once I reminded them that you both would be quite angry, they realized being trapped with Cara in a helicopter for hours would be unwise."

I have to smile, despite the stress of all of this. "You're a smart man Jonas."

"I know," he says simply, taking my hand and leading me carefully through the snow, following the path of their footsteps to the helicopter. He doesn't touch me often, but every time he does, I'm reminded of my place in his world, inside his small circle of trusted people. It's a privileged place to be.

"Thank you for being my friend Jonas. And for looking out for me." His cheeks redden, and he squeezes my hand gently as he hands me up into the helicopter. Declan and Zach follow with our bags and jump in. I catch a glimpse of the motel owners as we lift off and lean over Declan to wave at them.

I'm sad to leave, which is stupid. Those scary guys are still down there. We were in a tiny room, and I'm sure we would have eventually run out of food or heat or something if the storm dragged on. But it was also a perfect little bubble filled with strangers who didn't care if Declan and I held hands.

Now we're headed into the viper's den. Ok, the bunnies' den. If the bunnies were a bunch of gossiping men. I've lost the analogy here, but the Brash brothers gossip. No two ways about it. And I'm going to be the target of it, I have no doubt.

"Zach, if you don't stop staring," I say, glaring, "I'm going to come over there and fuck up your hair." He rears back, spooked, as he should be, and very deliberately moves his gaze to the ceiling of the helicopter. He's been watching us way too carefully. I think he knows something is up. I can't decide if I want him to figure it out or if I want to stick to this stupid plan. But maybe the plan is a blessing in disguise. It would be way worse to date publicly and then break up. I couldn't stand the looks and the questions. No, this is better.

My confidence in our plan fades as Declan completely ignores me for the rest of the flight to Vegas. The Helicopter sets down, and we pull off our headsets and move to disembark. The guys jump down, Jonas turning to offer his hand, but Declan's there first, nudging him out of the way. For the first time in hours, we connect. His hands wrap around my waist, slowing my jump down to the helipad. Our eyes lock, and the whap of the blades fades into the background as we look at each other. In his eyes, I see frustration, desire, and want, all echoing my thoughts.

He releases me, and we turn to join Zach and Jonas at the edge of the roof. Lost in my thoughts, I didn't pay attention when we landed, but holy crap, I missed a lot. We're on the top of a massive building, the Las Vegas Strip and beyond stretching out in front of us. The view's incredible.

As we descend the metal steps, all the men reach for me as if to stabilize me, but I march down those stairs like I'm wearing sneakers instead of stilettos, strutting past them with a smirk. Two uniformed staff are waiting at the door to the hotel, giving us a smile and a little bow as we pass.

I barely take in the opulence around us, the mirrors, the gold, the plush carpeting. Now that we're here, I want nothing more than a minute to myself. My emotions are pinging all over the place, and I don't think I can stand all these eyes on me for much longer. "Can you show me to my room?"

Zach nods and leads us to an elevator. We travel down two floors. The doors open, revealing a hallway with only a few doors leading from it.

"We have the floor. We put you down at this end near Jonas and me. Dec," he says, nodding over his shoulder, "is rooming with Nick down that way." He hands me a key, and Declan brings my bag to the door, blocking the guy's view of me with his body.

"Can we connect later?" he whispers urgently.

"I can't do this," I whisper back. His eyes flare. "I don't want to pretend we hate each other. It was a stupid idea. Can we just...not do that?"

He sags. "Yes. God, yes, we can drop that whole thing." He wets his lips. "Does that mean we can...can I touch you?"

I'm hyper-aware of Zach and Jonas' eyes on us and step back involuntarily. I don't want to pretend we hate each other, but I'm also not ready to broadcast our relationship to everyone. I see the hurt in Declan's eyes before he shakes it off, winking at me. "Text me when you're ready to meet up. I'm going to have to adjust my plans for our next date, but I think I can come up with something great now that we're here."

"I'd like that," I tell him with a smile. Unable to look at him any longer or risk throwing myself at him in front of his brothers, I scan my card and let myself into the room. It's pure luxury, of course. Which I've come to expect when I travel with the guys. They've completely ruined me for budget travel.

As I fill the massive tub, I check my texts with Bree, a little miffed that she seems completely unconcerned that I dropped off the face of the planet for a day. Tossing my phone onto the bath mat, I pour in some lemony bath oils, letting the fragrance loosen the tension in my shoulders.

Despite my love for luxury, I'd still rather be back in that motel room with Declan than here by myself. But now, away from the confines of that room, I'm stuck with my whirling thoughts.

Sinking into the water with a moan, I rest my head back and ponder the massive twist my life has taken. Not just this weekend but that night. With Tyler. I prided myself on having my shit together, but ever since that night, I just feel...wrong. Like I don't fit into my own life the way I used to.

I guess it's understandable. Something horrible happened. I did something horrible. But it feels like more than that. Like I was moving through the world with blinders on, and now, they've been stripped away, showing me what the world is really like.

The new world, my world, is a far more complex place than I ever imagined. I feel stupid for even saying it, but despite all the shit I've been through, things have always worked out for me. Sure, I struggled, but I felt in control. That control has been stripped away, leaving me unbalanced.

Wrapped up in a plush robe, I stand in front of my suit-case, filled with old me outfits. I haven't been wearing them the same way I used to. With skin out, boobs on display, everything tight. At first, it just felt better being covered up. Now, I can't figure out why I don't want to wear them. Why I can't just go back to being me.

The knock at the door startles me. Pulling my robe tighter,

I check the peephole, then rest my head on the door with a groan.

"Why are you here?" I grumble, annoyed I didn't get a little longer to get my head straight.

"We need to talk, Cara. Please, open the door," Ransom asks quietly. The impatience in his voice is clear through the door.

"I need a minute." There's no point in putting this off. He'll stand there, like a fucking wall, until I open the door. He's so damn stubborn.

I throw on my dirty leggings and another of my sexy shirts, then throw Declan's hoodie over that. Then, after a few deep breaths, trying to remind myself to stay Zen, I open the door.

"You're a fucking asshole. You betrayed my trust, and I'm really pissed at you."

Ok, so I'm not that Zen.

I turn and stalk to the other side of the suite's living room, then turn to face him, hands on hips. He closes the door carefully, eyeing me, then drifts to the couch.

You'd never know, looking at him, that he's a billionaire. That he's ruthless. That he always gets what he wants. He's in full weekend mode, complete with dark track pants and a henley. He's still wearing a watch that costs more than I earn in a year, though, and I get paid really well.

The lines on his forehead and between his eyes seem more pronounced. "You look like shit," I tell him. He nods but doesn't say anything, just sits and stares at me, waiting. Finally, begrudgingly, I flop into the chair near him, leaning back and crossing my arms. You know, just in case he didn't get the idea I'm pissed at him.

"Are you ok?" he asks, elbows on his knees. He's about as close to my bubble as he can be without being in kicking distance. The man knows me too well.

"You mean, despite being stranded and nearly killed in a

snowstorm and then forced to share a motel room with—" I clamp my mouth shut, not sure how to finish that. Share a room with the man I love? The guy I was crushing on? The guy who's broken my heart more than once over the last few years and doesn't even know it?

"Yeah. Despite all that."

"Peachy," I say flatly.

"I owe you an apology," he says, brows lowered.

I tap my fingers on my arm, already done with this conversation. He just stares at me. I raise my eyebrow. This motherfu— "In order to apologize, you have to actually say sorry fucknut. And mean it."

He chokes out a laugh, which is infuriating and reassuring at the same time. The man has never once called me on my attitude, despite being my boss. Yeah, he's done it in fun, but he's never tried to curb who I am.

"I'm sorry. You're right. That was half-assed." He rubs the back of his neck. "Everything got so fucked up."

"Why did you do it?"

He groans, drawing it out into a sigh. "I wanted to give you guys a few hours together."

"To relieve Declan's guilty conscience?"

His lips twist. "No, to give you time to tell him you're in love with him."

30

CARA

I s my mouth hanging open? Pretty sure it is.

"Wait…what? I don't…that's not…" I mumble. What the hell am I supposed to say?

"It's ok, you know."

I can't look at him. "It's not ok. It's pathetic." A horrifying thought occurs. "Did you all know? Did he know? Oh my god, you guys probably gossiped about it behind my back. You're worse than the water aerobics biddies at the Y."

His lip curls. "What do you know about water aerobics, Cara?"

"Nothing," I mutter, staring at the ceiling. Why the hell did I just give him that ammunition? He's still smirking. "What? It's really good exercise, ok? Fuck off."

He's laughing. Not even trying to hide it. Hanging onto my mad is getting harder and harder as I struggle to contain my embarrassment. Thank fuck, no one else is here for the conversation.

"Do you seriously go to the Y and do water aerobics? How the fuck did I not know this about you?"

"There's a lot of shit you don't know about me." And yes, I go to the Y. Those gossiping biddies are also funny as hell and keep me going back to work out. It's not cool, so it's not like I broadcast it, but there you go.

His smile fades. "Yes, I suppose there is." His jaw clenches and his hands curl into a fist, then loosen, over and over. "Why didn't you call me?"

"Because I was pissed at you. Then we didn't have cell services, then we were in a fucking—."

"Not then," he says, slashing his hand through the air. "That night. When you were attacked. Why didn't you call me?"

"Well...Colt was there," I say dumbly. He knows this, and I have no idea why he's bringing it up now.

"But what about after? Would you have called me?"

"You're my boss. I would have called in sick and told you then. "

"But not before?"

"Why would I?"

If I hadn't spent the last three years reading him, I wouldn't have seen it. But I do. He flinches. It's barely there, but for him, it's the equivalent of Declan tipping out of his chair.

"Ransom, why does that hurt you?" He opens his mouth, but I cut him off. "And don't give me some story. You're hurt by that, and I want to know why."

He stands, pacing around the couch, his hands locked behind his neck. I have never seen him like this. It's a bit like discovering there is no Santa Claus. Ransom's always felt larger than life, and I don't recognize this version of him.

"I didn't expect you, you know," he says, glancing at me. "By the time you walked in for that interview, I was beyond pissed. I'd spent the morning talking to a bunch of ass-kissing Harvard grads who saw this job as their ticket to something bigger. It was annoying as fuck. Then you walked in." A small smile plays on his face. "You strolled in wearing that leather jacket and those pointy shoes and told me I was an idiot, and saved my fucking life. If I'd had to hire one of those fuckers, I would be in prison right now. Guaranteed."

I smile at that because he's being dramatic, but he's not wrong. He would have no patience for someone compliant and overly enthusiastic in my role. He needs to be challenged.

"I thought we were a team, Cara."

"We are," I say dumbly.

"Then why the fuck didn't you call me when you needed help? I thought you knew you could depend on me for anything?"

"I guess I didn't see the point in bothering you."

He stares at me dumbfounded. "Are you fucking kidding me?"

"What is happening here? What am I missing?"

"It didn't even occur to you to call me?"

So maybe I roll my eyes a little bit. We're going around and around in circles. "That's not how this works. I'm your employee. I don't call you when I need help. You call me."

He nods slowly. "Got it. Is that all I am to you? Your boss?"

A flush travels up my chest. Oh God, no. "Are you trying to tell me you have feelings f—." His horrified glare shuts me up pretty quickly.

"That's gross. It would be like kissing my sister." His who body shivers, and he even gags a little bit, which is insulting but also really comforting. "I thought we were more than co-workers by now, Cara. I thought you knew that you could come to me with anything, and I'd be there for you."

I take a few steps toward him, tilting my chin to look up at him. It feels weird not being eye-to-eye with him. "I guess I do know that. But I've been on my own for a long time. Honestly, I'm used to being the one fixing the problems."

"I get that, but would it kill you to depend on someone?"

"Maybe," I mutter. "Look, you know how weird you guys are, don't you? The way you operate is not normal. I mean, letting your employee coerce you into giving her your credit card for a trip to Miami is not normal."

He smiles at that. "You earned it. But maybe that's where our disconnect is. You stopped being my employee a long time ago."

It's my turn to look dumbfounded. "Wait...what? I'm still getting a paycheck from you. Pretty sure you're still my boss."

"I have lots of employees, Cara. You're not one of them." He steps forward, cupping my shoulders. "You're one of mine now. You have been for a while. It's been a long time since I brought someone into the fold. I guess it didn't occur to me that you needed that spelled out."

"One of yours?"

"Yeah, kid. You're family. I think you're the only one who didn't realize it."

"F-Family?" I ask with a choked breath. Flashes of family play in front of my eyes. The dinners, bedtime stories, and calling dad for rides in the middle of the night. Family feels big and permanent. Even though I know all too well that it's not.

"Yeah. I can't say we ever wanted a sister, but you just wormed your way in there. You grew on us. Like a fungus."

"Asshole," I mumble through my tears. I keep my eyes wide, hoping they'll dry up quickly. "I didn't really know that."

"Yeah, I see that. *Now.* I've been pretty fucking pissed with you this month. Having you move into the building is the first time I felt like you might be ok." He cups the back of my head, bringing me into his chest. "You call me. Don't pull this shit again, Cara. If you need me, you call. When you and Declan figure your shit out, I'll accept being moved to your second call. But that's it, no lower."

I lean in, letting him hug me. Taking the comfort he offers so easily. I've seen him do this with his brothers. For a bunch of guys, they're pretty damn affectionate, always slapping backs and hugging.

"Have you always been a hugger? Did you teach them to like it?"

A chuckle rumbles from his chest. "We were all starved for affection. But it took some time for them to trust me."

"Why did you do it? I've always wondered what motivated you to pull them all together."

I feel the rise and fall of his sigh against my cheek. "Simple answer? I wanted a family that couldn't be broken."

"What's the not that-simple answer?"

He pulls back, holding my shoulders. "I needed a family." He winks, changing the subject. "So, what are we going to do about you and Dec?"

I roll my eyes and groan. "Do we have to? Can't we talk more about your mysterious past? Got any skeletons in your closet you want to pull out and show off?"

"Too many to count, kid. But you're not getting out of this. We're sick of seeing you and Dec dance around each other. It's time to shit or get off the pot."

"Gross. Don't talk about my love life like that."

He cackles and drops back to the couch. "C'mon, let's figure this shit out. Boy's got no game, despite Zach's best efforts. I need to know how badly he fucked things up between you."

I press my lips together and study him. "What exactly do you know about it?"

"I have eyes, Cara. You've been hooked on him for a long time. And his reaction to you has been funny as fuck to watch. We all thought he'd sort himself out soon enough. Obviously, we were wrong." He wrinkles up his nose. "That's the only reason I agreed to Colt's stupid plan. I thought it would give you both the chance to straighten shit out."

I feel a little bad for assuming this was just about Declan. I'm a little squishy knowing he was trying to help me, but I'm also still a little pissed over their methodology. But the outcome...that's yet to be seen, but it's promising.

"Tell me what happened," he coaxes. Like, I'm really going to spill my guts to him. Bree yes. Him? Nah. I'll keep my mouth shut and j—.

"He beat up two guys."

Ransom's gaze sharpens. "Ok. And?"

"He just...did it like it was no big deal. He was really relaxed about the whole thing." And so in control.

"And that's a problem?"

"No. Yes. No." I drop back into my chair and rest my head on the back. "I don't know that part of him. Like, at all. I didn't even know he was capable of that."

"And it scared you?"

"What? No. Not exactly. It just made me realize I've been chasing this idea of him. Not the actual him."

"Did you get to know the actual him this weekend?"

"If I say yes, Colt's going to be a giant pain in the ass."

His lips twitch. "Probably."

I tip my chin and stare at the ceiling. "A bit. We were in a bubble, though. It's not real life."

"Maybe it was more real than anything. No distractions. Nothing to hide behind."

The man may actually have a point. I drop to the couch next to him. "Maybe. But..."

"But what?"

"What happens if..."

He chuckles softly. "Planning for contingencies isn't a bad thing, Cara, but when it comes to people, it's not as easy to do. People are complicated, messy, and unpredictable. At least, my brothers are. But your position with me is secure. No fucking way will I let you go anywhere, no matter what happens with my brother."

"But if shit goes sour, I'll have to see him every day."

"How is that different from now? You see him every day, and shit's been tense."

"It's not the same. If we try and then he..."

"I doubt that's going to be the problem, Cara. He's been stuck on you for a long time. I know my brother. He's got it in his head that he needs to be the man you deserve. He's not going to stop until he's got you."

"Jesus, you guys have a way of saying sweet stuff in a really creepy way."

He laughs, leaning back on the couch. "What can I say? It's a gift."

"So what do I do?"

"Just spend some time with him. That's all."

"And Colt?"

"He's holed up with Evie. Keeps calling her his bride and getting teary. He'll be distracted today, guaranteed. Don't worry about tomorrow. Grab Dec, and go explore Vegas."

I roll my head toward him, studying his open face and kind eyes. "Ok. But I need to do a little shopping first. And I'm charging it to the room...Boss."

He shakes his head, chuckling. "I'd expect nothing less."

31

DECLAN

I wipe my hand down the side of my pants because, of course, I'm sweating. I'm next to the most beautiful woman in the world, and she's mine for the day...as long as I don't fuck it up. She's dressed a little differently, in new, shorter leggings that end below her knees. And another one of her shiny, soft tanks that makes me want to touch. Everything makes me want to touch, but those tanks are on a whole other level. I know firsthand how soft they are.

I sneak a glance down at the space between us, then at the numbers ticking down on the elevator. Just before the doors open to the lobby, I make my move, cupping her wrist and sliding my fingers down along her palm until we're holding hands. We've been off balance since that helicopter landed at the motel, and I'm half afraid she'll brush me off.

She doesn't.

Shooting me a small smile, she squeezes my hand, then shifts to thread our fingers together. I'm thirty-three years old, and I've never done this. Walked with a woman I'm crazy about, holding hands. It's something so simple, and yet it's never mattered more. I can't screw this up.

The doors open, revealing the ornate lobby of the hotel. A

weird mix of Asian and modern that looks expensive and cold. Not my style, but judging by the lines of people at checkout, a great investment.

As usual, when I'm at a property like this, the staff converge. Not all physically, some of them just smiling and nodding, but there's always a group that comes to 'bow and scrape,' as Nick puts it.

"Mr. Wilder," a polished man in his fifties says. His suit is on point, the little pocket square folded precisely. His shoes are so shiny I can see our faces in them. "Is there anything I can help you with?"

"Arrange for a private table for us at the restaurant," I ask, naming the one with a celebrity chef. "We'll walk for a bit first."

"Of course, sir. I'll have it set aside immediately for you. It will be ready whenever you return." I'm sure it will be. We own the fucking thing. If I want a table engraved with my name and left ready for me at all times, they'd do it. One of the perks of being the owner I guess.

I nod my thanks and lead Cara through the maze of people, exiting to the courtyard off the strip. I pull her into a quiet corner.

"Hi," I say dumbly, lost in her gorgeous blue eyes. Every time I see them, I can't stop myself from fixating. I can't stop myself from remembering what they looked like after I kissed her. All hazy and sleepy.

"Hi back," she says with a cheeky grin. She looks different today. Shorter.

"Your shoes are different!" She's wearing a pair of sparkly sandals. They're flat. "I've never seen you in anything normal like that."

She snorts, laughing at me. "Normal? Whatever. I just thought this might be a better choice for today. What are we doing?"

"Well, I had all these elaborate ideas, but I thought it

might be nice to just spend a bit of time relaxing. We could walk, or I've got us spots at the spa. Or we could find a movie or a show. I kinda ended up in analysis paralysis."

"Analysis paralysis," she echoes, looking at me questioningly.

"Yeah," I mutter, studying our feet. Her toes are polished a color so dark it's either black or almost black. It makes her skin look paler than it actually is. "It happens sometimes. When the stakes are high, I end up in a loop of indecision."

"How do you get out of it?"

I meet her kind eyes. "My brothers. I use them to bounce ideas off. It helps to get another perspective. In this case, that would be pointless since the only perspective that matters is yours."

"Oh, ok. Well, then, I really like the idea of walking around in the sun. I took a bath, but I still feel like my bones are cold."

Images of Cara in the bath, and all the ways I could help her warm up flash through my mind. I clear my throat. "Then let's do that. We'll play tourist and buy shirts that say, 'What happens in Vegas stays in Vegas.'"

"I like this plan," she says, backing out of the corner and tugging me with her. "Maybe we get some of those giant drinks, too, and see where the day takes us."

"IT'S NOT THAT BAD. WE COULD TOTALLY DO IT," SHE SAYS, leaning way back into my chest to get a better look. She's a tiny bit drunk. The kind of drunk that makes her lean on me a little more, touch me a little more. Tiny bit drunk Cara is addictive.

I shift my focus to the roller coaster perched on a skyscraper way the fuck above the strip as I tighten my arms around her. "Yeah. We could totally do it. No big deal." We both nod, staring, able to hear the faint screams from the street.

"I'm a wee bit drunk," she says, reaching back to pat my face without looking, ending up slapping me instead. Laughing, I catch her hand and nip at her fingers. "Maybe we'll come back after we've had some food. You know, to soak up the booze."

"That's a good idea. We'll come back after food." We turn, and I throw my arm over her shoulder —I love those flat shoes— and wander back down the strip.

For the third time.

The first time, we decided it was too sunny, and it would be better to do the ride when the sun wasn't in our eyes. The next time we came back, we decided we needed a bit of liquid courage. This time, the excuse is food.

We're never getting on that roller coaster, and I'm not mad about it. It's cute as fuck, the way she tries to psych herself up. If she really wanted to do it, I'd go, but I would really rather save myself the worry.

That's new too. Worry. I've never felt protective like this with anyone I'm dating. Cara's about the most capable woman I've dated, so logically my need to keep her safe when I didn't have the same overpowering drive with other women, doesn't make sense. But I can't turn it off. I'm constantly sweeping the street in front of us, watching for danger. Is this what Colton's always feeling? If so, then I feel bad for giving him so much crap about it.

It's powerful shit.

Pulling her closer to me as we walk, I revel in the feeling of being Cara's man. It feels really good having the right to hold her. To be the one to escort her. To be touched by her. In public, no less.

I have never been with anyone with her kind of appeal. Everyone looks at her. Even toned down in her short, tight pants, she's stunning. All the men look and admire, and so do the women, though not the same way. Some of the women's eyes are warm, others not as much. It took me a while to figure it out. The ones who'd look us up and down, looking kinda confused, were the skinny bleached ones. It's like they can't figure out why she'd ever date me.

I get it. I don't know why she'd date me, either. I may have bulked up a bit, but I'm still the geek. Sure, I call myself a hacker, cause let's be honest, I can get into any system I put my mind to, but it still isn't that cool. I've never been the athletic guy or the guy that the women flocked to for his looks. It's always been my money attracting them.

There, in the back of my mind, is a tiny worry that my money might be a part of why she's dating me, but the more rational part is screaming at it to shut up. Cara works in a building with eight billionaires. If she wanted to date someone with money, she has a fuck of a lot of choices. But for some reason, she wants me. No fucking way do I want to waste any more of my energy questioning why. Instead, I'm going to make damn sure she doesn't regret it.

"Should we head back to the hotel? That table's waiting for us."

She hums, spinning out from my arm, nearly knocking into a camera-toting, sneaker-wearing couple. "Sorry," I mutter as I reel her back in.

"Let's get grease." She spins again, shading her eyes from the glare of the neon around us. "There," she says, pointing excitedly, then takes off towards a hole-in-the-wall burger joint with a lineup fifteen people deep. She hops into the line, waving at me to hurry up. I run the last couple of feet and move in behind her.

"This place has got to be awesome. Or cheap. Either way, guaranteed it'll be greasy. I can smell it from here."

"Well, as long as it's greasy." I study the heads in front of us, noticing quite a few people in hotel uniforms. If the locals are eating here, maybe we are in for a treat.

"When I was in high school, we'd end up at this diner downtown after parties. I'd always get a cherry coke and a burger and fries. It was so good. We'd sit there for hours, just talking and flirting. It was so much fun."

"It sounds fun." Teenage Cara would have been a sight to see. I'm sure she would have left teenage me a hormonal mess.

"I guess you never got that, did you? High school parties and sitting at diners with your friends."

"No, not really. I was younger than everyone else, and my home life was different. I didn't have a mom and dad checking on me the way they did. Me and the guys spent time together instead. At the apartment, mainly. When we got busier and started making more money, we sometimes splurged and went to a diner. But it was hard to get all of us together sometimes."

"But you all lived together?"

"Yeah, but by then, everyone was starting to scatter. A few of the guys would disappear to their girlfriend's places. I was at school a lot of the time or hanging out at gamer bars. Micah was obsessed with his custom builds. Ransom was always out and would come home with the weirdest shit. He came home with a raccoon once. Fucker said he won it. That's what he said every time he came back with something. 'I won it.' I never could figure out if he was lucky or really good at cards. I mean, why would he want to win a raccoon? I never figured it out."

Cara's riveted by my story. "What did you do with the raccoon? Was it in a cage?"

"He brought it home in a cage. Mav thought we should set it free, so we opened the apartment door and the door of his cage. He just sat there, wandered out, looked outside, then came in and slept on one of our sleeping bags. He lived with us for almost a year."

"You guys are fucking weird," she mutters. She doesn't make it sound like a bad thing.

"Yeah, you're not the first one to say that."

"So what happened when you got some money and could afford your own places?"

"We scattered and saw even less of each other. We'd go on vacations together, and we'd see each other at the office, of course. God, in the beginning, we were all sharing offices in this small leased warehouse on the south side."

"So then, how did you end up at the high rise?"

"That's all Jonas and Ransom. They got it in their heads that we should all be together. They had the plans drawn up and had the contractor picked before any of us saw it."

"But you didn't have to move in, right? You could have sold off those apartments for a pretty penny."

"Yeah. Some of us talked about it. But Ransom kept having these meetings with the designers, and they started talking to us about how we'd want our places finished and what kind of furniture we wanted. By the time it was built, all of us were so fucking invested, no way would we let anyone else stay in the apartments we designed."

"He's so smart," she says with awe.

"Yeah, he is. It turned out great, though. I didn't realize how much I'd missed everyone until we were back together. Now we're always meeting up, either at each other's places or at work, or in the gym. We're closer than ever, which is mostly a good thing. Except when they see too fucking much and start interfering in our lives."

"Fucking Colt," she says with a sneer.

"Fucking Colt." I agree, biting down my laugh. She's so adorable. I'm having a really hard time holding onto my mad at Colt. At least until I think about white-knuckling it during that drive. We're really lucky things didn't go a whole lot worse.

Cara slaps her hands on my chest. "We need to," she stops, staring at her hands, sliding them down to my pecs and squeezing. "Beep, beep," she mutters, then shakes her head and looks up at me. My chest shakes with laughter. Fucking adorable. "Colt. We need to teach him a lesson. What do we do?"

I let my evil genius smile play on my lips. "I have so many ideas."

"Remember to play it cool," Declan whispers in my ear just before we pull the door open.

"Shut up. This isn't my first rodeo. I know the plan. Keep cool, let him apologize, and we nail him when he least expects it."

"Right," he says, bouncing on his toes in excitement. "Let's go!"

It's been an amazing day. My drunk has mostly been soaked up by the world's best burger. We walked around, holding hands, being tourists. And we laughed. A lot. Seeing the world through Declan's eyes is an amazing experience. He's completely adorable explaining the differences between Pokemon while at the same time staring down anyone who gets too close to me. I've never felt that protected, that taken care of, maybe in my entire life.

It's different with parents. My dad was a pitbull when it came to our safety. I didn't think I'd ever find that again. But it was an overprotectiveness that bordered on crazy. Thank god he had two of us to split his attention. I never would have made it out of the house otherwise.

As a grown-ass woman, I can handle my life. And

honestly, if I had to deal with Colt's level of protectiveness, I would lose my ever-loving mind. Declan's, on the other hand, straddles that line between overbearing and sexy. The hand on my back, the insistence on walking on the curb side of the sidewalk, the way he uses his body as a barrier between me and a crowd. All of it feels really, really good.

But right now, all those protective vibes have been shoved to the side as he nearly levitates with excitement. He's standing there, bouncing, waving me frantically through the door.

"Ok, ok. I'm coming. Why are you so excited? Haven't you done this before?"

"No. Come on." He drags me towards the large group in the lobby. They're all there. All the brothers, Colton's wife Evie, her daughter Mia —currently on Zach's shoulders— Holly, and Becca. And they're louder than the indoor skydiving fan behind them.

Colt sees us and breaks away from the group, heading straight for us. Here we go. He stops right in front of us, eyes darting between Declan and me.

"I'm so fucking sorry. I never meant for any of this shit to happen." He drops to the floor and wraps his arms around my feet. "Please, tell me you'll forgive me. I promise never to fuck with...well, I promise to try not...shit, I promise I'll never arrange for you two to be stuck together again. I promise I'll never bribe pilots to leave you again. There. Those are true." He drops his cheek on the top of my foot pathetically.

I have to bite my lip to keep from laughing. I meet Declan's eyes, and he's not laughing. He crouches down next to Colt.

"Brother," he says, waiting for Colt to roll over and look at him. "I get you were coming from a good place, but what you did is fucked up. And it could have been really bad. You and me, we'll be having words later."

Colt seems to relax at that. He and Declan exchange nods, then focus back on me.

"You're supposed to be my friend Horsey. Friends don't manipulate and lie and force people to do things. That's not ok."

He lets go of my feet, rising to his knees, head almost at boob level. "I know. It was a complete dick move. If it's any consolation, Evie almost called off the wedding when she found out what I did."

I glance at Evie. She's wearing a gentle smile, the same gentle smile she wore the night Bree and I showed up at the hospital. She gives me a nod.

"That actually makes me feel a little better." I lean down, tucking my cheek against his. "You made me feel like I didn't matter," I whisper. "Don't do it again."

He swallows thickly, eyes glassy. "I only did it because I think you two should be together. I never meant to make you feel that way."

"I know. But what would you do if some guy manipulated Mia the same way?"

His face blanches, and I see it finally click. "Right. Fuck that. I'd tear the fucker apart."

"Right. So I accept your apology, but please understand, you started a war, my friend, and I will finish it."

I turn and stroll away to look at some warning posters on the wall, letting my smile free. That tinge of fear in his eyes is everything. Declan and I are going to destroy him.

IT DOESN'T SEEM LIKE IT WOULD BE A HARD THING, GETTING A bunch of grown men into wind outfits. But it's actually a shit show. I'm still not convinced I want to do this, though it seems a hell of a lot safer than the roller coaster. I would have gone back to ride it. Maybe. Ok, no way was I ever getting on that thing. But Declan doesn't need to know that.

Turns out, I don't have to worry. I don't meet the weight guidelines, and, thank god, I get to sit this out. We all gather around the instructors. It was one younger guy, but when they saw the level of enthusiasm in our group, they got more help to wrangle us. Now a college kid is trying to give us the safety lecture and not getting very far. Every time he opens his mouth, another brother pops off on a tangent.

"Hope you didn't eat too recently. Can you imagine blowing chunks in there? It would fly right back in your mouth," Kade mutters to Micah. Becca, beside him, grimaces and casually elbows him in the stomach then eases to the back of the group, scowling at her boyfriend. She stops beside me, patting her stomach.

"Asshole fed me Sushi before we came. I did not know we were coming here, and I really don't want to think about them puking."

"I just ate a burger the size of my head and fries to soak up the very big drink I had. Too bad I can't go," I say with a very fake sigh.

"Want to blow this joint? We could call a cab, go hit the town on our own."

"We could, but we'd miss them," I say, pointing at the guys looming over the instructor. "And that's going to be worth watching. Trust me."

She bites her lip, studying the guys. Finally, a smile breaks free. "Yeah. You're right. Ten bucks says Kade pukes."

I shake my head. "Suckers bet. They're definitely puking. The only question is whether it's inside that wind tunnel or not." I turn to her. "Would you actually want to do this? If you could, I mean?"

She grins maniacally. "Oh yeah, I would. But I really don't want to taste my Crispy Crunch roll on the way back up, so I'm ok missing out today."

"Agreed," I say, thinking of how not delicious my burger and fries would be the second time around.

Plan settled, we drop onto a long bench to watch. Holly wanders over with a wobbly-lipped Mia. "Evie's in the bathroom, so Mia and I are hanging out. But Miss Mia is not happy," she says with a gentle smile.

"Hey, little bit," Becca says. "What's the matter?"

"I no go," she says, dropping her head to Holly's shoulder. "I too little." She says little with a 'w' and it's freaking yummy. "Who you?" She asks, staring at me.

"My name is Cara. I work with your new step-daddy."

She lifts her head, looking at me in confusion. "Step?"

I look at Holly and Becca, but they don't look like they're planning to step in. I am not a kid person. I didn't babysit when I was younger. Instead, I got a job at the concession at the football field as soon as I was old enough. I thought I'd get way more time to watch the guys in their tight pants, but nope, I was run off my feet every game. Not my brightest plan.

"Um...a step-daddy is when your mommy marries another man, so he becomes a step-daddy." There. That was easy.

"Mommy no been married. I don't got's a daddy."

"Oh, well. I think people will still call him your step-daddy."

She frowns, looking towards Colt, currently arguing with one of the young instructors.

"It's not discrimination, sir, I assure you," the kid says. I can see his throat bob from here. "It's physics. You're simply too large to get any lift."

"Well then, just crank up the wind."

"Sir, I can't crank it up high enough for you to get off the ground."

"Are you calling me fat?" Colt's voice is rising in pitch. He slaps his hands on his hips. The suit he insisted on putting on, the suit that billows around the rest of his brother's bodies is clinging to him like a second skin.

The kid's face is bright red. "No. Sir, of course not. It's just the aerodynamics. The fan won't give you any lift."

"Any reason why I can't go in there and give it a shot?" he asks as he crosses his arms, staring down at the kid. He's completely intimidating, and the kid backs up with a gulp.

"Well, no."

"Good, let's go."

The guys file into the round padded room, and we step up onto the viewing platform. Becca's studying the guys, frowning.

"I weigh less than some of those guys. Why the fuck can they go, and I can't?"

Holly points to the sign over the door behind us. "They obviously got that same question more than once. Says right there, 'women carry their weight lower and have a different center of gravity, making it harder for them to balance.' See, perfectly reasonable."

Becca snorts. "Whatever," she mutters under her breath, not looking at all happy with that answer.

We all lean forward for a view into the round padded room — walls and floor— with a huge fan-looking grate taking up the floor. The instructor is giving them more rules, so I tune out as I mentally undress Declan. The flappy suit hides everything but the width of his shoulders. Even his eyes are hidden by funny-looking goggles.

"So," Becca says, nudging me with her shoulder, "how did things go between you two at that motel?"

I glare at her, and trust me, my glare has made more than one man shrivel, but it doesn't seem to have any effect on her. She grins at me, folding her hands in her lap and blinking exaggeratedly.

"Fine," I say shortly. Evie joins us on the long bench, stopping to kiss the back of Mia's head before sitting.

"What did I miss?" she asks, looking between all of us.

"Cara was just about to tell us how she and Declan handled being snowed in," Becca says cheerfully.

"I really wasn't," I say flatly.

"You don't have to tell us anything," Holly says, scowling at Becca. I like her. I've only met her once or twice, but she seems like a kind, thoughtful person. "Besides, pretty sure by the way you two were looking at each other, there was some fornicating in that motel room."

I take it all back. She's a vicious harpy.

"I don't do this," I say, waving my hand around. "I don't gossip about my love life, and I really don't chit-chat. Why don't we watch the guys, huh? Isn't that why we're here?"

It works briefly. We turn our attention to the wind tunnel just as the fan is turned on. The guys all look ready to leap, and it's clear the instructor is way over his head handling them. Suddenly, one of the guys, Nick, I think, swan dives into the middle. For a minute there, I think he's going to make it. He gets a bit of lift, then wobbles, arms outstretched, before getting blown sideways right into a couple of his brothers. All three of them fall back against the padding. There's a hell of a lot of hooting and laughing.

"Lord," Evie mutters, "we'll be lucky to get out of this city without a trip to the hospital."

Smiling, I wink at her. She's right. That would be pure luck. When these guys get together and are this excited, one of them usually ends up bleeding.

"Doesn't gossip imply going behind your back?" Becca asks, dragging us right back into the conversation.

"Maybe. But why should I spill my guts to a bunch of women I barely know?" That kind of attitude is usually effective at chasing people away, but it seems to have no effect on these women.

Becca laughs, and I have to fight the urge to push her backward off the bench. "Because all of us have spent a ton of time with him. We know him really well. A wise woman would use that to her advantage and pump us for information. Besides, we're a package deal. You might as well get used to us now."

"You may have a point," I mutter grudgingly.

"Look, we love Declan," Evie says. "He deserves someone great. And according to Ransom, you're the smartest, most capable woman in the world. If you want any insight, you just let me know. Just...don't hurt him, ok. He's soft-hearted, and if you're not serious, then tell him that."

"Are you warning me off?" Why does that hurt so much? They're assuming I'm this man-eating harpy, and while I don't mind that image when it suits me, I don't want these women thinking that.

"No. Just asking you to communicate with him. He's not as confident as the other guys. I just think you'll need to be aware of that." It almost feels like they want me to back off, despite what they say. And I can admit I'm a little hurt by that. I'm tough. I've never denied that, but it doesn't make me heartless. I'm just...focused.

A loud cheer goes up, drawing our eyes back to the wind tunnel just in time to watch Colt dive into the wind, spread eagle. I wince in sympathy when he lands face-first on the grate. He didn't slow down at all.

"That's going to leave a mark," Evie mutters, picking up her purse and rifling through it.

Not a minute later, Colt's sitting on the bench between Evie and Holly, holding a paper towel to his nose, looking sad.

"It's okay, baby. You tried," Evie says consolingly, patting his big shoulder.

"I really wanted to fly," he says in a nasal voice. "Maybe I can buy one of these things. But a bigger one. A more powerful one. I can take my little princess on it, too."

Evie's eyes widen, but Holly gently pats his hand. "Sweetheart, any fan that would hold your body weight would launch Mia into space."

He eyes Mia resting on Holly's chest. They study each other. "You're right," he says to Holly, then shifts his attention to Mia. "One day, you'll be big enough to go in there too. You'd like that, right?"

Mia studies him, her finger in the corner of her mouth. She leans towards him, arms outstretched, and he reaches for her at the first movement. Not an ounce of hesitation. He's completely wrapped around her finger, and she's completely secure in that knowledge. When she's settled, she examines his nose. "Owie?"

Colt carefully lifts the paper towel, revealing a slightly crooked nose. "Yeah, honey, I'm okay."

She studies him, not at all convinced. She turns to Evie, "Mama, we take Daddy to hospital?"

This moment feels too big, too personal for me to watch, but I can't take my eyes off them, off Colt's face. I watched him moon over the picture of Evie for months and then obsess over her and Mia for months more. Now they're married, which I'm still sad I missed, but from the look on his face, this moment, the moment Mia called him daddy, is the moment everything truly changed for him.

I watch those words settle on him, sinking through the skin and bone all the way to his heart. They lodge themselves deep. I can see how deep, in the tremble in his hands, the glassy eyes, and the rhythmic swallowing. Evie, sitting beside him, hands over her mouth, doesn't even try to wipe away her tears.

"We go hospital, Daddy?" Jesus, this kid is smart. She knows exactly what she's doing. She's claiming him. She doesn't want a step anything. She wants a daddy.

He can barely speak through his tears. "No, princess. I'm okay. Uncle Nick will fix it for me later."

She plants a sloppy kiss on his cheek, then plops down on

his lap to watch her uncles fly. Colt holds her like he's been given the most precious jewel. His eyes fall closed as he lets the tears fall. Evie leans into him, crying too, knowing how big the moment is.

I focus back on the brothers, but my thoughts are a million miles away. On the future I thought I had all worked out. And the big gaping hole that sits there now. I could still end up in jail. I know that. But if I don't, maybe my future could be something I never even imagined.

And maybe I am a kid person.

I sit, dazed, until we're suddenly surrounded by all the men. Declan's eyes meet mine, but I'm too lost in my own thoughts to engage, giving him a small smile instead.

"No way we're letting this party end," Nick crows. "Let's hit Freemont Street."

"Let's go!" Becca yells, running ahead. She stops, spinning back to us. "I smell puke. Which one of you blew chunks?"

33

CARA

I'm not sure if there's a buffet etiquette, but if there is, the guys definitely aren't following it. We're still in the lineup and already there's been complaining, shoving and they've done a little too much looming over the other people in the line. Declan's eyes have been on me the whole time. If we're supposed to be keeping what's between us private, then he's doing a shit job of it. Trying to distract myself, I turn to Jonas.

"Your hotel has way nicer restaurants than this, and there's a buffet there, too. Why exactly are we here?" This place isn't fancy. It's not even particularly well-kept. But the lineup to get in was out the door, so obviously, it has something going for it.

"Meat," Jonas grunts, eyeing the front of the line impatiently. Nick snickers and elbows him. Jonas elbows him back distractedly.

Nick leans in to be heard over the noise of his brothers. "He means the guy who owns this place is a master with the smoker. We come here every time we're in town. It's been too long this time. I swear my stomach is about to eat me from the inside."

"So when we get in there, we should stay out of your way?"

He grins, his teeth gleaming white against the tan of his skin. "Pretty much."

Somehow, I'm lucky enough to be at the front of the line. Colton has Mia on his shoulders and Evie tucked under his arm. They're bickering happily over god knows what. His nose is still swollen, but it doesn't seem to be bothering him any. Mia leans down, and she and Colt start whispering to each other.

I turn back to Nick. "Where did you learn to fix broken noses? I mean, you snapped it back in place like it's your job."

Nick laughs. "It pretty much was. We lived in cramped quarters for a few years on Knight Street. We didn't always handle it well. Someone got punched weekly. I'm not sure how I ended up being the go-to, but it turns out it's still a handy skill to have."

"I guess it is," I say distractedly. Something is up. Colt and Mia look sketchy. As I'm watching, Mia throws herself dramatically onto the top of Colt's head.

"Daddy, I so hungry," she wails pitifully. She sniffles, but her dark curls hide her face. Then the sobs start. Colt awkwardly reaches up, patting her back.

"Oh, my poor princess. She's wasting away. Mia, baby. I'm so sorry. It's important to wait your turn." He starts patting his pocket, dramatically turning them inside out to show how empty they are. "I'm sorry. I don't even have a crumb to give you."

A sweet older lady starts rifling through her purse, and Colt's eyes flash with panic. "We'll get you your macaroni soon, I promise."

Mia, fucking three-year-old con artist Mia, sniffs dramatically. "My tummy hurts. I need macaroni." Then she gags dramatically. Jonas gags next to me, and I clamp my hands over my mouth and drop my head onto Nick's shoulder. He's shaking, but he doesn't make a sound. Mia gags again, and Jonas follows suit. Colt starts up too. Now the baby and two giant men are gagging. The people around us clump together as far from us as possible, not wanting to be in the line of fire.

And oh my god, it works. Soon people are moving sideways, clearing a path to the register. Jonas swipes his card, and we weave through the tables, following a wide-eyed waitress to a grouping of tables. The guys start moving chairs, and before I know it, they have a long table set up with spots for everyone.

They stand around, staring at Evie, who drops her head on the table. "Just go," she mutters. And they're gone. That was weird.

"What the hell was that?" I ask.

She snorts, propping her head on her hand. "We went to a buffet yesterday after the ceremony. We got kicked out. They fell on it like wild dogs, and I might have scolded them a bit."

"You scolded them? Those very large men?" I mean, I've done it at work a time or two, but it's kinda my job.

"Yeah. I'm trying to get them to set a better example for Mia...Jesus. Fuck." She slaps her hands over her eyes, and I spin in my chair to see what's going on. I don't bother to hide my laughter this time. Mia, now riding on Declan's shoulders, is double-fisting meat. She's got a drumstick in one hand and a steak in the other and seems to be doing some sort of war cry as Declan fast walks to the next food station. She tears into the chicken leg, dropping bits of chicken and juice into Declan's hair. The rest of the guys seem to be coordinating some sort of attack, led by Micah, as they sign to each other across the room.

"Sorry, Evie, it looks like the lunatics are running the asylum now."

. . .

I'VE BEEN TO VEGAS ONCE BEFORE. THE YEAR AFTER BREE graduated, I took a couple of days and flew in with a friend from college.

I don't remember most of it, but I do remember those drinks. The really tall ones in the cups shaped like ladies. Most of the guys have one. Colt, Declan, Holly, and Ransom seem to be the self-appointed sober delegation as we run amok down the street. How are they still so enthusiastic about everything? They each ate enough meat to satisfy a full-grown lion. After that, it seemed to me that heading back to the hotel and dropping into a coma should be the next order of business, but nope. They're running around like freshmen on spring break.

It's a good thing I don't embarrass easily. After some coaxing by Mia, Declan, Kade, Colton, and Zach have all stripped their shirts off so they can get their bodies painted by an artist set up on the sidewalk. Mia's already sporting a real-istic monarch butterfly on her face. She wants them all painted like her favorite animals.

I settle onto a bench a dozen feet from the guys, not surprised when Becca and Holly wander over. Becca's already wobbly, and Holly seems to be fucking with her, gasping and skittering backward here and there, making Becca jump.

"This whole place is invested," Becca announces dramati-cally, raising her feet as she slurps at her drink. "There's spiders eeeeeverywhere."

I shoot a look at a laughing Holly. *Invested?* "Yeah, totally infested. Better watch out."

"Mmhumm, they can't get me. My feets are up."

Holly's cackling, Becca's slurping, and I'm wishing I'd grabbed another one of those drinks, too, instead of the beer I'm sipping. The one I had earlier is long gone from my system.

Ignoring the very drunk woman beside me, I turn to

Holly. "Congratulations, by the way. I'm really happy for you and Micah."

"Thank you," she says, dropping her hand to her belly. I see a hint of an extra curve, but it's not enough for a stranger to guess her condition. "It's been a bit of a whirlwind, but we're excited."

"Excited now, you mean? Something in your voice made it sound like you weren't before."

She sighs, watching Micah, Maverick, and Jonas paw through the interior of a souvenir shop. "I've been pregnant before." I should maybe mind my own business, but the women are right. They're a part of the brothers' lives, and judging by how much the men talk about them, the women aren't going anywhere. So I want to get to know them. Besides, according to Ransom, I'm like their little sister. It's my job to get in there with the wives.

"Since you don't have a child, I'm guessing..."

"I miscarried. Right around this time, actually."

"Jesus, you must be stressed the fuck out."

"It's been better this time. Last time I was in a really different position."

"Different because it was with your shitty ex?" I know a little about what she's been through. She ran from her abusive ex with Evie's help. But after two years, he found her. Well, found Becca. Who proceeded to break several bones in his body. She's sort of a ninja.

"Partly, yeah. It's hard to imagine having a baby with a man who seems hellbent on destroying you. Can you imagine? Being connected forever to a man who beat me nearly daily?"

"No, I really can't. I honestly don't have a frame of reference for that kind of experience. I've never been hurt that way."

"I'm glad," she says softly. "I wouldn't wish it on anyone.

Things this time are different. This time...I'm excited. For this baby, and to see how Micah is as a daddy."

"Babies are awesome," Becca mutters beside us. Her eyes are locked on the body painter and, more specifically, on her man. "I want babies with Kade."

"Seriously? Don't you think you'd better marry the man first?"

"Yep," she says, still staring. There's a calculating gleam in her eye.

Holly looks dumbfounded. "He's been sort of asking you for months. And you've been giving him shit about it. Now you're ready?"

Becca smiles, and suddenly she doesn't look quite so drunk. "He was asking for the wrong reasons and he hasn't proposed in at least a month. He knows I'm not going anywhere now. He's settled down. And I want to keep him, so we should get married. Plus, I need to keep him on his fucking toes. When he thinks I'm going to zig, I'll zag like a motherfucker."

She smirks, then sticks her tongue out, searching for her straw as her hand waves. None of us mention it when she accidentally sticks the straw up her nose. She puts her drink down on the sidewalk next to her and watches the world go by, that smile never leaving her face.

Well alright then," Holly says with a roll of her eyes. The body painter works fast, and soon enough, the guys are striding over to us, proudly showing off their paint.

"Kade," Becca says, looking up at him. "Let's get married. Right now."

His mouth drops open. He searches her face. "You're fucking with me?"

"Nope. I'm serious. There's a chapel right over there," she says, pointing at one of the hotels across from us.

"Are you sure?" His throat is bobbing.

She reaches up, pulling him down to her. He drops to his knees, pressing between her thighs, smearing the brown body paint along his sides. "I love you. That's never changed. And I want a future with you. So yes, I'm sure. I'm not interested in the dress, or flowers, or any of the planning that comes with a big wedding. I just want to be married to you. So will you marry me? Now? With all our friends around us?"

"Fuck yeah!" he yells, planting a deep kiss on her, then hopping up and running around to all his brothers. "I'm getting married fuckers. Let's go, right the fuck now."

And that's how Becca, slightly sloshed, clutching her drink like it's a bouquet, marries Kade, painted like a gorilla, contoured chest and all. In the audience are a lion, a rhino, and a unicorn. And don't try convincing Mia that a unicorn isn't a real animal. I try and end up ninety-nine percent sure that they actually are. That kid is going to be dangerous as a teenager.

Kade's gazing down at Becca, love shining from his face. "You're the best fucking thing to ever happen to me. Thank fuck you didn't let me fuck it up. I promise I will love you, cherish you, and give you whatever the fuck you want for the rest of our lives."

We're all laughing. The man has no problem throwing F-bombs in his wedding vows. I've never met anyone who curses as much as he does.

Becca laughs with us. She knows him. Knows everything about him and clearly loves it all. "All I want is you. I promise to call you on your shit. I promise to wear that little outfit you bought me at least once a week, and I promise to stick it out and fight with you. I won't give up on you. Ever."

I try to hide my wet eyes, but when I look around the room and realize nobody else is, I give up. A smiling Micah is holding a sobbing Holly. Becca finally turns to her, exasperated, "Get a fucking grip, woman."

I really do like these people.

Smiling, I listen to them make a few more racy vows. And when Declan steps beside me, casually brushing his fingers over the back of my hand, it takes everything in me to resist leaning into him. My need to keep this private competes with my need to feel connected to him. So I memorize his small touch. It has to be enough for now.

When it's over, a laughing Becca turns to us, chucking her thankfully empty plastic glass at us in lieu of a bouquet. Her aim is shit, so she banks it off the wall before sending it straight into Zach's hands. He scowls at her and drops it into the trashcan on the way out.

We spill out of the chapel into the casino, beelining for the slots. Well, except for Ransom, Nick, and Jonas. They head to the poker tables, convinced slots are for suckers, which of course, they are. But it's a lot of fun pulling those little arms. The push-button ones aren't nearly as satisfying. We're riding a love high, Kade and Becca in the center, spending more time making out than gambling, but other than a couple of side eyes, no one pays them much attention. Clearly, they're not the worst Vegas has seen.

Declan, Zach, and I settle at a row of machines, waving goodbye to Colton and Evie with their very sleepy Mia. We're definitely getting some looks. Zach's unicorn paint is sparkling, thanks to the flashing lights of the slots, and Declan's the most built lion I've ever seen. I can't even count how many women are sneaking glances. The older ones don't even bother pretending they're not staring. The guys don't seem to care, so I ignore it, along with the waves of heat I feel coming from Declan, and just play.

Turns out gambling is a lot more fun when you're doing it with someone else's money. Ransom pressed a black card into my hand before he disappeared further into the casino. When I saw the balance available, I almost swallowed my tongue.

The business owner in me wants to cash out and use this money to invest in a new bar, but vacation me has decided to say *fuck it*.

We don't notice them at first. We're too busy laughing and whooping when we get tiny payouts. But gradually, the smell of baby powder and muscle relaxant cream invades our senses. As a unit, Declan, Zach, and I turn to look behind us. The sea of seniors standing there suddenly scatters, trying to look busy. One old man with the gnarliest nose I've ever seen in real life just looks straight up to the ceiling, clutching his walker. Like if he doesn't make eye contact, we won't be able to see him.

"What the fuck is happening?" I hiss, spinning back to my machine. Declan and Zach are both grim-faced, shoulders tight.

"Fucking lurkers," Declan mutters.

"We're not moving," Zach shouts, looking back over his shoulder. "Not again fuckers."

"Wait, what? What am I missing?"

"They're lurkers. They're going to wait, and when we leave our machines, they'll swoop in and steal the payout. No way. Not this time."

"This has happened before?"

"Last time we were in Vegas," Zach mumbles, yanking the handle down aggressively. "We left for a few minutes, and the ladies that took our machines walked away with a couple of grand. It's not happening this time."

"Damn right it's not," Declan vows.

I spin, looking for Micah and Holly, searching for a shred of sanity outside the looney pool I'm swimming in. Holly's looking baffled as Micah hunches over his machine protectively.

"Do you guys not realize you're rich?" I say, turning back to my machine. "You don't need the money."

Zach sneers at me. "It's not about the money, Cara. It's the principle of it."

"Oh, right. Of course, the principle. What's the principle again?"

Zach's lips firm, and he deliberately turns his stool away from me. I turn to Declan, hoping for a smidge of sanity, but nope, out of luck there.

I get a drink from a passing waitress and settle back in my chair, relaxed, playing my slot. We chill, still aware of the white hair around us, for a couple of hours. At some point, Kade and Becca, deep into a very public make-out session, tip off their chair and hit the floor. They barely come up for air long enough to wave goodbye, then they're heading out. Holly drags Micah out, hand on her belly, soon after. Smart of her. She's the only one who was likely to get him to move. Before he leaves, he slaps hands on Zach and Declan's shoulders. "It's on you." Then glancing at the lurkers behind him, he signs to them. They nod grimly and turn back to the machines with renewed purpose.

"What did he just sign?" Micah's always used a combination of sign and speech, though his speech is coming more easily now. But the guys still use it to communicate all the time.

It's Declan who answers. "He told us to stop drinking. And not to give in."

"He doesn't want you drunk?" I don't really get it. We've been drinking all night.

"He doesn't want us to lose our machines because we need a bathroom break."

Yep. They're crazy.

Three hours later, closing in on midnight, I'm convinced of it. Declan and Zach are both doing a seated version of the pee-pee dance. And it's no wonder. I abandoned my machine an hour ago, needing the bathroom. Declan and Zach got into a heated argument with a blue-haired woman pushing eighty, but she won. Apparently, saving someone's seat is against the rules. I don't see any rules posted, but the guys backed down after she shoved them. They didn't move, of course, but were wise enough not to push her back. They're crazy, not vicious. So now they're sitting there, two hulking men on either side of a little old woman, determined not to give in.

"Guys, maybe it's time to call it." I don't really mean it. This is way too much fun.

"No fucking way," they mutter in unison. Declan can't stand it anymore, wiggling off his seat to dance beside the machine. I could leave and go back to my room. I'm pretty sure Declan would pull himself away to escort me. That protective streak in him is alive and well. But I kinda want to stick around and see if one of them pisses themselves. God, that would be an amazing Vegas story to tell over and over. And over.

I nearly lose it when the lurkers start up.

"Gee, I sure could use a big glass of water. I'm parched," an old man says next to them.

A tall, stylishly dressed lady, somewhere between sixty and eighty, chimes in. "Norm, do you remember that trip we took to Niagara Falls? The water was just amazing. It poured over the edge like a wave. Just whooshing and pounding. I've never seen that much water in my life."

A round cherub cheeked woman joins in. "Oh my, we should go see those dancing fountains while we're here. I can't wait to see that water spray up in the sky like that."

The guys resist for a good ten minutes, but when one of the ladies orders a pitcher of water and empty glasses from a passing waitress and proceeds to pour everyone a glass while standing right between the guys, they break.

With curses and an exchange of middle fingers with two ladies wearing matching pink sweat suits, they bolt for the nearest bathroom. But they're still in earshot when the sirens on Declan's machine wail, paying out one of their tormentors.

I laugh the entire way back to the hotel, plastered between two very grouchy men.

"Fucking lurkers," Zach mutters, leaning against the cab's window forlornly.

"Fucking lurkers," Declan echoes with a sigh.

34

DECLAN

"Where are you going?"

I nearly jump out of my skin at Zach's voice. "Jesus. Fuck. Don't do that," I whisper yell at him, spinning in the hallway to face him.

He smirks, leaning against his room door, still covered in unicorn paint but somehow making it look cool. It's late. I thought I'd be safe from prying eyes. I thought no one would catch me.

"So jumpy," he says with a snicker. "Seriously, where are you going?" My intentions must be written all over my face. He shakes his head. "It's one in the fucking morning. You go to her room right now, it's a booty call. Is that your plan?"

I roll my eyes and shove him back into his room, following him in. There are way too many people who could come across us. His suite is just like mine and Nick's. Big living area, view of the city and desert behind, then two bedrooms. The door on the left swings open, revealing Jonas in his white boxer briefs.

"I thought I heard voices," he says, studying me. "Are you having Cara problems again?"

"I am not having Cara problems," I nearly yell. "We're

fine. I think. Or maybe not. I don't know," I scratch at my beard, frustrated by my inability to get a read on the situation. "We had such a good day, but she avoided being alone with me since then."

"Shit," Zach says with a wince. "That could be bad, but maybe she just doesn't want to broadcast your relationship?"

"Relationship?" I ask with a squeak. We haven't broadcasted anything. Cara wanted to keep it between us, and I'm trying to honor that.

"Nuances and body language are challenging for me," Jonas says, "but even I could tell that you and Cara have become much closer. The way you look at her is similar to the way Colton, Micah, and Kade look at their women."

"Oh god. Does everyone know?" So maybe we're a little more obvious than I thought.

"Probably," Zach says. "None of us are good at minding our own business. We've been speculating on how you guys were doing all weekend."

I collapse onto the couch and drop my head into my palms. This is all so fucked up. "She's going to run."

"What makes you say that?" Jonas asks.

"We're a lot to fucking take. She has to deal with us all day at work, and now she has to handle interference in her personal life too? Why would she stick around?" She gets hit on all the time. She could have any guy she wants.

Zach drops onto the sofa. "Because she likes you. I would think after several years of chasing you, that would be obvious."

"But I fucked it up."

"And you fixed it," Zach reminds me.

"Right. I did. I apologized. She forgave me."

"So then, what's the plan now? Why are you knocking on her door this late?"

"I just need to talk to her. We were in a little bubble, just the two of us, and now there's so much noise...I'm just—"

"Flipping out."

"Yeah. I need to reconnect with her somehow. We're flying home tomorrow morning, then we're back at work, and I don't know how the fuck we're supposed to act."

"Then you should talk to her. But make your intentions clear right from the beginning, so she does not misunderstand you," Jonas says.

"Yeah. Ok." I hop up, done with this little distraction, and head to the door.

"Dec," Zach says, stopping me with my hand on the door. "You and Cara have spent a long time dancing around each other. You're going to have to be straight with her. Don't let her misunderstand your intentions toward her. She's still our employee, and things could get very messy if it's not handled right."

I study the luxurious gold and blue rug under my feet, resisting the urge to lash out. This is nothing I haven't already considered and already talked about with her. But the reminder hits hard. What the fuck am I doing, going to her room in the middle of the night?

"Right," I mutter, ready to head back to my room with my tail between my legs. I'm such a fuckup. I pull open the door and, with a brief glance down the hall toward Cara's room, turn and head back to my suite.

The door to Nick's bedroom is closed. I head into mine and shut the door behind me, dropping onto the bed. Every time I think I know what the right next step is, one of my brothers reminds me that I don't. The last thing I wanna do is corner Cara or make her think that I'm trying to take something from her. Yeah, I've been fucking obsessed with her for years, but that doesn't mean that I can't fucking control myself.

I hop up, my body wanting me to go to her, to explain to her how much I care for her and how serious I am about this thing between us. I can't leave it like this. I can't not talk to her or tell her what I'm feeling. Our disconnect this evening has been too scary. I'm afraid we're falling back into the way things were just a week ago. Pulling out my phone, I type out a quick text.

> Me: I had so much fun with you today. It seemed like things were a little off between us tonight. Is everything ok?

The dots pop up, showing me she's typing immediately. I can't sit, jumping up to pace as I wait for her response. When it comes, the ground I'm standing on feels shakier.

> Cara: Maybe we're moving too fast.

Fuck this. I'm out of my room and sprinting down the hall to hers in seconds. I tap gently. Her voice comes through the door.

"Declan, this isn't a good idea."

"Cara, we need to talk. Let me in. Just talk, I promise." I'm begging, and I know she can hear it. "Nothing else needs to happen, but we have to talk."

I wait, holding my breath, willing my heart to stop pounding so loudly so I can hear her through the door. Finally, I hear the slide of the chain, then the deadbolt unlocking. One stunning blue eye peeks out, looking past me.

"It's just me. No one else knows I'm here."

Her lips firm, but she swings the door open enough for me to slide through, then she closes it and locks it again. She leans against the door, eyes shuttered. It feels like she's a million miles away from me, and I suddenly feel like that stuttering idiot all over again.

"Did something happen today?"

Her eyebrow rises questioningly. "Something? Lots of things happened today. Could you be more specific?" I curl and release my fingers over and over, trying to loosen some of the tension in my body. Her tone is ice cold. Her voice almost robotic.

"What the fuck happened? Cara, if I said or did something wrong, you need to tell me, so I can fix it." I'm mentally replaying everything I've said and done since this afternoon. It's a lot, but I can't pinpoint a moment that would make everything go to shit like this.

Her face softens, and she takes a few steps away from the door. "You didn't do anything wrong, Declan. It's just...everything feels different right now. And today, I was reminded that maybe us...maybe this isn't a good idea."

My heart is in my fucking shoes. "What do you mean you were reminded? Why wouldn't this be a good idea?"

She shrugs, but the movement isn't casual. There's a tension in her body that I don't like. "Maybe we're just too different. Maybe you need someone sweeter...or softer."

"Doesn't exist. No one's sweeter than you."

A slight flush colors her cheeks. "I'm not an easy person, Dec. I'm just not. I'm nothing like your sweet gamer girls. I just—"

"Enough," I bark, striding towards her. Her eyes widen, and she backs up until she bumps into the door. Planting my hands on either side of her head, I lean in close, eyes locked with hers. "I've had sweet gamer girl. I'm not a fucking monk. I've dated. I've fucked around a lot. If I wanted that, I could have it."

I press my cheek next to hers, the shell of her ear at my lips. "The day I met you, Cara, those women ceased to exist. They were just gone. You were all I could see. All I could think about. All I want. So whatever bullshit is in your head right now? Let it go. But if you can't, or if you don't want to, then it can all go back to the way it was, except this time I'll keep my fucking eyes off you, and you'll keep your hands off me." I back up and put a few feet between us so I can really look at her. My throat feels tight. There are shadows in her eyes, and Zach's words echo through my head. I can't risk her thinking I don't want her.

"It would fucking kill me, Cara, but I would do it if that's what you want." I wet my dry lips. "Do you? Do you want me to walk away?" She studies me, chest heaving, mouth slightly open, and doesn't say a fucking word. I'm suddenly cold, my future stretching out before me in a big blur of nothing. Dropping my eyes, I head toward her, carefully reaching for the door handle so I can get the fuck out of here and find a big bottle to climb into. Her hand covers mine.

"Wait," she says quietly. I freeze, but I can't look at her. I can't show her the devastation on my face or the tendril of hope unraveling. "Your family thinks I might hurt you."

Back teeth clamped together, I let a wave of rage shudder through my body. "They had no right to say that to you. It's none of their fucking business. I am not a child that needs protecting."

"But what if they're right? I'm not an easy woman. I've been told I'm a ballbuster by more men than I can count. I ju—"

"Shut up."

Her eyes flash, her mouth opens to give me hell, and I swoop in, taking her mouth. Plundering, stroking. Cupping the back of her head, I hold her to me, not letting her escape me. Escape us. Because this? This fire between us? It's the equalizer. That's what nobody else seems to understand. I back off, just the tiniest bit, letting her breathe.

"You are a ballbuster. You are tough. You are strong and independent. You are all those things. But you're also soft, and emotional, and overwhelmed sometimes. You showed me your soft spots, Cara. You showed me you. So why the fuck should we care what anyone else thinks? You and me? We work. And I don't want to walk away from the possibility of us. Do you?"

She wets her lips, eyes still hazy. She slides her arms

around me, hands fisting in my t-shirt. "No. I don't want to walk away."

I kiss her again in relief. In want. In need. She returns it all, matching it with her own. Pulling her tighter to me, I lift her, walking us over to the couch. I drop down, and she climbs on, straddling me. I'm desperate for another taste of her, but she pulls back, eyes worried.

"What happens tomorrow? What happens at work?"

I brush back her hair, tucking it behind her ear. My heart is pounding, but not with fear this time. I hear the hope in her voice, matching the hope in my heart. "What do you want to happen? They all have a pretty good idea of what's going on between us. But we can keep things…quiet if you want."

"I don't want that. I don't want you to run away from me anymore." The echo of hurt in her voice kills me.

"I won't, I promise. I'm done running. If I can't think of something to say, or if I get overwhelmed, I'll just do this." I kiss her. Long, slow, deep. Until I can't tell where I am in the universe.

"Good plan," she gasps, trying to catch her breath. I hug her close, loving the feel of her lush body in my arms. She feels right here. Like it's where she's always supposed to be.

"Maybe we keep it mostly professional at work, then after…"

"Then after, we date?" I ask hopefully. "I've been thinking about the dating part, and I could take you to some of those fancy—"

Her fingers press against my lips. "Why don't we play those by ear? I don't really need fancy restaurants. I like diners and walking and just spending time with you."

"Me too," I choke out.

She leans in, giving me little nips on my jaw. The bite to my earlobe just about launches me into space. "Ah, if you don't want to take this any further tonight, then now would be a good time to stop," I squeak out.

She drops her forehead to my shoulder, giggling. "Declan, remember those bases?"

"Um...yeah," I croak.

"Let's round a couple," she whispers against my ear. She does a slow, rolling grind against my cock, and every single noble thought in my head leaks out of my ear.

"Wha—what base is this?"

"No idea. Would you like me to stop so we can discuss it?"

"No," I yell, clutching her hips, pulling her harder against me. Her moan drives me higher, and I buck up into her. We haven't removed a single piece of clothing. Her hands are around my neck, mine are at her hips, and already, this is by far the hottest moment of my life. How have I survived this long without this feeling? Maybe it's good that I didn't know how hot we'd be together...I would have lost my fucking mind over the last three years.

"Declan," she moans against my throat, in between teasing bites, "harder."

"Yes, ma'am," I say, widening my legs, forcing her knees out further, giving me more room to move. I pull her down to me and start a matching roll. Judging by the long, low groan coming from her, I'm hitting just the right spot.

I read a lot. I absorb everything and retain it. An article I read in some waiting room once pops into my head. It was in some women's magazine, and the author was complaining about how most men make the same mistake in bed. They find something their partner likes, but instead of sticking with that and making her come, they'll stop and try other moves, leaving their woman unsatisfied.

So instead of changing up my movements, I double down, pushing my hips higher and pulling her down lower. She fights me, but a quick look at her face assures me she's not hurting. No, she's fighting to control the rhythm. But this is my fucking show. I may be a geek. I may struggle to find the right words. I may obsess over my hobbies. But I know how to make a woman scream my name.

Thank fuck, I'm not a virgin. Thank fuck I can please her. I keep her hips planted against me, the feel of her heat making me feral. She rears back, throwing back her head, hands planted on my shoulders as she mumbles. I don't catch the words, but her meaning is clear. So I don't stop, don't falter, and she rewards me by falling apart.

Cara shuddering through her orgasm is the most beautiful thing I've ever seen. I'm so fixated on her that my own release takes me by surprise, kicking out of me against my briefs. I throw my head back, gasping. Cara drops her mouth back to mine, and together we ride out our release.

"Holy fuck," I mutter, breathing into her mouth. "I think I died."

She giggles, and I pull her in and soak up her laughter.

"We have an early flight in the morning," she mumbles against my neck.

"Yeah, we do."

She gives me one more nip on my neck this time, then jumps out of my arms, laughing at my growl. "I'll see you tomorrow. Maybe we can sit together?" How can she move? How do her legs work? How does she look so energized? What the fuck is she talking about? The flight?

"You better not try to sit anywhere else." I blow out a breath, wishing I could stay right here with her. I want her in my arms tonight. Every night. But the last thing she probably wants is me skulking down the hallway in the morning. I move to the door and psych myself up for the sprint down the hallway to my room. If the guys catching me before was bad, I don't want to think about the jokes they'll make when they see me running down the hall with cum stains on my jeans.

"Oh, remember, operation destroy Colt starts tomorrow. You ready?"

I give her a cheesy wink. "Woman, I was born ready. He won't know what hit him."

Her evil cackle echoes in my head as I run to my room. The woman is perfection.

Now all I have to do is not screw it up.

35

CARA

I see him coming long before he gets to me. He's hurrying, giggling to himself, and it's somehow both adorable and hot.

"He's coming!"

Declan skids to a stop in my office, then leans on the edge of my desk, attempting to look casual, crossing and uncrossing his arms. He's going to give us away if he keeps this up. I slide my foot out of my stiletto and run my toes up his calf. His arms drop, and his eyes lock on my foot as it travels up his jeans.

"You gotta calm down. You're the one that told me we're playing the long game here. You're going to give it away if you don't chill."

"Chill. Right. I can chill. Totally." He doesn't look up. He doesn't take his eyes off my foot. I let my smile grow. The last few days have been frustrating yet magical. Our flight home, on the Brash jet this time, was uneventful. Declan and I sat together, but the rest of the plane kept side-eyeing us the whole time, so it was uncomfortable and frustrating.

But the teasing glances and casual brushes of the hand at work have been such a welcome change from the last few years. Hell, even from the last few weeks. The way his eyes warm when he looks at me has knocked down almost every layer of brick in that wall I had built to protect myself from him. Colton and Evie stayed in Vegas an extra week with Miss Mia, of course. So Declan and I have had plenty of time to really perfect our plan. Today, his first day back, we're setting everything into motion.

"What the fuck?"

I have to bite my lip to stop from laughing as Colton's voice rings out through the hallway. We're starting small, with small annoyances. But clearly, Colton's already had a rough morning.

"Tell me again what you did to his truck?"

Declan giggles and covers his mouth. "I fucked with his radio. It's blaring Death Metal. Every time he turns it off, it comes back on. It's been amazing. I can control it from my office." It is amazing. Colt is all about the eighties. I mean, the man had a long-haired, leather-wearing Bon Jovi imperson- ator officiate his wedding, so the Death Metal would be making him ragey.

"Declan!" Colt yells as he gets closer. "What the fuck's going on with the elevator?"

Dec wipes his smile off his face and tries for a concerned expression. He's shit at this, but it's adorable. Luckily, I'm great at deception and misdirection when I need to be.

"What do you mean?" I ask as he fills my doorway. "Is it still not working right? Declan, can you please get your guys to check on it?"

Colt's glower fades as he studies me. "You had problems too? Every time I tried this morning, it dropped me off on the wrong fucking floor. I've been to the basement three fucking times!"

I pinch a tiny bit of skin on my thigh to keep myself under control. "Oh no. That's so frustrating. Declan, what the hell's going on in your department?"

He chokes and rubs his hand over his beard, trying to hide his smile, I'm sure. "I don't know. I'll get my guys on it." He winks at me and slaps Colt on the shoulder as he squeezes past. Colt studies him suspiciously, brow furrowed, then turns back to me.

"Everything ok?"

"Everything's fine. How was your mini honeymoon? Did you guys have fun?"

The suspicion clears, replaced by a post-honeymoon glow. "Fuck yeah, we had a blast. I had no idea there were so many things to do in Vegas with a kid."

My smile's real this time. Yeah, I'm still pissed at him, but I'm also so glad he's happy. "You'll have to take a kid-free honeymoon later. You know your brothers will babysit."

"They're desperate to. But I really like having her with us. She's pretty amazing. You know?"

"Yeah, I do. Being a dad looks good on you."

He puffs up, his already massive chest getting bigger. "She calls me daddy now," he says proudly.

"I heard, big guy." Now we're both blinking back tears.

"Good talk," he mumbles, turning on his heel and disappearing into his office.

Sappy fucker.

I spin around and slide into my desk, ready to lose myself in work. A couple of hours later, I stand and stretch, heading for Ransom's office. I knock and poke my head in, waiting for his 'enter.'

I plop into my chair and drop the blueprint on his desk. It's the guest chair, but I use it the most, so it's mine. "So, what exactly are you planning for that site?"

He leans back in his chair, studying me. "A commercial building. Like the plans say."

"With a six story underground garage, and a whole floor for a daycare? Not to mention the twelve-bay custom garage at the back and the warehousing. You're not building this for anyone else, are you?"

His lips quirk, and he shakes his head. "When I made the offer, it was going to be three twenty-story office buildings."

"And now?"

He shrugs, suddenly looking tired. "I miss Micah. It's time to bring him back into the fold. If I can get him excited about that garage, I can get him and Holly out of Knight Street. And the daycare..."

"Mia."

"Mia and the new baby. And if things keep progressing the way they have been, there will be more kids. A daycare makes sense. And we don't have the space for it right now."

"True. We're kinda busting out at the seams here."

He nods. Knowing I'll have more to say. I always have more to say.

"How are you handling all of this? Your brothers coupling up?"

He picks up a pen, a simple Bic —no fancy pen for Ransom Kyle—"It's been an...adjustment. Except for Kade, none of them had really disappeared into a relationship before. It's odd not to see them as much, but it's nice to have the women around. Even Becca, but don't tell her I said that."

"I won't, I promise," I say through my laughter. Their relationship is fun to watch. She needles him, and he plays the grump. It works for them, and that woman is fucking Teflon. Nothing gets to her.

I tap the blueprints in front of me. "Are these plans finalized? Should I send them out for bids?"

"Yeah, they are. Unless there's anything you'd like to change?" There it is again. What boss asks his assistant if there's anything she wants to change on the plans for their new office building?

"Does my office have a window in the new place?"

"Two of them."

"Then nope, nothing else to add. Oh, when I send it out for bids, I'm going to let a new firm send a proposal, too."

One black eyebrow swoops up. "What new firm? I have the top players on that list already."

"Top male firms, sure."

"Male firms?" he repeats carefully.

"Yep. There's a woman I know from school. She and her sister, and some friends, started a construction company. They're up-and-comers. You should give them a chance to bid."

He doesn't look convinced, but he knows me well enough by now to know that I wouldn't suggest it if I didn't think they could do it. He waves a hand, clearly done with the conversation. "Whatever. Do your thing. We'll look at them all."

"On it boss." He snorts at 'boss' and mutters about bossy females as I leave the room. There's no heat in his voice. No challenge. He's laughing, so I let it pass.

I spend the rest of the afternoon putting together a package for tender and putting out minor fires. It's amazing to me how many people think that they need Ransom to solve their problems. I swear, this place would fall apart without me handling all this shit.

My cell rings, and my stomach drops when I see the D.A.'s name. I don't want to answer it, but I also don't want to risk pissing him off.

"Hello," I say, trying for cool and casual. I succeed, mostly.

"Miss Davis. How nice to hear your voice." Something in the way he says it makes me shiver, tendrils of dread creeping up my spine. He's always creeped me the fuck out. On the surface, he's an attractive man. But the way he looks at me, like he wants to slice into me and watch me bleed, is scary. Thankfully Marty, my lawyer, is usually the one talking to him.

I hum but can't respond. My throat is closing up. Is he calling to tell me all the charges have been dropped, or is he about to blow up my life?

His chuckle makes my stomach twist. "How was Las Vegas? Cheeky of you to leave the state. You aren't supposed to do that."

"I haven't been charged with anything. There's no reason I can't travel. My lawyer said so." He also said to not speak to this guy without him present, but I can't seem to hang up the phone.

I can hear the anger in his voice. "Well, it's still unwise."

"Mr. Jackson, you should be speaking to my lawyer. Do you need his number?"

His rusty chuckle is horrible. The man can't be more than mid-forties, but he sounds decades older than that. I wonder what's aged him so much. Maybe the gritty voice is a reflection of his black, tattered soul. "No, lovely, I have it. I just thought I'd warn you to get your affairs in order. When you go away, it's going to be for a long time."

I tap the end button, no longer caring if I'm rude, and carefully place my phone on my desk, then curl my fingers into my palms and will them to stop shaking. It's going to be ok. It's got to be.

When four rolls around, thanks to that call, I'm already mentally fried. Leaving my shoes under my desk, I wander off to find Janey. She's been a bright spot in my life over the last month, helping me process some of what happened. She's recommended a counselor too, but I haven't been ready. But maybe I am now. It's getting harder and harder to bounce back.

I take the elevator down to the tenth floor and head toward the HR offices. I'm not likely to find her here, but it's as good a place to start as any. Janey spends most of her day wandering through the building, talking to people. She's almost never in her office. So I'm surprised to find her there. She's on her phone, texting, but startles when I walk in. She fumbles the phone in her hands, slapping it to her chest with a little scream.

"Cara. My god. You scared me!"

"I can see that. Who are you texting?"

Her cheeks flush, and my curiosity roars in, distracting me from that shitty phone call.

"Um," she stammers, batting at the brown flyaway hair on her cheek. "It's just someone I've been seeing."

"Janey, you have to give me more than that. Who is he? Is he cute? Where'd you meet?" She's such a sweet woman, but I've never seen her with a man. Judging by the flush on her cheeks, she's into him.

"We met online. We've been talking for a while, and we're going on a date." Her voice rises at the end, a mix of giddiness and nerves.

"That's good, right?"

"Right. It is, yes."

I close the door, then cross the room, dropping into a chair across from her. "You don't sound so sure."

"I don't have a lot of experience," she whispers, a blush staining her cheeks.

"That's not a bad thing, Janey. In fact, a lot of men prefer innocent women."

"Oh, I'm not innocent. I've...well, you know."

I do know, and that has nothing to do with her innocence. It's not about being a virgin but the way she seems to walk in the world. Always hoping for the best from people.

"Gotcha. But you don't have a lot of dating experience? Are you worried about that part?"

She nods, dropping her hands in her lap. "I just never know what to talk about."

"Talk about the same things you do when you're texting.

Just remember, you're amazing, and he's damn lucky to have your company."

"Amazing. I'll try," she murmurs, a shy smile curving her lips. "How are you? What brings you here?"

I needed to talk, but I don't want to anymore. I want to sit with my friend and be excited about her date. I don't want to think about Tyler, or the D.A. or jail. I just want to look at pictures of handsome men and gossip about dating.

"Just wanted to catch up, that's all. So...got any pictures?" I ask with a wink.

36

DECLAN

"**M**y fucking computer keeps shutting down."

I hide my smile, which is really fucking hard to do, and turn to Colt. "Shit, man. That's frustrating. I'll get my guys on it." I type out a quick bit of nonsense, then tap the mouse. "There. Done."

He's studying me, dissecting me. He's not dumb, and he can't be sure I'm fucking with him, but he's wondering. "We still haven't talked about what I did"

"No, we haven't."

He sits on the window ledge and crosses his arms, studying me over my monitors. "I didn't mean to fuck up that bad. That's not me. I don't even understand why I went through with it other than you were so pathetic that I knew you were never going to get anywhere with Cara if you didn't have some help."

There's that word again. Pathetic. It's not the first time one of my brothers has used it to describe me, but today it seems to dig a little deeper. Now that I'm batting so far out of my league with Cara, it grates on me. I usually just shut my mouth and don't say a damn thing about how much it bothers me. As much as I hate to admit it, he's not totally wrong. Stammering and stuttering, unable to speak to the woman I have been crushing on for years. But today, I can't let it go.

"What gives you the right to fuck with my life like that? Do you really have so little respect for me?"

He stands, dropping his arms. "Brother, no. That's not it. I swear. You're just...not really a ladies man. It just felt shitty watching you two dance around each other. I love you both, and you both seemed to want the same thing. It seemed like a good idea to help you guys along."

"I could do without your kind of help. You stuck your nose in where it didn't belong, and shit went sideways. What if we couldn't have made it out of that storm?" My hands are shaking." She could have died out there on that road. No fucking way I could have lived with that. Could you?" Just the idea of being stuck in a snowstorm watching Cara fade away makes me nauseous. It was way too close, and it's not okay.

"No, man. I couldn't," he says tightly.

"Right. Then stay the fuck out of my love life." He goes to open his mouth, and I glare at him. "I'm serious. You were so far out of line, it's not fucking funny. Stay out of it. I'm a grown man, and whatever happens between Cara and me is none of your business."

He nods tightly, throat working. "I hear you. I'll stay out of it. Promise." He reaches out, gently tapping the Yoda bobblehead on the edge of my desk, then turns and leaves. I feel a little bit like I've just kicked a puppy, but I'm not gonna call him back. I'm not going to apologize for standing my ground. I'm right on this.

I spin back to my screens, answering a few emails and messaging my techs to check in. I never wanted this job. I honestly didn't think I could do it. Sure, I know computers, and I fucking rock when it comes to digging for information, but I didn't think I could manage people. But that's the thing with Ransom. If he sees something in you that you don't see yourself, he will push you and push you to step up. So often, it's easier to just give in, and so far, I've ended up realizing that he was right. The only thing that makes him somewhat bearable is that he's never smug about it. He just pats you on the back and goes on about running our empire.

I get a solid hour of work done before my next interruption. I don't mind. This is how it always works in the daytime here. Brothers popping in, staff with questions, it's all good. If I have shit I really need to get done, I stay late. I've slept on my office couch more than once. I raise my head to see Zach at my door. His face is a weird mix of wired and confused as he drops into the chair next to my desk, staring down at his clasped hands.

"She emailed me back."

I don't need to ask him who. She's been pretty much all he's come to me about over the last couple of months. Maya is a mystery, and it's pissing him off. I've seen the woman's work. She's a brilliant marketer. But so is Zach. So are a lot of people who work here. There are probably a dozen people capable of doing what she does, but he's fixating now. Women don't ignore him, ever.

"That's what you've wanted. You've been trying to get her to work in your department for months. What did she say?"

"She wants to do a video interview."

"Okay...and that's a problem?"

"No," he murmurs, frowning. "I guess not. I just don't get it. Why now? She's been completely ignoring me for months, and suddenly she wants a video interview? You didn't find anything?"

"No, I didn't. There's no family to speak of. She doesn't seem to have any attachments to the city. She grew up in Cali and moved to New York for University. From what I can tell, she lives a quiet, dull life."

He taps his fingers on the arm of his chair, staring out the window at the winter sun, low in the sky. "Okay. Well, maybe she came to her senses. I'll talk to her and see where we want to go with it."

"Set it up soon, yeah? Before she changes her mind?"

He scowls harder like the possibility never crossed his mind. He slaps the arms of the chair and stands. "Maybe we should do it now?" He pulls his phone out and starts tapping.

"We? It's not really my department, man. I'm not sure what you want my help for?"

"I don't fucking know. I just can't get a read on this woman. I think having more people in the interview is a good idea."

"Okay, but maybe Janey would be a better choice? Or Colt? I'm not exactly a people person."

He grunts, and taps some more on his phone, then wanders over to the couch and drops down. All of our offices have couches. They're all laid out the same, so I'm not really sure why he's camping out here, but it doesn't really bother me. I focus back on my screens, getting lost in what I'm doing. A throat clearing pulls me back to the room.

Janey, standing in the doorway, smiles at me. I smile back automatically because who wouldn't? Then I startle when I see Jonas sitting calmly on the couch next to Zach. I didn't hear or see him come in. I get like that sometimes, so in the zone, a bomb could go off, and I wouldn't notice. Course, all Cara has to do is sneeze down the hallway, and I'm focused on her, ready to fetch her tea or a tissue. I'm totally whipped.

"What's happening?" I ask dumbly, looking between them.

"Maya. Video call. Now." Zach says shortly, the toe of his shiny black shoe tapping on the carpet.

"Ah, okay. Send me the de—"

"In your inbox," he says shortly. What the fuck? This is not like him at all. He's usually cool and unruffled. If this woman sets him off this badly, then maybe we shouldn't do this. But judging by the stubborn look on his face, he's not interested in hearing that right now.

I skim the email, then get the video call set up. They all shuffle around, dragging chairs to settle around me. I let Zach move to the center of the screen, sliding sideways and behind Jonas, who's fussing with Janey's chair, adjusting the lumbar or something.

Suddenly, the screen in front of us is filled with a woman's face. It's a striking face, an odd mix of features that don't seem to go together but somehow make you want to keep looking at her. Her dark hair is pulled loosely back from her face, leaving the focus on the dark slash of her eyebrows over deep brown eyes. Her mouth is a little too wide, a little too lush.

We're all staring at each other until Janey, thank fuck, clears her throat. "Ms. Miller. Thank you so much for taking the time to speak with us. I'm Janey. I work in HR here at Brash. Mr. Lee thought it might be good if we all spoke with you."

Maya's dark eyes shift slightly, her face softening slightly. "That's fine. It's better to be judged by everyone at once."

Zach straightens in his chair, frowning again. Fucker usually avoids frowning, not wanting to get wrinkles, probably. "Ah, we hadn't planned on judging you, we j—"

"Of course you were," she says with a snort. "You're trying to decide if I'm a good fit for your company. I'm doing the same thing. Trying to figure out if I could be happy there. I'm not convinced I will be."

"Then why did you agree to this meeting?" Zach's words come out clipped and harsh. "I've been trying to contact you for months. Why now?"

"Because my circumstances have changed, Mr. Lee. Why else?"

Zach opens his mouth, and Janey lays a hand on his arm, patting gently. His eyes drop to it, and he exhales heavily.

When he looks up, his face has lost some of its severity. "Right. Well, we appreciate it anyway. Are there any questions I can answer for you?"

"A few," she says quietly.

The next half an hour is one of the strangest of my life. I've never been interviewed for a job, but I have hired staff, and not once has anyone asked me about the average temperature of the building. Or the average decibels in the office. She had a ton of questions about the dress code, which I'm not even sure we have, and a bunch of other shit that doesn't seem to have anything to do with actual work.

Janey, Jonas, and I hang back, letting Zach handle the interview. Zach barely keeps his shit together during the call, getting more and more frustrated at her inane —his word— questions. Finally, he can't take it anymore. "Ms. Miller. We've answered a lot of...questions for you. Are you going to ask about the water temperature next, or can we move on?"

Maya's mouth tightens, and her cheeks color. "You're making fun of me," she says flatly.

"Nope, not making fun of you. Obviously, you care about the answers to these questions, but I don't see how any of it is relevant to the work I'm looking to hire you for."

"It's all relevant. I find it difficult to concentrate in certain environments. It doesn't make sense for me to agree to take a job that would force me to work in distracting conditions. I would be miserable, and you'd regret you'd hired me."

Janey smiles, leaning forward. "Ms. Miller, I think you'll find that we're very accommodating and accepting of differences here. If there are things we need to modify or arrangements we need to make to make things easier for you, then we're happy to do that."

The small lines between Maya's brows slowly disappear as the tension in her fades. "I see. Well, that's refreshing."

"Does your current employer know you're considering

taking another job?" Jonas asks, pushing his glasses up his nose.

"They do."

"What was their reaction?"

"They offered me a twenty-five percent raise." I whistle through my teeth, and Zach slaps me on the stomach.

"And did that tempt you to stay?"

"No," she says softly, so softly I lean in. "Nothing could convince me to stay here."

Janey's mouth twists in sympathy, and Jonas nods. There's pain in Maya's face, but also a clear 'do not ask' sign hovering over her head. Zach's head is tilted, studying her. "So you're planning to leave? The only question is, where?"

"Yes."

"And how many companies are you talking to?"

"Six."

Well shit. She's even more in demand than I understood.

"I see." Zach's fingers are tapping again. "I can email you a formal offer this evening. Then you'll have the information you need to make a decision."

She nods, and the call ends quickly after that. The four of us huddle near my computer, studying each other.

"Is it just me, or is she a little weird?" I finally ask.

Zach snorts. "A little? She's weird. But weird isn't a deal breaker around here."

Janey's cell pings and she excuses herself with a blush. Jonas watches her walk away with a focused look. He looks at her like that a lot. It doesn't seem to bother Janey, so we've stopped commenting on it. When she's left the room, he turns back to Zach.

"She'll be working directly for you. Are you going to be able to handle her? You seem to be quite reactive with her." Trust Jonas to point that shit out. Zach doesn't try to deny his frustration with the woman.

"She'll be in my department. I won't be working side by side with her. It's fine. We'll stay out of each other's way."

He sounds so confident, but I'm not so sure he should be. Something about the way he and Maya looked at each other tells me he's in for a bumpy road.

If she accepts the job, that is.

37

CARA

The guys' regular after-work meeting is just breaking up when I head back to my office. I return smiles and comfortable touches as we pass in the hallway. They're mostly a touchy-feely bunch, with each other and with me, and I like it. Declan's the last to leave, and he leans against the wall, watching me with a look that makes my blood heat. He doesn't speak, doesn't move, but his eyes track his brothers over my head. Suddenly, he darts in and grabs my hand, and we're running down the hall. He swings me into his office, shuts the door, and presses me up against it.

I'm a little breathless, partly from the sudden run but mostly from the feel of him against me. The hard planes of his body are pressed against my curves. Without my heels, he has to duck his head to kiss me. Something about having to tilt my chin up to kiss him does it for me. I'm tall, I'm curvy, and it's not often I get to enjoy this feeling of being surrounded, of being taken over.

His intensity is off the charts tonight, and I'm here for it. For his wandering hands and frantic panting. Heat washes through me as his tongue sweeps in to dance with mine, and his hands grab my ass and pull me into him.

"I've missed you so fucking much," he murmurs against my mouth.

"Me too." I really have. It hasn't been the same since we got back. It's been hard to find time together. The flu's been working its way through my entire staff, so Bree and I have been working extra shifts to cover. Normally, I'm happy to be there, to be needed. It's a place I feel totally in charge, and I need that. Especially since a lot of my life feels completely out of my hands right now.

"Come home with me tonight," he begs as his hands knead and press. I want to say yes so badly. I want to close the club and lose myself in Declan.

"I have to be at the club," I say. He stiffens, hands tightening on me briefly, then blows out a heavy sigh. His reaction puts me on the defensive. I clamp my mouth shut so I don't say something shitty and just give him and myself a second.

"There's no one else who can go in?" he finally asks.

"No. There isn't."

His lips tighten, but he nods. I appreciate him dropping it, but I don't like the emotional distance that's between us now.

"If I could get out of it, I would. But I've got a bunch of sick staff members, and if I don't show up, I won't be able to open tonight."

"Would that be such a bad thing?" he asks with a raised brow.

I stare at him, honestly surprised. "You know, I sometimes forget how different our worlds are, then you say something like that, and I'm reminded."

He scowls. "We're from the same world, Cara."

"We really aren't. In your world, if you decide to close the office for the day, do you still pay everyone?"

A dawning realization comes over his face.

"Yeah. Maybe you do. But I can't afford to pay people not to go to work. So I show up, and everyone still gets their paycheck. I really don't have any other options. People need to eat, the lights need to stay on, and my landlord expects his check on the first of the month, or I'll be out of business."

The tips of his ears are red. "Right. I knew that, but..."

"But you haven't had to think like that in a long time. I'm not trying to make you feel bad, I swear. It's just I have to think like a business owner. I know you own Brash, but day-to-day finances aren't your area, so I get why it might not have occurred to you. But I have to think about shit like this, or I'll lose everything I've built. Most of my life feels out of my control right now, so I can't just—"

"I get it. I do," he says, cutting off my words, cupping my cheeks, and pressing a gentle kiss to my forehead. "I just wish I could spend more time with you. But I'm starting to understand how hard you've worked for your business, and I would never want to fuck that up for you."

I press in to hug him, pressing my forehead against his jaw, blowing out a relieved breath. There's been this little thread of tension between us every time I mentioned the club. It wasn't all him, I know. I've been mentally tensing each time I bring it up, expecting the worst from him, which probably isn't fair. He said some really shitty things over a month ago. In the three years before that, he never said anything negative to me...if you don't count the running, at least. I'm choosing not to count it.

"Hey!" he says, pulling back to look at me. "Why don't I come to work with you tonight? I'm sure there's something I can help with."

I'm a little surprised he offered. It's very sweet of him. "Ah...have you ever worked in a club?"

"No. But I've been to a bunch of them." Obviously reading the doubt on my face, he strokes his thumbs over my collarbones. "Come on, it'll be great. We'll hang out, and after you're done, we can spend some time together."

"Friday nights are usually pretty crazy. Are you su—"

"Then you need the help. You told me you were short-staffed. Isn't some help better than none?"

Is inexperienced, enthusiastic Declan going to be any help at all tonight? Maybe. Is he going to be a serious distraction for me? Yes. Am I going to take him to work with me, anyway? Yep.

"Alright, you're on."

I almost feel bad for him. He's so happy. He has no idea what he's in for tonight.

None.

HE'S USELESS, BUT HE'S TRYING SO HARD, I CAN'T BE MAD ABOUT it. So far, he's failed spectacularly as a waiter, repeatedly forgetting drink orders and having to go back to the tables to ask them to repeat them. He was so adorably flustered no one gave him any shit, which is a miracle.

He's behind the bar now with Bree, his hoodie long gone, white t-shirt soaked with sweat. A gaggle of women are at his end of the bar, flirting up a storm, teasing him about taking his shirt off. I can't decide if I want him to or if I'm a jealous ho-bag with double standards. I play up the sex when I'm on shift. It's great for the tips and fits the vibe of my club. But Dec doing it? Not sure I'm a fan.

He shoots a panicked look my way. Grinning, I move past his admirers and duck under the bar. His eyes are wide, the white all the way around his brown eyes visible.

"I have no fucking idea what I'm doing. What's a Sex on a Beach? How do I make an Orgasm?"

Choking on my laughter, I turn to the women, many of whom are regulars. "You guys are awful! Seriously? Who ordered a Sex on the Beach?" One of the women in the back cackles, and I shake my head at their ridiculousness. "Tanya, since when do you drink shit like that?"

"Girl," she shouts back, flipping her tight braids off her

shoulder. "Don't ruin it. We almost had that shirt off! Every time we ask him for something he don't know how to make, he sweats a little more!"

I cross my arms on the bar, drop my head onto them, and laugh. These conniving women.

"Wait...you've all been torturing me this whole time?" The shock in his voice makes me laugh harder. "So you don't want an Orgasm?"

Jesus. The women are in hysterics, catcalling and generally treating him like a piece of man candy they want to take many bites out of. His face is getting redder and redder. I should take pity on him, I know, but I can't help thinking about those women chasing him out of that cooking class and I laugh more.

His eyes dart between the ladies and me. His eyebrow quirks, and he grabs the bottom of his shirt. "All for this? You just want...what? A peek?" He raises the shirt, making some of the girls yell, then drops it. They boo and shout for him to take it off. Some of the more brazen ones even fish out bills and start waving them around. They're treating him like a stripper. I take a closer look at Declan's face, and far from the panic I heard in his voice only minutes ago, he looks...intrigued.

I move to the corner of the bar, so he's in full view of the women, and lean back against it. I don't want to get in the way of the show, and maybe I need the support. The way he's rubbing his hands over his stomach, through the shirt, has my knees a bit wobbly.

I almost feel like I'm watching a really hot butterfly come out of its cocoon. Declan's always been so shy, awkward even. I've seen another side of him the last couple of weeks, but tonight, in front of these women, he's realizing how sexy he is. And I don't plan on stopping it anytime soon. Aside from the fact that Dec's enjoying himself, the women are going to be talking about this for months. You can bet they'll be back, looking for the hot bartender. If he actually takes his shirt off, I'm damn sure revenues will go up.

A small grin curls his lips as he teases the women. "You really want my shirt off? It's just a chest, you know. There's nothing special about it." They make damn sure he knows they don't agree. His smile widens. He turns to me, and I send him a wink. Let him play. I sure as fuck would enjoy the show, too. He laughs, shaking his head. "You're not going to save me from this?"

"Baby, you don't need saving. They're all eating out of the palm of your hand. Just look." His eyes lock on mine, heating, before finally turning to the women.

He studies them, finally seeing that behind their teasing is true interest. Any one of these women would go home with him in a heartbeat, and they have no idea how much money he's worth. It's all sexual, primal, and he's finally clueing in.

A touch of confidence, the kind I usually only see when he's talking computers, enters his eyes. He raises his arms, reaching for the back of his shirt. My panties are in serious trouble now. It's such a man thing to do, and it shows off his powerful arms and wide chest. I clench my thighs together and resist the urge to drag him back to my office. We're definitely going there later, but right now, I want the fucking show.

He winks at me, then grins at the ladies. "Is this what you wanted?" he asks, then pulls his shirt off right there in the middle of my club. The women are going insane, begging him to come closer so they can touch. Some of them are tossing money at him. And he's standing there, wide-eyed, realizing for the first time that he is a sexy beast. A seriously sexy beast.

I can't take my eyes off him.

The first time I saw him with his shirt off, I was not in the headspace to appreciate it. The second time, I didn't get enough of a view before those gorgeous muscles were covered up with body paint. But tonight? Oh, my god. His skin is a light golden color, with a hint of white where his jeans dip down. The dusting of hair on his chest makes me think of running my fingers along it. Of pulling at it. I wonder if he likes a hint of pain with his pleasure?

One of the ladies kneels on the bar, and my brain comes back online. "Woah, now. Settle down. This is a look but don't touch kinda place. Bree!" She's been watching the show in between serving the big group of guys in front of her. She's been playing with them all night, kind of like the old Bree would have, and I am so relieved. She flips a bar towel over her shoulder and wanders down to us, a massive smile on her face. She stops next to Declan, studying him up and down.

"Goddamn big guy. Cara never mentioned how built you are." She reaches out and pokes one of his ab muscles, making them contract with his inhale. He pulls away from her with a little laugh, and I store that away. He's ticklish, and I want to see what reactions I can pull out of him. I want to find all his sensitive spots. I just...want.

She turns to the women, grabbing drink orders, distracting them. I move to my man, grab his hand, and lead him away from the bar, through the crowd, and down the hallway. I don't need to pull. He keeps his big body nearly pressed to my back the entire way. He doesn't say a word, and the fire between us is a living, breathing thing. My hand is on the door of my office when his arm bands around me, pulling me into his body.

"You open that door, Cara," he growls, "and we're not stopping. I don't care if the club catches on fire. I need to be in you."

38

CARA

My mind is being blown over and over again tonight. Declan chipped in at my club, his willingness to help out softened my heart in a way I hadn't expected. Then watching him strip sent my blood pressure through the roof. Now Dec, sweet, nerdy Dec, is pressing his cock into my ass, grabbing me like he's about to take what he wants.

Yes, please.

But after all this buildup, you can be damn sure I'm going to make the man work for it.

"Ah baby, I want that too, but..."

His arm tightens. "But what, Cara?"

"I've been a little...unsatisfied for a while now. It might be safer for us to wait, maybe pick this up at your place later, and you let me go in here alone so I can...take care of things."

"Take care of things?" he chokes out. I bow my head, smiling, pushing my ass into him, savoring his groan.

"Yeah, baby. Cause if I don't. If I let you take me in there? You might not make it out of there alive. I'm too needy. I might...take too much from you."

His whole body shudders and my smile grows. It feels so fucking good to know he wants me as badly as I want him. That he's desperate for me. Suddenly he shifts, pressing me tightly against the door so I can feel all of him. His mouth comes to my neck, and I tilt my head, giving him room. I expect the gentle touch of his lips. I expect reverence. I don't expect him to sink his teeth into my skin, biting. My head drops forward, and my knees give out. Declan's arm is the only thing stopping me from falling to the floor in a puddle of goo.

"Open the fucking door, Cara."

It takes more effort than I'm proud of to slap my hand on the doorknob. It takes even more effort to turn it. Then his arm tightens, and I'm lifted off my feet. We're spinning, and my back is suddenly pressed against the door, our fronts pressed together.

Declan presses his forehead against mine. We're both panting. I'm on the verge of coming from that bite, and I can't wrap my head around that Declan. Biting Declan.

"We need to have that conversation, Cara. I'm clean. I haven't been with anyone in a long time. And I've been carrying condoms in my wallet since that motel."

"Ah...clean. I'm on the pill, but..." Aside from the logistics of bare, which I've only heard about and not personally had to deal with, I'm not sure I'm ready for that...yet.

"Condom. Got it. Anything else I need to know?"

"I don't know. Just touch me, for fuck's sake."

"You have to tell me if you don't—"

"Declan, if your hand isn't in my panties in the next five seconds, I'm going to—"

I suck back a breath, my entire focus narrowing to his hands. Those big, capable hands, diving under my skirt, yanking down my tights. He drops to his knees, letting out an impatient grunt as they get stuck on my shoes. He pulls off my stilettos and then the tights, lifting up each foot, giving it a quick squeeze. He shoves my leather skirt up around my waist.

Then he's pushing his way between my legs and threading his arm through until my knee is resting on his shoulder, and I'm open to him. All I can do is feel. And moan. Ok, there's some yanking on his head too.

I've never felt anything like this. Like him. Never before has someone listened like this. Or read my cues and found exactly the right way to drive me higher. The brush of his beard, the softness of his lips, and the gentle sting of his teeth on my clit make me fall apart too quickly. I'm falling before I get a chance to savor him. Savor this.

I shudder and moan through my orgasm, afraid my body will just fly apart. My hands fly out to hold on to something, maybe the doorframe, but Declan surges up, and I cling to him. He holds me so tightly, yet so carefully, as I ride out the waves, murmuring encouragement and praise against my ear. I can't make out the words, too lost in sensation, but as I slowly come down, they start to penetrate.

"So beautiful." A kiss on my ear. "Ride it, baby." Hands stroking up and down my spine. "You taste so good. I want more." That one sends an aftershock through me that makes me moan and lean on him harder.

I want to tell him how amazing he is. How amazing that was. How I've never felt anything like this. How good he just made me feel. What comes out is, "Yeah...good. Woah."

His body shakes with his laughter. I can't even be mad. I don't think I can ever be mad at him again. He's a sex god, for sure. Thank god I didn't know this about him before. My obsession with him would have cranked up to stalker level. I almost don't know how to be this woman. This falling apart, sexually satisfied version of me is brand new.

I loosen my grip on his shoulders and trail my hands over the firm muscles of his back, and down into the ass of his jeans. Thank fuck the waistband is loose. They're skintight at his thick thighs, but there's just enough room for me to caress his ass. His groan settles me. I may be totally lost in him, but he's lost in me, too. We're together in this, and that makes everything ok.

Finally, feeling my feet underneath me, I step into him, driving him back to the couch. He's nipping and biting at my neck, my chest. He tilts my head so he can take my mouth in a toe-curling kiss. My office is long and narrow, and the couch is at the back of the room. We bounce off the desk as we pass it, then, finally, I have him right where I want him. I reluctantly pull my hands out of his jeans and shove him down. He goes willingly, dragging me with him.

I wanted to take control. To be in charge. But that's not happening. But it's strangely wonderful because he's not in charge, either. We're both driven by desire, by feeling. And maybe, tonight, there's no place for power dynamics.

Our hands clash at his waistband, both of us eager to get his pants open. Laughing into our kiss, I brush his hands away gently and take over. Unbuttoning him and sliding down the zipper oh so carefully, fingers between it and the fabric of his underwear, echoing all the times he did up the zipper of the hoodie I was wearing. It was hot when he did it. It's hot getting the chance to do it to him. And judging by his hissed 'fuck', he thinks so too.

The first time with a man is always strange. You never know what you're going to get, and I learned early on that I need to school my reaction. Some of the biggest guys are packing the smallest pistols and indicating that it's anything other than amazing when I have it in my hand is a guaranteed limp dick and an end to the fun. Because that's what it was. In high school, it was fun. It felt good, and I felt a bit like a rebel, sneaking out to have sex. As an adult, it was still fun, but it was mainly to scratch an itch.

Sex with Declan is already washing away the faces of the men in my past. None of it ever felt this big, this intense. It was always two separate bodies coming together. I don't feel separate right now. The connection between the two of us is palpable.

I felt him against me that night in Vegas, and when I get him in my hand, I don't need to pretend or flatter. He doesn't need it. He's packing plenty to work with, thank god. I rub my thumb over his tip, spreading his pre-cum.

His hand covers mine. "I'm on the fucking verge here. Don't play with me."

So maybe he does think he's in charge. "Playing is my favorite part. Don't ruin it for me," I murmur. Thanks to the soft glow of the lamp on my desk, I can see the lines of strain on his face. The tightness of his jaw and the desire in his eyes. I want to break him a little bit, just like he broke me.

Sliding off his lap, I drop to my knees and pull him into my mouth, drawing him in and out to the rhythm of the pumping bass in the club, muffled back here but still strong. His shout isn't quiet. I want to hear it again. I want more of his hands digging frantically through my hair.

I've just hit my stride, driving him wild, when with a snarl, he pulls me back and up into his lap. I'm panting, about to complain, when his fingers spear into me. His satisfied murmur when he finds me soaked makes my breath hitch.

He pulls away, holding me with one arm as he grabs his wallet, pulls out a condom, then chucks his wallet at the wall like a major league pitcher. I lean my head back, laughing, as he fumbles between us.

My laughter cuts off with a moan when he lines us up and presses in. It's been a while, and I'm tight, but the man is a sweet talker, whispering in my ear to let him in, and before I know it, I do. I give an experimental wiggle, and Declan's arms clamp around me.

"Wait. Just wait," he breathes."I've never felt anything as good as you." I tighten my hands around his neck because that's the best thing anyone has ever said to me, and just breathe with him. It's not weird or awkward. We just...look at each other, connected. It's the closest I've ever felt to anyone. Then his eyes darken and his voice lowers in a way that arcs fire to my core. "You played. Now it's my turn."

He thinks he can boss me around in my own club? I give another wiggle just to fuck with him. The stinging slap on my ass makes me clench, and we both moan.

"I want your shirt off. Now. Show me those pretty breasts."

Ok, he can be the boss.

I shimmy out of my tight lace top. His hands are there, unsnapping my bra, and then his mouth is on me. It's so good. He can do whatever he wants with me as long as he keeps making me feel this good.

We're heaving breaths and frantic hips. My body's wetness makes sounds that would be embarrassing if we weren't both frantic. We're sweating, sliding, and all I can think about is chasing the next wave. When it crashes over me, I let it take me, falling limply against Declan. Unable to hold my position.

He stops for just a second, separating us, then I'm on my back, legs splayed as he pushes back in. His thrusts are making the waves come harder, faster. I throw my hands back, clutching the arm of the couch above my head, and hang on for the ride. Then he's shuddering, groaning, pressing me down, grinding into me in the perfect spot to light me up again.

When I finally catch my breath. When I can see again, I realize I'm fucked. It's official. There has never, in the history of the planet, been sex this good. Never.

"I hope you know," I mumble, staring at the ceiling as he presses soft kisses on my chest, "that you're never getting rid of me now. I'll expect you to service me daily, twice a day on the weekends. Minimum. You're my boy toy now."

"Oh. My," he says dryly. "How ever will I survive?"

I want this forever. The laughter. The teasing. The man who looks at me like I'm the whole world. We haven't said it yet. But it's there, between us. It's early. We've come together in weeks. But it's also been three years in the making.

This is love.

But we have time. There's no panic to say the words. Not yet.

I believe it. All weekend. In his bed. In mine. On the floor and in the kitchen. I believe it.

I believe it when we walk into work on Monday morning holding hands. I believe it when we laugh over Colton getting locked out of the building.

But when the cops show up for me with handcuffs at lunch, I realize I was a fool.

39

CARA

He's been sneaking kisses all morning like he can't get enough of me. Leaving his office, casually walking down the hall towards me, then ducking in to kiss me senseless. Ransom's caught him twice, just rolling his eyes and walking the other way. We've officially been outed to most of the brothers, and none of them have made a big deal out of it.

After the weekend we just spent together, I need that connection too. Going from being within a couple of feet of each other all weekend—most of that time naked and pressed up against each other— to this distance is dumb. I want more of him, always.

I'm still laughing, sliding my feet into my shoes to go grab some lunch, when I hear the whispers. Always ready for good gossip, I pop out of my chair to see what's going on. It's stupid, I know, but never in a million years would I have guessed I'd see the group of five police officers led by that fucking D.A. walking toward me. I vaguely register Ransom's large presence next to me, but I can't take my eyes off the uniformed men.

His hand spreads on my back. "They have a fucking warrant. We had to let them up. It's complete bullshit Cara, and I will not let this stand."

The smarmy D.A.'s eyes bounce between us, looking gleeful. A good person would look subdued when they're about to destroy someone's life, but not him. But the boys already told me he's not a good guy. So did my gut every time I talked to him.

The group stops in the hallway, blocking Ransom and me in my office.

"I warned you this was coming, Cara." The D.A. says with a sneer. The way he says my name sends panic down my spine. The filth coating his words makes that tiny spot of dread that's been living in my stomach for more than a month grow like one of those foam toys in the capsules, the ones that you put in water and you get a sea creature in a couple of hours. "You're hereby under arrest for manslaughter."

He steps aside, and two officers move in, one focused on Ransom. The other comes to me and pulls out his cuffs. Ransom's growl makes them both freeze. "Are you fucking kidding me, Jackson? She killed the man who was trying to kill her sister and nearly killed her. You're taking this grudge too fucking far."

The cop closest to me studies Ransom and the D.A. His mouth tightens, and he turns to me almost apologetically. Ransom and Jackson are shouting, and it's all a blur. All I can focus on is the feel of the metal on my wrists, the calluses on the cop's hands as he secures the cuffs in front of me, and the firm grip he takes on my elbow as he guides me down the hallway. I walk numbly, nothing penetrating the dread until we approach Declan's office. Nick and Colton are there, physically holding him back as we pass. All three of their faces are hard, eyes burning with rage, but I can't focus on anyone but him.

I have a brief moment of hope that what he told me back

in Colorado is true and that he's going to be able to get me out of this. But the moment is brief. I'm in handcuffs, surrounded by police, and this isn't a fairytale. As much as they might want to, I don't think the brothers are gonna be able to get me out of this. And it really fucking sucks.

I feel my tears fall, and I reach up awkwardly to brush them away with my cuffed hands. It's ridiculous, these cops have seen worse, but I don't want them to know how scared I am. How close I am to falling apart.

I try to hold my head up, but I can't look at anyone as I pass by. The people I've worked with for years are watching me get marched out of here. It's only when I see Janey in the lobby that I crack just the tiniest bit. She comes straight for me, completely ignoring the wall of cops. They aren't immune to her warmth, and with a few words, she's in front of me, folding me into her arms. I lean down and drop my head on her shoulder, letting a few more tears fall.

"Stay strong, Cara. We're all here for you. We'll be right behind you." She's petting my hair, sliding it behind my ear and it's so comforting, in a moment that's got me scared shitless.

"A word with my client, please." Maverick pushes in next to us and wraps us both in his arms. He presses his lips next to my ear. "I called Marty. He's already heading down to the station. We're going to get you in front of a judge this afternoon. We're going to take care of this, I promise you."

I lift my head to take a good look at him. He looks wrecked. Like this is all his fault. "Okay. I'll be okay." I reassure him. Maybe I'm reassuring myself, too. I have to be okay. This has to be fixable.

Sitting in the back of the police car on the way to the station, I have a moment to wonder how the hell I got here. I mean, I know what I did. I know that Bree would be dead if I hadn't come home in time. I know in my heart that I was just trying to survive. I don't deserve to go to prison for protecting myself and my sister.

For the first time, I wish I'd never taken this job. Yeah, there are a lot of perks to working for the brothers. My life has been changed, but it's all put me in the back of the police car. This is because of them, because of something in their past. I'm just the pawn in all of this, and I'm powerless to do anything about it.

It doesn't matter what I actually did. Jackson is going to destroy me to hurt them. He believes that they care enough about me to be hurt by this.

He might be right.

They love me, and they're going to flip this town upside down to try and fix it.

Holding so much anger and gratitude, and fear in my body at once is exhausting. I'm checked out by the time I get to the police station. Cold and calm through the fingerprints and the mug shots. I'm even okay in the holding cell, though wishing I'd worn a lot more layers. It's fucking freezing in here.

But when they take me across to the courthouse, and the judge says those words, 'bail is set at ten million,' I thaw slightly. I don't have a chance of coming up with that, but before I can even worry about that, Marty's cool voice rings out.

"We're prepared to post bond immediately."

The judge scowls at that, which seems weird to me. Aren't they supposed to be impartial? Why does he look so mad? I don't have time to ponder it as I'm herded out the door, in cuffs again. Glancing back, I meet Declan's warm eyes, soaking in their comfort before he's gone from my sight. They came. They didn't leave me. I hoped they wouldn't, and I believed they wouldn't, but a tiny niggling voice in the back of my mind wouldn't let me rest easy in my faith. I've learned the hard way that sometimes, despite people's best intentions, they can disappoint you.

I don't have the capacity to sift through my overloaded emotions right now. All I can do is take one step, then the next, hoping that at the end of the road is freedom.

40

DECLAN

"None of this is fucking right," Maverick mutters. We're all huddled in the parking lot of the courthouse, waiting for Marty to finish up. Posting bail should be easy. Ransom's had our bankers on alert since the cops showed, ready to courier over a certified check. No way will we let her spend even a night in jail. Just the idea of her locked up at all has my heart racing. I can't imagine how scared she must be.

Ransom grabs the back of his neck with both hands. "We knew Jackson was gunning for us. But I didn't think it would actually come to this. Why the fuck would he do this? No jury will ever convict her, so why? And what the fuck was up with that judge?"

I've been wondering about that too. For the crime she was charged with, for her resources, the bail he set was ridiculously high. There's a fuck of a lot more going on here than we realize. For the first time in the hours since those cops took her from me, my brain is firing the way it normally does, and I don't like the picture that's starting to form. "He's fucking in on it."

My brothers all look at me grimly. They're feeling it too. This is all fucking wrong. Burning in me is the need to unravel this, to take it apart, to expose it to the light.

"We need more information," Ransom says, nodding at me. I take it for what it is, a directive to start digging. Not that I need the nudge. My files on Jackson are pretty fucking complete, but this judge is a new player. Maybe now I'll be able to find a few more threads to tug. Usually, when this feeling comes over me, I chase it to its end. Nothing's fucking safe from me. But all I want right now is to stand here and wait for Cara. I need my hands on her. I need her safe with me.

"I can't leave her."

"I fucking knew it," Colt mutters, eyeing me. I don't even care. We've been fucking with him all week, and it's been fun because Cara was having fun. Without her, I don't care about any of it.

Ransom's heavy hand lands on my neck. "I know, brother. But we need to figure out what the fuck is going on. And you're the man for that job. I will stand right fucking here until Marty brings her out. I won't leave her alone for a second. Colt will stick with me. I promise we've got her."

"But she needs to know that I..." Love her. Want to be here for her. Am thinking only of her.

"I'll make sure she knows why you're not here. I got her. Go help her the way only *you* can. Find the dirt on these fuckers fast."

My brothers all have their game faces on. They know we're in for a fight, and they're all ready to pitch in. But Ransom's right. I am the only one who can find what we need now. "Fine. But I want a call the second she's out. I need to talk to her."

"I'll call you, brother," Colton vows.

Nodding, I turn to Jonas. "I'm going to need you. If the

302 | JENNA MYLES

fucking judge is in on it, then this goes way beyond a grudge. I've got to follow the money." Jonas nods, already heading to his van. I pin Colton with a look. "Take care of her. Don't upset her. And call me the second she's out of there. I need to hear her voice."

He pounds his fist on his chest, eyes fierce. "I fucking promise."

Satisfied, I turn and jog after Jonas, my mind already sifting through probabilities.

TWO HOURS LATER, WHEN MY PHONE RINGS, I DIVE FOR IT. I'VE been focused, but not like I usually am. On a regular day, digging for dirt like this would make the entire world disappear. I've spent entire days in a research fog, forgetting to eat or sleep until I find what I'm looking for. Since Tyler, I've spent many nights like that, looking for dirt that would help Cara. But it wasn't enough. But today, knowing how scared she has to be, I can't focus. I need to know she's okay.

"Hello," I yell into the phone.

"Declan," Cara says. I fucking wilt, collapsing back into my chair.

"Cara. Baby. Fuck, tell me you're okay. Where are you?"

Her voice is thin. I can almost taste the salt of the tears she's trying to hide. "We're in the car. We're heading home. Are you there?"

"Yeah, baby, I'm here. Jonas and I are working to figure out this mess. I fucking swear I will fix this for you."

"Okay," she murmurs. She sounds like she doesn't believe me. And why the fuck should she? I told her I would take care of it, and I didn't.

"Cara, come to me, okay? When you get home, come up here."

Her hesitation fucking kills me. "I—I need Bree right now." I bite back my words. I won't beg her to come to me. I can't force her to need me. To want me. Of course, she wants her sister. But I really want to be there for her.

My mouth is so dry. "Later?"

"Later," she agrees quietly. "Goodbye."

She's gone, and I can't help worrying that she's pulling away from me. She's been through some shit today, so it's not all about me, but I fucking failed her. She has to feel that. She has to remember what I promised.

"Is she okay?" Jonas asks. We're camped out in my home office, papers spread everywhere.

"No. I don't think she is. She sounds...lost."

"She's going through something very difficult."

"I know. I just wish I could help."

He pushes up his glasses. "Should I ask Janey to come? She and Cara seem to be good friends."

If I can't be there for her, then someone needs to be. Bree is her sister, but she's still recovering from everything that happened. She's too close to this, too emotional. "Yeah. Call Janey."

Jonas makes the call while I stare blankly at the wall of monitors in front of me, feeling like the most important person in my world is slipping through my fingers.

"HOLY FUCK," I MUTTER, STARING AT THE MESS AROUND US. At the layers of corruption we've uncovered. "Holy fuck."

Jonas pulls his glasses off, rubbing at his tired eyes. "Exactly. We need to call everyone."

"Yeah, we do." I send a quick message to the family chat, then drop my phone on my desk. "What time is it?" My stomach is a gnawing pit of hunger. I push up, groaning at the pop and pull of my muscles.

"Nine," Jonas says with a yawn, standing and stretching too. We've been at this for seven hours. And it paid off.

Battling between twin urges to run down to Cara's apartment or stuffing my face, I beeline for the kitchen, freezing in my tracks as I take in the wrapped plates on the counter. I don't stop to question my luck. I grab forks, pass one to Jonas with a grunt, and still standing, barely chewing, we inhale the food. When the edge of our hunger has been dulled, when our plates are clean, I lean back against the counter with a sigh.

"Are you and Cara...okay?" Jonas asks.

"I don't know. This weekend was so good and now everything's fallen apart. I should have caught this sooner."

Jonas looks at me like he's trying to pull the top of my head off and peek inside. "The judge was the missing piece. Without that information, we wouldn't have unraveled everything. I don't see how you could have caught it sooner unless you'd investigated every judge in the city. That seems like a waste of time and resources."

"You're right."

"I know," he says simply, jumping up to sit on the counter. "Do you think Cara is mad at you? Because she was arrested?"

"Yeah, I do. I told her back in Colorado that I was going to fix this. And I fucking failed. She never should have been put in this position in the first place."

"Perhaps not. But wishing things were different won't change anything."

Sometimes, Jonas's straight talk is a little much to take. Especially when he's right. Which he often is. "Do you ever just feel like you don't fit? Like you haven't figured shit out yet?"

His hands move to grip the edge of the counter, knuckles whitening. He drops his eyes to the floor. "Yes. A lot lately."

"What do you do when you feel that way?"

"Shift my attention to things I know I'm good at. Feeling unsure is...uncomfortable."

"It sure as fuck is." I lift myself onto the counter opposite him and stare out the floor-to-ceiling windows at the moonlit night. "Computers and hacking are the only things that make me feel capable. I've been trying to be more...grown up for a while. I think I've changed, outside at least. But I don't feel that different. I still feel like the useless little brother."

Jonas raises his head with a frown. "I don't understand why you would say that."

"Come on. You have to see it. I am not like the rest of you. You're all so confident. You seem to know exactly what your place in the world is. And I'm the fucking kid playing video games."

"That's one of the stupidest things I've ever heard you say. And I once listened to you and Colton argue over whether Mario or Luigi was the better plumber."

I'm still right on that. Luigi's height gives him more torque. "Good thing you didn't try for a career as a therapist. You're not supposed to tell people in crisis that they're stupid."

"You're not in crisis. You just aren't looking at things correctly."

"Oh yeah? And what's the right way?"

His gaze is piercing and too knowing. "We're an organism. A living, breathing system. Just like a body can't function without a liver, or a heart, or kidneys, we can't function without each other. Together, our parts make up a whole. If you weren't you, then none of this would exist."

That may be one of the best things anyone's ever said to me. I let myself sit with it for a minute. Rolling it around, testing its edges. Wondering if it's true. "But the guys rag on me for playing video games."

He shrugs. "So? They also play with you sometimes. And you tease me about my puzzles all the time. But sometimes you sit and put them together with me. I'm not sure we would function as a unit without annoying each other."

Chuckling, I drop my head back. "You're probably right."

He still looks so...not him. "Jonas, what makes you feel like you don't fit?"

His mouth firms into a line, and he pushes his glasses up his nose. If I were to ask some of my other brothers this same question, they'd brush me off or make something up. Not Jonas. If he didn't want to answer, he'd just tell me. The fact that he's talking tells me how much it's been bothering him. "Recently, I have discovered a...fascination with a woman. I'm finding it difficult to see a clear path forward."

"With Janey?" He's been more than obvious in his fixation on her. To an outsider, it probably just looks like he's being friendly, but for Jonas, it is the equivalent of dropping his pants and saying, 'come and get me'. He has never shown interest in another woman. I mean, he asked her to call him by his first name. I wouldn't be surprised if he bought a ring already.

His eyes shutter. "Yes."

"And you don't see a clear path forward because?" Any woman to end up with Jonas would be damn lucky. And Janey is amazing.

The door opening saves him from answering. It's time.

An hour later, the plan is in place, and I'm closing the door behind Jonas and Janey. I turn, leaning against it, eyeing Cara at the windows. She's standing, arms crossed tightly over her chest, looking out over the lake. Her face is shadowed, but the ravages of the day are stamped on her features. She looks like she's one second from a full meltdown. And I don't know how to make it better.

But I do know something I have to do.

Moving to her, I stop behind her, raising a hand before dropping it again. We study each other in the reflection of the glass, this moment feeling too precarious to face each other.

I clear my throat nervously. "I am so fucking sorry. I told you I would make this go away, and I didn't."

"I know," she says, voice low and thready.

"Do you hate me now?" Have I ruined everything? Please, let her give me a second chance.

"I don't know."

41

CARA

"I don't know," I murmur truthfully.

I can see my words strike him like an arrow. And I wish I could call them back at the same time satisfaction roars through me. Finally, I'm not the only one hurt by all of this.

I'm not being fair. Declan isn't a wizard in one of those games he plays. He can't just wave a wand and make all of this go away. But I'm still mad.

"What can I do?"

I have to laugh. "What can you do? Aside from turning that Delorian into a time machine and going back to that night?"

"I wish more than anything I could go make and stop Tyler from hurting you."

"Not that night. The other night. The night Colt's brother killed that man's cousin and set all of this in motion. The night a bunch of kids made a mistake that I'm now paying for." Clenching my shaking hands into fists, I turn to him. "I killed someone in order to save myself and Bree. But it gave this guy an opening. Now my entire life is being toyed with because he hates you guys. And I'm so fucking angry about it."

He flinches, rocking back on his heels. "I don't blame you. All of this is out of your control. But this plan will work. We'll go in there and make sure they never come after you again."

"Sure. It'll all work out perfectly. Why wouldn't it?" I'm verging on hysteria, and I don't care. "Oh, right, because you're talking about blackmailing a Judge and the D.A. into dropping the charges against me. What could possibly go wrong?"

He reaches for me, brushing his hand down my arm, then dropping it. I don't know if I want him to hold my hand, to hold me, or if I want him to leave me the fuck alone.

Ok, I do know. Alone is horrible. Alone means too much time with my thoughts, worrying about what will be left of my life after I get out of prison because my brain has gone all the way there, straight to being convicted and locked up.

"Blackmail's an ugly word. We're just showing them we know all about their fucking shady dealings and encouraging them to make the smart choice."

"Right. Blackmail. Pretty it up all you want, but this plan could land you in prison, too."

His words are low, firm. "No chance. These guys don't want this shit out there. They'll cave. It's a game of chicken, and Ransom never backs down first. He's got this."

"Maybe. There's a lot that could go wrong." It could go so, so wrong. And leave me destroyed. I don't care what anyone thinks. Being men and being really rich is almost like being a superhero in this world. They can get away with almost anything.

But not me. I'm no one in the grand scheme of things.

"Nothing will go wrong. I'll be there. I have all the information. It's fucking airtight."

On the list of the worst days of my life, this one's just cracked the top five. It's fucking bad. Not parents dying bad.

Not Tyler attacking Bree bad. But bad. And I'm so tired of holding myself together.

Declan's hand is threading through my hair, and he's pulling me to him. I resist, for a nanosecond, then collapse into him. Letting him hold me. Letting him tell me it's all going to be alright. And I try to let myself believe it. But I can't stop the tears or the sobs that follow them. And just like that morning in the motel room, he's steady, cradling me, soothing me. Being exactly what I need, despite my pain and misplaced anger. This isn't his fault. I know that. Doesn't make me any less angry, though.

He walks me through his apartment, the place I left this morning, and I feel like I've aged a decade since then. Sitting me on the edge of his bed, he pulls off my ridiculous, fluffy kitty slippers, then tucks me into his cool sheets. He pauses only long enough to strip down to his boxer briefs, then he follows me in, pulling me tightly into his arms.

"I've got you. For right now, I've got you. Nothing can get to you in this building. Nothing."

I snort out a surprised laugh. "Except all your brothers, their women, and my sister."

I can hear the smile in his voice. "Right. Except them."

Burrowing closer, tucking my head into the crook of his neck, I share the boogeymen living in my heart. "I don't want to leave Bree. She's lost so much. She needs me with her. And I don't want to lose the club. I've worked so hard to build it. And if I go to jail, it'll fall apart. And I look horrible in orange. Do all prisoners wear orange? Do you get to pick what color jumpsuit you wear when you get there? That would be better. And you better send me really good shampoo. I can't handle that sulfate crap." I sniff pathetically. I wouldn't blame him for laughing, teasing me, or telling me I'm being ridiculous.

He does none of those things. Instead, he kisses my head and murmurs, "Tell me more. Tell me everything that's scaring you."

So I do. I tell him every scary thing that's crossed my mind in the last month. Every random thought, every nightmare, every silly wondering. Pretty sure I tell him I'm afraid I'll have to eat beans in prison. I hate beans, the canned disgusting mushy ones, and somehow the idea of having to eat them in prison is more upsetting than the rest of it. How dumb is that? And he listens like the rest of the world doesn't exist. He doesn't try to tell me I'm dumb. Or that my fears are stupid. He just holds me.

When I wind down, exhausted by my fears, I gaze sightlessly out the window at the black night sky. There's only a hint of the moon peeking out from between the heavy, drifting clouds. "What if this plan fails? What if I still end up going to jail?"

Declan tilts his chin down, meeting my eyes. "Won't happen."

"You can't know that."

"Yeah, I can. It won't fucking happen. If something goes wrong, then we'll handle it. If you end up being prosecuted, then you can be damn sure no jury would ever convict you. Besides..."

"What?"

"If worse comes to worst, I will have you out of here so fucking fast. You and Bree, wherever in the world you want to go, whatever you want to do, I got you. We could go anywhere, as long as there's not an extradition treaty. That still leaves us with a lot of options. There's a big world out there to see, Cara."

I can't decide if that's the sweetest offer I've ever heard or the most terrifying. "You said 'we.' You...you'd go with us?"

His arms tighten around me, his chest moving with his deep inhale. "I can't imagine being here without you anymore. Seeing you has been the best part of my day for years. Years, Cara. Now that you've let me hold you...I'm done for."

I stare out the window as his words fill up the rest of the space in my chest. The elation they bring competes for space with the fear and anxiousness that overwhelmed me today. I want to tell him I feel the same way. That I have for a long time. That the last couple of weeks have been the best. But I can't. Not yet. My life is a runaway freight train, and I need off this ride.

I press a reverent kiss to his chest, but I can't hold his gaze. His eyes shutter. I've hurt him, not saying the words back. I see it. But he's so good, he just pushes it aside. Like it doesn't matter. Like his, feelings don't matter.

His grin is sad. "I always knew you were out of my league," he mutters. Something in his tone bothers me. I sit up so I can get a better look at his face.

"What do you mean? You think I'm too good for you?" I ask in disbelief.

He sits up and leans against the padded headboard of his King bed. "Exactly that. You are totally self-made, Cara. You have a drive in you that I can't even begin to understand."

"But you guys built all this," I say, waving my hand at the massive room in the massive high-rise they built. "That doesn't make any sense."

He raises a knee, draping his arm on it. He's so beautiful, hair mussed, his strength on full display. "I've always felt like," he frowns, his hand curling into a fist, "like I wasn't as important to our success as my brothers were." An instinctive denial leaps to my lips, but he shakes his head, silencing me. "I don't need you to convince me I'm wrong. I talked to Jonas about it a bit. He said we're all a part of this and that without all of us, we wouldn't be here, and that makes sense. It does. But it took nine of us to do this, Cara. And you did it alone."

"But I didn't do it alone. Colt invested--"

"You would have found other investors."

"Probably. But I still needed investors. I had friends help me at the beginning with discounts on liquor and free labor.

Bree worked the bar when she wasn't at her day job. She didn't cash any of her paychecks for the first year. I took on a lot of responsibility, yes, but I had lots of help too. You guys had each other. Is needing help to build something a bad thing?"

His lips twist. "No, I guess it isn't. I hadn't really thought about it like that. I think I just feel like a loser sometimes, sitting in the background behind my computers, like I did today. I really wanted to wait for you at that courthouse. It was all I wanted. But—"

"But you had to do what you do. I understand. I really do. Did I wish you were there? Yeah. But Ransom explained it." This man. "I was obsessed with you for years. And most of that time, I figured I wasn't good enough for you."

His eyes bulge comically. "What? Why the fuck would you ever think that? Was it the money?"

"No, actually. It was you. You seemed so shy most of the time." Am I really going to tell him this? "I dated a lot, Dec. A lot. Men love me, and they're fun. And the ones I hung around with tended to be...easy. They were simple guys, happy to party, and not too challenging. I felt...in charge, maybe? Then you came along." I didn't know what I expected on his face. I hoped I wouldn't see judgment or jealousy, but the grin on his lips surprises me. "You're smiling," I say dumbly.

"None of this is news, Cara. The first time you cornered me at work, I knew you were hell on wheels. You were so fucking confident. And beautiful."

"I felt like that at first. But I think some of my confidence wore away when I realized you weren't going to take me up on my offer. Men don't turn me down, Dec. Ever. The self-doubts started creeping in. I felt...less and less like me."

His smile falls. "I never meant—"

"I know. I do. You have no responsibility for any of that. That's not why I'm bringing it up. I just wanted you to understand that it's not an either-or thing. It's not like you have confidence or you don't. I can feel like I have the world in the palm of my hand in one area of my life, while another might be a dumpster fire. I think a lot of people are like that. I know for a fact Ransom's confidence in business does not extend to you guys. He worries about you all constantly. Everyone has their own shit to handle."

"How'd you get so smart?"

"By being stupid for a long time."

"Cara...I'm done being stupid. I will be the man you need. I will prove it to you."

I reach out, running my thumb over his lower lip. "I love you just the way you are. You don't need to prove anything to me."

Woah. I just let that shit fly. So much for not being ready.

42

DECLAN

I'm hallucinating. No way she just said those words to me. She's staring at me expectantly. There are so many things I want to say. I want to jump around the room and yell it from the rooftops. Instead, I ask the dumbest question a man has ever asked a woman.

"Like a friend, you mean?"

Gouging my eyeballs out would be less painful than living in my skin right now. A bead of sweat trickles down the back of my neck. Thank fuck, the room is dark.

She makes a choked sound, but to her credit, she doesn't slap me or call me a dumb fucker. "Ah...is that what we are? Friends? I've never let my friends stick their tongue in my—"

I dive at her, cutting off her words. She's shaking with laughter beneath me, and I bury my head in the lushness of her breasts. "I didn't mean that," I mumble, slightly distracted by her softness. I can feel her warmth through her thin t-shirt. "I'm so fucking in love with you, and I honestly don't remember a time when I haven't been. I'm sorry I keep saying the wrong thing. You just make my brain go numb sometimes."

Her hands thread through my short hair, locking at the

back of my head. "Declan," she breathes, making every single one of my senses leap to life. "Look at me."

I reluctantly raise my head because...boobs. Plus, I'm afraid to say anything else that might ruin this moment. Her face is so soft. I want her to look at me just like that, forever.

"I like the scattered, say-the-wrong-thing version of you. That's the guy I fell for all those years ago. Please don't change."

Smoothing my thumb over her cheekbone, across to her mouth, I thank god or whoever made this woman apply for this job. The day she showed up at work and knocked me out of my chair was the day my entire world got brighter.

"How the hell did a woman like you ever fall for a geek like me?"

"Surprised me too. But you're so deep in me now, I can't remember anyone else."

"Good," I mumble, already sliding back down to those breasts. I want...I need this connection to her right now. Before we face the men gunning for our destruction. And judging by her moan so does she.

While she's on her side, I drag her loose pants down her legs, brushing kisses as I go, then, unable to resist, pull her panties aside and spear two fingers into her. Her wetness and warmth surrounding me is the best fucking drug in the world. Pressing my thumb against her clit, I find that textured part of her with my fingers and rub over it.

She bucks. "Jesus, Dec. Again."

"So bossy," I mutter against her stomach. But I love her shouts, her moans, her threats of bodily harm if I don't make her come. She's as fiery in bed as she is in the rest of the world. It's only when I've pushed her over the edge that I get soft Cara. She makes me work for it, as she should.

The way she's riding my fingers as she clutches my head ratchets my desire up to a million. Pulling my fingers out, I push her onto her back. I rise over her and suck on my fingers. "You taste so fucking good." I'm fucking torn. I want more of her down my throat, but I'm desperate to get her wrapped around my cock. Her gasped, 'fuck me,' is the tiebreaker.

When I slide home, we both suck in a breath. I plant a fist next to her head, the electric currents running between us making me dizzy in a way that nothing else ever has. I dip my mouth down to hers, sipping from her as I give her all of me.

"I thought pushing myself to the edge on a racetrack, testing my limits, was the most thrilling thing there is." Her collarbones need some of my attention. I trace the line of them with my tongue, loving the salt of her skin. "I was so...so wrong. Because being with you, Cara, it's better than anything I've ever felt."

She wraps her arms and legs around my back, pulling me down to her. Being pressed against her sends tingles down to the tips of my toes. But I have to move. I'm powerless not to. I manage a kind of awkward scoot.

"Jesus, Fuck. Do that again," Cara orders, yanking her mouth away from me and biting into the cord of my neck. I oblige, pushing against her over and over. Breathing labored, she pants, "yes, yes," against my skin, over and over.

My rhythm isn't perfect, but apparently, it doesn't matter. She falls over the edge with a yell, squeezing around me like a vise, setting me off like a rocket.

My ears are buzzing, light flashing behind my eyes. My hips can't stop thrusting. That's when the extra wetness registers. My fucking stomach drops through the bed to the ground some thirty stories below.

"I didn't use a condom," I admit, freezing. I've never not worn one. Ransom drilled safe sex into us before I even realized what my dick was for. His detailed explanations of diseases successfully freaked me the fuck out. But now, with this woman I love in my arms, I lost my head.

Cara, still panting in my arms, flops a hand against my back. "S'ok," she mumbles.

I let her lack of concern calm me down. Carefully, I pull out of her warmth, watching her closely. She smiles up at me. "It's really ok...except," she says with a frown, "I can feel it leaking out." She slaps at my shoulders, "Move, move."

I shift off her, grinning, quickly wiping my smile off my face when she glares at me. She slides off the bed and hobbles to the bathroom, legs pressed tightly together, and I lose it, letting my laughter roll.

"Careful big boy," she yells from behind the door, "you tease me about this, you won't get in me bare again."

Panicked, laughter dying, I leap off the bed to follow her. "Hey baby, why don't I run you a bath?"

I spend the next few hours pampering my women. There's laughter, but beneath it is the understanding that before dawn breaks, we're heading into war.

43

DECLAN

"I don't like this," Colt mutters from the backseat. I don't either, but no way could I get Cara to budge on this. She insisted on being here.

It's only right we do this at Knight Street. It's the place where everything started for us. And we know every inch of this place. We can lock it down.

Cara turns to glare at him. "This is my fucking life, Colt. I am not going to sit by while the men fix this." He growls and crosses his arms over his chest. He's protective as fuck. It used to annoy the shit out of me. But I get where he's coming from now. Cara's mine, and I don't want her anywhere near this either.

"You promise you have this locked down?" I ask him. For the millionth time. To his credit, he doesn't show a hint of impatience at having to answer again.

"Swear. My guys are everywhere and have been since we sent that message."

It's early, but in this area of town, a few of the businesses are waking up. But we've got a few hours yet before things get busy. We have the night to ourselves.

We could have waited, maybe. Done this later tonight. But I want this done for Cara. I want them out of her life for good.

"And the other thing?" I ask him. He glances at Cara, then back at me, and nods. Good. This will be done soon.

We all roll up, all my brothers here to support Cara. Once we're in the office, I pull her to the side. "You're here. I won't fight you on this. We've done everything we can to make this safe, but I need you to stay where I put you." She opens her mouth to argue, and I cover it gently with my hand. "No. I will not risk you getting hurt. You'll be in there with us, but you're going to be safe behind one of the cars. These men have a lot to lose, and that makes them dangerous. Promise me you'll stay hidden. I will not survive you getting hurt. You own too much of me now."

Her face softens and she slides into my arms. "Okay."

I'm terrified she'll expose herself, come out into the open, and be hurt, but I have no option but to trust her. I thought about locking her up somewhere to keep her safe, but taking away her control like that might break us, and I can't fucking do it. I can't risk losing her.

"I won't do anything stupid. I don't want anyone hurt, but I can't stand sitting around and waiting any longer. That's not me. I need..."

"You need some control back."

"Yeah, I do." Her face is white, eyes wide. She's scared, but I see her determination in the set of her shoulders. She's going to see this through, no matter what.

"Tell me again what the plan is."

"They'll arrive. Ransom will lay out some of what we've found and tell them that if they don't drop the bullshit charges against you, everything will be turned over to the police. They agree, walk out of here, and it's done."

"You say it like it's all going to be fine, but so much could go wrong."

"We weren't always on the straight and narrow...fuck, we

aren't now. This is not the first time we've been up against men out to get us. It won't be the last. We've got this."

EVERYTHING IS GOING TO PLAN. THEY SHOW UP, PREDICTABLY puffed up and threatening us, and Ransom is fucking ice. We're all scattered around the room, surrounding the two men, ready for anything. I can feel Cara's eyes on my back like a laser cutting through me. But she stays put.

When it goes off the rails, it's sudden. Jackson, faced with the mountain of evidence Ransom slapped on the hood of an old sedan, goes on the attack. "You fuckers are done. I'm the fucking District Attorney. I will have you all up on charges so fast your balls will shrivel. And all of this," he says, waving at the files, "is a desperate attempt to discredit me. I will spin this so fast, you'll lose everything."

The Judge, mostly silent up to this point, pastes a sneer on his face. "You have no idea who you're fucking with. In the court of public opinion, we will destroy you."

I catch Colton's eye, and he reaches into his pocket with a nod. When he nods again, I step forward. I am done listening to this. Done standing by. My brothers startle when I step forward, all but Colt anyway. "Time's up."

"Ah, Mr. Wilder. Your fingerprints are all over this. This is what you do, after all, dig for dirt? You're nothing better than a scavenger, hunting through garbage for the filth."

"Filth. That's a funny word coming from your mouth. You know all about filth, don't you, Jackson?"

Ransom steps back, eyes flat, to outsiders at least. I can read the *what the fuck are you doing* look on his face. This isn't me. I don't ever do the talking. I mean, *ever*. I've always been content to let my very capable brother handle things.

Not anymore. I shoot Ransom a grin. Time to have some fun. Because for the first time, I know I have this. These fuckers have no idea what's coming. There is even more shit in this guy's background than even my brothers know.

I turn back to the sneering Jackson, my entire body steady and calm. "I mean, the list of your filth is long. So why don't we start with the mistress you've got on the west side? Does Mrs. Jackson know about her? No? How about the three prostitutes you're paying hush money to? I saw their medical records, and you are a sick, sick, boy." His face whitens, but he shakes it off. Doesn't matter. I have so much more.

"So what is your plan exactly?" I ask him, honestly curious. "Frame us for...what? You don't have a fucking bit of evidence tying us to anything. You'd have to grease a fuck lot of palms to get any traction. And for a man as broke as you are? Not gonna happen."

He laughs. He has no idea. God, this is fun. "I have all the resources I need to put you away," he says.

I let my grin loose. "Come now, let's be realistic here. We're billionaires, asshole. Even if you had two-point-three million in a bank account in Panama, it still wouldn't be enough to fuck us over."

I relish the way the white takes over his face, washing away any hint of his earlier bluster. "Two...Two-point-three million?"

"Caught that, did you? Yeah. I know about that account. I know what's in it. Or should I say *was* in it. It's gone." I cleaned the motherfucker out last night. I have plans for that money.

Jackson erupts, lunging for me. Not at all surprising and easy to put down. An elbow to the face, and he's facedown to the hood of the car, bleeding onto the evidence of his sins. I lean down right next to his ear. I want to make sure he feels the rest of this.

"You thought you could destroy an innocent woman's life to make a point. That's bad enough. But you went after my woman. So I'm going to destroy you. That wire you're wearing right now, we've hacked the feed. My brother Colt has a fancy little remote in his pocket, and he's in control of it now. You won't be using it against us. And with everything you've said here, we've got plenty on there to tear you apart. And we will." He chokes at the mention of the wire. I catch Ransom's raised eyebrow, but I want this done. I'm sick of dealing with this man's filth. "So, here's what's going to happen. Judge over there, he's going to walk out that door and go back to his life. But I have crawlers on him." I turn to pin the now shaking Judge with a glare. He's dirty as fuck, and the out he thought he had is gone.

"You vowed to uphold the law, Judge. You broke that vow. You're going to pay for that. From this minute on, I own you. You want your family to stay blind to your corruption? You're going to answer to me. You make any move towards any of us, I'll know it. Probably even before you think it, I am that far up your ass right now. You will find instructions in your office on where to make a sizable donation...you're giving away all that bribe money you took. I'll have more instructions for you soon, trust me. You have any objections, Judge?"

He wraps a shaking hand around the neckline of his thick coat. "No...no." He darts a glance to Jackson, then hurries out the door, followed closely by Nick, who shoots me a wild grin.

My brothers are all staring at me, game faces on, but behind their steely masks, I see their surprise. I shove Jackson's face a little harder into the hood of the car. "You fucked with the wrong family, asshole. You should have let it go."

Soft footsteps approach, Cara's light lemony smell drifting around me. I'm a little pissed she's not staying back, but I'm rational enough to realize shit's under control. And she has a right to face the fucker that's trying to destroy her. Jackson hasn't clued in that she's right here.

"Would you? You fucked with my family. Would you have

let it go?" His voice is muffled against the cold steel of the car, but his vitriol is clear.

"Nope. I respect your motives. I even understand them. If anything ever happened to someone I love, I'd be murderous." I glance back, meeting Cara's shining eyes. "But your execution is all kinds of pathetic. We never would have involved an innocent. The fact that you did tells me everything I need to know about the kind of man you are."

"So what? You're going to own me now?" I gotta give the guy credit. He still manages to sound like a dick, despite the shit sandwich he's eating right now.

"Nah, I don't want anything to do with you. I already told you I'm going to destroy you. But I'm not like you. I won't hurt innocents. So I won't take everything. Your wife and kid will still have a roof over their heads. But you? I'm going to leave you with nothing. Not your reputation, not your job, not your pride. Nothing."

I pull him off the car, spinning him to face Cara. Jackson grimaces, teeth painted red from all the blood. Cara plants her hands on her hips and studies him. Her fingers tap against the leather of her skirt. She's dressed in leather from head to toe, jacket, skirt, and knee-high boots. Fishnet stockings covering her thighs. I'm sure she's fucking freezing, but she doesn't betray a hint of discomfort. She looks powerful and dangerous. And judging by the glint in her eye, she's going to take a piece out of him.

Colt slides up behind her, covering her back, but making no move to stop her when she smiles, steps forward, and with a powerful kick, plants the tip of her pointy-toed boot into Jackson's dick. He collapses with a wheeze. I let him go as he falls hard on the concrete. I wink at my woman, loving her fire. Of course, she kicked him in the balls. Why wouldn't she?

"You're a piece of shit," she says flatly, face calm and composed as she watches him writhe on the floor. "Your family is going to be way better off without you." Then, without another word, she backs up to lean against the door of a bright red mustang. My brain briefly short circuits. Against the backdrop of that sexy car, she's a fucking pinup with her leather, blonde hair, and blood-red lips.

Really done now —the sooner we get this done, the sooner I can get Cara alone— I yank Jackson up and march him to the door, straight outside. His luxury sedan is parked right outside the door, and I shove him into it. "Go now. Drive safe."

He glares at me, blood dripping from his chin onto his white shirt. He's confused, not understanding why I'm letting him go. He'll know soon enough. His eyes are full of hate as he guns the engine. His gaze turns sharp.

I lean in close, still blocking him from closing the door. "Don't even think about it. Any of it. You do it, and your family will be collecting welfare by the end of the week. Then I'll make my way through the rest of them until even your mother is living in a tent underneath the train tracks." Any plans he had of running me or anyone else over die a quick death.

His chin drops nearly to his chest. "What was I supposed to do? He was family."

"He was a gangbanger, out to hurt all of us. What the fuck did you think was going to happen to him? If it wasn't us, it would have been someone else. He was never going to live long. I get revenge, but you should have thought about the family you have now. But don't worry. Cara's right. They'll be better off without you. I'm sure some other man will step in and show your wife what a real husband and father should act like." I slam the door, stepping back as he guns it, backing out of the lot, and screaming down the road.

I listen to the growl of his engine as it fades into the early morning cold. The door opens behind me. A heavy hand lands on my left shoulder as soft, warm fingers rub along my right palm. I curl my hand around Cara's, a relieved breath leaving my chest. We did it.

My brothers fan around me, confusion still written on their faces. "What the fuck just happened?"

I pull Cara closer, tucking her safely under my arm. "I found so much fucking dirt. I just couldn't let him get away with it. I know what the plan was, but I had a backup. And he talked so fucking much, he buried himself."

"So what happens next? You just let him drive away." Maverick asks.

Colt steps forward. "We'll have all the evidence delivered to the cops. And the media. Everyone will learn how dirty he is."

"So it's over?" Cara asks hopefully, eyes shining.

"Yeah, it's over. Without Jackson pushing for prosecution, the case will die. No other prosecutor will touch it. Besides, we've got a Judge in our pocket now."

Ransom smiles but tightens the hand he has on my shoulder. "Next time, you mind cluing us the fuck in? I mean, that was epically awesome, but for fucks sake, warn a brother."

Zach snickers. "When you decide to step up, you do it in a big way. What happened to letting Ransom do the talking?"

Pressing a kiss to Cara's head, I turn and rest my cheek against her hair. "This was my fight."

"Well fuck brother," Nick mutters, "when you get in the game, you do it in a big way. But I gotta know, what did you do with his money?"

"The town we got stranded in. In Colorado. It's dying. They're going to get a cash infusion. Maybe they can build the world's largest spoon or some other tourist trap to bring people off the highway. And the motel owner? She and her husband were incredible people. They deserve a tip. So I'll pay off their mortgage."

Cara tips her head back with a laugh. "That's one hell of a tip!"

Laughing, we wander back into the garage, making our way into the break room to get the coffee going. In the bays, I grab Colt's shoulder, pulling him to a stop. "Jackson's going to end up in the Pen. We need to get Joker out before that happens. Jackson's still fucking pissed, and it's only going to get worse. He doesn't have a lot of pull. In fact, he put a lot of those guys behind bars, but having Joker and him in the same place is a bad idea."

Colt frowns, rubbing his beard. "He doesn't plan to apply for parole. I think he's afraid of getting out. He's been in there nearly half his life."

"We'll pull some strings. He's going to have to adjust. We'll help him, but it's time to push it. We've got the Judge to write a recommendation. Joker just needs to be convinced that it's in his best interest to get out."

He nods grimly, already anticipating Joker's reaction. He's changed since he went away, but I don't think he's changed that much. He's going to be royally pissed at us interfering in his life. But it has to happen. It's time. Eighteen years is long enough.

Cara's laughing with my brothers in the break room, clutching a cup of coffee like it's the only thing keeping her together. Her eyes are warm, and a smile curves that lush mouth. I can't fucking help it. I stride to her, put her coffee mug in Zach's hand, and draw her into me for a kiss. It's a kiss full of relief, love, and passion.

"Declan and Cara, kissing in a tr—." Muffled curses, banging, and a few groans sound behind us. I don't pay a second of attention. Colton can handle himself, and I have better things to do.

44

CARA

I shouldn't laugh. It's not funny, really, but I've never seen him like this, and I can't look away.

Zach's teeth are gritted as he holds up a pair of flat women's shoes. "Where is she?" I shrug because I honestly have no idea. Maya's been working here a week, and if I've learned anything, it's that the woman is impossible to predict. "How does she do this? Just wander around and lose her shoes? It's completely unprofessional."

"You say this every day. You told her there was no dress code, remember? You told her there was no dress code, remember? She even cleared it with Janey."

"Don't get me started on her wardrobe," he mutters with an eye roll. He shifts the plain black loafers into one hand, running the fingers of the other through his hair. He's frazzled, his shirt unbuttoned at the collar, his tie hanging loose. It's a hot look, not that he's ever not hot. But he's been way too busy fixating on Maya to obsess over his looks lately. It's like watching a slow-motion car crash. One day, maybe one day soon, she's going to knock him on his ass. He doesn't know what's coming.

"There's nothing wrong with her wardrobe."

"No, not if you're fine with shopping at Frumps 'R Us."

"Zach, you're a complete snob." Yes, her style is quirky, but it's so totally her.

"Cara, I simply have standards. Standards that she is not meeting."

"Oh, I see. So she's not performing? She's actually awful at marketing?"

He scowls at me. "She's amazing. Everything I hoped she would be, in that aspect at least."

"Then I don't see the problem."

"Cara, we travel all over the country for work. Looks matter. And her looks are...I mean, she's pleasant to look at, and she's..." his eyes go hazy, and I hide my smile, turning to tuck my stuff into my bag. "Anyway, I need to do something about her wardrobe." He stares at the shoes in disgust. "This can't continue."

The elevator ding draws our attention across the office. There she is. The now infamous Maya. She's a bit of a chaos gremlin, leaving a mess wherever she goes. And she's completely oblivious to it most of the time. She meanders toward us, alternating between taking bites of her muffin, dropping crumbs, I'm sure, and ducking her head into cubicles.

I turn my head, covering my laughter with my hand. It's adorable and a scene I've been treated to multiple times already this week. The woman seems to hate shoes and abandons them sometime during the morning. Then she spends an inordinate amount of time looking for them at the end of the day. I'm considering stocking up on flip-flops and storing them in my desk drawer just so we have something for her if she ever can't find them.

As she passes Declan and then Jonas's offices, they emerge, smiling. Jonas chats casually, with Maya, unbothered as she darts away from him and out of sight, then reemerges. Declan follows them, grinning, peeking into the odd cubicle. The woman has two billionaires searching for her twenty-dollar target shoes. And they both seem happy to do it.

I love these men.

And I really love my man.

I catch his eye, sending him a wink, savoring the blush covering his cheeks. Zach mumbles a goodbye, marching towards the slow-moving group. He stops in front of Maya, and even from here, I can hear the scolding in his tone. She casually takes another bite of her muffin, not bothered in the least. She swallows, nods her thanks, and takes her shoes from him, wandering away down the hallway. Zach shoves both hands through his hair, watching her walk away in her flowy, flower-patterned dress. It's hideous, and yet on her, not. The bohemian style suits her. With a shake of his head, he and Jonas follow her to the elevator.

Sliding my feet into my stilettos, I head out to meet my man. He sees me coming and leans against the wall, watching me walk toward him. I put a little more sway in my hips, and lick my lips, satisfied when his eyes narrow dangerously. Leaning into him, I run my fingernails up and down the zip of his hoodie. "Hello, handsome. Fancy meeting you here."

My smile widens, remembering saying those words to him only months ago. That was the day everything started to change. I walked out that day so fucking low, but today? I'm higher than I've ever been. I have a sexy man who loves me, I have a sister that's healing, and I'm a badass business owner. Life is fucking perfect.

Declan's low growl makes my legs wobbly. God, that hits me right in the gut. Combine that with the way he yanks me to him, and I know we're not going to make it home before I get him inside me.

Tugging my head back, he nips at my chin. "We're supposed to be heading to family dinner. And now, thanks to you, we're gonna be late. Are you happy now?"

"Not yet, baby, but with a tiny bit of effort, I will be."

Laughing, he takes my mouth, plundering, seeking, stroking. At some point, I stop relying on my legs to hold me up, trusting Declan to do it. All I can focus on, all I can think about, is him and his fabulous tongue. And all the places I want that tongue to taste tonight.

The family text chime makes Declan groan into my mouth, pulling away to check. "We're supposed to stop for ice cream on the way home. Holly's desperate for mint chocolate chip."

I straighten up immediately, thoughts of being spread out like a feast on Declan's desk moving to the back burner. No fucking way am I messing with a pregnant woman. She's gotten grumpy and bossy. Micah seems to be eating it up, but the rest of us are treading very lightly around her. "Let's go."

"She could wait a few minutes," he complains.

I spin, walking backward as I give him the evil eye. "A few minutes? Really? Is that all it takes?"

"Baby, all I need is a few minutes, trust me." Jesus, he's almost got me convinced, but another ping from his phone sends me spinning, running for the elevator.

"Jesus! Fuck! Cara, you're going to break your leg. Slow down," he yells.

"I told you I could run in these shoes."

He catches up, yanking me off the ground into his arms. Shaking with laughter, I let him herd me into the elevator. "Dammit, woman. You've got to be more careful in these things. Those shoes are deadly."

"I could stop wearing them. Switch to nice respectable flats?" His snarled 'fuck no' makes me laugh. I've started dressing like me again, only with a touch less see-through material. The sexy clothes were a weapon, an effective one, and there's still a place for them, but I don't need them the same way I used to. And Declan honestly loves me wearing anything or nothing. But the shoes? Turns out my man loves the way those shoes look draped over his shoulders.

I do too.

The elevator doors open to the lobby. It's late, the place is empty except for Janey, waiting at the windows, and Jonas a few steps behind her, unmoving, hands tucked in his pockets.

"There he is," she says excitedly, waving a quick goodbye to all of us, then darting to the sleek sports car pulled up at the curb. She's gone in seconds, leaving a stoic Jonas staring after her.

We stop next to him, and Declan lays a hand on his neck. "Are you ok?"

"She has a boyfriend," he says flatly, not looking at us. " He didn't even open the door for her. Did you know she's seeing someone?"

I move in front of him, concerned at how off he sounds. "I knew she's been talking to someone. It's obviously progressed."

"Yes, well. Of course, she has a boyfriend. She's lovely."

My heart is breaking at the sadness in his voice. He's lost her, and he never even had her. And he's so very aware of it, of what he's missed out on. I want to wrap him in a hug.

"Jonas," I ask, putting my hand on his sleeve. "Can I give you a hug?" I expect him to say no. I've offered in the past, and he would smile and say no. But today, he doesn't answer. Just steps into me and drops his forehead onto my shoulder. I wrap my arms around him, squeezing tightly, and gradually, I feel his body relax. I meet Dec's sad eyes over Jonas's head.

We stand, the three of us connected, until Zach storms off the elevator, grumbling. He stops, concerned, checking in to see if Jonas needs him. He's so connected to his brother, so present for him all the time. He doesn't let just anyone see it. But he can be off duty tonight. Jonas is ok. The problem he's facing tonight isn't something Zach can easily fix.

Finally, Jonas straightens, glancing briefly at me, then away. "Thank you, Cara."

"Anytime, Jonas." His eyes are still lost-looking, still sad. I want to chase it away, at least for a little while, so I throw my man under the bus.

"Jonas, can you tell me why Declan has your face tattooed on his ass?"

Declan's gasp of outrage combines with Zach's hysterical laughter and Jonas's snicker. Their laughter and arguing carry us out to the parking lot, Declan and I heading to my car while the brothers hop into Jonas's minivan. We don't say goodbye, simply stopping the conversation until we all get home, where it will start up again as if there wasn't a pause.

As I speed towards home Declan relaxes in the seat beside me —he did take me to the track, and I did prove to him I'm an excellent driver— I marvel at how light I feel. The shadow of arrest is gone, and the D.A. is being prosecuted for his crimes. Bree is doing so much better and has been brought into the fold. We've both been told that family dinner is mandatory, and we've been wrangled into hunting for hamsters more than once. It's loud. It's chaotic. It's family. Something Bree and I have been without for too long.

I pull to a stop in my spot in the secured parking area. Laughing as Jonas and Zach shove each other on the way to the elevator, stopping only to yell at us to hurry up as they pass my car.

"Thank you for giving me this," I say.

"What?" he asks with a small smile.

"Family. I missed it. Bree and I have been on our own for so long."

"Never again. You'll always have us, I promise."

He lifts my hand from the gearshift, pressing a kiss to my palm. "You are the best thing to ever happen to me. I love-- Shit! Shit! We forgot the ice cream."

I snatch my hand back and turn on the ignition. "On it." I back out of the space with a squeal. Declan rolls his window down to shout at his brothers.

"We forgot the ice cream! Holly will murder us." They

laugh and wave us off, but we both know that if we don't get back fast, there will be hell to pay.

I stop at the top of the ramp onto the street, Christmas lights on the street flashing, lighting up the car. Declan grins at me, eyeing the clear road in front of us, and puts his hand on top of mine on the gearshift. "Hit it, baby."

Laughing, I press the pedal to the floor, and together, we roar out into the night.

~

ABOUT THE AUTHOR

Jenna lives in Canada with her family, both human and furry. She's a proud adoptive and foster parent, and has a soft spot for people from hard places.

Made in the USA
Las Vegas, NV
13 February 2023